I0677959

EXPRESS INTENT

A GOLD AND COURAGE NOVEL

KAREN S. GORDON

Copyright © 2020 by Karen S. Gordon

All rights reserved.

No part of this book may be reproduced in any form or by any electronic or mechanical means, including information storage and retrieval systems, without written permission from the author, except for the use of brief quotations in a book review.

Express Intent is a work of fiction. Names, places and incidents are the products of the author's imagination or are used fictitiously. Any resemblance to actual events, locales, or persons, living or dead, is entirely coincidental.

ISBN: 978-1-7336064-6-2 (Ebook)

ISBN: 978-1-7336064-7-9 (Print)

ISBN: 978-1-7336064-8-6 (Audio)

For my great-grandmother Martha Renneaux. Family lore has it she could tell a story like no one else.

1

FORT STOCKTON, TEXAS
240 MILES EAST OF EL PASO

Josh Dominguez tapped the brakes. A tanker hauling liquefied natural gas up ahead had slowed.

Every corner of Texas had a speed trap and the last thing he needed now was a traffic stop. He glanced at his phone. Just after midnight. A horse trailer passed going the other way, heading west on Interstate 10.

Thirty minutes ago, the fax machine in his rented condo had awakened him from a dead sleep. The news was bad. There had been a breach at the research and development lab.

The sprawling complex, much of it underground and located in a remote area, was harder to find at night. He leaned forward on the wheel, squinted, slowed, and turned the Range Rover onto a long driveway leading to an underground tunnel. The high beams lit the metal gates. He powered the window down, pulled the side mirror in, and stopped adjacent to the keypad.

The guard shack, usually staffed by uniformed security personnel, was empty. He pressed his finger on the security pad; the gate didn't respond. His finger felt moist and sticky. Reaching overhead, he switched on the dome light.

Wash your damn hands after eating, man.

He plucked a moist towelette from the dispenser in the center console, wiped his finger, leaned out the window and cleaned the sticky brown substance from the keypad.

Wadding the towelette into a little ball, he dropped it in the cup holder and tried again. The gates chuffed open on the second try like wings on a moth.

He drove slowly through the tunnel, down three levels in the empty garage, and parked in his assigned slot. His heart pumped as he jogged the stairs up to Underground Level 2, triggering the motion-activated lights as he went.

Exiting the stairwell, he hurried the length of the hallway, passing dark offices, some with shades drawn, and others with mirrored windows until he reached the laboratory. Other than the suite number, the heavy door was unmarked.

The hallway went black.

Jesus Christ. He'd complained to security about slowing the intervals on the motion-activated lights, but management was under pressure to reduce the building's carbon footprint.

He felt for the lock, and pressed his index finger on the biometric keypad. Nothing happened. He bent over, looking closer, but it was too dark to see.

He waved his arms overhead, cueing the lights. Darkness. He pulled his cell from his pants pocket, activated the flashlight and pointed it at the lock. The handle was broken. He pushed on the door. It opened, and his movements activated the banks of overhead lights inside.

The large steel workbench where the prototype was stored at night was empty, its black shroud spread on the floor near the table legs, as if a wicked witch had melted. His heart pounded and he couldn't breathe.

Millions of dollars of R&D. Poof. Gone.

Hands shaking, he auto-dialed security from his cell. The call went to voicemail. He ran to the garage, drove to ground level, cut the lights, and parked near the gate. He got out, walked a few steps to the guard shack and shined his cell flashlight into the window. Tilting the beam down, he saw a body on the floor. He tried the knob. The door was unlocked. By squatting, he could reach inside and feel for a pulse. The man was dead, but the body was still warm.

Something stuck to the sole of his boot. He stopped to knock his heel on the concrete, but whatever it was clung to the bottom of his shoe. He pogoed to the keypad, and balancing on the pole, squatted and looked.

What the . . .?

He stumbled backward, using the door of the SUV to break his fall.

Oh, God.

He flicked a human finger from the leather sole of his shoe.

Heart racing, he ran back to the guardhouse and panned his cell light across the body. A small pool of blood glistened near the man's right hand. His index finger was missing.

He started the Range Rover, did a quick U-turn, and headed to the all-night gas station to use the pay phone.

Roy Pompadour answered on the second ring.

L auren Gold hurried beneath the blanket of stars covering Antelope Creek Ranch, to the shed behind the lodge where the ranch owner, Roy Pompadour, stored the recreational vehicles. Selecting a sparkly orange-and-white one, she sat shivering on the cold seat and started the engine, hoping Davis Frost would hurry.

Davis arrived a few minutes later. "I didn't expect you'd beat me here."

She rubbed her hands briskly. "Why's that?"

"I figured you might not show up at all. I know how much you hate the cold."

"All these years working together and you think I'm not going to be dependable?"

"I like this one," he said, taking a seat on an ATV with a desert camo paint job.

"You didn't answer my question."

"I've never seen you so gaga for a dude before."

The way she felt about Vance Courage was that obvious? She feathered the throttle on her off-roader. "I'm not *gaga* for him."

Vance had stayed at the ranch after his live-aboard sailboat sank in Miami and he hadn't decided where he planned to hang his holster permanently. If he had, he hadn't said yet.

She'd seen him when they'd arrived yesterday; gaga was probably a good way to describe the way she'd felt. She cringed at the thought and wondered if Vance had noticed, too.

"Okay, boss. It's too early to argue."

A minute later, she led the way along the lighted gravel path to the guestrooms.

A shadow stepped out from under a veranda in front of one of the rooms.

Her heart skipped.

"Keep it down, for chrissake. Some of us are trying to sleep." The man in a bathrobe went inside and slammed the door.

They pushed the off-roaders on foot the rest of the way to Davis' room; she left hers there and went to her room to warm up while he packed and loaded both vehicles with the video equipment they'd need for their shoot.

She'd have preferred to stay in bed in her PJs but one ATV wasn't big enough to carry all the gear. He'd insisted they go out an hour before sunrise. Good photographers—Davis was one— refused to be rushed, especially when it came to sticking to Mother Nature's schedule.

Davis tapped on her door. She zipped her jacket, followed him out, slipped her off-roader into neutral gear and pushed it on foot away from the rooms, tires crunching the gravel. Once past the lodge, they fired the engines and caravanned to the location Davis had picked to set up.

The week after New Year's, Roy Pompadour had invited them on an all-expenses-paid trip to scout the ranch. He'd hired her to produce a promotional video to market the ranch on the Internet. Davis had been awestruck by the natural beauty of West Texas from the moment they'd arrived. He'd set his sight on a berm about a city block's distance behind the lodge, beyond the ranch's private airstrip that would double as base camp from which to fly the drone to capture the aerial scenes.

There were two berms that looked like the aftermath of an ax dropped on an eighty-foot-long watermelon, the two splintered pieces falling facedown in a wide V-formation. Davis had dubbed them "the humps."

The creosote bushes and mesquite trees rooted in the sandy soil along the base of the berms provided natural cover. The vegetation would camouflage the camera cases and ATVs from the aerial drone shots. Davis said the location would also give them natural shelter from the sun and wind, and because the berms opened like a fan facing the mountains to the south, they'd have privacy from the guests, too.

It was a rough ride along the dark, desert trail. Lauren gripped the steering wheel as the ATV twisted and bounced beneath her. The L-shaped headlights mounted like parenthesis lit the path immediately ahead. Unlike a proper road, there were no streetlights or painted lines to follow.

Damn Davis. He's driving too fast.

She coughed and her eyes stung from the dust. She covered her nose and mouth with her sleeve, trying to keep pace.

Davis, a big man weighing in at almost three hundred pounds, rammed the left front suspension into a hole. His off-roader nose-dived. She jammed the brakes on hers. He leaned forward, clutching the steering wheel. His machine teetered on two wheels, the beginning stages of a side rollover. Graced with fast reflexes, Davis shifted his weight, counterbalancing the ATV. It straightened but didn't stop. It pounded the ground, then bucked on the back wheels and slammed down before coming to a stop.

"Are you okay?"

Davis didn't answer. Her heart raced. He was slumped facedown on the steering column, motionless. Maybe he'd been knocked unconscious. Or worse. Maybe he'd had a heart attack.

She ran through the dust cloud, shining her cell phone flashlight.

He popped up, and seeing the look of terror on her face, clutched his enormous gut, belly-laughing. Other than a transport case held by a bungee cord listing to one side, the equipment was in good order.

Maybe if he'd paid for it, instead of her, he'd have been more careful. "It's not funny. That could have been the end of the shoot."

To which Davis leaned forward and roared more loudly.

It wasn't a joke. She hadn't gotten out of bed in the pre-dawn hours and braved the cold to watch him hot-dogging. She wanted to get to the site as quickly as possible so he could unload the gear and she could head back to the lodge to warm up.

She led the way once back on the trail, letting Davis eat her dust. They stopped at the backside of the southeastern mound and unloaded.

Davis peeled his jacket off and slung it over the roll bar. Beneath it, he wore a wife-beater exposing rolls of fat and flabby skin hanging from his arms like pizza dough. At least he'd waited until it was just the two of them before he'd stripped down.

Davis was a contradiction. He did little to improve his appearance yet had a keen eye for beauty. Which focused on women.

She'd been waiting for the right time to bring up an issue with him, and this seemed about as right a time as it was going to get. "I think Jake's daughter feels uncomfortable around you."

Davis looked up. He'd been kneeling in the dirt assembling

the drone, lifting parts and pieces housed in the molded cutouts, using the ATV headlamps for lighting.

His icy blue eyes didn't mask the hurt. "You really think that?"

She nodded.

"Why?"

There was no delicate way to say it. "You stare at her."

"I do?"

He couldn't be serious. Could he? When she spotted him ogling the girl, she could have draped his tongue around his neck like a scarf. Twice. "Yes." She had to choose her words, massage them into something softer. "I know you didn't mean to upset her. She's a beautiful young girl. I get that. But you can't just stare at her like a stalker."

His face burned red. It was awkward but it had to be said.

He tinkered with the settings without speaking.

She checked her phone, shivering, giving him a moment to process it. The sting would wane. He'd get over it. Quickly, she hoped.

"Okay. I didn't mean anything by it. She's just beautiful, is all." He kept his eyes on the tablet, adjusting the focus and iris, toggling the joystick. "I was studying her."

"Studying her?"

"Yeah. I've been testing a theory."

"What kind of theory?"

"Davis Frost's theory of photogenics."

"Sounds like a skin care treatment."

"Very funny. Don't you wonder why some people look so much better on camera than in person? And vice-versa?"

"Yeah, but I haven't given it a name." She sat on her hands and patted her feet on the ATV floorboard, trying to generate body heat.

"That girl race car driver we worked with is the perfect

example. The one who couldn't cut it on the race track."

Lauren raised her eyebrows. Once again Davis aimed a bit too high when it came to critiquing women.

"Princess Diana was the same way."

"You met *Diana*?"

Davis snorted a laugh. "No. Someone I know did and he said he wouldn't have given her a second look on the street."

"What's your point?"

"If faces are symmetrical, cameras love them."

"Does your camera love Caitlin?"

"I don't know. But my guess is yes."

"Is that why you've been staring at her?"

"It's one reason. The other is it's kinda hard to believe she's Jake's kid."

"I know." Lauren laughed. "Not only is she beautiful, she's sweet."

"Which makes it seem impossible." Davis swung his big Saint Bernard head from side-to-side and grinned. He'd moved past his hurt feelings.

Lauren stood and kneaded his bare shoulder. "I wish I didn't have to say that to you, about Caitlin."

He twisted away from her. "I know, boss."

"I'm heading back. The next stage is frostbite."

"You're such a wimp." Davis stopped building the drone and grabbed his jacket from the seat of the four-wheeler. He draped it over her shoulders. "I don't need it."

"I'll be back in about an hour to help you haul stuff back. Sound good?"

"Perfect." Davis fired-up his camo-colored ATV, moved it to the base of berm and snapped branches to cover it

The orange-and-white metallic paint on hers twinkled like night stars. The motor produced a jungle sound, too throaty for a riding lawnmower but not muscular enough for a V-8. When she goosed the gas in neutral, the engine noise traveled to the foothills and echoed. She clamped both hands firmly on the wheel and grabbed the gearshift. She saw Davis' lips moving in her periphery. He came closer but she still couldn't hear him. She killed the engine.

"I just wanted to say I'm sorry about being a creeper."

"Don't obsess. I'll be back."

Davis powered the drone and revved the engine with the joystick. It lifted like a tiny helicopter, creating a small puff of dust. It was almost as loud as the gas-powered four-wheeler, but had a much higher octave. The low notes of her ATV blended with the high ones of the drone and traveled freely across the desert as she hurried back to the dining hall to thaw out, and meet Vance Courage for breakfast.

She ducked about thirty yards or so from the lodge. The drone was less than three feet from the top of her head and the noise was deafening, overpowering the ATV. Davis was showing off his operating skills, working the drone like a puppet. He flew it ahead of her and turned it to face her, hovering in place. Lauren flipped a bird overhead, knowing Davis would see it on his tablet. It did a barrel roll. She laughed.

The drone danced, dipping side-to-side, seesawing for a few seconds, before it spun in place, making her a little dizzy watching it. It bowed with its nose down, buzzing as loudly as a swarm of bees. Lauren clapped at the impromptu show. He piloted it toward the lodge's back outdoor patio lined with burning butane heaters as tall as young trees, and slowed it as it approached the dining hall.

Suddenly the drone reversed and sped back toward the berm.

She smiled, imagining the horror on Davis' face when Jake and Caitlin appeared on his handheld tablet that doubled as his monitor. The way he'd spun and hightailed it away said it all.

3

Vance Courage sat beneath the amber glow of the deer antler chandelier in the dining hall nursing a mug of coffee. Though not much good at it, he worked the *New York Times* crossword from an old paper he'd found in the lobby.

66 down, *Cheap cigar, slangily.*

Ah ha.

He filled in the boxes: *s-t-o-g-i-e.*

He'd awakened by alarm clock at oh-dark-thirty, and not caring to do a face plant in the gravel pathway, used the light from his phone to hopscotch across the courtyard to the main lodge.

____ *and circumstance.*

Wow. He'd gotten two answers in less than a minute. He was about to fill in the blank when his cell buzzed. UNKNOWN NUMBER.

He'd been getting fewer robocalls since he'd been forced to buy a new smartphone after getting doxed by Zack Wisenberg's minions, the founder of the world's largest social media company. He set the phone screen-side down on the wooden table and resumed his puzzle, writing *p-o-m-p* in the blank squares. The next clue stumped him: *A yellow spice used in garam masala.*

His phone dinged. He turned it over. What the . . .? A fraud alert from a credit card company? Seriously? It was too early for this shit. He tapped the link to the sign-in page, typed the information and pressed the SEND button.

User Name and Password Do Not Match.

What? He tried again. The same message repeated with an identical warning. On the third attempt an autoreply popped up.

`Your Account Has Been Locked For 24 Hours.`

Are you kidding me?

He didn't know if he'd forgotten his password or typed it wrong three times. He pulled his wallet from his pants pocket. All his cards were accounted for.

What's the combination? He smacked his forehead. No sign-in revelations came.

He set the phone on the wooden table, rolled the newspaper, and swatted the screen with a crack. How the hell was he supposed to remember dozens of login and password combinations for his accounts when he was too pigheaded and paranoid to autosave the lot of them?

"What's wrong?"

He hadn't noticed Jake Fleming and Jake's teenage daughter standing over him. Unsure how long they'd been watching, he set the paper down gently.

Caitlin held her palm out. He handed her his phone. She grimaced. "Ouch. Maybe your credit card was stolen?"

He heard the ping. She turned the screen so he could see it: A message from the identity theft protection company instructing him to call immediately.

"Sorry," she said, as if it were her fault. "Do you want me to wait? Until you figure it out?"

"Morning." Jake Fleming sounded half-awake and disinterested.

Caitlin was graced with many things her father was short on. Empathy and patience were two of them.

"No. I'll figure it out," Vance said.

"Figure what out?" Jake asked.

Caitlin showed him Vance's phone.

Jake looked at the screen filled with green text bubbles, then looked back to his daughter admiringly. "Did you know she's a long-distance runner being scouted by the college recruiters and she's only a freshman in high school?"

The girl wore dark-colored sweats with a lightning bolt on the outer seam of each leg, an oversized University of Michigan sweatshirt, and sneakers, obviously dressed for a run.

"Impressive," Vance said, staring out the huge south-facing window of the dining room. It was still too dark to see the Chinati Mountains, the international boundary dividing Texas from Mexico. "Be careful out there."

Jake put his big hand on Caitlin's shoulder. "I'll walk you out." Using an open arm, he gestured toward the back door leading to the open desert.

She hesitated, eyeing the phone she'd returned to Vance. "Are you sure? I feel bad leaving you to figure it out."

"I can handle it," he said, watching Jake lift the loose strap of her red backpack onto her shoulder and tuck a bottle of water into a side pocket.

Jake cursed and ducked as he opened the door. A swarm of bees stormed the back patio. The noise filled the dining hall. "Damn it!" He waved his hands over his head and rushed back inside, shielding Caitlin.

"Dad. That's Davis' drone. Gosh, now he's creeping me with *that* thing." She covered the top of her head with both hands.

REE-aw-REE-aw.

REE-aw-REE-aw.

Vance shook his head and snorted. Davis Frost had the uncanny ability to annoy people in ways he could never picture and he had an active imagination. The high-pitched sound prickled his eardrums and he pushed his finger in one earhole to stop the tickle. He'd give Davis a piece of his mind, but it would have to wait.

The drone spun a one-eighty and disappeared into the pre-dawn sky.

He heard another noise, the throaty growl of an off-roader approaching. He looked out the window. Lauren Gold parked the ATV parallel to the low adobe wall behind the building and cut the lights. She strode toward the lodge, rubbing her hands briskly.

JAKE HOGGED THE DOORWAY. He was on a knee, tightening one of Caitlin's shoelaces. He looked up. "He's very irritating."

Lauren squeezed past him. "Good morning to you, too." Standing inside, hands in pockets, she said, "I talked to him."

Jake struggled to his feet, using the doorframe for support. "Talked to who?"

"I'm talking to your daughter." Lauren flipped her chin toward Caitlin. "I had a chat with Davis. He's harmless. I told him he makes you uncomfortable. He promised to be mindful in the future."

"Then why'd he almost give me a haircut with that—"

"—Daddy."

Lauren said, "I doubt he knew it was you. He was having a little fun with me."

Jake patted his daughter on the arm. "Tell him my daughter can outrun half the boys on the track team."

"I'm sure she won't have to run from him." Lauren stepped inside, hunching over from the cold, and joined Vance.

"What was that all about?" he asked her, tapping his pen on the unsolvable crossword hint.

"*Dad.*"

Jake did a U-turn and waddled to the doorway. Lauren followed and stood in front of the window, her warm breath fogging the glass. No doubt his daughter brought the best out in him; it was heartwarming to watch them.

Jake held Caitlin's forearm and led her to the narrow patio just outside the window where the butane lamps burned rings of blue fire.

Caitlin lifted her arm, holding something against her wrist with her thumb.

Jake fished his readers from his shirt pocket, tilted her wrist beneath the light shining down from the security lamp on a pole, and fiddled with the strap.

Caitlin pulled the sleeve over her wrist, then kissed her father on the cheek.

He straightened the visor on her forehead, centering it.

Lauren opened the door to let him inside.

"Be careful," he yelled.

"I will, Daddy."

Beyond the porch lights, in the pre-dawn sky, her silhouette blended with the background and she disappeared on the horizon. Lauren looked at her watch. It was just before 7:00 in the morning and it was shaping up to be a busy day; the sun hadn't risen and the dining room began to fill with guests.

She sniffled and dabbed her nose with a napkin, poured herself a mug with hot coffee at the self-serve station and join Vance at the table. "Turmeric."

He looked at her blankly. "Two-what?"

"T-U-R-M-E-R-I-C. '*A yellow spice used in garam masala.*' It's also an herbal supplement used to help reduce inflammation."

"Who knew?" he mumbled, filling in the blanks on his cross-word puzzle.

Yesterday afternoon she'd made good on her promise to take Caitlin on a trail ride. The girl was a bit of a daredevil, badgering Lauren to let her gallop the horse. The animal she'd picked for her was too feeble to do much more than trot a few steps.

She gave in and when the horse picked up the pace for a couple of steps, Caitlin hunched over and clamped a death grip around the old horse's neck. At the tender age of fifteen, most things still looked a lot easier than they were. She smiled at the thought, checking the time on her phone: just after 7:15.

4

G od. What was happening?

Caitlin's bones rattled inside the dark container, joints aching from sitting on the metal floor above one of the axles.

A ribbon of light streamed through the slit above. Heaving, she flexed her abdominal muscles, fighting the urge to vomit as she closed her eyes and tilted her head back, letting saliva fill her mouth. She forced the bile back down, her lips sealed tightly with a strip of bitter duct tape.

Breathe.

Breathe.

Sickened from the diesel fumes permeating the trailer, she tucked her nose into the elbow of her dad's sweatshirt and inhaled. As the urge to vomit faded, she ran the backs of her bound hands over her upper lip, hoping to hook the tip of the zip tie binding her wrists under an edge of the tape. Instead, she almost poked herself in the eye.

The dark box rocked like a train on a track.

It'd happened fast.

Her attacker had pounced like a jungle cat.

Neck muscles aching, she tried to keep her head from bobbing. She pressed her left shoulder against the interior wall, closed her eyes, and shook her shoulders. The plastic tie cut circulation and she wiggled her tingling fingers, hoping to pump enough blood to her hands to bring back feeling.

How had she not seen him? He'd sprung from nowhere and ambushed her. She played it back in her head over and over but her brain was a broken record. The movie clicked off the moment before he grabbed her, then the sequence of events started over.

She'd said goodbye to her dad before she'd left the lodge to go for a run. After seeing that Davis Frost had set up behind the small hill to the left, she started her morning run heading west, away from him, around the adjacent berm, hoping he wouldn't see her. Lauren said he meant nothing by it, but him ogling her —practically drooling—gave her the heebie-jeebies.

Davis worked for her dad as his boat captain and she'd complained that the fat man tracked her every move with his eyes. Lauren had promised to speak to him, to share how uncomfortable he made her feel.

Her nostrils stung and her eyes welled.

She'd gagged on her own saliva earlier. If she barfed now, she'd choke on her vomit.

Get it together.

She sniffled, fighting the tears.

If she'd known Davis was going to be at the ranch, she would have canceled the trip, and asked her dad to reschedule. If he hadn't been there, this wouldn't have happened.

Lauren said she'd talked to him. What good did that do? He'd buzzed them at the patio door. He was spying on her. Her dad saw it, too. And so had Lauren. He'd flown the thing right over the tops of their heads.

Why was she being held prisoner inside this container?

The road vibration rattled her teeth. She craned her sore neck sideways and lifted one shoulder in an attempt to rub her ear. Suddenly the axle beneath her hit a pothole, snapping her neck.

Think. Think.

She'd left the lodge from the back patio door, heading to the hill opposite the one where Davis had set up to start her morning run. As dawn broke, she heard his drone flying overhead.

The bottle of water her dad had packed sloshed inside her backpack. She'd decided not to carry it on the run and stopped to find a place to stash it, planning to pick it up on the way back. She'd looked for a landmark and spotted a large boulder with a reddish tint, big enough to sit on: It stood out and would be easy to spot from a distance. She looked in the direction where Davis was flying the drone. So far, he hadn't noticed her.

She dropped the red backpack from her shoulders and tucked it behind the big red rock, set her fitness tracker for five miles, then started running.

The sky was full of fading night stars and as she sprinted, she opened her palms, looking skyward, pretending she could catch one if it fell from the sky. The temperature was perfect and the air light and dry, unlike home in Miami where it was like running in a sauna.

As the sun crept up and the stars disappeared, she changed course, running more inland, away from the mountain shadows where the sun could warm her neck. Turning to the west, she ran parallel to the foothills for just over two miles, then stopped and rested. Bending over, she'd held her knees and inhaled crisp desert air.

Turning for home, heading east, she'd been spellbound by the morning sun casting a golden light, outlining the mountains like a giant cardboard cutout. The blue sky was on fire with brush strokes of orange and red, dissipating fast. When she neared the westernmost berm where she'd started her run, she stopped again to look at her fitness tracker. The five-mile run was complete

She'd checked the time: just after seven-thirty. Cutting a diagonal path, she'd headed to the spot where she'd dropped her backpack. Walking the last hundred feet, she tilted her head down and split her ponytail into two handfuls, pulling her hair taut in opposite directions in the elastic band.

Adjusting the visor to better shade her eyes, she looked in the direction where Davis had set up. She couldn't see him, but she heard the drone, now a faint buzz. Looking up, it flew south, tiny in the sky like a hawk, heading toward the mountains. If she ran straight to the ranch now, he wouldn't see her.

That's what she should have done.

Sniffling, she dabbed her eyes with the sleeve of her sweatshirt. The vehicle towing the trailer sped up and diesel fumes wafted into the container. She tightened her abs again, fighting off stomach heaves.

The tape in her head rewound to the beginning.

Focus. Focus.

Her thoughts restarted, visualizing the boulder, recalling its size and shape, its reddish color against the landscape's gray tones.

Her mind went blank again.

Think. Think.

She had the boulder in her sights and she'd sprinted toward it. That prompted another memory. The ATV. The one Lauren had been driving. The orange-and-white one, headed for the berm where Davis set up, a rooster tail of dust chasing it. Lauren was halfway there when she suddenly stopped in the middle of the desert.

She squatted behind the mound of dirt, sipped water from

the bottle in her backpack, adjusted the visor to shade her eyes from the rising sun, and spied on Lauren, wondering what she was doing sitting on the off-roader.

That's right. She'd hoped Davis was bringing the drone in for a landing. That would give her a chance to sprint back to the lodge. Instead, he flew it low, eye-level, slowly, at a walking pace. What was he doing that for? Did he see her and plan to fly it around the berm where she was hiding? Was he playing hide-and-seek with it, planning to surprise her?

Her heart sped up. She could hardly swallow.

More events flashed into focus. She'd seen something rustle in the bushes. It had startled her; she'd jumped to her feet when she'd spotted a desert pocket mouse, not much bigger than her thumb. The tiny rodent stood on its hind legs like Stuart Little, twitched its nose, then froze, staring at her with inquisitive black eyes too big for its small head.

She'd set the water bottle down and fetched her phone from her backpack. Stuart cocked his head, posing. She giggled and clicked a picture.

Then Davis' noisy drone had snapped her back into reality. She'd covered her ears and leaned forward. Davis flew it low, screwing around, like he was bringing it in for a landing, except he didn't. What was he doing? She remembered now she'd wished he'd hurry up and finish so she could run back to the lodge.

But instead of landing, he'd sent it back up vertically until it was a dot in the sky.

That's right. That's what happened.

She'd been stuck. She shouldn't have stopped. She should have run to the ranch. She'd wondered then: *How long am I going to be stuck hiding behind the berm?*

A loud noise rattled the contents of the trailer; a semi tractor-trailer passed, buffeting it, causing it to sway.

The movie in her head started back up. She'd peered around the mound of earth and had seen Davis and Lauren packing the ATVs with the video equipment.

Oh, my God. That's what happened. She'd been about to take another picture of the pocket mouse when she saw something out of the corner of her eye.

What was it?

Think.

She'd turned her head to see. The screen in her head went black.

What happened next?

She couldn't breathe. Her heart raced.

That's right.

He had the advantage.

She'd jumped to her feet. Tried to run.

Focus. Focus.

Her flight instinct had kicked in. When she'd turned to run, he'd grabbed her upper arm and spun her around. Her legs buckled like a thumb puppet.

That's what happened. She'd been abducted by a man with a gun.

"Help!" she'd yelled. But Davis and Lauren couldn't hear her. The sounds of the off-roaders had drowned her out. "Help me!"

"Shut up," the stranger had growled.

She'd frozen like a deer. He'd loosened his grip on her arm, testing her. She didn't move. Her heart pounded beneath her shirt.

"You open your mouth again, and I'll strangle you with my bare hands."

He'd pulled her body closer until she could smell his stinky breath. She'd arched her back, trying to keep her distance but he'd pressed the tip of his gun into her belly and clamped his hand tighter on her forearm. *Ouch!* He'd pushed the gun harder against her tummy, her knees slackening from fear and pain.

"Do you understand me?"

She'd bobbed her head. Every nerve in her body fired as an infusion of adrenaline raced through her system.

He'd torn something from the shoulder of his T-shirt: A strip of duct tape, and slapped it across her mouth. She couldn't breathe, couldn't take in enough air through her nostrils. Her heart pumped as if it would jump from her chest and her every muscle twitched.

"Put your hands together." His dead eyes stared into hers. He panned the gun back and forth, left and right, across her chest.

Her heart thrummed now, like it did then.

She'd obeyed, lowering her hands, pressing her wrists together. He'd traded hands, holding the gun in his left hand, using his thumb and forefinger to thread the plastic tie around her wrists, pulling it taut with his teeth.

She could have head-butted him. But then what?

"Try to run and I will shoot your pretty face off."

It was like it was happening all over again. She sucked air through her nose to keep from passing out.

She'd let him tape her mouth. And bind her hands. Why hadn't she fought back? Same answer: *He would have killed her.*

Trapped, bones rattling, mouth parched, the non-stop clattering of metal and vehicle vibrations were interrupted occasionally only by louder sounds of semi tractor-trailers passing.

She'd heard a siren earlier.

Her hopes were dashed when the truck pulling the trailer slowed and the siren shrieked as it streaked past, then faded.

She'd been ambushed and lost her backpack in the struggle.

Without her phone, what could she do?

She swallowed hard.

What did he want?

And why didn't anyone see him get away?

Yes. There was more: the strange machine.

She banged her head on purpose against the metal siding inside the trailer, the incessant road vibration that wouldn't stop, the flexing of the axles twisting beneath her, driving her insane.

More came back, in pieces.

The thing took up most of the space in the trailer.

He'd *flown* it.

She tilted her head down and felt her forehead with the back of one hand. Her visor was gone. The wind had ripped it from her head. She'd tried to catch it. She pictured it now, sailing in the wind.

Was her mind playing tricks? Was it a dream? No, not a dream.

The man's eyes were too close together, like a pit bull's. And there was something else. He had a tattoo on his left arm. Yes. She'd seen it for just a second as he forced her into his strange flying machine.

Flying machine.

Imprisoned, bound and gagged inside this dark container. This was no dream. It was real.

Everything she was remembering was real.

Someone had to see something.

She prayed that help was on the way. Tears welled and streamed down her face.

Why hadn't someone stopped him?

My God. No one knows, because no one saw it happen.

5

"What crawled up his boxers and croaked?" Lauren asked. She sat across from Vance and both of them watched as Jake paced, shaking his fist, yelling at someone on the phone.

Vance grinned. "Boxers? Not briefs?"

She glared at him. "Will you ever let it go?"

She'd made the mistake of sleeping with Jake Fleming, then followed it up with an unforced error: Admitting it. When the chance to razz her about it presented itself, Vance seemed unable to pass it up.

"At least I let the croaking thing go. Mostly because I don't want to know."

She narrowed her eyes and studied Jake for a moment before shifting her eyes back at him. "Whatever's going on, it sounds like he's pretty pissed off."

"Apparently, someone stole his credit cards."

"Seriously?" She pulled her phone from her jacket pocket and looked at the screen.

"First me, then him. Someone must have hacked the wireless. Jake's taking it harder than I am."

"Don't you think it's weird?"

"That you have better karma? Not really."

"Not that. What I was thinking is how weird it is that Jake shape-shifts into Mister Perfect Dad when his kid is around."

He grinned. "Apparently, his irresistible charm isn't limited to his daughter."

She volleyed back. "My poor judgment in men might not be limited to him, either."

"Oh, come on. I'm just teasing you."

She'd observed the father-daughter dynamic for the first time yesterday afternoon. It was hard to believe. She'd sensed Jake was devoted to his kids but seeing it was another matter. The way he walked with his arm draped over Caitlin's shoulder, nodding attentively while she chattered as the duo toured the grounds.

Her more familiar opinion of Jake returned when he yanked the bench, slapped his phone screen on the wooden table, and sat. "The whole country is so dumbed down. I was on hold forever and when I finally got someone, I could barely under-stand a word he was saying. Some call center in a third world country halfway across the world."

"A call to somewhere halfway around the world doesn't exactly constitute the dumbing down of the 'whole country,'" she said.

"Fine. The whole planet is stupid because they can't fix my problem. The identity theft folks canceled most of my credit cards. So much for fraud protection." He rolled a cloth napkin and smacked the tabletop like a bullwhip.

"Geez. Don't take it out on the furniture," she said.

Vance smiled.

"I'm going to mooch off you two 'til I get back to civilization where I can go to the bank and talk to a human who speaks English as a first language."

Vance said, "You might have to mooch off her. I didn't cancel my cards, but my bank might have."

Jake stared out the big south-facing window framing the mountains. "Did you guys see Caitlin?"

Vance shrugged.

She shook her head. "Not since Davis tried to give you a buzz cut."

"That girl loves to run. Go figure," Jake said. "Sure doesn't come from my side of the family. It hurts my hips just thinking about it."

Lauren's phone pinged. She looked at the screen. "I gotta get going. Davis needs help with his gear."

Jake's phone dinged just as she stood to leave. It was face-down on the long wooden table. Instead of checking it, he pushed it an arm's length away. The kettle in Jake's head was about to whistle and this was a good time to go.

A young couple passed the table, smelling of alcohol.

Jake craned his bear head and lifted it, sniffing.

The woman carried a champagne flute. A mimosa. The man gripped a glass tumbler with a celery stalk spouting from tomato juice.

"A little early, don't you think?" Jake grumbled at them.

LAUREN DROVE toward the berm to meet Davis. She stopped midway to watch him. It appeared as if he were trying to shoot from the point of view of a hiker, inspiring her to start editing the scene in her head.

Another photographer would have strapped a Go-Pro to his forehead and walked the shot. Davis' approach was more cerebral, a smoother shot with a wider lens creating a more panoramic view of the mountains, tempting the occipital-temporal brains of the most jaded web surfers.

Translation: When vacation planners saw it, they'd click the BOOK IT NOW button.

When he waved to her, signaling she wouldn't ruin the shot, she drove toward the hump. His eyes flicked back and forth from the screen to the sky until he appeared almost walleyed, keeping one on the tablet, the other on the drone as he brought it in for landing.

She covered her ears to muffle the noise, and when the drone was two feet off the ground, she watched the retractable legs open. The dark-gray machine descended gracefully, coming to a rest in the powder of dust it kicked up at each leg. He killed the engine, lifted the drone, wiped the dust off with the tail of his wife-beater and set it on the seat of her ATV.

He had a sloppy grin plastered across his face. "Check it out." He shaded the tablet screen with his hand and pressed the start button, his expression alternating between surprise and glee.

"It's gorgeous." Roy Pompadour was going to be impressed with the footage he'd just shot at Antelope Creek Ranch. The drone could fly places otherwise inaccessible. A natural water-fall appeared on screen, crystal water streaming down the face of a rosy cliff. "Wow. Where did you see this?"

"I got lucky."

"It's incredible."

What was even more amazing is that Davis hadn't seen the gear until yesterday afternoon. She'd bought it from an online outfit in New York City and had it FedExed straight to the ranch: $31,500.

"This place is almost as pretty as home," he said. "In a different way, of course."

Wow. Davis had done a lot of whining after Hurricane Irma whacked the Florida Keys, flattening his rented duplex. He'd been living aboard Jake's 60-foot Maritimo yacht, the *Arm & A Leg*, working as the captain. He hated Freeport, Texas where Jake docked his yacht, and didn't hold back calling the place an eyesore. Saying something positive about West Texas was a step in the right direction.

Davis finished packing the gear and they caravanned back to the lodge.

"I DIDN'T THINK anyone used those things anymore . . . except as packing material," Davis said to Jake.

It was worse than being in the middle of an old married couple.

Jake lowered the newspaper and glared at Davis. "It's not a *thing*. It's a newspaper. And I'm not *using* it. I'm reading it."

Davis headed to the buffet.

Lauren sat across from Jake.

Jake yanked the paper open and covered his face. "Did he get some good pictures?"

"Do you want to see it?"

"Not really." He lowered the paper. "Did you see my daughter out there?"

"She's not back yet?"

"Would I ask you that if she was?"

She grit her teeth.

He adjusted his nerdy horn-rimmed readers. "How long's your friend Davis going to be here?"

"Couple of days."

He turned the paper around so she could see it.

Nothing caught her eye. "What?"

Jake tapped the headline. "Zack Wisenberg's company stock price hit an all-time high last week." He folded the newsprint four ways and set it down, removed his glasses and twirled them. "You know what they say?"

"No, I don't."

"The rich get richer . . . and the poor get on social media." Jake laughed at his own joke.

Zack Wisenberg was the social media tycoon they'd tangled with before they'd sold the ranch back to Roy Pompadour. They'd had the misfortune of getting in Wisenberg's crosshairs.

Jake looked out the big picture window. "I'm sure Wisenberg loves how dysfunctional Congress is."

"I don't know about that," she said. She could care less about politics. Or D.C. Or lobbyists. Or legislation. She just wanted a guy like Wisenberg with that much power to leave them alone. "Do you think he's done trying to intimidate us?"

Jake shrugged. "Who knows? He's got bigger problems. The European Union is going after his company for taxes."

"Couldn't happen to a nicer guy." After his PR goons spread click-bait stories about her, Vance, and Jake, accusing them of being involved in some shady business dealings, she'd talked to Vance about it. He was a lawyer. Couldn't they sue him for libel? Wisenberg's company had deep pockets.

Money wasn't the issue. The problem was, Vance reminded her, that in Zack's attempts to discredit them, his pit bulls had come close to exposing the truth.

They *had* been involved in some shady deals. Specifically, they'd salvaged millions of dollars of illicit drug cash sunk off the coast of Miami. Money different entities believed belonged to them. For one, the US Justice Department thought it belonged to the Treasury. Cuban relatives and former associates of the now-defunct Los Guapos drug cartel thought it was theirs, too.

A cold sweat broke under her blouse. She, Jake, and Vance had bought Antelope Creek Ranch to launder a few million dollars each. As the temporary owners, they'd accidentally exposed Wisenberg attempting to manipulate the courts to protect his business interests. Even though they'd sold the ranch back to Mr. Pompadour, Wisenberg coming that close to the truth, presumably by accident, spooked her.

Jake sighed. "That power-hungry prick says the stock hitting a new high 'proves the business model is solid.'" When he glanced up and saw Davis coming, he stopped talking.

The fat man's plate was piled high with crispy bacon on one side and chocolate éclairs on the other. He set it down in front of the tablet he'd left at the table and mounted the bench next to her. "Did you look at any more footage?"

Jake hid behind his newspaper. "We were having a conversation."

Davis wrapped a bacon strip around an éclair and bit into it.

"Did you see my daughter while you were out flying your toy chopper?"

"Um, no." Davis looked at Lauren.

"She's not back yet," Lauren said.

Davis chased the bacon-wrapped pastry with Coca-Cola. "I'm sorry I made her uncomfortable. She's a very pretty girl."

Jake lowered the paper. "She's fifteen, buddy."

Jake Fleming had aced his ACT tests in high school, scoring in the top fifth percentile. He'd graduated cum laude from a top Midwest school before slogging, elbowing, and butt-snorkeling his way up the corporate ladder on Wall Street. None of it compared to drying out from booze. He was coming up on nine months sober and the one thing that motivated him most to keep on the straight and narrow was his daughter, Caitlin.

For her twelfth birthday, he'd promised her not to drink. Instead, he got blitzed, embarrassing her in front of her friends. Worse, he drove her home from the party, arriving two hours late with a blood alcohol level that could have killed a moose. He'd infuriated his most recent ex-wife, Ann.

He shuddered at the thought. What would have happened if the cops had pulled him over? Or something worse happened? It had taken six months of verifiable abstinence before his daughter answered his calls.

It was her idea to go on the father-daughter trip. They'd had a special bond long before his drinking had spun out of control. Kids favor one parent over the other. Jake had. He'd idolized his dad and struggled with his mother. Caitlin's attachment to him was baffling.

He'd wondered how partial he was. Didn't all parents have blind spots when it came to their children? His daughter was bright, thoughtful, and wholesome. He thought it; everyone else said it.

His son was a different story. He'd invited him to come along on the trip but the boy was holding a grudge. Jake couldn't blame him. He'd been shit-faced for most of their childhood.

Jake lowered his paper and made an attempt at civility. "How's the drone thing going?"

"Amazing," Davis said. "This place is cool. I piloted it up to a thousand feet and the pictures are unbelievable, like nothing I've ever seen. It's against FAA regulations to fly higher than four hundred feet, but who's counting? We're in the middle of nowhere, right?"

Jake felt his presence. He looked over his shoulder. Roy Pompadour loomed over the table like Osiris guarding the Underworld.

"There's law enforcement out there, son," Roy said. "A lot of it. Federal, state, county, local . . . you name it. Don't get lulled into thinking you can fly under the radar. Bad pun." Something caught his eye. He pulled a white handkerchief from his starched shirt and strode toward the bookshelf.

Roy ran his cloth-wrapped finger along the shelves, looked at the results, creased his brow, stuck the hanky in his pocket and headed back to the table, sitting on the bench next to Jake. "Where's your daughter?"

"She went out for a run."

"By herself?"

"Uh-huh."

"We usually tell the guests not go out alone." Roy squinted

until his eyes were slivers. "Especially on foot. There's wildlife —"

"She promised not to go far," Jake said. "She's a smart kid. She's probably looking for a frizzy hair or a chip of black nail polish. She's crazy about that old rock star that stays here. He's older than me, and I'm a geezer dad." Jake grinned, exposing his off-center upper teeth.

"I think it's refreshing, that people can remain relevant when they're that old," Lauren said. "Has anyone seen Vance?"

"I saw him a little while ago," Roy said. "He was meeting someone."

"Who?"

Roy shrugged. "He didn't say."

"A guest?" she asked.

"I don't know. I bumped into him in the courtyard. He said he saw someone he wanted to talk to." Roy stood to leave. "I'm sure he'll be back soon."

Long before Lauren met Roy, she'd read the infamous feature story about him in *Texas Monthly*. Rumor had it he'd agreed to the interview to tout the painstaking effort he'd gone to restoring the ruins of Antelope Creek Ranch, his luxury West Texas resort.

The writer went off track, submitting an exposé on Roy as an eccentric ex-'Nam war hero whose obsessive-compulsive disorder drove him to near madness resurrecting the pre–Civil War fort. Roy wasn't angry. He was livid and tried to kill the story. It was too late and it went to print anyway. The writer got fired.

Why hadn't Vance mentioned he saw someone he knew? That was weird.

She plucked a tissue from a pack in her pocket and dabbed her nose on her way to the guestroom that Roy was inspecting for readiness.

Why did it seem like the desert was the place that activated her allergies? Wasn't it supposed to be the other way around?

She stopped. Roy stood sideways on the threshold of the room she and Davis had picked out as the best one for shooting interior shots. Roy squeezed his body between the maid's cart and the doorway, pulling a hanky from his pocket.

Lauren texted Davis: It might be a while. Will let you know when room is ready.

Her phone pinged. K.

The turquoise pool in the courtyard reflected blues and reds from an American flag sailing atop a metal pole, a recent addition. A hawk circled overhead. Roy emerged from the room and planted one hand on his hip, gesturing to someone still inside. One of the housekeepers poked her head out. Roy showed her the handkerchief.

Oh, God. She sent Davis another text. Might be a LONG wait.

She stopped at the front desk to say hello to Rosa, who was huddled on the other side of the counter, talking to a young fellow she'd seen earlier working the reception desk.

Rosa brightened when she saw her. "I heard you were here."

"And I heard you were pregnant."

Rosa looked down and ran her hand over her belly, smiling.

"How far along?"

"Eight months."

Wow. In a month Rosa would be a mother; she'd last seen her as a new bride. "How's married life treating you?"

"Pretty good. Josh's been traveling for a couple of months. Now that we're married, he took a job in Fort Stockton."

"Doing what?"

"Some project of Roy's. He doesn't talk about it much. And you, what are you up to?"

She told Rosa about the video she and Davis were working on.

"Maybe it'll drum up some new business. Especially this summer. How long will you be here?"

"A couple of days."

"I hope you don't take this the wrong way, but I have something for that."

Lauren raised her eyebrows.

Rosa grimaced, walked around the counter and reached into a drawer. She handed her a red-and-white box. "Take one. It'll dry your nose up."

Lauren turned away from Rosa and dabbed her nose with a tissue. "Oh," she said.

The young man standing next to Rosa said, "Be sure to get rid of them if you're going to Mexico."

"Why?" She looked at the box with the brand name label.

"It's by prescription south of the border," Rosa said. "We had a bit of a situation last year."

The young man said, "One of the guests, a regular, was arrested in Mexico."

Rosa crunched her nose. "I didn't know."

Lauren looked at the box again. "I don't know if I should take these."

"They're safe," Rosa said. "Supposedly the ma and pa dealers were using the pills to make street meth so the Feds cracked down on sales. Some people. I guess it worked because I haven't heard any recent stories about neighborhood meth labs blowing up." Rosa shook her head.

Lauren had forgotten all about those stories that had so often made the news. She stuffed the pack of pills in her pocket. "Will I see Josh while I'm here?"

"Maybe. It depends on how long you stay."

She forced a smile at the young man, sniffling and patting her nose with a tissue. "You must be the new guy."

"Oh." Rosa threw her head back and laughed, an electric-blue lock of hair falling out of place. She brushed it from her face. "Pardon my manners. This is Adam. He's the new front desk officer."

"'*Front desk officer.*' It sounds so, um, official. Nice to meet you. I'm Lauren Gold," she held her hand out.

"Aren't you one of the owners? I mean previous owners?"

"Yes. I owned it for about a nano-second."

Rosa said, "After Roy bought it back, he promoted me to general manager."

"So I heard. Congratulations."

Roy approached.

"Back to work," Rosa said. "Good to see you."

Roy handed two neatly folded handkerchiefs to Adam, who unfolded the top one and studied it as if it were some sort of treasure.

"Place looks great," Lauren said to Roy.

Roy guffawed. "The room won't be ready for at least another four hours."

She could kiss the day goodbye.

Roy said, "That dust that belongs outdoors, son."

The young man blinked, wide-eyed.

Roy held his hand out and took the handkerchiefs back. "We all wear many hats, young man. One of yours is to check the lobby for fingerprints and dust. Have you taken any calls for me this morning?"

Adam shook his head.

Roy looked at his watch. "I have a meeting scheduled. His name's Mack Twane. Call me on my cell when he arrives, which should be any second now that he's officially one minute late."

"Uh . . . okay." The landline rang. Adam cradled the receiver on his shoulder. "Antelope Creek Ranch. How may I help you? . . . . No, I'm sorry, we're completely booked this week."

When Roy was out of earshot, Rosa returned. "Go easy on him. I'm kinda surprised he didn't cancel the shoot."

"Why? What's wrong?"

"He hasn't been the same since it happened."

"What happened?"

"His niece passed away last month."

"Oh. I didn't know about that."

"It's sort of a secret. He spent a fortune trying to help her."

"Help her, how?"

"She was a drug addict."

"Is that how she died?"

"Uh-huh. Found with a needle in her arm in a public bathroom."

"Oh, my gosh. That's horrible. Where did it happen?"

"At Union Square, in Denver. Mr. Pompadour flew out to identify the body. What a mess. He brought her home and took care of everything. He's not been himself since." She patted her pregnant belly. "She was like Josh to him. The daughter he never had."

"That's so sad."

"Tell me about it," Rosa said.

LAUREN STOOD over the table where Jake sat and cracked the cap on a bottle of sparkling water. "Is Caitlin back?"

"Not yet." Jake looked at his phone. The screen blew up with text bubbles. He scrolled through the messages.

"Maybe she's in her room, showering," she said, patting dust from her pant leg. "It's pretty easy to get dirty out there."

"Speaking of dirty," Jake said.

She followed his line of sight. Mr. Pompadour stood on a chair running a cloth over the top of a large oil painting hanging in the lobby.

"You should cut him some slack," she said, wondering if Jake knew about Roy's niece's recent drug overdose.

"I thought he was bugging you," Jake said. "I figured his white-glove inspections must be slowing down the project."

"I'm in no hurry."

"Your friend Davis might be. Said something about buying a non-changeable ticket because the weather was supposed to be perfect all week."

"If he has to pay to change it, I'll take care of it."

"I really wish you hadn't scheduled the shoot while I'm here with my kid. It's like there's no escaping him. Seems like you two waited until the last minute to book your trip."

"I didn't know you'd be here."

"Davis did. I had to notify the school in advance. And get permission from my ex to take her out for a few days. You should try dealing with Ann."

"No, thanks. We all have our own schedules. Maybe you should have changed yours if you didn't want to be around Davis."

Jake scowled, picked up the paper and snapped it open.

8

Vance peeked his head around the corner of the L-shaped hacienda housing the guestrooms. He spotted Roy crossing the courtyard. It was impossible getting anything past the old eagle eye. Roy waved to him.

Shit.

He detoured and said good morning, trying to keep it short.

"What's the rush?" Roy asked.

"I think I saw someone I know and if I hurry, I can catch up with him."

"Then off you go," Roy said.

Vance walked the opposite direction he'd planned to go, keeping an eye on Roy. He stopped behind Lauren's room and waited a second.

If anyone saw him heading on foot toward the highway, especially Roy, it would draw attention. He cut back toward the courtyard and squatted behind the chest-high hedges bracketing the pool area where he had an unobstructed diagonal view into the dining hall.

Jake sat alone reading the paper. When the path was clear,

he strolled behind the building and jogged to the four-lane blacktop.

His phone pinged in his pocket. He looked at the screen.

Where are u?

He shoved it back into his pocket and stopped near the shoulder of the road, beyond the purview of the security cameras atop the massive iron gates.

Was it possible he'd seen a UFO? It sounded crazy without even saying it aloud.

It'd flown low, hovering three, maybe four feet off the ground, traveling in a northeasterly direction. He swore he'd caught the tail end of it out of the corner of his eye.

Would he put his hand on the Bible and swear to it? Maybe. With the morning sun rising from the east, he couldn't be certain.

He'd been hurrying in the direction it was traveling to spy on it when Roy spotted him. The short encounter had cost him. By the time he got to the road, all he saw were the taillights of a trailer way off in the distance.

Maybe he'd seen a dirt bike pulling a forever-wheelie, showing off. He'd seen ATV riders and bikers riding near the property before. If that were the case, wouldn't there have been a dust cloud?

A semi tractor-trailer approached from the west. Using the pyramid of rocks flanking the gates as cover, he crouched and continued looking to the east. He closed one eye, and holding his forefinger and thumb together in a C-shape, squished the tiny white square—the back of a trailer—in a gesture of frustration as it disappeared on the horizon.

The long-distance hauler rumbled by. After it passed, he lobbed a rock across the highway, to the other side of the desert.

Maybe the hard-pack surface explained no dust. Maybe his eyes were fooling him. Desert sunlight could do that. It could create mirages of all kinds. Water. Snakes. Humans. Aliens. UFOs.

But that didn't square, either. Mirages formed during heat waves. He'd seen plenty of phantoms in the hot summer months. This morning the sun was too low and the cool March temperature wrong for refracting light.

Maybe it was the opposite problem: not enough light. He closed his eyes. An image popped in his head of a cartoonish mountain bicycle with big round fenders lying on its side. It wasn't his imagination. He'd heard it, too, a small combustion engine.

What sort of machine could hover across the desert and disappear? Whatever it was, was a moot point now.

He walked back to the lodge, dictating a text message to Lauren and sent it: See u in 5.

She pinged back instantly. Meet me at the airstrip.

LAUREN FOLLOWED the group of guests heading outside and was halfway to the private airstrip when Vance caught up with her.

"Check it out." She pointed to a dot in the sky. "The Oil Baron's flying in."

"The Oil Baron?" Vance cocked his head.

"He's practically a celebrity."

Oil and gas executives were a big part of the ranch clientele and one old wildcatter, the Oil Baron, still piloted in on a single-engine prop plane. Watching him land it was a coveted event. She could see why. If an airplane could get drunk, this is what it would look like.

The plane buffeted as it approached, wings dipping errati-cally, one coming perilously close to skimming the top of a mountain of crushed limestone piled adjacent to the runway. As it bounced, the back end fishtailed on the plane, skidding to a stop inches from where the runway turned to dirt.

She saw something out of the corner of her eye. "Is that Jake?"

Vance craned his neck over the small crowd of people gathered to watch the small plane land. "What do you think he's doing over there?"

She looked at her watch. It was just before ten in the morning. "I don't know. I think he's looking for something." Jake was hunched over like a candy cane, walking slowly along the backside of the berm, opposite to the one where she and Davis had set up earlier.

"Are you done for the day?" Vance asked.

"Hardly."

"Roy said you saw someone you know? Who'd you see?"

"Speaking of Roy," Vance said, "where is he?"

"I don't know. He's probably micromanaging housekeeping. I overheard him say something about a meeting he was having with a guy who's running late."

She saw a giant microwave tower in the distance, beyond the runway, with various-sized satellite dishes running up and down the pole. "Jeez, that thing is ugly. I don't remember it. Do you?"

"It wasn't here when you sold my ranch back to me. It's a boon for the cartels."

Crap. Where did Roy come from? She smoothed her hair in the breeze, wondering if he'd heard her snide remarks about micromanagement.

"How's it help the cartels?" Vance asked.

"It's Five G. Unbelievable bandwidth. Now I wish I hadn't deeded that land back to Texas Parks and Wildlife. That monstrosity wrecks my view."

That was gracious of Roy to take the blame for releasing the acreage. He wasn't the one who'd deeded the land to the TPWD.

She, Vance, and Jake had when they'd bought the ranch, before they'd sold it back to him.

"He's a character, isn't he?" Roy said about the old wildcatter who'd parked his plane and climbed down from the wing.

Roy led the way to the lodge with the lookie-loos following. He held the door to the dining hall open and let the guests in ahead of her and Vance.

"I'm rescheduling the shoot 'til tomorrow," Roy said to Lauren.

"May I ask why?"

Vance licked his finger and held it in the air behind Roy's back. She had to look away.

"The rooms aren't up to snuff."

The old wildcatter, a fast-talking, wiry fellow who obviously loved the attention, pushed past and headed to the reception desk.

A group of stylish men she guessed to be fortyish, moved across the lobby like panthers. They looked all business, and out of place.

"Who's that?" she asked Roy.

"New arrivals," Roy said in a low voice. "Last-minute booking. Flew in privately late last night."

"Where's their plane?" Vance asked.

"Charter."

"Are they hoping to meet venture capitalists?" Vance asked.

Roy shook his head slowly. His expression was contemplative. "No. They're working on something."

What would a bunch of suits be working on at Roy's luxury guest ranch?

Vance watched them. "Where are they from?"

"They're Israeli," Roy said.

Vance looked at her and raised his eyebrows.

That was a weird. Why would a group of Israeli businessmen

convene at a historic fort in the middle of the West Texas desert? If it were a working vacation, surely, they'd have picked a place that looked a little less like home. If they were in the technology sector, they'd have known the big players had moved on. As a playground for the tech tycoons, Antelope Creek Ranch had fallen out of favor last year when Zack Wisenberg badmouthed the ranch in the media. The only entrepreneurs coming now were wannabes.

"They're not dressed for hunting," Vance joked. "Maybe they're here to fish."

Roy ignored him as the Israelis streamed past, dressed in Italian loafers and custom suits, tight jackets fastened with a single button, the edges of their straight shirttails cut just below the waistline of their trousers.

Vance tried a different angle. "Maybe they're sniper training."

"They're already firearm proficient," Roy said.

Lauren cocked her head.

"Everyone has to join the military at age eighteen." Roy turned toward the table where the six men had taken seats and huddled. "Even women and girls. Mandatory conscription."

"Like the draft?" she asked.

"Don't you two have something better to do than grill me?"

Lauren couldn't help herself. "How do you know they're Israeli?"

"I still have friends in D.C., mostly career military. I avoid the civilian bureaucrats. They're a bunch of lawyers from fancy schools. When my military buddies need a favor, I help when I can. They're here on US Justice Department visas."

That was a mistake. Now Vance wanted to know more. "Who are they?"

"If I tell you, will you stop with the questions?"

He nodded.

"They're with Unit 8200."

Lauren had never heard of it. "What is that?"

Roy scowled. "The *last* question was supposed to be the *last* question."

"They're Israel's version of the NSA," Vance said. "The National Security Agency."

She glared at him. "I know what the NSA is."

"I'll leave you two to duke it out." Roy stopped talking when the big wooden front door swung open and a woman charged past the wildcatter now chatting with Adam at the desk.

It might have been the most purposeful walk Lauren had ever seen. The woman nodded at the two men at the desk as she stalked by.

She wore a dark ensemble that could have been from the same clothier who'd designed the suits the men wore. Except her version had a snug skirt cut at the knee. She was bare-legged with shapely calves: an athlete, not a beauty. The heels of her black leather pumps double-clattered on the Saltillo tile like hooves on cobblestone. Her hair was pulled so tightly it gave her face a lift, accenting high cheekbones. This was not a woman to cross.

"Who is she?" Lauren asked.

Roy rubbed the bristle on his chin. "She's their boss."

"Whose boss?" Vance asked.

"Unit 8200." Roy fixed his gaze on her as she approached the men sitting at a long table.

The men scrambled from the benches to their feet. She motioned them to sit and pulled out the ladder-backed leather chair at the head of the table, the one the men had apparently left vacant for her. She sat, then grabbed the seat with both hands, scooted forward, crossed her legs, smoothed her skirt, and laid her forearms flat on the tabletop, all in one fluid motion.

Why was Israeli Intelligence at Antelope Creek Ranch?

"Their identity is confidential," Roy said. "I trust you'll respect that."

The back door to the lodge burst open. Jake rushed past in such a hurry he brushed the shoulder of one of the seated agents. The man looked up, annoyed. Jake ignored him. He was on a mission.

"I . . . I . . . my daughter," he stammered, "my daughter, Caitlin. She's—" He was breathless. "She's . . . missing."

"How do you know?" Roy asked.

Jake held up her red backpack. His face was chalky. "I went out looking for her. I called her phone and it kept going . . . to . . . voicemail. Then I thought I heard it ringing. It was in the brush, behind the dirt mound, beyond the runway." Jake snapped his neck in the direction of the berms. "It was behind that one."

He pointed out the big picture window framing the mountains, to the hump west of where she and Davis had set up for the drone shots.

"Maybe she left it there. Maybe she's coming back for it," Davis said.

Uh-oh. Where'd he come from?

Jake's tone turned ugly. His eyes bulged. He slammed his fist on the table. The Israelis flinched in concert.

"My daughter is an elite high school runner. She's not going to disappear for almost three hours. She's not going to leave her phone stashed in the desert. And she sure the hell wouldn't worry me like this."

The lodge fell silent.

Lauren didn't know what to say. Neither did anyone else.

Vance treaded carefully. "Has she ever done anything like this before?"

"No," Jake snapped. "She's the most reliable kid I've ever known. Everyone says that about her. If she's five minutes early, she thinks she's five minutes late. Something's wrong. How many kids leave their phone behind?" He fished inside her backpack and held Caitlin's cell up.

The Israelis stared at them. Roy headed their way. Jake followed him. Roy held his hand up signaling Jake to stop. Then the two had words. Jake waited off to the side while Roy talked to the guests.

Davis grimaced. "Sorry."

Up until now, it hadn't been his fault. But what he'd said just now ticked Jake off.

Vance glanced around the room. He lowered his voice. "Did you guys see anything weird?"

"Like what?" she asked.

"You know. Anything suspicious."

"When?" Davis asked.

"When you were out shooting. When you were wrapping things up."

Davis shook his head.

"What do you mean by suspicious?" she asked.

"Seems weird that she would just disappear. Since you were out there, I thought maybe you saw something."

Lauren glared at him. "Don't you think we would have mentioned it?"

"Well, we didn't see anything suspicious," Davis said. "If we did, we would have told you. Jake's going to think this is my fault."

"He'll blame Lauren, too," Vance said.

"Thanks," she said. "What if she *really is* missing?"

Vance turned on his heels and walked toward Roy and Jake, who were huddled in the corner.

Lauren saw Rosa heading toward the desk and headed her off to talk with her privately. "He found her backpack."

Rosa's eyes widened. "I wondered what was going on." She chewed the cuticle on her index finger. "Where?"

"Behind one of the berms."

"Maybe she left it there and is coming back to get it."

"Almost three hours ago? With her cell in it? Do you know if anyone's checked her room?"

Rosa bared her teeth apologetically. "I did. I peeked inside. Just for a minute. I know, it's none of my business, but I overheard you guys talking about it earlier. Housekeeping was cleaning. It didn't look like she'd been back. The shower floor was dry. No one's seen her?"

"No," Vance said, surprising Lauren. "Not since sunrise."

"Jesus." Rosa chewed her lower lip. "This isn't good."

Vance narrowed his eyes. "Jake says it's completely out of character."

"Completely."

Jake's voice startled them.

"My daughter is a Polly Anna. She's never even been to prom because she doesn't want to give the boys the wrong idea."

"What do you think we should do now?" Lauren asked.

"Holy shit," Davis yelled from the dining hall. "You all better take a look at this."

9

Caitlin's jaw throbbed. Muscles she didn't know she had ached from contorting her face, trying to loosen the duct tape sealing her lips. She'd closed her eyes and drifted off, for how long, she didn't know. The cramp in her calf had awakened her. The space she was folded up in was no more than a three-foot square, like an airplane seat, without the chair. She blinked at the pinprick of sunlight flickering from a slit overhead while her rolling prison rumbled forward.

She could have outrun him, could have outrun most people. But he'd held a gun on her. He'd pulled the cover off something hidden in the thick brush near where she'd dropped her backpack. She steadied her breathing, trying to focus, the way she did at the start of a race. The tarp was lightweight, like parachute material. The group of young military personnel she'd seen at the airport leaving Miami wore the same camouflage pattern.

He'd pulled the cover like a David Copperfield trick revealing a vehicle like nothing she'd seen before. Dull, dark gray, and futuristic. It looked alien, like a UFO.

The ranch was in the middle of nowhere. Wasn't it the kind of place where people reported UFO sightings?

Like the place in Nevada, right? She'd seen a post on social media, a spoof inviting people to storm Area 51. Over a million people planned to go. A lot of people believed the government covered up information about UFOs and UAPs—Unidentified Aerial Phenomena.

She'd been recording a new TV series and had watched interviews with trained Navy pilots — not crackpots — who reported sightings that defied physics. Unidentified flying-what-ever objects. Her science teacher told the class the US govern-ment was forming a new branch of the military. The Space Patrol? No, the Space Force.

Maybe she'd imagined the whole thing. UFOs weren't real. Maybe she was experiencing a false memory. People had those, right?

She stretched her arms, wincing at the soreness of her wrists bound with the plastic tie. She leaned forward and reached as far as she could and touched the tarp with her fingertips.

What she felt was real. And she could smell it, too, the aroma reminding her of a gasoline-powered lawnmower that had been used recently. The machine took up most of the trailer.

Bits and pieces of what had happened began to fall into place. The man who'd grabbed her was no alien. He was a human predator with beady eyes, like the pocket mouse that had scurried away when the trouble started. Except the rodent had bright eyes and the man's were as lifeless as dried mud.

It was the element of surprise that tripped her up. Why didn't that pervert Davis see what happened? For all the times he'd stared at her, why wasn't he leering then? Or Daddy's friend, Lauren? If they'd looked her way, they'd have seen what was happening. They could have stopped it.

She'd tried getting their attention, silently begging God to make them turn and look. But they didn't notice because they were busy with the video. She'd seen Davis land the drone, and as soon as the buzzing stopped, she'd heard them talking. Just the underscore of voices, too far away to make out the words. The man surprised her, things happened fast, he slapped the tape over her mouth.

One ATV had started up, then the other. The sounds of the vehicles driving back to the ranch faded. A wake of dust billowed behind the off-roaders, then disappeared. It was so quiet she could hear him inhaling, exhaling, his shoes crunching the hard-pack ground.

He'd forced her to kneel next to him, pushing her head down by the back of her neck, concealing the two of them behind the berm. He'd wadded the tarp and tossed it in on the front seat of the bizarre machine. He ordered her to sit behind him, using the nose of his gun as a pointer.

The machine was loud, but not as loud as the off-roaders. A moment later they were airborne, like a Disney ride. She'd missed her chance.

She couldn't swallow, or breathe. She'd felt for her visor on the top of her head, recalling that her dad straightened it right before she'd gone for her run. But it was ripped from her head during the short flight.

Flight.

Her eyes had stung from the dust. And welled from terror.

Where was everybody? Where was her dad?

Her heart jackhammered under her sweatshirt.

He'd landed the thing behind a white trailer hitched to a dark pickup truck with big wheel wells and dual back tires. In ten more seconds, the back door to the trailer swung open. He pointed his gun at her, barking orders, instructing her to help him push the hovercraft into the open container. It had been easy; it was on wheels.

Her bones and joints vibrated.

A car whooshed by, then another, and another, rocking the container, breaking the mind-numbing staccato of the tires chewing at the blacktop, axles bouncing and squeaking beneath the metal flooring where she sat, cornered. The repetition of noise, and the vibrations, and being trapped was driving her crazy.

Suddenly the trailer fishtailed violently. She tumbled sideways like a sack of potatoes, unable to break the fall with her hands. A horn blared, as if the driver were laying on it. A series of honks followed, shrill beeps, and toots, and deep blasts, coming from different directions.

The trailer jerked left, then right, and again, convulsing in a mechanical seizure, jackknifing sharply at first, its swing slowing like a pendulum. The payload slid sideways, bumping into the metal siding on one side before swaying back toward the middle. She tightened her knees, and pulled them against her chest to keep from being crushed.

Pushing her heels against the cargo, she pressed her back against the bulkhead. The roller-coaster ride wasn't over. The trailer bounced as though it left the road, and rumbled onto the shoulder.

Caitlin wiped her forehead with the backs of her hands, then pressed her feet flat on the metal flooring and inched backward on her seat bones, folding her body into the corner like a grasshopper.

The trailer picked up speed and settled back onto a straight track. She closed her eyes and drew deep breaths through her nose, sucking the air spoiled by gasoline and burned rubber until her heart rate slowed.

In the darkness, she worked the left sleeve of her sweatshirt up, using her chin. She tapped the screen on her fitness tracker with the tip of her nose. The display fogged up. She lowered her hands, letting the face clear and checked the time: 9:40 AM. The Low Battery Warning blinked.

She rested her hands on her knees until the device switched to SLEEP MODE. The screen went dark. She raised her right shoulder and twisting her neck, used her nose and chin to work the cuff of her sweatshirt over the fitness tracker strapped to her wrist.

Without her phone, how would her dad find her? How would anyone know where she was? He'd be panicked by now. Maybe they'd search and find her backpack hidden in the brush. They'd know the spot where she'd disappeared.

The truck hit a pothole, the front axles bounced, the trailer jumped twice, sending her and the payload airborne a few inches, snapping her neck, throwing the back of her skull against the bulkhead. How many bruises did she have?

Her head pounded, and her neck ached while her brain shuffled through the various pains, settling on the sharpest one, the plastic tie cutting into the skin on her wrists. Rolling onto one hip, she stretched one leg, her strained calf muscle responding with another painful contraction.

She asked her mind to forget the pain. She closed her eyes, picturing the trail where she'd gone horseback riding with Lauren. They'd ridden to the top of a mesa with a panoramic view of the ranchlands. She'd felt afraid from that vantage point, like being in the middle of the ocean.

Beyond the ranch there were no houses or businesses, no street lamps, or highway signs. Past the massive electronic gates flanked by pyramids of rocks stacked twenty feet high, there were just miles of blacktop and telephone lines. Her thighs burned on the ride back to the barn. She recognized the pain from training, the response from lactic acid, a byproduct of muscle metabolism.

She didn't use those muscles, the adductors, when running

and training, the long ones on the insides of her thighs. Now it hurt if she flexed her hamstrings. She changed position, slowly stretching the leg with the cramp until the sole of her running shoe stopped at the payload.

What was this thing in front of her? She tried lifting a corner of the tarp with her toe.

Aw . . . aw . . . aw. Another leg cramp.

If only she could stand and stretch. Taste water to soothe her achy tongue, mouth dry as cotton.

She'd flex her wrists and massage her aching joints.

The machine left barely enough room for her; she was cornered like a circus animal.

Something rattled on the metal beneath her. Feeling the flooring with the heels of her palms, she heard it roll out of reach. She kicked at it with her shoe.

Her mind went back to the elevated lookout, miles of desert flat lands broken only by the ranch buildings, no bigger than matchboxes. The natural creek, a serpentine of turquoise, threaded itself across the ranchlands while the Interstate—traveled mostly by long-distance haulers whose gears she'd heard all the way to the foothills—cut a straight line east and west.

Antelope Creek Ranch felt safe inside, like a fortress. She'd been so excited ahead of the trip she'd searched the Internet, marveling at the ancient pictographs carved into the rock walls where humans lived thousands of years ago.

Where was she now, and why was she being held against her will? What was going on? She sniffled and wiped her eyes on her dad's old college sweatshirt. She held the sleeve over her nose and breathed deeply, taking in the faint scent of his cigars. A smell she'd always hated, now so comforting.

Her heart ticked faster as the truck pulling the trailer slowed to a crawl. A minute later it came to a full stop. It lurched forward, rocking the trailer on the hitch, the diesel engine growling and clattering as the truck slowed for a two-beat before turning left. She put her ear against the metal wall.

Light street traffic replaced the highway noise.

Raising her hands to her chin, she tilted her cheek against her wrists and worked her sleeve up to reveal the screen on her fitness tracker. She tapped it with her nose. The Low Battery light blinked faster.

The truck stopped. The door on the back of the trailer creaked open. A shard of sunlight pierced the darkness.

Caitlin twisted her neck away from the light, burying her face into the shoulder of the sweatshirt to shield her eyes. The silhouette stepped inside, grabbed the inside bar, and clanked it shut. She lifted her head and opened her eyes. A bright light blinded her. A cell phone flashlight.

Footfalls clunked. His shadow loomed.

"I'm going to take the tape off your mouth. You scream and I'll kill you, little bitch. Do you understand me?"

She nodded.

Holding the light two inches from her forehead, he picked at the tape. Up close, she smelled that he needed a shower. She held her breath and closed her eyes as he dragged the tip of his fingernail across her upper lip, back and forth, feeling the seam to loosen it. Finding an edge, he pinched the skin above her upper lip and ripped the tape from her mouth. She grit her teeth to keep from yelping.

He held a plastic bottle to her lips.

Water.

Squinting, she grasped for it with her elbows pressed together, clumsy like a baby, palms opening and closing like a clamshell, as she gulped.

"What the fuck?"

Blood surged in her veins. He'd seen something. *Oh, no.*

The light from her fitness tracker glowed from beneath her

sweatshirt. He grabbed her wrists. Water splashed on her face and clothes. Wrapping one huge palm around her hands, he shined his light, looking for it.

Shoving her sleeve up, he twisted her forearms. Her body contorted. He tapped at the screen with his thumb. She dared not look up. The screen lit up. He rotated her hands until they turned at the elbows.

She rolled onto her knees, pulling away in pain. But she was no match for him. He shoved his hand against her throat, his thumb and forefinger opened to a V.

"Get up. You try anything and I will squeeze your pretty little neck until it snaps. You understand?"

She blinked. Her neck was in his grip, his palm pressing on her windpipe. She could barely breathe. Pushing her shoulders against the trailer, she struggled to get to her feet. He unfastened the tracker and stuck it in his pocket. Shoving the heel of his right hand into her chest, he slammed her body against the trailer. She went limp, collapsing at the knees, crumpling in a heap. Tears welled but she kept silent.

"Food and water," he barked, dropping a plastic bag at her feet. "And use this.'"

His cell light was on a plastic bucket.

"To relieve yourself."

She nodded. Out of the corner of her eye she saw him pull a knife from his pocket.

He tossed a roll of paper towels at her, thumbed the knife, snapping the blade open with a clack. She recoiled.

"Calm down. I'm gonna free your hands so you can do your biz." He inserted the blade between her wrists and sliced the plastic tie, releasing her wrists. "You have one minute," he said, sidling toward the back of the trailer. He opened it, hopped down, and shut the door.

Caitlin felt for the pail. She didn't have enough room to

squat. She had to hurry. Yanking her leggings down, she balanced the plastic bucket between her bent knees, quickly peed, and pulled her tights up.

Light filled the trailer. He hopscotched toward her, took a new zip tie from his back pocket and tied her wrists. He picked up the pail, stuffed the paper towels under his free arm and squeezed past the cargo, crabbing toward the exit with both shoulders braced against the wall to balance.

The container was twelve, maybe fifteen feet long and the space between the cargo and trailer wall so tight he'd had to scale his way to the exit. When he pushed the back door with his palm, it swung too wide. He had to set the bucket down and jump off the ledge to catch it from opening all the way.

The bright glare burned her eyes, as if leaving a dark movie theater at noon on a sunny day. Shading her eyes with the crook of her elbow, she processed the scene. It was a public place with a building in the background.

A rundown convenience store made of corrugated siding. With posters in the windows. Beer signs. Lottery tickets for sale. In English and Spanish. She recognized the smell: fuel. He'd stopped at a gas station. There were no landmarks other than the faded pumps and desert flatlands.

He held the strap of the fitness tracker between his thumb and forefinger, dangling it like a carrot in front of a horse. Then he released it, lifted one leg at the knee and smashed it with his boot. He held up the remains, grinning like the devil.

She cast her eyes away and down.

The metal door clanked shut with a bang, followed by the grating of metal-on-metal—the T-bar being set into place. The trailer rocked gently. She cowered in the back corner like a broken marionette.

It went pitch black. The dampness of perspiration and the water he'd spilled on her clothing chilled her core. But her mouth was free. She opened it wide, like at the dentist, and rotated her jaw. Her face was sore. She licked her lips, tasting the bitter residue of the duct tape.

Her eyes readjusted to the darkness. It was the first chance she'd had to see his face since he'd first captured her. The cell flashlight in his hand lit his upper body like an actor on stage, except the spotlight was pointed the wrong way, at him. She'd seen enough to describe him. Yes. A pit bull with eyes set too close to his nose.

Twisting her body to the left, she raised her right shoulder and rubbed her stinging lips with her thumbs, hands clamped together like the lobsters with banded claws she'd seen for sale in fish tanks at the grocery store.

A moment later, the trailer was back up to speed. She twisted the rosy metal ring round and round on her finger until it hurt, sobbing.

10

"Can you replay it?" Lauren sat next to Davis.

Vance and Jake hovered over the tablet while he ran through the video, forward and reverse, switching between the PLAY, PAUSE, FORWARD, and BACK buttons.

"Come, come on, come on," Jake said.

Davis fast-forwarded to the beginning scene when he'd landed the drone, paused, and backed it up a few seconds. He stopped on a frame that looked down at the desert from couple hundred feet up. A fairly wide shot.

Lauren saw her miniature sparkly orange-and-white ATV heading toward the berm. Davis put the tip of his index finger on the HAND tool shaped like a mitt and moved it around the screen, advancing the video one frame at a time, one thirtieth of a second.

"There we are." Davis pointed to the upper right corner. "And I think that might be her."

Her heart skipped. "Back it up a hair."

Davis tapped the reverse ARROW a few strokes and stopped.

"Did you record time code?" she asked.

"Uh-huh."

"What's it say?" She and Davis had had plenty of disagreements about it. From his old days in TV news, Davis had the habit of recording the time of day in GMT. It was confusing, the way the long sets of numbers skipped between recordings. She preferred using the length of each video clip, always resetting the time to zero for each new scene. But now his way could be very helpful.

Davis paused the video. It was in military time. "Oh-seven-four-hundred."

7:40:07:12 AM, to be exact, expressed in hours, minutes, seconds, and frames.

Jake leaned closer. "Can you reverse it and slow down it down more?"

"Sure."

Jake balanced one hand on Davis' shoulder, watching.

Davis clicked the ARROW tab on the lower right side of the keyboard and tapped it, moving one frame at a time, stopping so Jake had time to process each scene.

"Stop," Jake said.

The figure in the upper right corner of the screen was as small as an ant. Davis had caught it accidentally while landing the drone. He tapped one frame forward as the figure on the screen ran toward the hump opposite the one where they'd set up.

Jake put his finger on the screen. "That's where I found her backpack."

The drone landed, followed by a quick shot of Davis' feet and one hand reaching into camera view, then the screen went black.

"What the fuck?" Jake snapped. "What's wrong with you?" He glared at Davis, who leaned away. "She was going to get her backpack and you didn't follow her."

He'd been warned to stay away from her.

Davis tapped the FORWARD button and returned to the first frame where she'd come into view, and paused the video. Positioning the HAND tool with his finger over the image of Caitlin, he tapped the ZOOM key, enlarging it. The more he magnified the shot, the fuzzier it got. But it was clear that the teenager was alone.

He pressed the PLAY button and twenty seconds later, Davis' ankles and shoes appeared again on screen. His hand reached into the frame and picked up the drone. Then the screen went black again.

"Shit." Jake yanked the hair on his head.

Davis recued and played it back again. It went quickly in real time. Caitlin was a speck in the corner of the wide shot for one, maybe two, maybe three seconds.

Jake stared at the screen. He pounded his fist on the table. After a moment of silence, he turned to Davis and said, "I'm about to lose my shit. Why didn't you follow her?"

The Israelis sitting at the nearby table turned and stared at them. Again.

"What are you looking at?" he growled at the group.

Davis defended himself. "I didn't see her."

It wasn't fair of him to blame Davis. "I know now it looks like we should have seen something, but we were focusing on the drone," Lauren said.

"If you'd been paying attention, you'd have seen it happen," Jake barked.

What nerve.

Vance intervened. "Wait a minute. I know you're upset. But you can't blame them."

Davis went back to the last image of Jake's daughter: a speck in the corner on the screen

Where was he, her dad, when she went missing? What was

he thinking, letting her go alone? She had an idea. "Go to the final shot of the airstrip. Maybe there's something there."

Davis closed the open video file and a row of thumbnails popped on the screen. He tapped the last one in the sequence. The file opened to a new video player. Davis pressed the PLAY icon and the shrill buzzing startled them. He tapped the mute button.

"Stop," she said.

Davis saw it, too, and stopped, tapping the video forward, one frame at a time.

Her eyes were finely tuned from thousands of hours of editing. "There. Stop the shot."

The scene from the drone flying over the top of the airstrip was almost perfectly lit by the morning sun. The video showed amazing detail.

Just before Davis had started to pack up, Lauren had thought of one more shot—it was a producer thing. There was always *one more shot*. After arguing for a minute, he'd restarted the drone and sent it back up to record a flyover of the private runway. It was a major selling point for the ranch and it might help Roy attract certain new clients.

Davis objected because of the big pile of limestone dumped adjacent to the airstrip. She'd convinced him she'd find a way to edit around it.

"Stop. Right there," she said.

It was a wide shot of the hump and surrounding area, a five-hundred-foot radius, less than an acre. The tracks from the ATVs were visible as thin threads, crisscrossing from the ranch to the eastern berm.

"That's weird," Vance said. "There're no other tire tracks. Does your drone record GPS?"

Davis nodded. "I saved the coordinates. I was thinking I might get a shot from the same spot at sunset. If we go back, I can do a visual overlay. I can get us back to almost the same exact spot."

"We should call the sheriff," Vance said.

"No way." Jake was adamant. "Do not call that poor excuse for a lawman."

Vance's shoulders squared and his chest puffed up.

"We really should call the Marfidio County sheriff," Lauren said, "and initiate an Amber Alert."

Vance glared at her.

"What are you saying?" Jake asked.

"I'm not saying anything." She should have kept her mouth shut. She was getting ahead of things.

"Come on. Let's talk to Roy and see what he thinks," Vance said.

Jake raked his scalp with his fingernails. "What do you think happened?"

"I don't know," Vance said. "We need to start a search."

She'd been warned there were mountain lions in the foothills. His daughter couldn't outrun one of those. What if that's what happened? What kind of grisly scene might they find?

An Amber Alert? What was she thinking? They were in the middle of no man's land, thirty miles from the closest neighbor. No post office. No school. Not even a gas station.

Her intuition told her the search wouldn't lead to the girl. That she was gone. The way Vance glared at her, she suspected he thought the same thing. He just couldn't say it aloud. Not in front of Jake.

11

THE SEARCH

Vance opened the rear passenger door and Lauren made room for herself in the middle seat between him and Davis. Roy Pompadour sat behind the wheel of the Hummer. Jake rode shotgun.

It was Vance's idea to take one vehicle, suggesting only one set of tire tracks would make things less confusing. Roy parked a two-minute walk from the humpback where Jake found the red backpack. The five fanned out on foot.

He and Lauren walked in lockstep, heading toward the berm.

"Whoa . . . whoa." He held his arms out to his sides to stop her. "Wait here." He walked around the base of the mound where the topsoil was subtly groomed into a large swirl pattern.

Weird. One set of footprints crisscrossed inside the semicircle. Outside the perimeter, a different set of prints. He knelt to get a closer look.

Jake joined Lauren. He shaded his eyes from the sunlight. "What's he looking at?"

"I don't know."

Vance hurried over. "Let me see the bottom of your shoe."

Jake did as asked.

"The footprints inside the circle look like yours." The same sets of prints from a flat leather sole led to the swirl pattern and zigzagged inside it, consistent with Jake searching for a ringing cell phone.

Jake furrowed his brow. "What do you see?"

"Look at the pattern on the ground." He gestured to the semicircle of freshly smoothed dirt arching from the base of the berm. "Then look over there." He pointed to the two sets of footprints outside the circle. "The flat ones are yours. The others look like running shoes."

Lauren placed her hands on her hips. "There should be prints leading away."

Jake heated up. "What are you suggesting?"

Vance squatted on his heels, looking closer. "I'm not. I'm assessing." Jake's were the only shoe prints inside the circle of smooth earth ending at the base of the humpback.

"I don't understand," Lauren said. "What would make that kind of a pattern? And why aren't there tracks from her running shoes inside it?"

He looked up at her. "I don't know." That wasn't entirely true. If what he'd seen was real, a flying object, the pattern made perfect sense. If it were some sort of low-flying aircraft, the blades could have wiped the existing footprints prints from the topsoil when it lifted off.

Jake took one step inside the circle.

"No!" Vance jumped and grabbed his arm. "Don't disturb the crime scene."

Jake wrinkled his brow. "Crime scene?"

"I didn't mean *crime scene.*" He did mean it, but saying it was an involuntary response.

"I heard there're mountain lions out here," Lauren said.

"If that happened, there would be forensic evidence. Like—"

"Oh my God," Jake said. "Someone has taken my daughter."

Davis hollered from the opposite berm, the one where he'd set up earlier. "Hey. I found something."

He and Lauren ran over to see what. Jake hustled the first few steps but couldn't keep up, breaking into a fast waddle.

Roy stood with Davis, looking at something. Jake caught up and elbowed his way past. He dropped to one knee and picked up the purple visor.

"It's hers. I'm positive," Jake said, stricken. "I bought it for her."

Jake's mouth was slightly agape and he stared into the distance, panning his head slowly from the daunting mountains in the background to the spot where they stood. "This doesn't add up. Her hat, how did it get here? Like you said, there would be footprints from her running shoes."

"Or tire tracks," Roy said.

"From a getaway vehicle," Davis said, kneading his hands.

Lauren brushed the hair from her face. "He's right. How could she disappear without more evidence?"

"Stay here." Vance signaled the others to wait, and he and Roy jogged to the berm with the swirl pattern, taking a wide berth around it, inspecting it from different angles.

Jake stood next to Lauren, clutching the visor to his sunken chest like a small boy holding a stuffed animal.

"The first twenty-four hours will be the best chance we have," Vance said, stepping back two paces, studying the scene. The berm in front of him was thirty feet tall and blocked the line of sight from the ranch.

The vegetation at the base was thick, at least four feet high and six feet deep, made up of creosote bushes and young mesquite trees, the former emitting a distinctive bitter fragrance.

Vance turned his back to the berm; the other humpback lay on an angle to his left, rotated to the south, facing the foothills. The two berms created a giant, wide open, V-formation with a twenty-foot-wide break between them at the apex. He walked between the mounds, heading toward the ranch. The airstrip lay ahead and the mountain of whitish, crushed limestone, stock-piled for maintenance, he assumed, was next to the runway.

The location provided cover from all directions: The perfect layout for an ambush.

A breeze kicked up and a dust devil spun, churning the topsoil, kicking up dust. "Wait here."

He jaunted around the perimeter of the circle, careful not to disturb the scene where it ended at the humpback. He shoved the toe of his boot into the slope and scaled five feet up the berm, crabbing along the side of it, using his hands to balance. Something had caught his eye.

He held onto the limb of a mesquite tree so he could slide a couple of feet closer. It was too far to reach. He let go, grabbing hold of the next nearest branch and stretched his arm as far as it would go, plucking whatever it was from a bush. Stuffing it in his pants pocket, he slid most of the way before jumping down. He showed it to Roy. It was a piece of torn fabric, no bigger than a dollar bill, thin and durable like parachute material.

Roy raised his eyebrows and felt it, rubbing it between his thumb and forefinger. "It's desert camo. Military grade."

Vance shoved it in his jacket pocket. "What do you think?"

"I don't know," Roy said. "Let me see it again."

Facing the berm for privacy, he handed Roy the remnant.

Roy studied it more closely. A worried look crossed his face. "Let's keep this between us. But you hang onto it."

"Sure." He put the evidence back in his pocket and they rejoined the others gathered around the Hummer.

"We have to call the sheriff," Jake said in an about-face. "Roy, you need to call in every favor you have."

"Let's think this through," Roy said. "We need to consider the unintended consequences."

"I don't care about unintended consequences." Jake's voice cracked. "*Fuck* unintended consequences."

Jake took Caitlin's phone from his pants pocket, padded six keys on the screen, and handed it to Lauren. She glanced at it and handed the phone to Vance.

Vance looked at the screen. "Why didn't you show us this before?" He was angry. "You have the password to get into her phone? And you're telling us now?"

"I . . . I . . . don't know. I didn't . . . ah . . . ah." He crushed the purple visor in his left hand.

Vance clicked on the texting app. No new messages. He opened the photos file. A blurry image appeared. He checked the time stamp: 7:43. He swiped right and looked at the picture taken before it.

Lauren stood next to him, eyes glued to the screen. The previous picture was of a tiny rodent with desert vegetation in the background. He swiped again. A picture taken at Miami International Airport with Caitlin in the foreground smiling: a selfie. He pulled up the pic of the mouse again.

"What is that?" Jake peered over his shoulder, blinking and swallowing.

Vance scrolled back and forth with his thumb and forefinger, flipping between the picture of the pocket mouse and the out-of-focus shot. He walked to the berm, holding the phone in front of him. The creosote plants in the background were exactly the same. "Something must have surprised her."

"What's the time stamp on the photos?" Lauren asked.

"The photos were taken two seconds apart at seven forty-three this morning."

"Oh, God," Jake said.

Davis wrung his hands. "This is my fault."

Lauren grabbed him by the wrists and shook his big arms. "No, it's not. I was out here with you. The ATVs and drone would have canceled the noise coming from over here."

Jake's upper lip quivered.

Vance said, "I'm thinking we're lucky as hell you were out here at all. And that we have her phone. Otherwise, we'd have even less to go on. Now we have a timeline establishing her disappearance."

Jake mouthed the word *"Dis-a-ppear-ance."*

Davis hung his head and stared at the desert floor.

Maybe age was slowing Davis down. These days he seemed to be two or three steps behind what was going on. He'd been working for peanuts captaining Jake's yacht, oblivious that he'd been the unsuspecting security guard, sitting on top of more than thirty-five-million dollars cash stashed in the hull. Now he was the hapless documenter of a live kidnapping.

On the other hand, his video production skillset was as sharp as ever.

Maybe she was being unfair. They'd been using him, exploiting him as a first line of defense like an alarm system. Davis wasn't stupid. He was gullible. That wasn't fair, either. He'd trusted her, and that had been his error.

They'd planned on moving the money out of the belly of the boat to a more secure location but hadn't come up with a workable plan yet. Soon, they'd all agreed, she, Vance and Jake, just as soon as they figured out a safe place, they'd move the money. When the time was right, and they no longer needed him to captain the yacht, she'd help him financially so he could go home to Florida. But the time hadn't come. Not yet.

Vance spoke softly. "It's not your fault, either one of you."

Lauren nodded and patted Davis on the shoulder. "He's right. There's nothing we could have done because we didn't see it happen."

Roy noticed how hangdog Davis was. "They're right, son. It's not your fault."

Vance walked the perimeter again, looking for clues he might have missed. There were no escape tracks. No tire treads or footprints. Nothing.

Roy read his mind. "I've never seen anything like it. Crop circles have explanations. But this . . . ." Roy shielded his eyes from the sun, swiveling his head left and right, scanning the desert terrain he knew so well. The old, retired Army commander who'd led a platoon in the jungles of 'Nam was trained to see things and knew the ranchlands better than the back of his hands. "It's mystifying."

Vance looked in the same direction as Roy, following his line of sight. The desert was as smooth as a beach after the high tide had gone out. How in the world did Caitlin disappear with no trace?

Lauren broke the silence. "What do we do now?"

Roy said, "Follow me."

12

CAITLIN IS MISSING, DAY ONE, EARLY AFTERNOON

E agle-eyed Roy was the first to spot the Marfidio County Sheriff's truck motoring up the gravel drive, in no apparent hurry. Vance stood with him under the awning in front of the main entrance as he rolled the brown patrol pickup to a gentle stop.

Jake waited inside, watching from the narrow vertical window with his arms clamped across his chest. When the sheriff walked through the front door and passed Jake, one could have cut the air with a two-by-four. The two men had a history.

Vance followed Roy, who led the way past the reception desk. The sheriff walked alongside the ranch owner, balancing a metal clipboard in the crook of his elbow, the heels of his ostrich boots brushing the tile.

Roy ushered them to the game room for privacy. He pulled up a chair at the poker table for the sheriff, who stood for a moment. Tooled leather belt, pale gray Stetson cowboy hat with a fancy band, and a MontBlanc pen in his shirt pocket. In place of a tie, a stringed bolo with snake rattles around the collar of his plaid shirt, held together with a jeweled map of Texas.

After the others were seated, Sheriff Manny sat, too. "You say you have video."

Davis jumped into action, switching seats with Lauren in order to sit next to the sheriff.

Manny rubbed the day-old bristle on his chin waiting for Davis to fire up the tablet.

Davis cued it, set the tablet in front of Manny, and tapped the PLAY button. When the frame with Jake's daughter came up on the screen, he paused it, and placed his finger beneath the tiny image of her in the upper corner of the screen.

"That her?" Manny asked.

"Of course, that's her," Jake snapped.

Vance raised his hand, palm facing Jake, who nodded and quieted.

"Yes. That's my daughter."

"Time of day?"

"Around seven-forty this morning," Davis said.

Manny opened the top of his metal clipboard and took the fancy pen from his pocket. "Full name."

"Caitlin Fleming," Jake said.

"Age?"

"Fifteen."

Manny pointed to the video screen. "This morning is the last time you saw her?"

Jake nodded.

"What time was that?"

"I don't know exactly. It was still dark out."

The sheriff plucked his phone from his pocket and tapped

the screen. A few seconds later, he said, "Sunrise was about seven-thirteen this morning. Huh."

Jake's tone turned ugly. "What's that supposed to mean?"

Manny looked out the window at the endless desert and narrowed his eyes. "You let her go out there before sunup?"

Jake pushed his chair back and jumped to his feet.

Vance intervened. "Hey." He blocked Jake from the sheriff and waited for him to calm down.

"What's this?" Manny asked Davis.

Davis leaned over to look. Manny ran his finger over a pair of pale blue lines superimposed just inside the outer frame of the video screen. The lines were thin, like strands of human hair.

Lauren craned her neck. "It's something called Safe Title."

The sheriff adjusted his cowboy hat side-to-side with his fingertips, and squinted at her. "What's it fer?"

"It's for broadcast TV," Davis said. "You see the entire picture on the web. But on a television set, there's a space, like a bleed line in printing."

"Huh," Manny said.

Lauren added, "It's mostly there for Chyrons, so the text on the screen doesn't—"

Manny held his hand up, as in too much information. "I'd like to see more of it. The video. Cue it to the beginning. And let me listen to it."

Davis dragged the player bar to the head and pressed the play ARROW.

"Dang, that'll bust an eardrum," Manny said.

Davis muted the audio coming the drone engine.

"Never seen it like this before." The sheriff appeared mesmerized. "Beautiful sunrise. What were you doing out there?"

Lauren said, "We're working on a video."

"Fer what?"

"The ranch. We're working for Roy."

"Is that so. Y'all should know better."

She snapped her head back as if insulted. "What's that supposed to mean?"

Jake pounded the green fabric on the card table. "My daughter is missing. Can we please focus on that?"

Vance jumped to his feet again, ready to intervene if Jake tried something stupid.

Manny ignored Jake's posturing and faced Davis. "Do you have an FAA license?"

"I do."

"Then you oughta know it's illegal to fly at an altitude of more than four hundred feet."

Roy, who'd just been listening up until now, said, "I'll take responsibility."

"Just a warning. This time. Got a lotta cartels flying drones near the border towns. Dropping kilos of meth and fentanyl and guns and other bad shit. New cell tower out there is a bonanza for the bad guys. Feds have us on the lookout for drones." He eased his chair back and stood. "Have the okay to shoot 'em down like clay pigeons."

"What about my daughter?"

"Roy says you found some a her belongings."

"I did."

"I need the stuff," Manny said.

Jake's face turned purple, like he might erupt. "Why?"

"You want help or not?" He flipped his metal clipboard closed with a clack. "Whatever ya got is evidence that could help."

Jake looked to Roy. "Evidence?"

Roy said to Jake, "Give him her things, the stuff you found at the scene."

Jake got to his feet and stood silently for a five-count, then ambled out the side door leading to the guestrooms.

When Jake was gone, the sheriff said, "I got kids, too. This kinda stuff makes my blood boil."

"What do you think?" Vance asked.

Manny fondled one snake rattler. "I dunno." He glanced at the ranch owner. "Roy says there're no tire tracks or footprints or anything suggesting a struggle. Or anything showing an escape route." He looked at him. "Didja see the same thing?"

He nodded. Roy didn't take exception that Manny looked to him for corroboration. As an ex-detective, it was natural the sheriff would ask him. "There is a pattern I didn't recognize."

"What kinda pattern?"

He did his best to describe the swirls.

The sheriff paused. "Darn hard to say what that could be. I'd like to take a look at the area she went missing."

Manny was about to say something else when Jake stalked through the doorway and dropped the red backpack and purple visor on the table.

The sheriff raised his eyebrows. "This everything?"

Jake sat back in the chair he'd left. "As far as I know."

Vance cast his eyes down at the big orange tiled floor. If Jake kept her phone, it would help them.

Manny stood to leave, slinging the backpack over his shoulder and hanging the visor over his wrist. "Y'all know the drill. She's gotta be missing for twenty-four hours."

This time Jake lunged at him and Manny leaned back on his heels. Vance stepped between them. Jake reluctantly put his hands up in an act of surrender, counted a two-beat, flattened his hair with his palms, then placed a hand over each ear and pressed.

"But this is a special circumstance," Manny said, checking his notes. "Fifteen years old. Right?"

"That's right." Jake shoved his hands in the pockets of his baby-blue Bermuda shorts.

"You don't suppose there's any way she's gone off with a boy, do ya?"

"No chance." Jake's voice carried through the open doorway. "No way."

Adam, at reception, craned his neck over the desk and stared.

Roy approached Jake. "You need to calm down. Let's think this through. I've been thinking I should call Barry Landeros' group."

Vance knew him, too. Barry headed up The Secondmen, an all-volunteer group that helped ranchers along the border spot cartels and coyotes moving drugs and humans. Roy had a good relationship with them.

Roy kneaded Jake's shoulder. "His guys know the terrain inside and out, better than the Border Patrol."

"I'm gonna call them, too," Manny said.

Roy cocked his head. "The Secondmen? Why?"

"No. Border Patrol. There's unspeakable stuff that goes on out there." The sheriff snapped his chin toward the window with an angle on the desert and mountains. "No one's safe. I wouldn't let my daughter go. Not alone."

Jake's forearms quaked and he stared at Roy. "Why didn't you warn me? If I knew it was dangerous, I wouldn't have let her go. I saw Lauren out there."

"I wasn't by myself," she said. "And I didn't go that far."

Jake's thermostat spiked. "What's that supposed to mean? You were right next to the spot where I found her backpack. Matter of fact, I can't believe you didn't see it happen."

The sheriff came to her defense. "Now don't go blaming others. Me? I wouldn't a-let no woman go alone." Manny squared his shoulders. "But you're a bunch of outta-towners not up on the local news, I reckon."

Vance had kept his mouth shut while Manny and Jake sparred. Time to intervene. "What local news?"

"The border's a hot spot. The cartels have been real active lately because every day some official in the government threatens to shut the border down an' it starts a stampede."

"What's that got to do with my daughter's disappearance?"

"Not sayin' it does. Just sayin'."

Jake's scary-movie-Freddy-Kruger voice got scarier. "Just saying what?" He stood and got too close to the sheriff.

Poised to diffuse what might happen next, Vance placed his open palm in front of Jake's chest and swore he felt Jake's heart thumping from a half foot away.

Manny said, "Not sayin' nuthin'. The cartels run the border. It's their turf. They do whatever they please."

Jake recoiled, staggering.

Vance reached for his elbow, steadying him as he slumped into the chair.

"This place is five hundred dollars a night," Jake whispered. "It's supposed to be safe."

Antelope Creek Ranch had been built over 150 years ago as a fortress to protect settlers from outlaws and Indians. It seemed as if it still had the same problem.

"Don't go lookin' fer her. Save your strength."

Jake looked up and around. A spider web of red lines mottled the whites of his eyes and dark circles hung beneath them. He opened his mouth to speak but no words came out.

Speechless was good. Jake's supersized ego had a way of fucking things up.

Then the sheriff kept on talking. "Cartels keep on getting smarter. First ones to get new technology. Faster than us, makes it hard for the good guys to keep up with 'em. Well, I better get a move on."

"I appreciate whatever you can do," Roy said.

The sheriff shifted his eyes to Jake. "This is gonna be the longest day of your life. But you're gonna have to keep it together. Understood?"

Jake nodded.

"We'll take care of him," Lauren said.

"I'll be in touch. Good day." Manny adjusted the red back-pack higher on his shoulder and tipped his Stetson.

Vance walked him to his truck. "I thought you wanted to look at the scene."

"Didja look at it?"

"Yep."

"Didja see anything I should know about?"

He reminded him of the swirl pattern, and lack of tire tracks, and the position of two sets of footprints. The sheriff was satisfied. "She coulda run off with a boy."

Manny was testing him. He didn't believe the sheriff thought that, even for a second. Running the scenario in his head of what he'd seen earlier, interrupted when Roy had intercepted him in the courtyard, he wondered if he'd seen the tail end of her abduction. Manny said the cartels had cutting-edge technology. What if they'd taken her? What if Manny was fishing? Trying to figure out if he'd seen something beyond what he reported.

Roy ran to the portico with his cell to his ear. Jake trotted slowly behind him.

"That was Barry," Roy said. "He'll be here at sunup. He promises fifty men."

"Sunup?" Jake sounded gut-punched. "What are we going to do until then?"

"Come on, Jake," Roy said. "Let's go inside and talk."

Manny motored down the driveway. The automatic gates

swung wide and the sheriff hung a slow right-hand turn, heading east onto the Interstate. A plume of dust billowed and rolled over the gates. When the air cleared, the brown patrol truck was gone. The same way the white trailer vanished on the highway. Like Caitlin had, too.

A new piece of information: If what he'd seen was a dirt bike or and off-roader, it would have kicked up dust, the same way the patrol truck just did. And Manny was going slowly when he left.

13

J osh Dominquez's stomach did a cartwheel recalling the severed finger stuck to his shoe. He powered the window down on the Range Rover, stuck his head out the window, and sucked air through his nose. The light up ahead turned red.

He composed a text while he was stopped: Hi sweetie. I'm in the neighborhood.

Rosa answered instantly. What a surprise. Your pregnant wife and unborn child can't wait to see you.

Waiting for the light, he replayed the events of that night in his head for the 99th time.

He'd hated calling Roy Pompadour in the middle of the night with the bad news that the prototype had been stolen, but he knew Roy would know what to do. He'd driven to the 24-hour gas station and used the pay phone. Roy told him to call 911 and go back to the lab and wait.

The local Pecos County Sheriff's Office had jurisdiction and two deputies responded to the initial call. A representative from the building's management team arrived next. By the time he'd been cleared to leave, the FBI had dispatched two agents.

He'd made statements about what he'd seen, and told both the local and federal investigators that he'd left the property briefly to call his boss. When asked why he didn't use his cell, he'd told them the truth: There were national security concerns to that.

He typed: love you, and sent it just as the light turned green.

He'd given them his contact information before driving back to his condo. After he returned to his rental, he'd shredded the document he'd received the old-fashioned way: securely, via fax.

The Israelis had selected the remote location for research and development and both parties, his and theirs, had gone to extraordinary lengths to protect the project from security breaches.

Was it an inside job? It had to be. Security was too tight for it to have gone any other way.

He'd called Roy again the next morning for an update. A group of Unit 8200 agents had been dispatched immediately and had already arrived at the ranch. They wanted to interview him.

Twenty minutes south of the ranch, he called Roy on his cell. Roy said to go to the Waffle House east of town and wait for his call.

He placed a napkin over his nose and mouth to filter the aroma of bacon and eggs. When the waitress handed him a greasy menu, he set it on the opposite side of the table and ordered coffee and water.

He checked his phone again. It was almost two in the afternoon. Roy hadn't shown up or returned his recent calls.

He'd personally done the background check on the man who applied for the job as the test pilot for the hovercraft. The veteran Army chopper pilot had flown everything from Chinook transport aircraft to the Army's premier assault AH-64 Apache. He seemed overqualified for the job. When his record came back clean, it allayed any reservations about hiring him.

The fax they'd sent from Tel Aviv the night of the break-in at the lab showed something different: a dishonorable discharge and a subsequent felony conviction for armed robbery in Florida. The Israeli's were light years ahead of the rest of the world when it came to intelligence gathering. Someone had obviously scrubbed the pilot's criminal record before they'd conducted the background check on him. He'd been calling the test pilot, but the guy had gone off the grid after the prototype was stolen.

Something else gnawed at him even more. The pilot came with a personal recommendation from Roy Pompadour. He'd kept that intel to himself during the investigation. Was it possible that Roy had made a fatal error in judgment and that the pilot was rogue? He'd wait for the right time, then he'd confront Roy about it.

After another hour passed, he left the restaurant and headed to the ranch. Rosa had been texting every half hour. Keeping her at bay indefinitely with no legit reason was going to raise suspicion. He'd have happily asked Roy for his blessing to show up at the ranch unannounced except he wasn't answering his calls. Better to be at Roy's mercy than Rosa's.

LAUREN WATCHED Jake from the window. He lumbered across the courtyard, hunched over, the soles of his loafers dragging on the manicured gravel path.

Vance joined her in the foyer. "How's he doing?"

"The way he looks." She twirled the ends of her blond hair. "He's calling Caitlin's mom."

"I wouldn't wanna be the one to do that."

"Me, neither."

They walked past Adam, who chatted with one of the Israelis at the reception desk. She followed Vance to the lobby exit. He held the door open as they exchanged hellos with two more Israelis heading inside. She sat next to him on the wooden bench under the portico, but waited until they were alone to ask, "I wonder why they're here?"

He shrugged. "Not me."

"Why not?"

"They're friends of Roy's."

She said, "You mean associates of friends of Roy's. Have you noticed Roy seems a little detached?"

"That's his façade."

She furrowed her brow. "What's that supposed to mean?"

"Come on. We all have one."

"I don't."

He laughed aloud. "Right. You're terminally unique."

Where was this coming from?

He kept at it. "We all project a picture of what we want people to think about us, what we think looks good. Some of us want to be liked. Others want to be respected. Some of us—"

"What do you want?"

"I guess I'd like to be respected."

"And you think people might not respect you?"

He laughed at that. "I guess you'd have to define respect." He lowered his voice. "I'm not sure I qualify these days, if you get my drift."

His "drift" had to mean the dirty money they were hiding.

He wasn't finished. "Most people aren't who you think they are. Most don't even know who they are because they don't have enough self-awareness to make a half-assed assessment."

Where *was* this coming from? Was he revealing inner

thoughts? Or was he dissecting Roy? As much as she'd have liked to dig deeper into his psyche, it had started with "Roy's façade," so she stuck to the topic. "Is that what you think about Roy? That he's a fake?"

"On the contrary."

"Care to elucidate?"

"Lucky for you, I know that word." He paused for a beat. "Roy's life has been carefully choreographed."

"By who?"

"By him."

"I get it. After the choreographer was done, he hired a set designer to build his façade."

"I find your sarcasm very attractive."

She said, "I don't think psycho-babble suits you."

"Maybe you're rubbing off on me."

She raised her eyebrows. "I'm not touching that line."

He chuckled and changed the subject. He reached into his jacket pocket, and removed a piece of fabric.

"What is that?"

"A clue."

"What kind of a clue?"

"I'm not sure yet."

"Where'd you get it?"

"Where Jake found her backpack."

"Maybe it was there for a long time."

He stood. "I doubt it. Look at it. The seams are freshly torn and it's clean."

"Where're you going?"

"For a walk."

"Can I go with you?"

"I'd rather go alone. I need some air."

He cut through the dining room. Lauren followed him,

hanging back far enough not to annoy him and watched as he strode toward the spot where Caitlin had disappeared.

He'd rather be alone? When she'd suggested that Roy seemed detached, Vance didn't say anything about Roy's niece overdosing. She'd just found out about it from Rosa. He probably hadn't heard the story yet.

Uninvited thoughts raced inside her head. What if he'd stayed at the ranch instead of returning to Miami with her late last summer after they'd sold the ranch back to Roy as a preemptive strike against the next stage of their relationship? He'd been upfront that he'd barely even been on three dates with the same woman, much less having been married to one. Maybe he was doing her a favor.

Maybe he needed more time.

Stop being so selfish. Jake's daughter is missing.

What if he moved in and they drove each other crazy? What if it didn't work out?

"Where's Vance?"

Jake's voice brought her to the present. He stared at her through glassy eyes.

"Did you call your ex?"

"No."

"Why not?"

"I don't need you nagging me about it."

She felt her face flush. "I wasn't trying to nag you."

"Excuse me." The Israeli woman, the one in charge, slowed, then passed between them. Her group had gathered around the pool area and when they saw their boss coming, they stood.

Jake walked out the front door under the awning, taking the long route back to his room. She took the back exit of the dining hall and looked out the picture window. The line of sight from the lodge to the south sides of both berms was blocked. When Jake distracted her, she'd lost track of Vance. She guessed he'd gone to search around the berm where the teenager had vanished.

A pit formed in her stomach. She'd been so close to the spot where the girl disappeared, wincing at the thought that she'd likely driven past while the abduction was in progress. That's what the video showed. Caitlin's attacker might even have seen her, seen them.

Could she have heard Caitlin if she'd called for help?

Did she have a façade?

Didn't Vance say everyone had one?

The turn of events was making her crazy.

She jogged to the spot where Caitlin had vanished.

Vance wasn't there.

She walked around the swirl patterns and footprints starting to dissipate, looking for anything they might have missed. Vance had found a piece of fabric. Maybe she'd see something. Climbing the berm, she scouted from a few feet up, sweeping her eyes in a grid pattern, looking. She saw nothing. Sliding to the base, careful not to disturb anything, she walked toward the airstrip.

Something caught her eye near the pile of limestone. A small blue and white tube of lip balm. She picked it up, opened the cap with her fingernail and sniffed it. The wax inside smelled like honey. It was a brand she didn't recognize. Maybe Caitlin dropped it. She put it inside her jacket pocket.

14

A hot shower revitalized her and settled her nerves. Holding her face under the jets, Lauren thought about where Jake's daughter could be. Was she still alive?

Lauren toweled her body, dressed, and peeked out the drapes of her corner room. The Hummer was parked in the circular driveway, doors open. Adam stood near the driver's-side window talking with Roy. A second vehicle was at the gate, a dark-colored SUV, a Range Rover.

She hurried to the reception desk and sneaked into the small office behind the counter where she could see the security monitors. The Range Rover had backed parallel to the gates and stopped on the shoulder of the four-lane highway. A person— ah, Rosa—walked into the camera frame, blocking her view of the driver. Who was Rosa talking to?

Lauren slipped out the side door leading to the courtyard and used the tall hedge dividing the pool area from the gravel driveway to spy on Roy. The Hummer idled, drowning out the conversation Adam and Roy were having.

She heard voices and leaned back, closer to the hedge. The

group of Unit 8200 agents filed past and climbed into the Hummer. Roy left with the Israelis.

Who was Rosa talking to?

As the gates opened, the awaiting Range Rover allowed Roy to pass, and with hazard lights flashing, pulled from the shoulder and dropped in behind him.

Rosa waved and started back up the driveway.

Lauren checked the time. Just after four.

Adam drove a golf cart down to Rosa at the main gate to give her a lift back to the lobby; he parked the cart in its designated spot and the pair walked inside.

"What was that all about?" Lauren asked.

Rosa ran her hand over her pregnant belly. "That was Josh. It was a surprise visit."

Antelope Creek Ranch was in the middle of nowhere. She didn't think people made surprise visits. "Where are they all going?"

"To an offsite meeting. Something came up at work. I told you, Josh works for Roy."

"I forgot, what kind of work?"

"I don't know exactly." Rosa gathered papers next to the computer and stuffed them in a folder. "Some sort of research and development project."

"Is that why Unit 8200 is here?"

"Who?" Rosa looked baffled.

"The Israelis."

"Oh. Is that who they are? I didn't know that. But you know how it goes. We get all kinds."

She'd been running motives in her head. Kidnappers demanded money. Wouldn't Jake have heard something by now?

Who knew about Jake's money? Those who did likely knew about hers and Vance's cash, too. But what if Caitlin's disappearance had nothing to do with money?

What if Caitlin been taken by one of the cartels? Wouldn't a beautiful fifteen-year-old girl be a target for the human traffickers?

She felt nauseous.

Didn't the sheriff say the cartels were always one step ahead?

The same fear that had haunted her in Miami for months after Davis was almost killed in the Upper Florida Keys, returned. It was her fault that Davis had been hospitalized. She'd brought him to the salvage deal, and deceived him, paying him handsomely in video production terms, but minimum wage compared to her share of the haul.

After she'd visited him in the hospital, she hadn't slept through the night for two months straight.

She should have seen or heard something when Caitlin was taken. There was no rational explanation for her disappearance, too much time had passed for that, and running possible scenarios in her head left her breathless.

Why didn't Vance have any theories? Wasn't that what detectives did? She shoved her hands in the pockets of her jeans to stop the shaking.

Davis startled her. "Are you okay?"

"Uh-huh. You just surprised me."

"This is all my fault." He hung his big Saint Bernard head.

"No, it's not."

If anyone was to blame, Davis Frost was last in line. He'd been a loyal friend and business associate and she'd played him. Without him, they'd never have recovered their half of the seventy-five million dollars in cash from the bottom of the ocean. He'd almost been killed, a gun pressed to his skull, his jaw broken.

Why didn't she stick to her guns and refuse her share of the money? If she'd listened to her gut, she wouldn't be here right now.

"We're going to find her," she said, rubbing his thick shoulder.

He kept shaking his head and repeating himself. "It's all my fault."

"I told you it's not. Stop saying that."

15

Caitlin leaned forward and dragged ten fingers along the vibrating metal floor. The sound, the pinging of a loose screw skipping and rolling nearby, was making her crazy. Her calf muscle ached from fishing for it with the sole of her shoe. The prick of sunlight emanating overhead flickered to a fading kaleidoscope of oranges and reds, signaling nightfall. Wedged into the corner, she rolled onto her right shoulder, using the covered payload for balance. The trailer was buffeted by a passing semi. She fell onto her elbow, onto something sharp.

Ouch.

The pinging stopped. Pawing the flooring in controlled movements, she rolled the screw from her elbow to her forearm until she was able to pinch it with her thumb and forefinger. Wrists bound, she crunched her abs to sit up and pressed her shoulders against the bulkhead. Rolling the piece of metal in her fingers, she positioned it in her hand like a pencil and scratched a line into the metal flooring. Feeling for the sharp tip, she rotated it in her fingertips and aimed for the plastic tie binding her hands.

Ouch.

The idea to use it like a tiny hacksaw didn't work; the edges of plastic dug into her flesh and she pricked the tip of her index finger. She dropped the screw, closed her eyes, and rested her head against the metal wall.

———

SHE AWAKENED when the truck pulling the trailer slowed. The sounds of oncoming traffic faded, the diesel engine labored, the exhaust wafted into the container when the driver turned sharply left. She leaned her body the same direction, away from the gravitational force, pushing her left shoulder against the metal siding.

The driver accelerated hard for an instant. The truck and trailer hopped the curbing, the axles and springs beneath her twisted and flexed, and the contents bounced.

Then the truck slowed to a crawl and stopped, the diesel knocking. A few seconds later, the driver made another turn to the left, a tighter one. She put her ear against the wall and heard voices, and cars, and new sounds.

The driver parked, shut down the engine, and got out. Jerking her head away from the siding, she sat erect, listening. But the highway noises played on in her head, like the tinnitus her grandmother complained about. Tilting her head and neck down and sharply left, she massaged her ear on the yoke of her dad's sweatshirt.

They had stopped during the night somewhere on the road. Shivering, trying to sleep with her chin on her kneecaps, she'd listened to the gears of the tractor-trailers. Some slowed to pass, others rumbled by, gaining speed. She'd guessed he'd stopped at a highway rest area, the kind she'd seen signs for on family vacations, with exits running parallel to the road, short runways, sheltered by trees. Places her mother would never let them stop to use the public restrooms. She'd dozed off there a second time, wherever they were.

She sat motionless, fingers trembling. The familiar scents and sounds of another fuel stop. She pushed her ear on the metal wall, listening for clues.

Her wrists had been hogtied for so long, if it weren't for the trembling, she wouldn't feel her hands at all.

Then more sounds just outside the trailer. The twist of the gas cap. The clatter of the gasoline handle taken from the pump. The clack of the metal nozzle entering the tank. She sniffed. Definitely fuel.

Voices nearby of people speaking in normal tones. Someone laughed, a child she thought. Her eyes welled with tears. Why was she being held captive? The sounds of normal life on the outside world faded, replaced with silence. Then her ears zeroed in on the sloshing of fuel rushing into the tank.

The gas nozzle clunked, signaling the tank was full. Then the gnashing of metal-on-metal—her captor hanging the fuel handle on the metal housing. A radio played in the background, an advertisement.

Her heart sank.

Someone fiddled with the back door. It went on for several seconds. A click, a squeak, a human harrumph, and then the trailer rocked as the back door cracked open and a silhouette appeared. It was dark out. The neon lighting stung her eyes. She was folded up in the corner like a grasshopper in her leggings, behind the payload. The walking shadow hopscotched around the cargo that had shifted closer to the back door.

Rocking the trailer as he moved, he held the door slightly ajar, moving toward the narrow gap between the tarp-covered craft, sidestepping to the corner where she was curled up.

Cowering, she rolled her shoulders forward and lowered her head, casting her gaze down.

"Get up," he growled, "slowly. No funny stuff."

Funny stuff? She could barely feel her limbs.

"Get up."

She wanted to ask how. *How* was she supposed to stand with her wrists bound taut, her aching joints stuck in place?

She couldn't see his face but it was her assailant, the same nasty voice she'd heard before. Raising her hands like an offering, she hoped he'd understand the message, that she needed help.

"I said, get up."

She scooted forward, rocking her shoulders and heels, seesawing forward. Once far enough away from the metal siding, she arched her back and used her hamstrings to push her shoulders against the metal siding. Clenching her jaw to work through the pain, she raised her torso to a squat. But she didn't have the strength to stand. Or hold the position. She slid down.

She closed her eyes and extended her arms again in front of her chest, then dropped them in defeat. "I need my hands. I . . . I can't get up without them," the words, barely a whisper.

"Put them up in front of you, where I can see them."

She opened her eyes. The sliver of light coming from the gap in the back door flashed so brightly it temporarily blinded her. She blinked, trying to regain her sight. Her hands were folded at the elbow, against her chest, and her wrists clasped beneath her chin, as if in prayer

He repeated himself. "I said, hold your hands out."

Her hands would not obey, as if some invisible force was stopping them.

"Gimme your fucking hands, you little bitch."

Her brain said to do it but her body would not comply.

The light reflected off a shiny object in his hand. The knife blade sprung open with a thwick.

Oh, God. She turned her head away.

He lunged another step, landing in the small place where she cowered in the corner. Clamping her wrists with one hand, he placed the knife handle in his mouth and held it with his teeth.

She turned her head away and squeezed her eyes shut.

"On your feet."

He clamped one hand around her wrists and yanked her arms.

She clambered upright.

"Your hands. Now."

She slit her eyes open and extended her forearms, as if serving herself up as an offering.

The sharp edge of the blade slipped between her thumbs, then a jerk and a snap.

Her arms splayed on either side of her rib cage. Limp. Sore. She wiggled her fingers, trying to make the pins and needles stop. She rotated her thumbs. But her hands vibrated and she crumpled into a sitting position.

"Get the fuck up," he said.

He backed away a half foot, giving her room. She leaned forward into the narrow passage, onto her elbows, and using her forearms for stability, switched from sitting to a kneeling position.

Headlights hit the vertical gap on the back door. The car lamps lit the interior long enough to see the indentations in the metal siding above her. She walked her tingling fingers up the side and when she felt the seam, used it to pull herself to her feet.

She looked past his silhouette, through the gap in the trailer door where the neon lights burned in the background.

"We're going to wait here together for a few minutes. And when we walk out, you're going to pretend everything is okay. Do you understand me?"

Caitlin Fleming nodded. This was the most he'd said without threatening her. He had an accent, very Southern. She wanted to ask to him what he was going to do to her, what he wanted.

The red haze from the neon signs seeped in though the gap on the trailer door lighting his jagged profile, a small nose planted between a jutting brow and receding chin. He'd changed clothing, now wearing a dull green T-shirt exposing more of the tattoo; his biceps muscled from weight lifting. Average height and medium build—she was sure he was same man who'd ambushed her at the resort.

"Where are we?"

He turned at the waist to face her, lifted the front of his T-shirt and flashed the grip of the gun stuffed nose-down in the waistband of his jeans.

He wasn't going to kill her, right.

If she went along with him, he wouldn't kill her. Right?

He crooked an index finger like a witch, motioning her to follow him to the opening where the red light spilled in. He pushed the door open and jumped first, then offered her his hand. She accepted it, hopping onto the pavement, landing next to him.

Holding one hand in her face, he turned his back, and used the other to shut the rear door, set the T-bar and clicked the padlock.

Eyeing the perimeter, he snapped his neck, motioning her to walk the narrow aisle between the fuel pump and the trailer. He followed so closely she smelled him. The gas station lights stung her eyes.

What time was it?

The voices she'd heard weren't coming from people nearby.

Rather the sounds had come from video screens built into the pumps. A handsome pitchman with a velvety voice hawked a gasoline additive. If only the actor was real. She could tap him on the shoulder. She could mouth "Help."

A minivan pulled into the lane two down from them. The driver got out and reached for his billfold. She heard the faint sounds of another advertisement begin to play. A woman, the man's wife she assumed, and three small children bounded out of the car and walked toward the convenience store. Her assailant grabbed the back of her sweatshirt, stopping her in front of the fuel hose draping across the passage between the pump and his pickup.

The little boy, the man's son, held the Mickey Mouse ears hat on his head as he skipped to catch up with his mother.

Caitlin tried to get the dad's attention by looking his way, willing him to sense trouble. She prayed in her head he'd notice something was wrong. He didn't even look to see where his wife and kids were headed. He watched the ad.

They probably looked like a father-daughter duo hauling whatever to wherever. There was nothing out of the ordinary, nothing to draw attention. Unless she did something now to attract it.

She twisted the pretty rose-colored band around her finger.

Her captor glanced over his shoulder, his eyes boring into her as he wrangled the nozzle out of the tank and hung it on the pump.

She stood motionless as he replaced the fuel cap.

Twisting it and closing the fuel door, he pulled her by the forearm and put his mouth near her ear. "We're going inside so you can use the restroom. But don't try anything funny. You'll get yourself killed and everyone else who sees us will die. Understood?"

She nodded.

Three cashiers inside rang up lottery tickets, gasoline, news-papers, and coffee. Coffee. There was a line in front of the coffee station. It wasn't nightfall. It was dawn. She looked outside, toward the truck. The rising sun had begun to reflect off the plate-glass windows.

Bins filled with rubber alligators flanked the counters, and *Who Dat Nation* ballcaps and towels hung from the ceiling, pinned to strands of purple, yellow, and green beads tied between slats along the water-stained ceiling tiles.

"I'll take five on two, and dis." The customer in front of them held a fifteen-ounce Styrofoam cup.

"Yes, sir." The cashier took his money and made change. "Dat all?"

Caitlin was next in line. "Can I help you, darlin'?"

"She needs the key to the Ladies' Room," her abductor said.

The big woman behind the counter craned her neck around them. "This young lady can't speak for herself?"

"Sure, she can."

The woman leaned forward and looked past them. "Dat yours?"

She snapped her head in the direction to the truck and trailer.

Her co-worker said, "He paid cash up front."

"That's right," the man said. "Now gimme the key."

She hesitated, squinting at Caitlin, as if something didn't add up. Then she smiled and handed her a plastic baton with a gold key tied to a leather lace. "Bring it back before you go now, ya hear. Don't forget. People do."

Her kidnapper followed her to the low-ceilinged hallway leading to the public bathroom, the beige linoleum marred with dirty footprints. A yellow bucket filled with brown water blocked the entrance to the Ladies Room. He used the mop handle to roll the bucket from the doorway, grabbed the door handle, and opened it.

"Nothing funny," he growled. "I'll be right here. Make it fast."

She went inside and felt for the light switch. The bulb flickered over a rusted sink and dripping faucet. She lowered the toilet seat. The paper holder was empty.

A moment later someone pounded on the door.

Hurrying, she washed her hands with cold water and wiped them on her leggings.

Her kidnapper stood on the other side. She followed him.

The place was busier. She stood in line to return the key.

"Excuse me, *sha*," a burly man said.

Caitlin looked at him blankly. The accent was bizarre.

He raised his eyebrows and tilted his neck sideways as in move out of the way. He reached behind her and pulled a newspaper from the stack on the counter.

The Daily Advertiser
WALMART SUPER CENTER OPENS IN LAFAYETTE.

Lafayette? Louisiana.

The big woman running the register reached for the bathroom key. "Thank you for remembering, darlin'. Any *sussie* dis mornin'?"

"Sussie?"

"You not from around here, huh? Something sweet to go?"

They were so friendly she could scream.

"Um . . . no thanks."

If she yelled for help, or told the woman she was being held against her will, he said he would kill her. He'd threatened to kill them all.

The cashier held her hand out, waiting for the key.

A surge of adrenaline coursed through Caitlin's veins. Now or never.

She stepped closer to the woman and leaned over the counter. The young mother with kids moved to the front of the line next to her and set down a hot drink and a box of sugary cereal. The mom glanced at her, managing a half-smile as she piled more junk food on the counter. The other cashier swept a handheld scanner over the items.

"I ain't got all day now."

"You heard the lady," her captor barked.

"Oh, sorry." She handed her the stick with the key dangling at one end.

The big woman grabbed it. "Thank you, darlin'. Y'all have a nice trip. Come back and see us."

It wasn't now.

It was never.

Her captor squinted with one eye—a warning—and held his arm out, motioning her to walk in front of him, herding her back toward the narrow path between the gas pumps and the truck.

A sharply attired man, one dressed more like her mom's friends, parked at the pump next to them and got out of an SUV. He went about his business, opening the fuel cap, entering his credit card, choosing the fuel grade, inserting the nozzle into the tank. The video screens were eye level. The man watched the ad play.

Her stomach roiled at the fumes.

She closed her fist and picked at the ring on her finger with her thumbnail. Two more cars pulled in, headlights out. There was enough morning sun to light the white license plates with Louisiana in red cursive above the blue numbers.

Her captor jabbed two fingers between her shoulder blades. A second warning to keep her mouth shut. She arched her spine, then dropped her chin to her chest, looking down. He unlocked the trailer door and cracked it open, ushered her to the opening, smacking the backs of her thighs with open palms. Holding the frame for balance, she stepped up.

Ow. Her muscles and joints ached.

He held a long zip tie in his fingers, stroking it like a pet. He motioned her closer and twirled the Flex-Cuff tie between his thumb and forefinger; she held her hands out as he bound her wrists. The man jerked his head sideways, toward the corner. She obeyed, scrambling to her spot in the trailer, dropping like a Halloween skeleton.

Her attacker watched from a gap in the doorway inside the trailer. When the SUV in the aisle next to them drove away, he jumped out, swung the door shut and locked it.

The axles squeaked as the dually truck lurched forward a few inches.

She picked at the rose-colored ring with her thumb. She'd asked her dad to buy the fitness tracker for her birthday. He asked her to send him the link to the online store so he could pay for it. At the last minute, the company had pitched the ring as an accessory. It was sneaky, but she'd added it to the online cart. She should have asked first, but he'd already agreed to buy it. It wasn't that much more money.

What good was it now?

Her captor had seen the fitness tracker on her wrist and confiscated it. Smashed it with his shoe and left it at the first stop. Without her phone or the tracker, the ring was useless. But it was all she had to hold on to. Better hide it. Or the stranger might take it away, too.

16

When the cable company offered Barry Landeros a significant discount to bundle his Internet, phone, and cable TV services, he might not have done it if he'd known about a new feature. Now, whenever the phone rang, the television muted itself and the caller, usually a telemarketer, came up as text on the screen.

His mobile buzzed. A graphic popped up on his seventy-inch flat screen, interrupting the *Science Discovery* program in progress. What a pain in the ass. He smacked the armrest with the remote before doing a double-take. MAYBE ROY POMPADOUR flashed on the screen. He fumbled for his cell.

The pleasantry was short. Roy got down to business. "You remember Jake Fleming?"

Barry considered it, but drew a blank.

Roy reminded him he'd met Jake who was the oldest of the three partners who'd bought his ranch last year.

That prodded his memory. "I do. What's up?"

"He's here, at the ranch, visiting. His daughter wanted to come and I'd promised him a father-daughter trip."

Roy was a man of limited words. This warm-up made Barry nervous.

"She went missing today."

"What do you mean, missing?"

"I think she might have been abducted."

He leaned forward on the sofa and pushed the phone against his ear. Most people who disappeared in the desert never resurfaced. He turned off the television. "How old is she?"

"Fifteen."

Fifteen? Jesus. "Teenage girls can be unpredictable. Maybe she ran off with a boy."

"Highly unlikely. What's the best predictor of future behavior?"

Classic Roy Pompadour. "Past behavior."

"That's right. Nothing about her profile suggests she would run off. I need you and the men here in the morning. We have video footage showing her running, but not enough to figure out what happened. Rally the troops. Tell them it's an emergency."

"What was she running from?"

"I don't know."

"What was she doing when she disappeared?"

"She'd gone for a run."

"Alone?"

"Yes."

"Out there? In the desert?"

"Uh-huh."

"Jake let her go alone?"

"Yes."

"Where did you get the video?"

Roy told him about the drone shoot.

He assured Roy he was on it and ended the call. Next, he sent a mass text message asking for help. This was different than the usual rally cry. The Secondmen were an all-volunteer border watch group who unofficially assisted US Border Patrol, ranch-ers, and sometimes even the migrants who'd been dumped in the middle of the desert by human traffickers.

By nightfall his phone finished pinging like a slot machine. No one said no. By his count, there would be fifty men gathered at Antelope Creek Ranch by sunup.

It was an eight-hour drive from Houston to Marfidio. He could catch a few zzs in the bed of the pickup when he got there. It wouldn't be the first time he'd slept in his old Dodge truck. He packed quickly and set out for West Texas.

JAKE STARED AT THE CEILING, his mind muddled with worry. He was exhausted, but couldn't sleep. He'd planned to call Ann but each time he'd gotten close, his fingers froze. It was almost midnight in Miami. What good would it do to drop the news on his ex now? There was nothing either one of them could do. He ran it through his head. He had nothing concrete to tell her. Why cause her a sleepless night? He dressed and went for a walk.

The stars were out and the night so clear he could see Venus, nature's LED bulb, overhead. It was also cold; the night tempera-ture had fallen thirty degrees.

Where was she?

Could she see the same constellations?

Was she cold?

Or hungry?

What had she run from?

Lauren said there were mountain lions in the foothills. At first, he'd panicked at the thought. But if animals had attacked her, there would have been *remains*. He'd overheard Roy say if she were dead, the turkey vultures would be out before sundown. They'd changed the subject when they'd noticed him listening. They'd been doing that all day.

He'd googled "mountain lions Chinati Mountains." They didn't hunt the desert flats, especially in the light of day. They stalked their prey at the higher elevations. At night. What if she were lost? Up in the mountains? What if she were fighting a lion now? He shuddered, his throat constricting.

The cool crisp air cleared his mind. He recalled the footprints, her footprints disappearing as if she'd been plucked from the sky. Vance had pointed out the swirl pattern on the topsoil. His daughter's shoe prints stopped at the edge, as if it were a swimming pool. What could have made that pattern on the soil?

The only other set of footprints belonged to him, a chaotic pattern inside the arc. Panic rose in his chest, the way it had when he'd heard her phone ringing, leading him to her backpack stashed in the brush at the base of the berm.

How could someone grab her without leaving footprints or tire tracks? The ranch was isolated in the middle of nowhere with no foot traffic to disturb the scene.

Crime scene, is what Vance called it.

He rubbed the skin beneath his collar with his fingers. A chill ran down his neck. Did Vance, the ex-detective, hide information from him? He balled his hands, digging his fingernails into his palms, willing himself to change the channel in his head.

That fucking Sheriff Manny.

They had a past. Manny had taken sadistic pleasure framing him for a DUI late last summer and then jailing him. Manny had all but licked his lips when Border Patrol dropped off three drug smugglers to hold overnight. He'd instructed his deputy to release them into the same cell where he was being held.

His head wouldn't let him change the channel.

He'd read an exposé by an investigative reporter, a Mexican

woman who feared for her life. Dozens of missing girls from Ciudad Juarez, a border town just south of El Paso, had been found mutilated, beheaded, bodies burned, charred remains. The murders had been unsolved mysteries until the reporter uncovered the truth: They were "trophy kills." The cartels raped and killed young girls to celebrate big drug runs across the border into the US.

His lungs stop working at the thought.

The scariest animals weren't the mountain lions. The human traffickers and drug smugglers were.

If Manny was hiding anything, he promised himself right then and there the sheriff would pay. He'd find out how that cocky rooster would fare in a federal prison. Prison? That wouldn't suffice. He'd hang the fucker from a cottonwood tree and watch the vultures peck his eyes out.

Get a grip. This rage boiling inside wasn't going to do squat to help him find her.

His alcohol addiction therapist told him anger was a trigger, one that led addicts to go "back out." His hands shook. He closed his eyes and tilted his head, staring at the stars.

What he'd do for a drink right now. A single shot of whiskey. He imagined the burn of hard liquor going down his throat. How great would that feel?

Except it was a bad idea. He'd have to wait. Let the fear go. Let the craving pass, too.

Fear.

That was strange to let the word enter his head.

He jumped to his feet, and detoured through the lobby. A few guests lingered. There were no familiar faces. He stopped by the fire pit in the courtyard. Fading embers crackled and sparked, sending several orange flakes glittering skyward before burning out.

The ashtrays were filled with big, gray eraser heads.

Someone had left a half-smoked cigar on the rock wall circling the pit. He sat on the ledge, breathing deeply, letting the smells of burned wood and tobacco fill his head.

The aroma of booze wafted. His nose followed it like a cadaver dog, to a glass with about a single shot of dark alcohol. He looked around. No witnesses. He shuffled toward the table and picked it up. He closed his eyes, placed his nostrils on the rim of the glass and sucked air.

A moment of calm fell over him.

Ahhhh.

He scanned the perimeter, again looking for observers. There were none. He placed his lips on the glass and tilted it up.

He yanked the glass away from his face and slammed it down on the rock ledge. The alcohol hit the last of the fire and lit it like lighter fluid.

That's right. Lighter fluid.

It sizzled.

The mix of fine tobacco and hot booze sent his brain into I-WANT-IT-NOW mode. He felt something wet in his hand. Under the warm light of the dying fire, he looked at his palm. Blood. He'd cut himself with the glass.

A warning from God.

God?

That was another odd thought.

He ambled to his room, stripped his clothes, splashed cold water on his face and climbed into bed. Squeezing the wad of Kleenex in his palm, he opened his fingers to look. The cut was superficial. But it hurt. Another sensation washed over him, another unfamiliar one that brought him some relief. He'd not succumbed to temptation.

Man, it was hard. He wrestled the pillow under his neck and closed his eyes.

Caitlin's phone rang. He leapt from the bed. His ex, Ann's

number, flashed on the screen. Jeez, it was after two o'clock in the morning in Florida. She'd already left five voicemails on his phone.

He placed the cell on his chest, waiting for the glowing screen to go dark.

The deal he'd made with Caitlin was that she'd give him password access to her phone if he paid for it. The combination was her idea: the last two numbers of his birth year, same for his son, and Caitlin's—oldest to youngest—making six numbers he could always remember. He'd promised to use it only in the event of an emergency.

Jake typed the number into the phone and listened to the first message Ann left for Caitlin.

It was from much earlier, chatty, with no hint of concern. He wasn't going to listen to the rest of them, especially the latest one. He had a pretty good idea what they'd sound like. He got out of bed and swapped phones on charge: his for Caitlin's. He set both on SILENT and resumed staring at the ceiling.

17

"Morning." Chef Gordy pushed past Lauren, on task, carrying a stack of foil-covered tin pans. He'd arisen long before sunup and was in the midst of loading a portable feast into the Hummer.

"How'd you sleep?" Vance asked, handing her a coffee.

"Not well."

"Look." He pointed to a flotilla of parked pickups and RVs lined up in the desert to the east of where Jake found his daughter's backpack. "Barry's guys. The Secondmen."

Roy stopped to chat. "I have a horse tacked up for you."

Vance looked puzzled. "A horse? For who?"

"Not for you. There aren't enough ATVs to go around. And since she rides, I figured she could go on horseback."

That meant they'd be separated. Her heart thrummed at the thought. A girl had disappeared out there.

"They can ride places we can't access by vehicle," Roy said.

Why hadn't he run the plan past her first?

"Who's going with her?"

"Josh."

Vance rocked back on his boots and folded his arms across his chest. "Josh? I didn't know he was here."

"Got in late last night." He looked at her. "You should stay inside and keep warm. The ranch hands are getting the horses ready. Josh'll call the desk when it's time to go."

It wasn't "late last night" when she'd seen Rosa meet Josh at the gate. It was afternoon and Roy was going somewhere with the Israelis. Josh—driving a Range Rover—had followed them, heading east on the Interstate. Rosa had said that Josh worked for Roy. Why wouldn't she know more about it? Maybe it had something to do with the Israelis. Unit 8200 was an intelligence agency. The more she considered it, the more sense it made that their arrival had something to do with Josh's job.

She watched from the window as Davis parked the four-wheeler near the low adobe wall and dismounted. He'd bungeed a black plastic case to the rear rack and had loaded a second one on the passenger seat of the ATV. He'd packed lighter than yesterday.

When Gordy finished loading enough food and drinks for fifty, he closed the back doors of the Hummer.

"See you later." Vance pecked her on the cheek. "Be careful," he said before going out the back door.

Vance helped Davis stack the cases into the middle back seat. Vance climbed into the third-row seat, letting Davis sit next to his gear, behind Jake and Roy.

Coffee in hand, she opened the door for an instant to test the temperature. *Brrr,* it was cold out. She headed for the front desk.

"Morning," Adam said, looking at the clock. "It's not even seven and the place is hoppin'." He typed the code into the main gate keypad.

She glanced at the security monitor and watched as the gates swung open and a brown sheriff's office pickup rolled up the drive.

Sheriff Manny didn't stop at the lodge. Rather, he took the westerly fork at the top of the driveway and drove the access road behind the guestrooms. Lauren walked to the south-facing window with the mountains in the background to see where he was heading.

When the pickup reappeared, the sheriff cut a diagonal line across the flat desert and drove toward the encampment. She headed back to the desk.

The landline rang. Adam held his finger up, as in just a minute. "No . . . . Yes, I understand . . . . Yes, it's a retreat . . . . I'll be sure to let him know." He hung up. "Some of the guests are complaining about the cars and trucks. I'm telling them Roy is hosting one of his charity events. It's not like I can tell them what's really going on."

Another vehicle appeared on the monitor. The truck was beefy, a dually with curved wheel wells so big they looked cartoonish. The driver opened the window and entered numbers into the keypad. The gate opened.

"Who's that?"

Adam looked at the monitor. "That's Daryl."

"Who is he?"

"A guy who knows Mr. Pompadour."

That was a long list, otherwise known as F.O.Ps: Friends of Pomps.

"Is he expecting him?"

"Not that I know of," Adam said. "He was here a few times last week."

"Doing what?"

"I think he was delivering some construction materials."

She watched from the vertical window with a view to the driveway. Daryl started on the same track as the sheriff, but rather than taking the fork behind the guestrooms, he turned left, making a wide arc, and stopped parallel to the privacy hedge lining the courtyard.

This could not be a friend of Roy's. He'd have had a fit if he'd seen the parking job. Folks relaxing poolside would have a mountain view to the south. But facing north, they'd see the rooftop of a truck and horse trailer.

Adam walked from behind the desk and stood next to her. "Is he going to leave it parked there?"

She raised her shoulders. "How would I know?"

"Mr. Pompadour will *kill* me if he leaves his truck like that."

"You could ask him to park somewhere else."

He didn't answer. He left his post behind the desk to walk outside to meet Daryl.

She zipped her jacket to her neck and followed him, noting that the trailer rocked side-to-side.

Adam raised his eyebrows. "Whatever's in it is alive."

Shivering, she folded her arms across her chest. "Have you heard from Josh this morning?"

"Oh, sorry. He called to say your horse is ready. I was supposed to tell you to meet him at the stables."

Lauren took a shortcut to the barn by squeezing through an opening in the hedge and crossed the courtyard.

She spotted Josh riding horseback toward the front of the lodge where the truck and trailer were parked.

She jogged to the stable. The little bay gelding she was familiar with, Smokey, was tacked-up and tied to the hitching post. She unbuckled the halter, mounted, and took the path behind the guestrooms, the way Josh had gone.

She arrived in time to watch Daryl unload. The horse hopped one step back toward the open end of the trailer, using its left hind hoof like a feeler, trying to find the ledge. The trailer swayed, metal horseshoes thumping the floorboards. Tap dancing backward in baby steps, the animal found the edge and dropped one hoof onto the dirt.

She rode closer to get a better view. A haze of chalky dust billowed inside the trailer like low-lying fog.

The horse made a bold final move. In a single lurch, as if dropping a standard transmission into reverse and popping the clutch, the horse jumped out, landing on all fours. It swiveled its head, ears pricked, nostrils flared, eyes wide, every ancient instinct on high alert, sizing up the new environment.

"Nice," Josh said, grinning.

A silver, jeweled leather bridle matched the tooled saddle atop a colorful Mexican blanket.

Daryl swung the trailer door sideways, then closed and latched it with one hand. He mounted in a single fluid movement, more gymnast than cowboy, and rode up to them, leaving the truck and trailer where he'd parked it.

"Lauren, meet Daryl Flood," Josh said. "Daryl Flood, meet Lauren Gold."

She nudged Smokey forward and sideways until the two horses were parallel and held her hand out.

"Nice to meet a woman who can handle a horse." His horse nipped hers on the neck and squealed. Daryl rested one hand on the saddle horn and petted his animal on the neck. "Name's Picasso. He's got a bit of an attitude."

"Daryl's a tracker," Josh said.

"A tracker?"

"He finds things the old-fashioned way. Like scent, freshness of footprints, sounds, broken branches, that kind of stuff. We're riding with him."

Daryl looked like he planned to be there a while. Saddlebags and a canteen were slung over his horse's withers, a stiff lariat clipped to a leather breastplate. And he had a bedroll neatly strapped to the cantle of his well-oiled saddle. The animal's coat sparkled with dollops of dapples, a sign of good care.

Josh reined his horse south, the direction of the mountains. "Let's get going."

Daryl trotted past her, and fell in behind Josh.

He wore an odd backpack over his shoulders, a large T-shaped canvas bag, Army fatigue green and camouflage colors, that reached from the back of his saddle to his neck.

His long black hair brushed his shoulders, both ears covered by thick braids with colorful feathers woven into the tips.

She cantered past Daryl to Josh, up front. Before she had a chance to ask a question, Josh said, "It was Roy's idea to have you ride with us. Did you know that when he served in 'Nam, he never went on patrol without a woman?"

"No. Why?"

"He thinks women have a sixth sense. Maybe even seventh and eighth, plus superior peripheral vision. Definitely better intuition. Stay tuned-in."

"Ah. Okay." *Tuned-in?* Whatever that meant.

"Shit," Daryl said. Picasso hopped on three legs. "Wait up." He stopped his horse and Picasso balanced like a tripod holding his left front leg, bent at the knee. Daryl jumped to the ground.

She rode closer to see.

He looked inside the hoof. A white rock, about the size of a walnut, was jammed in the frog. He dropped the backpack from his shoulders, unzipped it, and plucked a metal-tipped arrow from the quiver. Using the sharp end, he dug the rock from Picasso's hoof. He picked it up and put it in his pocket, then ran, leading the horse by the reins. Picasso trotted evenly on all fours.

"He's looks sound," she said.

"Looks like he stepped on a piece of limestone," Daryl said.

They hadn't ridden anywhere near the pile adjacent to the

airstrip. That didn't mean a rock hadn't found its way onto the trail.

"If there's a nail out here I swear this horse will step on it," he said, sliding his foot into the leather stirrup, slinging his right leg up and over.

The trio rode three abreast, walking.

"What kind of work do you do?" she asked Daryl.

Josh said, "He mostly works for the Feds."

"That's not entirely true. I freelance. Sometimes I get hired to go places inaccessible by other means." He shook his head. "I've seen a lot of things out here. Things I'd rather forget."

"Like what?"

"Bad stuff."

Her fingers trembled on the reins.

"The smugglers set fires to distract border agents. They kill ranchers' livestock, butcher and eat the animals. Human trafficking is the worst that they do. We find bodies. The morgues in the small border towns are overwhelmed with John and Jane Does."

Lauren felt a surge of bad chemistry in her veins. "Are you saying you think the cartels took the girl? Is that why you're here?"

"I don't know," Daryl said. "Roy's a friend. He asked me to help with the search."

Josh, who'd been listening, gathered the reins and stopped his horse. The other animals followed suit. Behind them the sun was an orange fireball coming up from the east. "Daryl's good at what he does. You'll see."

The encampment south and east of the ranch had grown. In the distance, fifty, maybe sixty men had set out on foot.

"They're doing a grid search on the ground," Daryl said, "while we ride to the foothills."

"What are we looking for?" she asked.

"Clues. Let's get a move on." Daryl smacked his lips and spurred his horse.

Picasso galloped. She fell in last, wiping her eyes and nose on her sleeve, welling from wind and dust. They rode south, toward the Chinati Mountains.

Roy Pompadour had influence. In about a half a day, he'd built an army now spread out for nearly a mile in the middle of no man's land.

18

Vance split from the search party and joined the head of The Secondmen. The pair sat on the tailgate while Barry scanned the flatlands through field glasses. He'd driven his old Dodge Ram eight hours last night, arriving before dawn and catnapping in the bed of the pickup truck.

Barry dropped the binoculars from his nose and shaded his eyes. "That girl's not out here."

He'd told Barry about the strange swirl pattern, the footprints, and the lack of tire tracks.

They sat quietly for a few minutes.

"I really appreciate you hiring my brother," Barry said.

It had actually been Jake's idea to hire Barry's brother, Karl, to keep an eye on the yacht while they were away at the ranch. He'd run the idea by Jake, and he'd agreed to split the costs two ways, instead of three. He hadn't run it by Lauren. If she didn't know, she couldn't accidentally leak to Davis that his temporary replacement was being paid daily what Jake had been paying Davis weekly.

"I met him. His name's Karl, right?"

"You did, when you and Lauren visited Jake. He's using vacation time. You had that fat guy keeping an eye on things. Gimme a break." He set the field glasses on his kneecap and rolled his light blue eyes.

Vance defended him. "He's a competent boat captain."

"I wouldn't have guessed. My brother says the harbor master told him the yacht hasn't sailed since it arrived."

The harbor master comment caught him off guard. It shouldn't have come as a surprise that people would notice Jake's yacht hadn't left the dock. The marina catered to middle-class enthusiasts, and a million-dollar yacht was conspicuous.

"It's a water ornament. You know how some people are. They want something and after they get it, they don't use it. At least Jake lives on it. You should hear him brag about not having to pay property taxes."

He told Barry that Jake hired a fulltime captain because he was worried about the increase in vandalism and petty crime—mostly stolen fishing gear. The marina's management warned the boat owners they couldn't afford round-the-clock security.

"Seems like crime is on the rise everywhere. If you can afford your own security, I'd do the same thing. But I wouldn't use that big guy."

Barry's point was valid. When it came to security, almost any pick was better than Davis Frost, who couldn't outrun a guy with a blood alcohol level five times the legal limit. Not to mention Davis knew nothing about the money stowed in the belly of Jake's 60-foot yacht. Neither did Barry nor Karl.

"Your brother's a cop, right?" Vance asked, remembering full well he was.

"Yep. Nineteen years on the force. Gonna retire next year."

"Why'd he become a cop?"

"You need a reason?"

"I did."

"That's right. I heard you're an ex-detective. My brother got his girlfriend pregnant in high school. Had two kids before he was twenty. The oldest is a special needs kid, a boy who's never leaving home."

"That's tough."

Barry said, "I don't think I could handle it. His wife's a saint. He's trying to come up with a second career. Pension plan is a mess with all the mismanagement and now there's mandatory retirement. I offered to help, but you know how it is." He flung his neck, cracking it. "Ah." He rolled his head from side-to-side. "Thanks for giving him some off-duty work."

"It's mutually beneficial. Lauren promised to hire Davis to work on a video out here at the ranch and Jake promised his daughter she could cut class for a few days on a father-daughter trip."

Barry picked up his binoculars. "He must be sick about her disappearing. I don't know what I'd do if it was my daughter. This is a dangerous place."

They sat in silence, the morning sun casting long shadows from the mountains separating far West Texas from Mexico onto the desert floor.

Igneous and metamorphic rock reached 8,000 feet at the summit, a reminder of a violent past. Thirty-five million years ago, the largest volcano in the history of the Trans Pecos region of Texas erupted, creating the Chinati Mountains. Deep crevasses webbed down the sides, an aide-mémoire of the lava flow and millions of years of erosion.

Thirty-five million years ago.

The area shaped like an upside-down Frisbee was so vast that Interstate 10 passed through it unnoticed. Maybe a place born of such violence could never escape it.

"Shit." He jumped sideways.

Barry followed suit, dropping from the tailgate, then laughed at him. "Jesus. You scared me. That's a common checkered whip-tail lizard. Native around here."

The reptile froze, blending with the sand and rocks, then went back to work, catching a bug with a quick lick of its tongue. It scuttled away, holding the insect in its mouth.

Barry hopped down and walked to the cab of the Dodge. He returned, holding a flattened ball cap with an American flag embroidered onto the front panel. Holding it by the bill, he snapped it with his hand, reshaping it, and popped it on his head. "I heard you have a tracker out here helping with the search."

"A tracker?"

"You didn't hear?"

He shook his head.

"Border Patrol uses Native Americans sometimes. One of them is here." He hopped up and sat on the open tailgate.

"What does Border Patrol use them for?"

"They travel on horseback, helping border agents. Look," Barry handed him the binoculars.

Three riders on horses rode away from them, toward the foothills, two women with one man between. That was odd. Two women. He figured the man was Josh. He turned the focus knobs in small increments, squinting. "Who's the woman?"

Barry laughed. "You need to get your eyes checked, dude. That's your girlfriend."

"No, not the blonde. The other one, the brunette. In the middle."

"Gimme those." Barry set the binoculars on the bridge of his nose. "That's not a woman. That's the tracker I was telling you about. His name's Daryl Flood."

"You know him?"

"I've heard of him." Barry passed the binoculars back to him. "Don't give me that worried look. He's here to help."

"Right," he said. In his world, the words 'here to help' always backfired.

19

Rosa compared the printed wholesale food invoice file to the one on her laptop. She'd taken a seat next to a butane lamp poolside where she had a bird's-eye view of the morning's search activities.

Her mobile rattled the outdoor tabletop: 9:21 AM. Adam at the front desk calling. She set her coffee down and answered it.

"It's the mom again. I let it go until the fiftieth ring. She's got us on speed dial. Some of the guests complained."

"About what?"

"Fifty rings. It's annoying."

"Tell her to hold on. I'll be right there."

Didn't anyone appreciate that she was eight months pregnant?

She picked up her warm coffee and paperwork, struggled to her feet and headed inside. Adam waited with the phone cord hanging around his neck. He tightened it around his throat like a noose and stuck his tongue out sideways. People dealt with stress in different ways.

He unwound it and handed her the receiver. She mouthed *not funny.* "Mrs. Fleming, I'm sorry to have kept you waiting."

Adam leaned with his back against the wall, listening.

"Uh, no—" Rosa said.

She looked at Adam and twirled her forefinger in front of her mouth, scowling.

"Uh-huh . . . . Yes . . . . As soon as I see him I'll let him know you called again."

She took a deep breath and exhaled quietly. Ann Fleming kept talking while she half-listened. There was no way she was going to be the one to tell Caitlin's mom that her daughter was missing. That fell to Jake.

"I know you've been trying to reach him. Like I said, as soon as I see your husband, I mean, Jake, I'll let him know you called again." She stared at the ceiling. "Yes, I promise, I'll make sure he calls."

She handed the phone to Adam.

"What do I do if she calls again?"

"Does she come up on caller ID?"

"Uh-huh."

"Answer it and hang up."

Adam's face turned into a pretzel. "Are you sure?"

"Do it quietly. This is Jake's issue. Not ours. We don't know anything."

She'd heard panic in Ann's voice, rising with each sentence. Since Roy Pompadour had promoted Rosa to general manager, this was the first time she didn't know what to do. Her job, as she saw it, was to handle things that Roy didn't care to deal with. Running to him and asking him what to say to Ann was precisely the reason he had a general manager.

Other than straightening pictures with a level and conducting white-glove inspections, he had no interest in the front desk.

"It's only a matter of time before the mother finds out."

Adam gnawed his cuticles. "I don't want to be the one to tell her."

"You won't be." She worked her thumbs on the keypad of her phone.

`Ur wife has called 50x. Call her.` She pushed the send button.

Jake didn't respond, of course. She waddled to the pool area and resumed her paperwork.

20

J ake's phone pinged. He glanced at Roy behind the wheel of the Hummer creeping along the shoulder of Interstate 10.

Ur wife has called 50x. Call her.

What he especially didn't need right now was one of Roy's employees harassing him. He deleted Rosa's text.

Both pants pockets of his cotton candy pink shorts had been vibrating all morning and he'd been doing his best to ignore the calls and messages. He used the tail of his shirt to wipe the dust from the face of his Rolex: 9:33 AM. A chill passed through his spine. She'd been missing for more than twenty-four hours.

His phone buzzed again. He took it out and looked at the screen. He pressed the red DISMISS button. That was sure to send Ann into a tizzy.

The one in his other pants pocket vibrated. Caitlin's phone. He fumbled for it and squinted at the screen. It was just like Ann to speed dial between the two cells, and now, the ranch landline. He let it go to voicemail.

Roy looked at him, curious.

"Don't look at me like that. I'll call her soon as I know something."

Roy leaned over the steering wheel and craned his neck past him, studying the area ahead on the shoulder of the road. "You haven't told her yet?"

"I will. When we find her."

Roy parked parallel to a barbed-wire fence held with thin metal posts set at twelve-foot intervals. The tops of some posts were painted white, others purple, and some not at all.

Jake asked Roy about it.

"Purple is Texas-speak for no trespassing. It's a moot point."

"How so?"

"I painted the purple markers myself when I owned this land, kind of like a dog marking a fire hydrant, I suppose. When I sold the ranch to you, you deeded twenty thousand acres back to the Texas Parks and Wildlife. It's their land now and people don't respect the law the way they used to. Those purple stakes used to stand for something."

Davis sat in the back with the drone on his lap, assembled and ready to fly.

Roy put the Hummer in drive and crept forward a couple of hundred yards. He looked out the window, on the passenger's side. "This looks like as good a spot to fly as any."

"This'll work." Davis lumbered out of the vehicle, carrying the drone. He stuck his head in on Jake's side to talk to Roy. "Can I break FAA regulations?"

"Do what you have to do," Roy said.

Davis had downloaded the drone software onto Roy's tablet the night before. He'd set it up as a second monitor, to mirror what he was shooting, and had left it with them so they could watch.

Climbing through a break in the barbed wire, Davis unfurled a towel and set the drone on the ground atop it.

When he started the engine, Jake powered his window up to drown out the sound.

Roy set the tablet on the center console so they could both watch and he and Jake stared at the screen for the next half hour, hoping to see something.

"I'm about out of battery," Davis said over the radio.

Roy pressed the talk button. "Let's check in with the others, see if anyone else has come up with anything."

Jake felt his face sag. "Don't you think they would have told us?"

"If they found her, yes. If they found a clue, not necessarily."

Davis opened the passenger door, carrying the drone under his arm free arm, and climbed in.

On the drive to meet the others, both cells alternately buzzed in Jake's pockets. When life moved along normally, Ann practically lived on the telephone. Holding her at bay was like sandbagging a house during a hundred-year flood. He had nothing to report yet. Maybe the others had seen something. Maybe he'd have something positive to tell her.

21

Primitive pictographs etched on the canyon walls reminded Lauren she'd ridden to the same spot alone with Josh late last summer, to a flat mesa a hundred feet up with a panoramic view of the ranchlands. From here, the berms and airstrip and buildings looked like a game board.

Daryl held his finger to his lips and closed his eyes. Josh gave a little shrug.

The horses stood motionless.

The tracker opened his eyes and studied the landscape below. The desert flatlands were cracked like shattered glass. The winter had been exceptionally dry, creating a web as far as the eye could see. Daryl panned his head, sweeping left to right, then stopped and stared intently at the humpback.

"The way I see it, the only way out is the highway," he finally said.

Josh took his binoculars hung over the saddle horn and peered through them. "There should've been tire tracks leading to the road."

"Do you see what I see?" Daryl squinted, looking with bare eyes. He reached into one of his saddlebags, removed a small telescope and put it against his right eye. "Look at the arc pattern near the berm."

They'd seen it from the ground.

Lauren held her hand out. "May I look?"

Josh handed her his field glasses.

She saw what he was talking about. There was a line of swirl patterns, too subtle to see from the ground. But up high, the continuous circles were easy to spot. They led to the highway on a diagonal path, heading east, and ended at the blacktop.

Daryl tilted his head back until his nostrils were parallel to the horizon. He flared them and took a long, controlled flow of air into his nose.

Smokey swished his tail at a fly.

Daryl exhaled. "The cartels are always one step ahead."

She shaded her eyes. "That's what Roy said."

Daryl patted Picasso's neck. "The only thing that would make a pattern like that would be some kind of flying machine. Maybe a drone of some kind."

"You think she could have been abducted by a drone?"

Daryl didn't answer.

Josh held his hand out. She passed his binoculars back to him.

Daryl fondled one of the feathers grazing his shoulder and studied the ranchlands below. "I don't know."

A shiver ran down her neck. "Do you think the cartels are using unmanned drones to smuggle more than drugs?"

Josh said, "I saw a spy video of a personal hovercraft on YouTube."

"A personal hovercraft?" She'd never heard of that.

"Yeah. They're in development. Even a runner as good as Jake's kid wouldn't have a chance against it," Josh said.

That peaked Daryl's interest. "The girl's a runner?"

Lauren twisted in the saddle. Smokey pawed the ground and

snorted. "Yes, and a good one from what I've heard. She's a high school track star."

"I wish I'd known that," Daryl said.

"Why?" Josh looked perplexed. "What difference does that make?"

"A lot of athletes wear fitness trackers. There's a good chance she might have been wearing one. They've been used recently to locate missing people."

It was beginning to seem as if the word tracker had found its way into every sentence. "I know she wore one," she said. "I saw it. Her dad helped strap it on her wrist yesterday morning."

"You sure about that?" Daryl asked.

"Pretty sure," she said.

"There's nothing else to see from here," Josh said. "Let's head back."

Halfway down the mountain Daryl stopped and shielded his eyes with his hand. "Look."

From the angle they sat horseback, the midmorning sun lit the whirl pattern, accentuating it. What if he were right? What if she'd been abducted by some kind of aircraft? The line of spirals ran across the desert floor from the berm to the shoulder of the road like the pattern of a commercial floor-waxing machine stripping wax. What would do that?

Daryl took the lead, riding down the decline, leaning back in the saddle, swaying side-to-side, nudging his horse down the mountain.

"Could it be small enough to fit in a trailer?" she asked.

"A personal hovercraft? Easily," Josh said. "Whoever stole it was smart enough to keep it out of sight."

She gripped the saddle horn. "Who said anything about a stolen one?"

"I'm just speculating," Josh said.

Daryl stopped and peered through the spyglass, fixing his

sight at the intersection where the swirl pattern dead-ended at the Interstate.

She reached down and scratched Smokey's shoulder. "Can you imagine how scary that would be, seeing a UFO in the middle of nowhere?"

"Especially if it abducted you," Josh said.

22

"Here they come." Vance tossed his head. "Don't laugh, but I'm afraid of them."

Barry looked puzzled. "Of what?"

"Horses."

"Bad experience?"

"Yeah. A birthday party when I was a kid. I was sitting on a pony and a clown with balloons ran up to us."

"Let me guess. The pony spooked and you fell off."

"And broke my arm when I got stepped on."

"Ouch." Barry grimaced. "Looks like you're going to have to face your fear sooner or later."

The Hummer approached, streaks of dust churning beneath the tires. Roy parked perpendicular to the old Dodge and got out to check in. "Do you boys have any news?"

"Nope," Vance said.

"You?" Barry asked Roy.

"Nah. Davis flew his drone but we didn't see anything."

Barry stood and rested his hand on Roy's shoulder. "She's not here, boss. Every bone in my middle-aged body says she's gone."

Roy squared his jaw and nodded. "I've been wondering whether or not it could have been a crime of opportunity."

Vance put one boot up on a wheel of the Hummer and leaned forward. "In my opinion, that's highly unlikely. The location is too remote. The chance that someone saw Caitlin and decided to grab her—what would they have been doing out here? The person or persons would have to have had a reason to be here."

"Jesus," Roy said, "I pray to God you're wrong about that."

"It's possible she was at the wrong place at the wrong time," Vance said, doubting what he was saying.

He knew the crime stats. Of the half-million missing children reports filed every year, over ninety percent were runaways or miscommunications reported by family members. Caitlin didn't check those boxes. An even smaller percentage of kids were abducted by strangers.

She did fit others, however. Most were girls. The average age was twelve-to-seventeen.

"I think you're right," Roy said.

"About which part?"

"That it's highly unlikely it was random."

Vance looked at Jake slumped in the passenger seat of the Hummer, staring out the windshield with his elbow and forearm on the window frame.

"You ready to face your fear?" Barry asked him.

Irrational terror rose in his chest as the three riders on horseback approached.

"You know what one of my greatest regrets is?" Roy asked.

"I give up."

"That I never learned how to ride a horse."

He swallowed hard. "Why didn't you learn? You have a ranch and horses."

"Because it's a lot harder than it looks."

Vance clenched his fists as the horses drew nearer. The tracker slung a bag over one shoulder. "What's he carrying?" he asked, squinting.

"A crossbow," Barry said. "I'm surprised you missed that."

He'd had a good thirty seconds to study the trio through binoculars but he hadn't noticed the T-shaped canvas bag. It was a rookie mistake. He'd been thrown off, mistaking Daryl for a woman.

He watched Lauren dismount and approach, leading her horse on foot. Roy intercepted Josh and Daryl, and the three men huddled, Roy on the ground, the other two on horseback.

"You okay?" she asked him.

"Sure." He backed away with his fists hidden in his pockets.

"I'll be back in a minute." She led Smokey to the Hummer.

The long-haired tracker dismounted mid-conversation with Roy, swinging his right leg over his horse's hindquarters and dropping to the ground, landing with a slight bend at the knees. He hung the crossbow strap over the saddle horn.

Daryl's horse's markings, swatches of rich colors splashed on a white background were striking, even from a distance. Daryl walked toward him, the horse following, head held high, snorting. Horse and rider stopped a few feet from him. The horse craned its neck forward, toward him.

He stepped backward, heart racing.

Daryl grinned.

He felt like punching him in the jaw.

"Ah, look what you've done." He massaged the horse's muzzle. "I think you hurt his feelings. I'm Daryl Flood. And you are?"

"Vance Courage."

"Nice name."

"Ditto." He backed away two more steps.

Picasso flared his nostrils, exposing the red velvet interior. Vance fought the urge to run, heart racing.

"Who knew the two of you would find each other so enchanting," Lauren said. "Here, hold my horse for a sec."

She tossed the reins to him. He caught them like a baby thrown from an open window, hunched over with open palms.

She ripped the packaging of a granola bar with her teeth and bit into it. "Relax. He's a golden retriever with hooves."

Barry returned with an armful of bottles of water and handed him one. He traded the water for the reins and crabbed sideways.

She laughed. "Do you want to pet mine?"

"No, thanks," Vance said. "I'd like to look, not touch. You know, the art gallery approach."

"Fine." She took the reins from Barry.

Jake stepped out of the Hummer, looking haggard. He did a double-take when he saw Daryl, who handed the reins to his horse to Josh. After Daryl introduced himself, he asked, "Did your daughter wear a fitness tracker?"

"I don't know." Jake rubbed his eyes. "What's a fitness tracker?"

Lauren said, "It's like a wristwatch. It keeps track of —"

"Yes." Jake shook his head in a series of fast moves, as if trying to clear his thoughts. "I helped put it on her wrist. Yesterday morning. She needed help with it. That was right before she left for her run."

"Do you happen to have her phone?" Daryl asked.

Jake took it from his pants pocket, tapped six numbers on the screen and handed it to him.

It filled with text bubbles. All incoming.

"Did you see all these messages?" Daryl asked.

"Uh-huh. They're from her mother. Can you look at her phone and get a location for the fitness tracker?"

Daryl paused. "Maybe. But it's not that simple."

Vance kept his distance from the horses. "I vote we go back to the lodge to debrief, so we can talk about the next step."

"Why can't you look at her phone now?" Jake asked.

"He's right," Daryl said. "We need to put the horses up and can meet back at the dining hall."

"Why does it feel like I'm the only one feeling a sense of urgency?"

Roy put his hand on Jake's shoulder. "We're all concerned. We're doing what we can to help find her. Look around at all the folks that got here before the sun came up. Most of them drove all night."

Roy seemed to calm him down.

"If you're all going back to the lodge, what about my guys?" Barry asked. "Are we done here?"

Roy lowered his voice. "Invite them to have lunch first. Then tell them to go home. Make sure they know how much we appreciate their efforts."

"I wish we could've done more to help," Barry said.

Lauren got back on her horse and rode up to him. Vance willed his feet to remain planted. "I'll see you back at the lodge," she said.

Roy opened the double doors on the back of the Hummer releasing the aromas of the moveable feast.

Barry sidled up to him. "I really do wish we could have helped him in some way."

A vehicle sped across the desert, heading toward them, throwing up a cloud of dust. Sheriff Manny hit the brakes and the patrol truck slid sideways, the ballooning cloud of dust rolled over the H-1.

"Jesus . . . Effing . . . Christ." Roy waved his arms in front of his face and slammed the back doors of the Hummer closed.

He and Barry covered their faces with the crooks of their elbows.

Manny powered down the window. "Folks back at the office ain't the best at checking phone messages. Seems like we got a couple of calls reporting some sort of low-flying UFO out here. One fella called it a UAP."

Roy squinted and raised his eyebrows.

Manny adjusted his Stetson. "That stands for an unidentified aerial phenomena."

"I know what it means," Roy said.

"Call came from truckers. Not them tree-hugging hipsters out looking at the roadside attractions. Best description we got of it." He looked at his small spiral notepad. "Some good ol' boy said it 'looked like Luke Skywalker's Landspeeder.'" He removed his wraparounds and wiped the dust from the lenses. "Now, ordinarily I wouldn't give a lizard's toenail about this kinda shit except it just so happens Border Patrol is on it, too. You know what that means."

Eyes danced but no one spoke.

"I'll help you out. It means me and my boys are gonna have to open an investigation."

Vance's eyes hadn't played tricks on him after all. What he'd seen earlier was real, a flying object. Luke Skywalker's Landspeeder. Damn. That was an accurate description. Now he wished he'd told Lauren what he thought he'd seen.

23

Riding back to the barn, Lauren wished she could have pulled Vance aside and told him about the extended swirl pattern they'd seen from the elevated vantage point, and that Josh may have slipped, revealing that a prototype hovercraft had been stolen. But Vance was too afraid of the horses for her to get a private minute with him.

Daryl twisted in the saddle and placed his hand on Picasso's rump. He was about to say something when his horse spooked, bolting as if the bell had rung at Churchill Downs and the starting gates had opened.

Her neck snapped as Smokey lunged forward from a walk to a dead gallop.

Shit. The reins were loose and she fumbled for a hunk of mane with one hand, quickly collecting the leather with the other. Josh had his horse on a short rein, and when the others bolted, his leapt vertically, crow-hopping in place like four attached pogo sticks.

"HO!" Daryl's horse obeyed and sat on his hindquarters, sliding to a stop.

Smokey cut left, avoiding a rear-end collision, unbalancing

her, throwing her to one side and forward. *Damn.* Her heart jackhammered under her shirt.

Josh rode up next to her and when he was within reach, leaned down and across, grabbing her reins, and checking up on both horses at the same time. The animals slowed to a trot.

"That damn sheriff spooked the horses, speeding across the desert like that," Daryl said.

A brown rooster tail streamed all the way from the road behind the guestrooms to the Hummer where he'd stopped his patrol truck.

"What an asshole," she said.

Daryl stopped his horse on the ride back. "We're not telling the sheriff what we know. It'll complicate things. I know what happens when too many of them start sticking their noses into stuff. It'll turn into a turf war that'll get in the way."

"I'm telling Vance."

"Does he work for the Feds?"

"No."

"Does he work for the sheriff?"

"No."

"Border Patrol?"

She shook her head.

"Does he want to find the girl?"

She glared at him. "What do you think?"

"Then fine. Tell him." Daryl kicked his horse and rode ahead of her to catch up with Josh.

"Oh, my gosh. Look at your horse's legs."

Daryl jumped to the ground, walked behind Picasso and knelt. He'd skinned his back legs on the sliding stop. Pinpricks of blood welled on his white stockings.

"Damn it." Daryl walked the rest of the way on foot, and back at the stables, looped the reins around a hitching post, then threw the saddle on the wooden railing. He led his horse to a concrete pad, turned on the water, and gently sprayed the blood from the horse's back legs. "I'll meet you inside when I'm done here," he said.

LAUREN DROPPED an everything-bagel in the toaster. She eyed the dining hall, expecting to see Manny mooching a late breakfast, primed to give him a piece of her mind about his driving.

The toaster popped. She put the crispy bagel on her plate, smeared a dollop of butter and joined the others at the table just in time to listen to Josh. Vance patted the seat next to him, inviting her to sit.

"She could have been taken by air," Josh said. "It would explain the odd swirl patterns."

Davis looked up from his tablet. "Air?"

Roy joined them a few minutes late and stood over the table.

Vance pursed his lips, as if thinking.

"There's been a report that a developmental hovercraft was stolen the night before she went missing," Josh said.

Roy's eyebrows went to full staff. He rubbed his temples with both forefingers, then scowled at Josh.

Josh leaned back and folded his arms across his chest. "We needed to tell them."

"The sheriff more or less just did," Roy said.

"What are you talking about?" she asked.

"The sheriff said there're eyewitness accounts. Multiple reports of some kind of unidentified aircraft. One person described it as Luke Skywalker's Landspeeder."

"This is my fault," Davis said.

She was running out of patience. "Would you please stop with that. We've been over it. Several times." She looked at

Vance. "What if it was hidden near the berm?" Then she elbowed him. "Show them what you found."

He narrowed his eyes.

"Just do it."

He reached into his jacket pocket and set the piece of torn fabric on the table.

Josh picked it up and examined it. "Where did you get this?"

"I found it near the berm."

Josh rubbed his jaw. "It's possible the hovercraft was out there and was covered with a tarp."

"Let's say someone did hide it. Caitlin could have been at the wrong place at the wrong time," Vance said.

Roy glanced at this watch. "If she was the target, we should have heard a ransom demand by now."

She held her breath. Both scenarios were grim.

"Here comes Jake," Vance said.

The conversation dropped to a whisper.

Jake noticed all eyes on him. "What?"

"Can you think of anyone who'd take your daughter?" Roy asked.

"No. Did you find something?"

The wooden legs screeched and the long bench rocked so hard she almost tumbled backward.

It was Davis suddenly scrabbling to his feet that unbalanced everyone sharing his bench.

"Hey." Vance leaned forward, grabbing the dining table to keep from tipping over.

"Check it out." Davis stood, looming.

Lauren leaned back and looked at the tablet. The others circled Davis from behind. He'd changed the picture to black-and-white and adjusted the contrast. When he replayed the footage from yesterday, the swirl pattern leading from the berm to the highway was clear as day.

Now, everyone was on the same page.

Jake reached into his pocket and put his readers on, studying the freeze frame on the screen. Beads of sweat welled on his forehead.

"I'm sorry to interrupt," Rosa said. "But Ann's on the phone again." She grimaced at Jake.

"You better to talk to her," Lauren said.

"She's threatening to take the next flight out of Miami." Rosa put her hands on her hips. "You need to talk to her. I can't keep holding her off."

"Go on, Jake," Roy said. "We don't know anything for sure."

Jake followed Rosa to the front desk. Adam stretched the cord over the counter and handed it to him.

"Look who's back." Lauren nudged Vance and tossed her head toward the front desk. Sheriff Manny strutted past Adam. She looked at Davis and funneled her hands over her mouth. "Put that away."

If the sheriff saw it, he might take it the way he'd taken Caitlin's backpack from Jake. She wanted to keep it, to study the video more closely.

Davis was a lousy sneak. He fumbled the tablet like it was hot.

"May I have a look?" the sheriff asked.

Davis laid the tablet facedown.

Manny put his hand out.

Trying to get his fat fingers under it, Davis launched it off the edge. The tablet smacked the tile and bounced.

Davis dropped to his knees, diving for it. Manny pressed the sole of his boot on his chubby hand.

"Ow," Davis said.

Manny pushed it from Davis' grasp with the toe of his boot. "I'll take that."

Manny high-stepped over Davis splayed on the floor like a

beached whale. Resting his elbow on the butt of the gun holstered to his tooled belt, he bent over and picked up the tablet.

"Show the sheriff what you showed us," Roy said to Davis.

"Okay."

Manny handed the tablet to him. Davis sat on the floor like Jabba the Hutt. The screen was in good shape after hitting the tile. Davis cued the video, pressed the PLAY button and handed it to the sheriff.

Manny watched for a minute. "Huh," he said handing it back to Davis. "Shut it down, please."

Davis did as asked.

Manny held his hand out. "Evidence," he said, taking it back from Davis. He strode toward the front desk, carrying his metal clipboard under his left arm, holding the tablet in his right hand.

Roy left to catch up with him.

Davis looked gut-punched.

She ran to see where Manny was going. Damn it. She stood next to Roy, watching the tail end of his U-turn as the brown truck headed down the gravel drive, toward the highway.

As the gate opened and the sheriff exited, a black Suburban turned left from the main highway and entered, motoring slowly up the driveway.

She hurried back to the table to check on Davis. He sat on the tile with his back against the bench, his chin touching his chest. Daryl stood over him.

"Where have you been?" she asked.

"Doctoring my horse." Daryl looked at Davis. "What's wrong with him?"

"Nothing," Vance said.

"I have an idea," Daryl said. "Who has a laptop?"

"I do," Vance said. "What do you need it for?"

"To do a little research on the fitness tracker."

Vance went out the side door and off to his room.

Jake paced the long side of the table, hunched over, shaking his head.

Daryl intercepted him. "Do you remember where your daughter got it?"

Jake was in la-la-land.

"Jake," she said. "Do you remember where Caitlin bought her fitness tracker?"

He shook his head.

Daryl said, "Sir, we're gonna need your help."

Jake cleared his throat. Then he perked up. "I think that's what I bought her for her birthday."

"Maybe there's a receipt on your phone."

Jake's face was a blank.

"Gimme your phone," she said.

He took his cell from of his pants pocket. His fingers trembled. He typed the code and opened the screen.

"Let me help you." She ignored more missed calls and messages, tapping the little blue envelope on the screen. His email opened. "Do you remember the name of the company?"

Jake shook his head.

She typed Caitlin's name into the email browser. Dozens of old messages popped up. "Do you remember how long ago it was?"

Jake paced, raking his fingers through his hair. "It was for her birthday. Check August."

That was seven, eight months ago. She added "birthday" to the search. A more manageable list appeared. She scrolled and stopped on the subject line: Purchase complete sweetie. Happy Birthday.

She tapped the link. There it was, the receipt. She forwarded it to her phone, then to Rosa's email, and walked to the desk.

Rosa was helping Adam, who was still learning the ropes. The black SUV idled beneath the portico. A well-dressed, fortyish man got out and strode toward the front door.

"He's a little overdressed for the West, don't you think?" she whispered, watching the man.

"You know how it is here. Anything goes," Rosa said.

"I need a favor." She asked Rosa to check her email and print the document.

Rosa disappeared through the doorway leading to the small office behind the reception desk. A moment later she returned with a copy.

The well-dressed man stepped up to the desk. Rosa excused herself to help Adam.

LAUREN SET the paper on the tabletop, in front of Vance, who'd returned with his laptop.

Jake looked frazzled.

"I guess we could use his phone," she said.

"I'll use mine," Vance said.

He looked at the receipt, typed the 800-number, then pressed the phone to his ear. "This might take a while. Sounds like a call center."

Jake sat next to Davis. "Let me see it again, the video," he said absently.

Bad on-hold music emanated from Vance's phone.

Vance covered the mic. "Will someone please explain to him what just happened?"

Roy put his hand on Jake's shoulder and squeezed it. "We don't have the video anymore."

"What do you mean?" Jake's voice rattled.

He'd been at the desk, on the phone with Ann.

"Listen to me," Roy said. "Don't overreact. Do you hear me?"

Jake nodded.

"The sheriff took Davis' tablet."

"What the—?" He scrambled to his feet and started toward the door. She'd never seen him move that fast.

Daryl and Josh each grabbed an elbow.

Jake's tone dropped to a growl. "Let go of me. I hate that mother—"

"I know," Roy said. "But letting your emotions get the best of you is not going to help. You need to calm down. Sit. Take a deep breath. If you want to find her, we all need to keep our cool."

Vance scanned the printout, running a finger up and down the columns. "Uh-huh. . . . Uh-huh. . . . Which numbers?" He paused, listening. "My name? Jake Fleming. . . . No, I don't have that. Uh-huh, yes, I can hold. . . . That's the only way? Yes, I understand."

Jake wasn't going to take this well.

He handed the mobile back to Jake, shaking his head. "They need the serial number. It's not on the receipt. It's on the box and on the device. Obviously, we don't have either."

All roads seemed to go nowhere.

24

Lauren took her boots off and fell into the leather club chair next to the bed. Vance hunched over his computer at the desk, browsing the 'Net. They'd gone back to his room to regroup.

"How come you never had kids?" he asked.

What the . . .? That question came out of nowhere. "I don't know."

He turned away from the screen and faced her. "I'm sure you've thought about it."

"Of course." Maybe the time had come to share something more personal. She hesitated, then took a risk. "When I was about ten, my dad told me I should never depend on a man."

He cocked his head, his expression softening. "That's tough."

"Yeah. Especially if you're old-fashioned."

"You consider yourself old-fashioned?"

"I do."

He turned to his computer. "What did your mom say about him telling you that?"

"She didn't know."

"Why do you think he said it?"

"I guess because he was an unreliable husband."

He looked at her out of the corner of his eye. "Still, that's a weird thing for a father to say to his daughter, kind of mean, actually."

Turnabout was fair play. "Why didn't you get married and have children?"

"Jesus." He leaned forward in the chair with his nose a few inches away from the computer screen.

"What? It's not fair to ask you the same question?"

"Not that. Look at this." He carried the laptop and set it on the bed, turning it so she could see the screen.

"Wow." She moved into a cross-leg position and put it on her lap. The website for a futuristic-looking aircraft called an *AeroHov*. "I'm sort of surprised they have a website."

He sat next to her, on the wide chair arm. "It's an expired website."

"How did you find it?"

"I did a Wayback Machine Google search for hovercrafts."

She tapped the keys. "They have a video." She pressed the PLAY arrow. An animation started. She craned her head closer to the screen, squinting, to study it.

No, not an animation, *actual footage*. Surreal. The person sitting in the forward seat, the driver—or pilot—or whatever, could have passed as a mannequin. Production value was high, meaning it was big budget work.

"Look at the location," he said.

The fractured terrain with mountains in the background looked a lot like Antelope Creek Ranch, except the peaks were snowcapped. The pilot made flying it look easy. The idea something like it was used to abduct Caitlin didn't seem so farfetched.

The website listed the potential benefits: landmine detection, pipeline inspection, crop-dusting, disaster-relief. Border patrol. According to the outdated website, the vehicle had been in the testing phase and wasn't FAA approved.

He took the laptop from her. "It's strange they didn't wipe the site from the 'Net."

"Can you do that?"

"You can do anything. If you know the right people."

"Maybe it's not a secret."

He clicked on the specs page and ran the mouse over the options. It weighed just over eight-hundred pounds, seated two, flew at a max altitude of twenty feet with a top speed of fifty miles per hour.

"Take off speed is zero."

She looked at him blankly.

"It means it can liftoff vertically, like a helicopter. We need to figure out who's developing these things and where they're testing them."

"Go to the Investor page."

The contact phone number started with 011972. He scrolled down to the physical address. "They're in Tel Aviv."

"This is getting weirder by the minute. Play the video again."

He toggled back to the page and replayed it.

"It looks cheap, like two big plastic fans molded together." The curved bodywork reminded her of children's shopping carts at the high-end grocery stores, except dull gray, not primary colors.

"It's hardly cheap. It's made of a composite material. Carbon fiber. Stronger than steel. That's the beauty of it. Very lightweight." He scanned the details that bored her to death. Engine specs, horsepower, drive-train, MPG. "It has an optional kit to make it amphibious, and it can be upgraded with airbags."

"Airbags?"

"We need to contact the company. If we can figure out who's

testing these bad boys, maybe it'll help us find her." His cell buzzed. The call was short. "That's a bummer."

She cocked her head. "What?"

"The fitness tracker. The company's website was hacked less than a week ago and all their customer files were deleted."

He was quiet for a minute, staring at the screen. "It doesn't add up. Companies have at least one backup system. Most of them cloud compute." He paused. "Maybe we can get hold of the original packaging. If we get the serial number, maybe we can go directly to the manufacturer instead of the retailer."

She grimaced. "You know what that means."

"Yup. Jake is going to have to talk to his ex again. He won't want to, but I'm sure he'll do whatever he needs to do to find Caitlin."

"Can you imagine? If it was your kid?"

Vance pushed the hair from her face. "I have an idea about how I can take your mind off it." He kissed her neck in three places, slowly.

"I can't. Not now."

He shrugged, nodded, and took his fingers off his zipper. A stroke of luck perhaps since he wasn't sure if he could summon the cobra. That was an alarming new development.

His phone pinged. A message from Josh: `come to the lodge - want u to meet a friend.`

Vance typed: `b right there` and pushed the send button.

"Come on," he said.

25

G uilt washed over Lauren as she hurried along the gravel path, past the turquoise pool and thorny purple bougainvillea rooted along the path. Even though she'd told Davis it wasn't his fault, she wasn't sure it wasn't hers. He'd been working. She'd been *watching*.

Jake looked worse. He stood over Davis and another person she didn't recognize, a millennial. Vance pulled one end of the bench to make room for both of them to sit. The screech pissed Jake off.

"Sorry," Vance said.

Josh made the introduction. "This is Fritz. He's offered to help."

"I'm no hacker," Fritz said, "but if she has a health app installed, and it sounds like she might, it's probably paired with her phone."

Vance told him about the snafu, that the seller's files had been hacked.

"Ah." Fritz nodded. "Sometimes I fantasize about catching one of them and using a meat cleaver to chop their fingers off so they'll have to hack with their toes and noses. May I see it? The paperwork?"

Jake handed him the folded document.

He studied it for a moment. "Hmm. Did your daughter have an account at the online store? Where she bought it?"

"Don't all the kids?" Jake started pacing again, the leather soles of his loafers slapping the orange clay tiles.

Fritz treaded lightly. "Mine don't, but that's because my wife won't let them. Do you mind? If I take a look at her phone to see if she has the shopping app installed?"

"Do whatever you need to do." Jake typed the password and handed him the mobile.

Fritz swiped the screen, located the icon, and tapped it, working his fingers on the screen like a clarinet player. He closed one app, opened another, and scrolled with his forefinger. "She shops a lot."

"Not exactly a news bulletin," Jake said.

Fritz squinted at the screen, then turned his palm so Jake could see it.

"It's a ring that can be paired with the tracker. It looks like she bought both at the same time. It's interesting."

"May I look?" Lauren asked.

He held it so she could see it. The device reminded her of a smart watch, and the ring looked like costume jewelry. "Do you think it's possible we can use this to track her location?"

"Depends," Fritz said.

"On what?" Jake asked.

"If it's paired with the phone."

"Look," Jake said, "I don't want to be an asshole, but her phone is in your hand."

"I know that. It lost connection with the phone yesterday, at seven forty-six in the morning." He squinted at the small font.

Jake's chest deflated and he hunched as if taking a boxer's

blow to the gut. "Yesterday," he repeated, knocking his temples with balled fists. "This is a nightmare. Fathers are supposed to protect their daughters."

"It's not your—"

Jake cut Lauren off. "You . . . don't have kids." He tried to sit, but his knees wobbled and he broke his fall, slapping both hands on the tabletop.

"Are you okay?" Fritz asked.

Jake composed himself and sat. "I'm fine."

He didn't look fine.

"It gives you a reliable timeline. It also confirms she's not, um, here," Fritz said. "Look, I have kids. I can't imagine—"

Rosa interrupted. "It's your ex on the phone again. She's freaking out."

"You haven't talked to her yet?" Lauren couldn't believe it. "What were you doing earlier, at the desk?"

Rosa glared at Jake. "He pretended to talk to her. Then he convinced Adam to lie and tell her he was in the men's room." Rosa narrowed her eyes. "And to tell her he'd call right back. She said she's done waiting. The next call will be to the police."

"You don't know Ann." Jake shook his head, slowly.

Fritz returned Caitlin's phone to him. "If it was my kid, first thing I'd do is call everyone I know to see if anyone knows anything about this technology. If that's a dead end, then I'd call the FBI."

She said, "Daryl told us they've used the fitness trackers to trace people."

Josh backed her up. "Maybe we should ask Daryl if he can help."

Rosa stood at the end of the table, with her hands on her hips, glaring at Jake, her eight months of pregnancy in full view over the tabletop.

"Shit." Jake stuffed Caitlin's phone in his pocket. "I'll be right back."

When he was out of earshot, Josh asked, "Do you know anyone who can help us?"

"I might." Fritz stared at the screen on his phone, typing. "There's always a backup file of everything. I doubt the call center where she bought it would have access to cloud files, but I bet the manufacturer does. All developers are about six degrees removed from each other, so I'm betting there's someone in my network who knows someone. I'm not making any promises, but I'm happy to give it a shot. I can make a few calls."

Jake returned to catch the tail end of the conversation. "I really appreciate it. Anything you can do to help me find my little girl . . . ." Jake paused. "Just let me know if there's anything I can do to help."

"You could look for the serial number. Your daughter might have kept the original packaging. That might help."

"Sure," Jake said.

"Hang on a sec," Fritz said, eyes glued to his mobile. "Mind if I make a phone call?"

Jake looked confused. "Why would I mind?"

"From your daughter's phone."

Jake pulled it from his pocket, unlocked the screen, and handed it to him.

Fritz's eyes shifted from the screen on his mobile to Caitlin's, back and forth as he pecked out an 11-digit number on the borrowed one. He tapped the green CALL button and put Caitlin's phone to his ear. A moment later he announced, "I'm on hold."

She glanced at Vance, who shrugged.

"Hello," Fritz said into the phone. "I wonder if you can help me. I'm on your website. I'm reading some of the posts on your community message board . . . uh-huh . . . yes."

He listened some more, then said, "I see here that you helped a customer find their lost fitness tracker. Uh-huh, uh-huh. Yesterday. Yeah. Uh-huh, it's paired with this phone. Uh-huh. Can you hold for a second?" Fritz covered the mic with his thumb. "They want to try pinging the watch. But they need a password."

"For her phone?" Jake asked.

"No, for the fitness tracker."

"I don't know it."

She whispered, "Try the same one as the phone."

Jake jotted it on the newspaper at the table, tore the edge and handed it to Fritz.

"Thanks for holding. Try 5-6-9-9-0-1 . . . Uh-huh. I don't know, I mean, I can't remember. Hold on . . . Do you know the date of purchase?"

"August tenth."

He gave them the date. "No, I don't mind holding. Take your time." Fritz drummed one thumb on the edge of the table. "I understand," he said. "Yep, this is a good number . . . Uh, yeah . . . . That's right . . . ah . . . no . . . I'm her dad." He looked at Jake and shrugged apologetically. "How long will that take? Okay . . . I really appreciate this . . . . Yeah, maybe we'll get lucky."

Lauren leaned on her elbows with her chin in her hands. "What was that all about?"

"They're going to try pinging the device."

Jake massaged his brow. "Then what?"

"Then they're going to call back to let us know if they get a hit." Fritz handed the phone to Jake. "Answer it," he said, "even if you don't recognize the number."

Jake shuffled out the side door. She and Vance watched him amble across the courtyard, leaning forward at the waist, as if heading into a strong wind.

The fitness tracker was the best lead they had so far.

"Do you know where Daryl is?" Lauren asked Josh.

"He's gone to see the sheriff."

"What? Why?"

"He'll be back soon enough."

She looked at the time. "Is he staying in town?"

Vance asked, "Why wouldn't he stay here?"

"The rooms are full," Josh said, "but he's not going home. He'll stay here overnight. He's going to camp."

"You mean like sleep on the ground?" she asked, recalling the bedroll tied to his saddle.

"No sense in him driving all the way to El Paso," Josh said.

Vance looked at her with raised brows.

"He went to see the sheriff," Josh said, "because a lot of the aerospace start-ups have hangars and warehouses around here. If someone's testing an experimental craft in the vicinity, Manny would have to know about it. Daryl's gone to find out what he knows."

Jake returned. His face was a mask. "My ex said she shouldn't have let me to take her out of school. My daughter could miss a month and still be at the top of her class. Ann's looking for anything that might have the serial number on it. She's very capable. If it's there, she'll find it." He squeezed his jowls with one hand, puckering his lips like a cartoon goldfish.

That was the first nice thing she'd heard Jake say about Ann. Maybe the first nice thing she'd heard him say about anyone, aside from Caitlin. He hung the moon on that kid and the way Jake looked now, he may as well have had the full weight of it hanging around his neck like a ball and chain.

Sometimes the worst situations brought out the best in people. Maybe Jake was one of them.

Jake's pants pocket buzzed. He pulled his phone out and looked at the screen, then stuck it back in his pants. The phone in the other pocket was the one ringing. He answered it, and listened intently. "I'll keep looking. Thank you." He shoved it back in his pocket, hands shaking. "They got a hit."

"Where is it?" she asked.

"They're gonna text me."

The phone pinged. Jake put his readers on, tapped the link, narrowed his eyes and handed the phone to Vance. "Take a look at this."

"A gas station off Route 90, in Comstock . . . around ten-forty yesterday morning."

Lauren searched Comstock, Texas on her phone. Holy shit. It was southeast of Marfidio, just miles from the US-Mexico border. She showed it to Vance.

"We need to go there," Jake said.

"It's a hundred and ninety miles," Vance said. "That's a three-hour drive. Let's see if the sheriff can help. It's still Texas. It'll be a whole lot faster if he knows someone in Comstock."

She said, "It's a small town. Population four-hundred."

"I know the place," Josh said. "I bet Roy knows someone who knows someone who knows the Val Verde County sheriff. It'll be a lot faster if they send a local deputy."

That was a better idea. She looked at the time on her phone. It was just after 10:00 AM.

"Maybe someone saw something," Jake said.

"Come with me and let's find out," Josh said. "Let's talk to Roy."

―――

WHEN THEY WERE GONE, Lauren said, "Take a look at this." A Google search for "Police department in Comstock, Texas" produced two hits. The first was the Val Verde County Sheriff's Department. The other, US Customs and Border Protection. The town was that close to the border.

She clicked another link and read aloud to Vance: "Border agents reported three incidents of deceased individuals on a local ranch last month."

She scanned a down a couple more paragraphs. "The terrain along the border is too rugged to travel by vehicle, and according to the US Customs and Border Patrol website, is a busy area for transnational criminal organizations. American citizens are advised to avoid the area."

She shuddered. If the mountainous area was impassable by vehicle, maybe it would buy them some time. If she'd been taken by one of the cartels, her kidnappers would have to find a place where they could cross into Mexico. If the teenager was still alive.

26

C aitlin had lost all track of time. The endless vibration rattled her bones to the marrow. The metal screw she'd used to etch a mark into the flooring had rolled out of reach and pinged like a BB. She sniffled, dabbing tears on her sleeves.

Maybe her mother had been right all along, that her dad was nothing more than a drunk. She winced at the memory, the day her mother said aloud her biggest mistake in life was marrying him. That she shouldn't have had kids with him. That he was an irresponsible father.

He'd defended himself in an equally awful way. If he hadn't been rich, he reminded her mother, she wouldn't have pursued him.

Recalling the days when her dad was wealthy, her mother and her mom's friends loved to compare their husbands' multi-million-dollar bonuses, as if it were some sort of contest. Her dad spent all his time at work and on the road. When he was home, he'd complain about the hundred-hour work-weeks, threatening to retire at age fifty.

He did it. One day he quit his banking job in New York City

and her parents announced they were selling their Connecticut home. The day they moved to North Carolina was the happiest of her life. Her parents started a real estate business together, buying parcels of land to build houses on, and fixer-uppers to flip. Trouble began because of something called the housing crisis. That's when her dad starting drinking all day. The more he drank, the more they fought.

Why didn't he just stop?

It made no sense.

How could he let a bottle of liquid ruin their lives?

One day she came home from school early. Her dad's car was parked in the driveway but he wasn't in the house. She'd gone room-to-room looking for him but he wasn't there.

It was late spring and the warmest day of the year so far. He liked to tinker in the garage, and if he'd been working there on a warm day, he'd usually open the overhead door. But, it was also one of the places where he hid his booze.

She passed through the mudroom leading to the garage. The light at his workbench was on. A surge of adrenaline flooded her body.

Oh, my gosh.

He was in there. With the neighbor lady. Her shirt was off and her dad's hands were on the woman's naked breasts. Screaming, she ran from the house, toward the woods.

Later that night her mother punished her for disappearing. Grounded for a month. Her father came to her room and sat on the edge of the bed and cried. He didn't deny what she'd seen. He told her he would to tell on himself. That he couldn't bear to see her taking the blame for what he'd done. He hugged her, said he loved her, and apologized.

Later that night she'd heard them arguing, and doors slamming. Her parents had the biggest fight *ever* and when she'd heard his car start, she'd looked out the window and seen him speed from the driveway. If only she hadn't come home from school early, none of this would have happened.

She'd thought a lot about his faults, his absences, temper flare-ups, endless apologies, broken promises, and mostly his drinking. Her mother accused him of not being *present*.

"Get help, Jake," she'd say. "Millions of others have."

If her mom had said it one more time, her head would have exploded.

A month later they sat her and her brother down at the dinner table and said they were separating. That meant they were getting a divorce. All kids know this. If her mother worried about him not being present, then how did she think a separation would help?

Over the summer, she listened to her mom badmouth him to anyone who'd listen. She ranted in the car on speaker. To the neighbors, to make sure everyone knew she wasn't to blame. One day a For Sale sign appeared on the front lawn. Summer camp canceled, vacations, tutors, music lessons, all postponed indefinitely.

They argued about the selling price for the house and her mom screamed at him they might have to file bankruptcy. That the million dollars they'd get from the sale would go to paying off debts for the unsold real estate they'd bought together.

That was the one and only time she'd seen her mother cry.

She'd have done anything to forget the look on his face that afternoon when she'd walked in on him, his hands cupped on that woman's bare breasts, that sad expression cemented on his face. The look of dull surprise plastered on that whore's face. The smells of the things he loved—potting soil, and varnishes, fertilizers, and paints—overpowered by the stench of second-hand booze. And sex, she assumed.

She'd sprinted through the woods, batting the foliage, stumbling, getting up, running until she could go no farther. She'd stopped by the creek and sat on the bank, watching the sun go down before heading for home.

Black iron lampposts flanked the long driveway leading to the house like a pair of lighthouses. She saw her parents through the kitchen window, their body language that of a pair of prizefighters worn out from landing jabs and taking punches. They'd surrendered. She slipped through the front door unnoticed and sneaked past the kitchen, covering her ears, blocking out their last words of resignation.

Sniffling and blinking back her tears, she recalled the relief she'd felt the day the house sold, along with the garage.

The whoop-whoop of a nearby siren pulled her back to the miserable present, recoiling as the shrieking came closer. She'd have covered her ears if she'd been able.

More hoots, short ones, followed. The truck pulling the trailer slowed to let the emergency vehicle by. The trailer shimmied as big rigs passed, some downshifting, others passing at speed. The siren didn't pass, rather it slowed, too, the sound now coming from directly behind. The droning of the trailer tires morphed into gnashing sounds where the blacktop turned to dirt as it rolled to a stop.

Her heart pumped.

She was being rescued.

She pressed her ear to the metal siding, listening. The ambient road noise was too loud to pick out specific sounds. She flinched as the siren near the back door wailed one last time, followed by a break in traffic, and then throaty idling of a vehicle stopped closely behind the trailer. The driver shut down the engine. A car door slammed.

The container she was trapped in rocked slightly as her captor got out of the truck; the interior huffed when he slammed the driver's-side door. She twisted the metal ring on her finger.

Breathe.

Her heart thrummed.

Pressing her elbows against her ribcage, she leaned forward and dug the toes of her track shoes into the flooring and arched her sore back. Her seat bones ached. The muscle in her right hamstring cramped. She lifted her knee but there was no room to stretch out.

Aw. Aw.

The trailer swayed gently from the winds of passing traffic.

How long had it been since she'd been taken, since she'd showered, or changed clothes. Or brushed her hair. She ran her tongue over her teeth and grimaced.

This was insane. Open the door. She wanted out.

She pressed her ear on the wall to listen.

She heard voices. Two men talking.

They were nearby, just outside the back door of the trailer, but she couldn't make out what they were saying.

She'd recognize her dad's voice. It had always been easy to pick it out of a crowd, a tone deeper and stranger than most. Then the voices faded, drowned out by passing traffic, mostly long-distance haulers, she assumed. She rotated at the waist, left and right, right and left, the muscle on the back of her thigh throbbing.

The car parked behind the trailer started up.

No, no, no, no, no.

The siren whooped.

Maybe another car?

More help?

The vehicle pulled from the shoulder at a break in traffic, crumpling dirt, popping gravel as the driver stomped the gas.

No, no, no, no, no.

The emergency vehicle left.

She lunged to her feet using her heels, scrambling over the cargo as if possessed, fumbling and stumbling and cursing and raging and pummeling the metal door, using the heels of her palms over her head.

She stood shaking, eyes following a pinpoint of light streaming from outside. She placed her eyeball an inch from it, like a peephole. She peered out, balancing on tiptoes with her right shoulder turned sideways against the back door. The highway was blank and the vehicle she'd heard drive in behind the trailer was now gone, fresh tire tracks and dust rising in its place.

Raising her sore wrists, she hammered the trailer door, jumping up and down. "What do you want?" she screamed, ramming her shoulder against the back door.

But no one answered. There was no one there. No rescue. Tears filled her eyes and her lip quivered. Knees slack, she collapsed like rag doll. Rolling forward, she rested her face on the tops of her wrists. Straightening her fingers and flattening her palms together, she began to weep.

Footfalls, just outside. Crunching the dirt.

She struggled to her feet and looked out the pinhole. The padlock clanked. He was outside fiddling with the lock. It dropped open. The T-bar clunked and squealed as he raised it. She scrambled backward, tripping, falling. The door creaked open six inches and sunlight spilled in.

He peered inside, his thick forearms grabbing the frame, squinting, expecting to see her in the back corner. But she wasn't there. He hopped like a chimp, and using his arms to pull his body up, landed inside, rocking the trailer. Squatting, he shined his cell light, looking for her. He spotted her in the corner immediately to his left, not near the truck bed, but near the back door of the trailer, between the cargo and the metal siding.

"What the fuck are you doing?"

A blast of adrenaline surged, her brain went blank. She

stood in a space with barely enough room for her feet, bent at the waist, leaning over the tarp covering the payload.

"Get . . . away . . . from . . . the . . . machine."

She had no space, nowhere to go.

"You have one second to get back to your corner," he growled. "Or I'll give you something new to cry about."

The threat didn't register.

"Stand up." He yanked the gun from the front of his pants and pointed it at her. "I said, get up. Get up. Now." Crow-hopping toward her, he braced himself against the metal siding and jabbed the nose of the pistol under her chin. "I didn't go to all this trouble to let you get away."

She squeezed her eyes and grit her teeth, breathing through her nose.

In out, in out, in out.

"Do you have a death wish?"

She kept her eyes down and shook her head.

"Good. Put your hands out."

She obeyed, lifting her head slightly.

He set the cell phone on the tarp and pulled something from his pants pocket. He snapped the blade open, stuck it in his mouth, grabbed her wrists with one hand, adjusted the cell phone on an angle, turned her hands over, and studied the marks from the tie.

"Ah. Look what you've done to yourself."

Bruises on the heels of her palms were ripening. He took the knife from his teeth, and cut the tie.

"I'm going out first. You wait for my cue. Do you understand?"

She nodded.

He hopped down like a zoo animal and closed the door. A second later he opened it and he reached inside. "Gimme your arm."

He guided her down.

"Walk in front of me, to the passenger door. Do not try anything. Do you understand?"

She nodded, fighting back tears.

"I don't wanna to hurt you, you spoiled brat."

She bowed her head.

Her hands were on fire. The numbness had been replaced with the sensation of electric shocks. Twisting the rosy metal ring on her middle finger, she wished to God she had her phone. With that, she could call her dad. He would come and save her.

27

Vance's phone pinged. He clicked the thumbnail of a photo and used two fingers to enlarge the image. The device on the pavement looked like a smart watch, the glass face, smashed.

A text from Josh followed: Found at a gas station in Comstock. Pic is from Val Verde S.O.

S.O. was Sheriff's Office. He showed the picture to Lauren who stared at the screen but said nothing.

He composed a text: Any leads? He pushed the send button.

Ding: Gas station clerk saw a dark colored pick up hauling white trailer — Florida plates.

That fit the basic description of what he thought he'd seen yesterday.

Florida plates. What were the chances?

Maybe there was surveillance video.

He spotted the software programmer, Fritz, running across the courtyard. The side door to the dining hall flung open.

"The ring that was sold with the watch is on the grid," Fritz caught his breath. "The wristwatch isn't. The two things are separated."

"How do you know that?"

"I have a contact who knows someone at the manufacturer. The watch stopped pinging in"—he looked at his handwritten note—"Comstock, Texas. But the ring is on the move."

"I don't understand," Lauren said.

Vance held his hand up, buying a few seconds to think. If Caitlin's assailant saw the wristband, he would have been smart enough to see it was more than a watch. He'd ditched it at the gas station. The picture Josh sent confirmed it. It made sense that her abductor missed the ring because it looked like plain jewelry. "Can I see the picture again? Of the tracker and ring together on the company website?"

Fritz clicked on a link and handed him the phone. "The company has gotten into some recent legal issues. They're hesitant to help."

Lauren cocked her head. "What kind of issues?"

"One of their devices was used to help arrest a murder suspect."

"That's a good thing," she said.

"Yeah, except it was stolen and they arrested the wrong guy. They were sued and settled out of court. Since that happened, they're gun-shy and their lawyers told them not to comply without a court order."

"Great. Another dead end," Vance said.

Fritz shook his head. "Not so fast. An old friend of mine owes me a favor. He's the one who got the hit on the ring."

"Where?" she asked.

"Alabama." He glanced at his notes again. "Around fifty miles west of Pensacola."

"Florida?" Lauren looked stunned.

Florida plates.

Fritz nodded. "The ring has its own chip, but it's miniscule. The battery life is two days, three tops when it's on standby. It's never sold without the watch because of the limited life."

"Tell them to turn it on and give us the current location," Vance said.

"We need to preserve it. Every time they ping it, it uses battery."

"Are you nuts? This is exactly the reason why we should ping it."

"I already told you, my contact is way out on a limb. Plus, they're suspicious about the story."

Vance raised his eyebrows. "They?"

"The manufacturer."

"Story?" Lauren asked.

Fritz shrugged. "They've heard it all before."

"Heard all what before?"

"The ruses."

Vance narrowed his eyes. "Ruses?"

"Yeah. They want time to authenticate the story. You wouldn't believe what the thieves do to steal technology. Bribery, hacking, pretty girls. Planting fake employees inside the company to steal secrets. The story about a missing fifteen-year-old girl? My source says the higher corporate echelon is suspicious. Rightfully so, I might add."

Lauren was getting a headful of steam. "Rightfully so? What does that mean?"

Fritz said, "I'm doing what I can. I told them it's true. I gotta go." He stood to leave. "I have your cell numbers. I'll keep you posted."

"Wait a minute," Vance said, "how do we know you're not a *bad guy*?"

"You see," Fritz said. "You don't. That's exactly their point."

"I need some air," Vance said.

WALKING off the bad news of another dead end, Vance's phone pinged. He counted twelve numbers. Caller ID: ANONYMOUS.

The first four were zeros. Maybe he should answer it and rip into the caller. Fuckers.

It pissed him off when the Russians, or the Nigerians, or the Chinese, or the Dutch, or whoever thought he was stupid enough to fall for some hacker in a dark apartment halfway around the world. Maybe he should toss his phone in the pool and go off the grid for a while.

He pressed the red button, instead, and dismissed the call.

His phone pinged.

He looked at the screen.

His heart thumped under his shirt.

Primo - GM is out.

He walked to the courtyard and sat at the edge of a chaise lounge next to the pool, watching the water ripple in the breeze. A wavy image reflected. Someone stood behind him.

"What's wrong?" Lauren asked.

"Nothing." He stuffed the phone in his pocket.

"You look worse than Jake."

"I told you, it's nothing."

"Whoa, don't take it out on me."

He took a deep breath and held it for a few seconds, then exhaled slowly. "I'm sorry."

The message had to be from his fugitive Cuban uncle, Tony, hiding in Panama. No one else called him *primo*. Cousin.

GM. GM. GM. Had to be Gregorio Marino. Who else would be *out*? Could someone else have sent it? How would Tony get his new number?

"Earth to Vance."

"Sorry. I'm just decompressing."

She sat on the lounge chair next to him.

Tony had been notoriously reckless. Driving Ferraris, wearing diamond-studded watches, tailored suits. It had finally caught up with him twenty years ago, forcing him to turn state's witness against his partner, Greg's father.

If this communication was from him, he was taking a big risk.

Gregorio Marino couldn't be *out*. That was impossible. Last he heard, Greg was being held in the Dade County jail without bond, awaiting trial.

"Okay." Lauren furrowed her brow and stood. "I'll leave you to your 'decompression.'"

What he really needed to do was get the fuck out of Dodge. He hopped on the ATV Davis had left parked on the path.

Feathering the throttle, he rode toward the backside of the L-shaped building where he'd have some privacy. Time to think. He pulled his cell from his pocket, scrolled through his contact list and tapped retired Sergeant Daniel Ruiz's name.

"To what do I owe the pleasure of this bi-annual call, *Gallego*?"

Gallego. Street slang for guy who can't get laid. He shook his head and mouthed *Mo-fo*. "Fine, thank you. And you?"

"Life's too good to be true," Daniel said.

He rolled his eyes and put his feet up on the ATV dash, pressing his neck against the headrest. "There's a rumor going around."

"What kind of rumor?"

"That he might be out on the street."

"That who might be out on the street?"

"Greg Marino."

"Where'd you hear that?"

"You know how rumors are."

"Speaking of rumors, how's the farm?"

"It's not a farm. It's a ranch. And we already sold it."

"Ranch, farm, whatever. What's important is that you took my advice." Sarge laughed into the phone.

He pictured his Jell-O gut billowing over his belt, jiggling to the beat. "What advice would that be?"

"You ran off with that horsey chick. That's what I told you to do. You bought the farm together. *Muy* romantic."

"A ranch." His fists turned into balls.

"Farm. Ranch. Zoo. Doesn't matter. What matters is you're together."

"Is Marino on the street?"

"Why are you asking me if you already heard it?"

"How'd he get out?"

"Bail. Turns out he had enough cash stashed to hire the Harvard Guys."

The Harvard Guys. Sleazy Ivy League lawyers who liked the South Florida lifestyle and who'd have cheerfully defended Charles Manson if he'd had the money. "I thought he was being held without bond."

"Guess you didn't see the news."

He hadn't.

"His lawyers got a change of venue. The new judge granted bail. You know how it goes. A technicality. Code for a sack of money with tickets to the Super Bowl mixed in. They're trying to get the charges dropped."

"Are you shittin' me? All of them?"

"Yep. The Ivies argued there wasn't probable cause to arrest him. Judge threw out the DNA results. I wish it wasn't so. The DA's not interested in charging him with conspiracy to murder his own father. No one gives a crap about an old cartel kingpin. Way they see it is one less mouth to feed on the taxpayer dime. I tend to agree. It's *super* expensive, keeping a prisoner in a *Super*Max."

"I'm talking about the sexual assaults."

"*Nada* without the DNA. Judge disallowed it."

The fucking Ivies. Sell-out pricks. "What about the gun?"

"Clean as a freshly diapered baby's bottom. Bought legally. Kid had a license and bill of sale. All on the up and up."

"How long's he been out?"

"A week, maybe."

"Anything else I should know?"

"There is one more thing."

"What?"

"Some cop's been asking questions about you."

"What kind of questions?"

"Reference-type questions. Said he was doing some off-duty work for you."

"What's his name?"

"I dunno."

"How'd he get your number?"

"He didn't. I heard it second-hand. You know, guys talking at the local Fraternal Order of Police barbeque. Someone saw me. Seeing me made them think about you. Said you must be doing pretty good if you're hiring your own security. That true? Do you have your own bodyguard these days?"

Sarge was a good detective in his day and there was a fifty-fifty chance he was bluffing. Vance needed to stay off the ropes and downplayed it, dodging the question with a question. "You remember Jake?"

"Hmm." Daniel paused. "The one had that romantic thing with the horsey chick? Your girlfriend, what's her name?"

If they were face-to-face, he might have kneed him in the nuts, if his knee could find an opening under his Jell-O gut. "Her name's Lauren."

"That's right. What about Jake?"

"His daughter disappeared two days ago." He heard Sarge breathing into the phone.

"What do you mean, *disappeared*?"

"She went out for a run and that's the last anyone saw her."

"Where'd she go running?"

He filled Daniel in on the details.

"Jesus, *Gallego*. That place is in the middle of Chihuahua-land."

Did Sarge just make a mistake? How'd he know it happened in the Chihuahuan Desert? He'd told him they'd bought a ranch, but he didn't recall saying where it was.

"How old is she?"

"Fifteen." He told him about the cryptic text that prompted the call.

"Holy mother of God. Are you thinking Greg Marino took her?"

"I don't know."

"You think your Uncle Tony sent it?"

"Don't know that, either."

"If the DA woulda charged that evildoer Greg Marino with the sexual assaults, the case woulda moved to the top of the prosecutors' docket. Too bad. It's an election year. The case would have gone all-Jeffrey Epstein. But without the DNA there's no proof he's the Internet Date Rapist."

"I can't believe they dropped all the charges."

"The prosecutor working the case pointed out while Greg was in custody, the assaults stopped. The judge ruled a reduction in date-raping was a long way from probable cause."

"How much was his bail?"

"Five-thousand."

"That's a joke."

"Let me know if you hear something. Watch your back. The kid thinks you stole his inheritance."

That was hardly a spoiler alert. "I know," he said, wishing Sarge hadn't said it on a cell phone.

He ended the call, thinking how Greg Marino had put Davis Frost in the hospital by busting his jaw, and how that piece of crap would have killed him and Sarge. And Lauren.

If someone had monitored their call, what would they have heard? That Tony might be on the grid. That Jake's kid was missing. That two ex-cops were talking about the Internet Date Rapist.

If Jake got wind his daughter might have been kidnapped by a serial rapist, he'd go insane.

If Greg Marino was the Internet Date Rapist, he was back out there.

The blood in his head surged.

If Greg had Caitlin, she would give that nasty piece of work a ton of leverage. He pushed the thought out of his head.

If Sarge hadn't sent the text tipping him off that Greg was out, who had? The list was short. His fugitive Uncle Tony was on it.

Whoever sent it was warning him.

28

Caitlin sat up front in the cab. She'd checked the digital clock on the dash. Three hours had passed since the last stop. The place where they'd last fueled-up advertised BBQ brisket, fresh coffee, and clean restrooms. She should have used the facilities when she'd had the chance.

"Do you plan to stop soon?"

Her captor didn't answer.

A small envelope addressed to the Mississippi Highway Patrol was tucked into the drink holder in the center console. When he caught her eyeing it, he snatched it, and slipped it under the visor on his side.

"I'm sorry . . . but I haven't *gone* for two days."

"What do you mean *gone?*"

So humiliating. "You know."

He looked over at her with dead eyes. "I asked you on the last stop. You could have taken a dump there."

He was so rude. "I didn't have to go then."

"You missed your chance."

"But I have to *go*."

"I ain't a limousine service." He knuckled the pickup's steering wheel. "You shoulda gone when you had the chance."

He glanced in the rearview mirror and slowed, letting a car pass and changed lanes. The trailer hitched to the truck lurched, jerking the cab two times hard enough to bump her head on the passenger window before settling back on pace.

"I'll find you a spot."

He reached behind the seat and tossed a roll of paper towels at her.

"What are these for?"

He removed the handgun from between his legs and placed it under his right thigh. "What do you think? To wipe your ass. Or your pussy. It'll work on both." He fixed his eyes on the road ahead.

Anger rose in her belly.

"Heard you're some kinda runner. The only time I run is when someone's chasing me." He flashed a wicked grin. "That's not true. Sometimes I do the chasing."

She locked her sore thumbs on her lap. A chill ran down her back.

"You run for fun. I'd never do that."

"It's not exactly for fun."

"Then why do you do it?"

"I like it."

"Why do you like it, Caitlin? If it's not fun, why run? I just made a poem. Did you hear that?"

"How do you know my name?"

"I know a lot about you."

"Like what?"

"All the basics. You're fifteen. You're a rich princess. Your dad's a crook."

"He is not."

"Is too."

Her head filled with steam. "Since you know my name, why don't you tell me yours?"

The highway traffic was steady. She glanced at her side mirror. A police car was closing in.

"Mack."

The cop car rode up on the trailer bumper, then suddenly changed lanes and screamed past on her side, lights flashing. The driver up ahead slowed and changed lanes, right turn indicator blinking. Mack had merged to the left and hugged the centerline, giving the cop room to pass and chase the speeder.

The Nissan pulled onto the shoulder. The black-and-white ducked behind it and parked, light bar flashing.

Her heart raced as she stared out the window, watching the patrolman step out of his vehicle.

She closed her eyes and took a deep breath. "I'd really appreciate it if you'd stop."

"You need to keep your mouth shut. What is it with women? This talking bullshit starts when you're in diapers and it never stops."

Mack slowed, activating the turn indicator. It clicked as he merged onto the off-ramp leading to the I-10 frontage road. He changed lanes again, taking the route north toward Highway 231. When the road flattened, she saw the sign for Cottondale, Florida. Population 933.

Oh, my God. They were in Florida.

"Nine hundred and thirty-three. Makes you wonder what they do when someone takes a dirt nap or some poor bitch pops out another puppy. Be smarter to use a chalkboard if you ask me. Nine-hundred-thirty-two on Monday morning," he mimed, swiping an imaginary eraser, "and nine-thirty-one on Wednesday."

The vegetation looked nothing like palm-treed South Florida. He passed beneath an overhead highway sign with mileage to Pensacola.

"Where are we going?"

"You bitches are all the same, I swear it. You just keep on yapping."

He slowed and rolled a thousand feet along the shoulder of the road, then stopped. "Get out."

"What?"

"You can *go* in the bushes."

"I'm not doing that."

"Have it your way, then." He put the truck in drive and looked over his left shoulder for a break in traffic.

"No-no-no-no." She released the seatbelt from over her shoulder.

"Wait here." He jumped out and sprinted around the front bumper of the truck, then motioned her out. "I'll be watching so don't get any stupid ideas. Like trying to flag a car down."

"Why can't we go there?" She pointed to the tall sign for the fast food place up ahead. "You can stand right outside the bathroom door."

"You going, or not? You got two seconds."

She stepped onto the shoulder of the road.

Mack reached inside the cab and tossed the roll of paper towels at her. "I told you, don't be stupid. And don't let a little snake bite you in the snatch when you drop those cute tight pants."

What a total creep.

What choice did she have? Protecting her face with her hands, she elbowed her way into the thick brush, and when she found a private spot with enough space, braced her shoulder against a tree trunk and squatted.

When she returned, Mack leaned against the side of the trailer looking skyward.

Oh, God, please don't put me back into captivity.

He gestured to her to get back into the cab of the truck.

She hesitated. She could bolt, definitely outrun him to flag down a car. But the traffic was light and the few cars on the road traveled westbound, on the other side of the median.

He brandished a gun from under his shirt. "Nothing funny." He pointed at the passenger door, using the barrel of the gun.

Caitlin stepped onto the running board and climbed in, eyes scanning the cockpit. She leaned over the driver's seat, powered the door locks and grabbed the traffic ticket from the visor. Mack strolled around the front of the dually and pressed the key fob. The truck chirped and the locks released. He climbed in the driver's-side and slammed the door closed.

"Nice try, locking me out. Gimme that," he barked, with his hand out.

She taunted him, holding the paper just out of reach, leaning against the passenger door.

He climbed across the center console. She recoiled at the stench of his breath and sour armpits, then at his body on top of hers.

He wrestled her in the passenger seat. She cowered, leaning against the door. He arched his body over hers, the sleeve of his jacket catching on the headrest, giving her a clear view of the full tattoo.

Before, she'd only seen part of it. The part she'd seen was the nose of a helicopter inked on his right forearm. It stretched from his bicep to his shoulder. There were letters in blue ink on the underside but she couldn't read them.

Snatching it back from her, he yanked his sleeve down and scrambled back behind the wheel.

"You're all the same. Keep your mouth shut." He started the ignition, the diesel clattering to life. "Stop trying to be smart."

She glanced out the passenger's-side window. The glass reflected the distorted image of a madman.

He leaned over her again. She flinched, twisting against the seat-back. He opened the glove box and riffled around. If she had a hammer, she'd have bashed it into his skull. When he popped up, he held out an individual-sized packet of pain reliever.

"Take this."

She took it from him.

He reached behind the seat and swished his hand inside a squeaky cooler, fishing a bottle of water from the crackling ice. Blotting the plastic bottom on his pants' leg, he twisted the top open, and gulped.

Caitlin fish-eyed him. *Double-Dutch jerk.*

He reached behind the seat again, this time for a large bag of pretzels. Opening it, he popped one in his mouth, then offered one to her.

She stared ahead.

"Come on. It won't bite."

She considered it. He'd eaten from the same bag. She'd seen him break the seal. He held it closer to her. She took the pretzel from him, inserted it in her mouth and chewed slowly.

"You need to do something about the attitude."

Me? Attitude?

She was on the brink of popping off at him but the salt from the pretzel tasted delicious. She asked for more. He handed the bag to her.

She fought the tingling sensation in her nose. Tears would make him angry.

She watched him from her periphery.

He held the paper toweling between his thighs and tore two sheets from the roll, then spread the toweling on his thigh. Reaching behind the seat, he scooped a handful of ice from the squeaky cooler. Eyes tilting from the road to his lap, he made an ice pack and handed it to her.

"Here. Put this on your wrists. It'll help with the pain and the swelling."

She set the ice pack on her thigh and raised the packet of pain relievers. "May I have something to drink?"

"Sure." He tossed the roll of paper towels over his shoulder and twisted in his seat, exposing the gun in the waistband of his pants.

She could try to take it. But then what?

He leaned around the center console, taking his eyes off the road. The truck drifted into the lane on her side.

"Watch out!"

He popped up, completed the lane change, and plunked a sports drink between his legs. He removed the cap and handed it to her.

"I'd rather have water."

"This is all I got."

She tore open the package of pain relievers, tossed the pills in her mouth and chased them with a gulp of lime-green liquid.

Her wrists throbbed from the ice pack, blunting one pain for another. She gazed out the windshield as he pressed the gas pedal, the diesel roaring as he switched lanes to pass a motorhome.

He'd left the pretzel bag between the seats. She took a handful and ate them quickly, chugging the sports drink, the coldness stinging the roof of her mouth.

She dabbed the dripping ice pack with the bottom of her sweatshirt, wishing she could change into clean clothes.

Brush her teeth.

Comb her hair.

Shower.

A hot shower. How amazing would that be?

She finished the drink, placed the empty bottle in the cupholder and set the wadded wet toweling next to it. He activated the left-hand turn signal and changed lanes, heading toward the elevated cloverleaf leading southeast.

She leaned against the passenger door, feeling the weight of the truck and trailer as it lurched forward, rhythmically chugging and hugging the circular path of the cloverleaf.

The view from high up on the curved overpass reminded her that Florida was flat and green.

"What do you want with me?"

He glared at her with bloodshot eyes. "I'm just doing a job."

"Who are you?"

That was the last thing she remembered before blacking out.

29

V ance needed to come clean about the cryptic message he'd received. "I didn't mean to bark at you but I got this weird text message."

"You mean decompress," Lauren said sitting at the edge of the bed in his room. "May I see it?"

He thumbed through the messages and pulled it up:

Primo - GM is out. He handed her his phone.

"Who's Primo?"

"Me, I think."

"Who calls you that?"

"My Uncle Tony."

"Why's he call you that? Doesn't that mean cousin in Spanish?"

"It's a childhood thing."

She gnawed on her thumb, staring at his phone. "Who's GM?"

"I'm not sure," he lied. "I called Sarge."

"You called Daniel? Why? Do you think Daniel sent the text?"

"He says he didn't."

"Why would he? Is it possible your uncle has something to do with Caitlin's disappearance?"

Hearing it out loud made his palms sweat. "I thought if anyone might know, Daniel would."

"Does he?"

"No."

She stared at the text message. "'Primo - GM is out.' It must mean something."

"May I have it back?" He held his hand out for the phone.

Was it fair not to tell her that GM could be Greg Marino? Was he holding back to protect her or to spare himself the trouble of an explanation? Did others in relationships have to ask themselves these kinds of questions?

She smoothed her hair, stood, and peeked out the drapes, nibbling her lower lip.

This was getting more and more complicated. Maybe his original instincts had been right all along. He'd treated marriage as a spectator sport, and perhaps it *was* best viewed from the sidelines.

On the other hand, if the odds were any measure, he probably shouldn't screw this thing up. If his math was right, a woman like her came around every forty years or so, meaning he'd have to chase the next one from a wheelchair.

"The timing is curious. I don't understand why you didn't tell me about the message before. Or that you called Sarge." She pushed her hair behind one ear. "I'm not made of powdered sugar."

"Come here." He lifted the sheet invitingly.

She rolled her eyes and stayed put. "Did Daniel have anything else to say?"

"That I finally did something smart and hooked up with you."

"Is that what we are? Hooked up?"

"Come on."

She folded her arms tighter around her chest.

"Oh, come on. Come here."

She inched nearer to him, fully-clothed, and using her elbows for balance, rolled onto her belly and faced him, chin in hands. "Sarge thinks I'm a good decision?"

"Uh-huh."

"Move over." She rolled onto her side and scooted back, pressing her shoulders into his chest. "I'm sentencing you to thirty minutes of hugging."

He clenched his jaw to keep from laughing and wrapped both arms around her. "I can handle that." He closed his eyes, letting the endorphins kick in. "You know, I improve your stats."

"How so?"

"You've been married three times and I've never gone off the plank, which means three divided by two equals one-and-a-half marriages each. Our one-halves could be re-categorized as annulments, or thrown out altogether."

She elbowed him playfully. "Measured another way, you're a zero."

The pounding on the door jolted them both to a sitting position. He jumped from the bed and looked through the peephole. "It's Jake."

"Has he heard of calling first?"

"Be right back." He stepped under the veranda and shut the door behind him.

Jake looked like he'd seen a ghost.

"What's up?"

He hyperventilated the words. "Ann's—been—in—an accident."

"Oh, shit. How bad?"

"I don't know."

"Holy crap. Wait here." He went back inside.

"What's up?" she asked.

"Jake's ex was in an accident."

"Oh, my God. What happened?"

"I don't know."

He let Jake in and pulled the door shut.

Placing his palms on his temples and pressing, Jake said, "I don't know what to do."

hit. The steering wheel jerked in Mack's hands, waking him. He must have dozed off.

The rumble strips vibrated beneath his seat. He shook his head in two short bursts, then steered the truck and trailer back between the white lines.

Reaching into his pants pocket, he removed a small glass vial, tapped it on the dash and opened it. Steering with his right kneecap, he scooped white powder with a tiny spoon and vacuumed the cocaine into his left nostril.

Dipping it again, he held his left nostril closed with his thumb and sucked powder into the other side. Wiping his nose on his sleeve, he put the vial back into his pocket.

He checked the time on the dash. Just after three o'clock in the morning. He activated his cell flashlight, and shone it on his passenger. She was slumped against the passenger's-side door, staring at him, glassy-eyed, mouth slightly agape.

Like a beautiful doll.

He'd prepared the dosage the way Greg Marino had told him to and added it to the sports drink he'd given her. Whoever dubbed Rohypnol the "Forget-me pill" should have had a big job on Madison Avenue. When she'd started to wake four hours ago, he'd pulled over and administered the second dose of the drug. Her eyes, they'd totally creeped him out as she stared at him blinking, swallowing the liquid. Fifteen minutes later, she was unconscious.

He squinted at the overhead sign up ahead. The next four exits were for Boca Raton. That meant he was about an hour north of Miami. He'd miss the worst of the morning rush hour traffic. He stroked the SIG Sauer M18 semiautomatic wedged under his right thigh, snorting and laughing.

Balancing his cell on the wheel, he scrolled through his contact list and called Marino.

"Where the fuck have you been?"

"Driving non-stop for a thousand hours."

"Do you have the goods?"

"Yeah. But it didn't go according to plan."

"What the fuck does that mean?"

"I had to fly the thing."

"What? Why?"

"'Cause that dumbass prison guard dropped it off behind a mountain of dirt."

"Why'd he do that?"

"I don't know. Why don't you ask him?"

"Do you have the girl?"

"Yeah, but it's a fucking miracle."

"What happened?"

"I snuck out to the ranch before sunrise, you know, to do a recon run to see where he stashed it. Left the truck and trailer down the road aways. Wanted to get the lay of the land. You know, figure out how I was gonna get it and grab the girl. Next thing you know there's a fucking drone over my head and people on ATVs. Then the girl goes out for an early morning run and on her way back, sees me."

"Shit. What didja do?"

"I grabbed her and kept her quiet. Then I forced her in it and I flew the fucker."

"Did anyone see you?"

"Not that I know of. Been on the move ever since."

"Where are you now?"

"Passing through Boca."

"Where's the girl?"

"In the passenger seat."

"You got the cargo?"

"Yep. In the trailer."

"You drug her?"

"Yep."

"How long ago?"

"Gave her a second dose 'bout four hours ago."

"The way I told you?"

"Yep."

"She'll sleep the rest of the way. She won't know what hit her. Call me when you get here."

"You got my money?"

"We'll talk about it when you get here."

Mack pressed the red button and dropped the phone in the center console. *"We'll talk about it when you get here."* What the fuck was that supposed to mean?

Mack had met Greg while they were both being held at the Dade County jail. Greg was awaiting trial. Mack was back in the pokey doing a stint for a DUI. He'd bitched to that dick, Greg Marino, that he'd flown helicopters for the US Army and that as a former convicted felon, he couldn't get a job with a private company. He couldn't even redeploy. Greg said he knew a guy, who knew a guy, who could wipe his record clean of the old felony. He'd help to get it done but Mack would have to go to

Texas and apply for a job testing some kind of developmental aircraft.

He'd robbed a liquor store in Kendall and got away with a couple of bottles of Captain Morgan. They threw the proverbial book at him, charging him with armed robbery. He'd spent a year behind bars.

The idiots at *AeroHov* had hired him. What kind of morons were they? Just because he was a US Army veteran who checked the "No felonies" box didn't mean he was telling the truth.

Ah, they weren't really idiots. During his three deployments, he'd flown almost every kind of helicopter, from special ops MH-6 Little Birds to the Chinooks he'd piloted deep into enemy territory. They were lucky as hell to get him.

He'd driven Greg's truck and trailer from Miami to Bumfuck, Texas to start the job test-piloting a toy he could have flown drunk off his ass, blindfolded. It was better than flipping burgers at a fast food joint for seven-fifty an hour, if he could get a job at one.

Then, out of the blue, they called him in and fired him. That meant he had to move up the schedule, tweak the plan. That's how it went on the battlefield. Shit never went as planned and contingencies happened all the time.

After they'd fired him, he'd had to salvage the plan to steal the hovercraft. He'd killed the night watchman. How else was he supposed to gain access to the building after they canceled his ID card? He'd cut off the guard's finger to gain biometric access. Then he helped load the prototype into an awaiting horse trailer.

Contacting the ranch owner, Roy Pompadour, to pitch him on the idea of starting helicopter service to his luxury guest ranch was his idea. The man was a former Army captain. 'Nam. They were brothers.

He'd had the idea before he got fired. It was supposed to be a way to scout the place first and check out the girl. Then the plan went to shit when they terminated him. He felt a little bad that he'd stood the guy up, like a paper cut.

When he'd signed up to steal the hovercraft, there wasn't any talk about a kidnapping. After he'd started the job, Greg changed the plan, convincing him a hostage would be their insurance policy. The stakes went up, but it kinda made sense.

Dropping the prototype in the middle of the desert behind a mound of dirt? That was the dirty prison guard's fucked-up idea.

When he'd heard the ATVs and the drone overhead, he'd had to scramble. How he'd been able to grab the girl and fly that toy at the same time without getting caught was a miracle.

It had to be God's plan. How else could he have pulled-off the near impossible without divine intervention?

If Greg Marino had plans to rip him off, he wouldn't live long enough to regret it.

Fuck the world. After three tours in the sandbox, half his buddies came home with brain injuries. The other half was missing arms and legs. All of them were fucked in the head.

He treated himself to another bump of cocaine.

31

Lauren peeked out the drapes in her room and spotted Daryl walking the path toward the barn. She freshened up quickly and caught up with him. "Josh said you went to see the sheriff."

"I did."

"What did you find out?"

"Not much."

"Did you hear Jake is going to Miami?"

"No. Why he's leaving?"

She told him about Ann's accident.

"Ah. Poor guy. That's rough. First his daughter, now this."

She told him about the new information, that they'd gotten a hit on Caitlin's whereabouts in Alabama. "An eyewitness saw Florida plates on a truck at a gas station in Comstock."

"Do they have surveillance video?"

"I don't think so. Just the eyewitness."

She followed him to his truck and trailer, now parked behind the barn. He climbed the ladder on the 4-horse trailer, cut a flake of hay from a bale tied atop the roof and tossed it on the ground.

"You must know the sheriff pretty well to go into town to see him."

"Well enough to know not to cross him. Everyone in the nut of Texas knows of him."

She frowned. "The 'nut' of Texas'?"

He stepped into the horse trailer and lifted Picasso's halter from a hook. He stamped his feet, leaving a chalky footprint of a cowboy boot on the dirt. "A little inside joke. Look at a map sometime and see if you see it. It's kind of a Rorschach test. Look for a body part. Male." He strode toward the pasture gate and whistled. His horse cantered to the fence. "When you look at it, maybe you'll see something different."

"I have looked at it and I don't recall seeing any anatomical parts. Male or female."

He opened the gate and slid the nylon halter over the horse's ears and led him to the rock wall behind the guestrooms dividing the stables from the vehicle path. Picasso poked his muzzle between the crook of his elbow and ribs, playfully stealing a chunk of hay. He tossed the rest on the ground, near the base of the wall and vaulted atop it, legs dangling.

He offered her a hand up and she accepted. The horse dropped his head to eat. The sky had turned pink and magenta, God's rose-colored glasses tinting the backdrop behind the mountains in the distance.

He handed her the lead rope, hooked the heel of his boot in a crevice on the wall, rolled his pant leg up and reached down, removing a pack of Camels from inside the leather top.

Tapping the pack, two smokes jutted out like magic, one sticking out farther than the other. Plucking both, he put one between his lips and offered her the other.

"No, thanks."

He removed a silver lighter from his pocket, flipped the

metal top, lit and drew on it, then released a thin streamer from the corner of his mouth. It wafted downwind, toward her.

She coughed. "What's the point if you don't inhale?"

"Ah. You're a reformed smoker. Sorry about that." He stubbed it out on the sole of his boot and stuffed it back into the pack. "Roy says Vance used to be a cop."

"He was a detective. Before I met him."

"How'd you two meet?"

That was a trick question. "A mutual friend."

"That's the best way sometimes. Roy's pretty shaken up about what's happened. He says Jake's an old friend."

"They are. They go way back to when they both worked on Wall Street. Jake's really not a bad guy."

"I never said he was." Daryl plucked a loose rock from the wall and tossed it. Picasso popped his head up and pricked his ears. "Easy." He held his hand out and the animal sniffed his palm. "How'd you and Vance meet Jake?"

That was a trickier question. "Jake was a client."

"Yours or Vance's?"

"Both, actually."

"I'm trying to figure out how that would work."

She laughed. "I can't remember."

"I don't believe that for a second."

It would be nice if he would stop sticking his nose where it didn't belong. "What's to know? We bought the ranch together, as an investment. Then we sold it back to Roy."

"Are you two a couple?"

"No."

He raised his eyebrows.

"It's complicated."

"What would you say if I told you I might know something about a missing hovercraft?"

"I would say tell me what you know."

"I'm thinking of why I would do that."

"Obviously, to help find Jake's daughter."

"I've been thinking about that and I'm not sure I can connect those dots. Not yet, anyway. Let's play a game."

"What kind of a game?"

"Let's call it an exchange of information."

"Hey, Lauren."

She turned to see where the voice was coming from. "Hey, Davis." God, he had to have the worst timing of anyone she'd ever met. When he lingered, she dropped to her feet.

"Have you met Daryl?"

Davis flashed his goofy grin. "Not officially."

"So, you're a treasure hunter," Daryl said. "Nice to meet you."

Davis lit up. "That was a long time ago. I guess she told you."

Her heart skipped. She hadn't said a thing to Daryl about Davis' stint as a wreck diver.

"Nah," he said. "Lucky guess, the coin around your neck. Sixteen-hundreds Spanish silver, Colonial."

"I dove for Mel Fisher in South Florida back in the 'nineties. He treated us like dogs but we got trinkets." Davis pulled the chain taut, crossed his eyes and looked at it. "I love the blue-water adventure. But this place is pretty cool."

"I've never lived near an ocean. I grew up on a reservation. My father still lives on one in Arizona."

"Wow," Davis said. "Like an American Indian reservation?"

"Uh-huh."

Davis fondled the coin around his neck. "That's cool. What's it like, being Native American?"

He laughed. "Compared to what?"

She wanted the conversation to end and motioned Davis to the follow her to the walkover bridge near the narrow creek where they'd have a little privacy.

He leaned on the railing, thumbing the armholes of his wife-beater. "I'm sorry to interrupt," Davis said. "But, well . . . with the shoot delayed, I thought I'd be finished by now, and, well—"

"If I can get you a progress payment, will that help?"

"Really? You could do that?"

Sure. She'd pay him cash out of her stash. He'd never know where it came from. "If I do, promise to keep it under your hat. At least for now."

"No problem, boss."

"There's another catch."

Davis smiled, his icy blue eyes twinkling. "Sure."

"You can't leave."

"Why not? I mean, why would I do that?"

Hurricane Irma had flattened his dilapidated Florida rental before he'd been able to get back in time to salvage anything. "Just making sure you'll stick around 'til we get the shoot back on track."

"When do you think you'll know for sure?"

"It depends on Roy. He's got other things on his mind."

Davis hesitated. "Not that. I know there's nothing you can do about what's going on. I meant, about the money, about me getting an advance."

"Consider it done."

"Really?" He looked relieved. "That's great. In that case, I'm gonna take the drone out tonight and get some sunset shots."

Davis headed to his room to prep his gear, she figured, before the sun set completely. Daryl waited atop the wall, watching his horse muzzle the last of the hay.

"American Indian, huh? Both your mother and your father?"

"Yeah. They go by *Tohono O'odham* now. Has a nice ring to it, don't you think?"

"Compared to what?"

"We used to be the Papago. It translates to bean-eater. Our rivals, the Pima, named us that a long time ago. The new generation of millennials thinks it's derogatory. Our new name means 'People of the Desert.' The Pima followed suit, changing their name, too, to *Akimel O'otham*. It means 'River People.'"

"They both sound Irish to me."

He laughed. "I see why Roy likes you."

"You're from Arizona?"

"Paradise Valley."

"Where's that?"

"In Phoenix, near Scottsdale. Before the planned communities and shopping malls sprang up, it was just a desert. When I was a kid, I could see the Superstition Mountains for a hundred miles. Now there's a permanent inversion layer, mostly from the influx of Californians that cashed out of their houses and moved east.

"My mom's a realtor in Phoenix. You know what she tells the transplants moving from L.A.? Get Arizona plates as soon as possible."

"Why?"

"Everyone hates them. The funny thing is, most of the haters came from California, too."

She reminded him of where they'd left off in their conversation, about the missing hovercraft and the "information exchange."

"If I tell you what I know, will you tell me where you got the money to buy Roy's ranch?"

A cold sweat broke beneath her shirt. "Sure. You go first."

"An Israeli group bought the technology from a US start-up. Roy has some kind of involvement with them."

She remembered the contact page for *AeroHov* on the dark web had a Tel Aviv phone number. "How do you know that?"

"Not so fast. How did you get enough money to invest in this place?"

"I inherited it."

"From who?"

"My uncle."

"The old rich uncle story." He chuckled.

"If I was going to lie, don't you think I could come up with something better?"

He hopped down from the wall and petted his horse on the neck. "Mossad has a venture capital division that funds technology companies."

"What's Mossad?"

"It's one of the Israeli Intelligence agencies. Their version of the CIA."

"Why would they partner with Roy? In Texas?"

"It's just for testing. Less regulations and more security. A lot of aerospace companies have set up shop in this part of Texas."

He was right. She'd read about it when researching the ranch. "Who else knows about this?"

"Very few."

"So that's why they're staying here."

"Who?"

"Unit 8200."

"How do you know that?"

"I saw them. They checked in yesterday."

"So that's why Roy couldn't fix me up with a room at the last minute."

The side door to the lodge opened and the stream of suits exited, stopping to huddle around the fire pit near the pool.

"That must be them. They look like Israeli intelligence." His jaw tightened and a bluish vein running from his hairline to his ear pulsated.

"Roy said they're here on US Justice Department visas."

He cocked his head at her.

"I think Roy called in some favors," she said.

"Meaning what?"

"How should I know? It's Roy. Six degrees removed from big things in D.C. How do you know what you know about Roy's involvement with the missing hovercraft?"

"I have a friend with the FBI."

"How's the FBI involved?"

"There was a murder at a research lab in Fort Stockton."

"A *murder*? Who was murdered?"

"A security guard."

"When?"

"Three days ago."

"How do you know that?"

"I told you. I have a friend with the FBI. When I heard about it, I called Roy."

"Why would you call Roy?"

"Because it happened at the R&D lab where Mossad is testing their technology."

She felt the blood leave her head. The background went blurry and she tottered. He hopped down from the wall and grabbed her elbow. The horse lifted its head.

"You okay?"

"Jesus. You knew this all along. You saw the swirl patterns and you knew the hovercraft had been stolen. You knew about the murder. They took Jake's kid. They'll kill her."

"Stop catastrophizing the situation. No one's going to kill her."

She placed a hand on her stomach. "You have nerve. You don't know that. They haven't made their demand yet. At least, as far as I know."

"You need to calm down. We'll find her. She'll be fine."

"Right. Ask J.C. Dugard, or Elizabeth Smart how *fine* they are."

"Those were freaks who kidnapped those girls."

"And some crazy person flying a stolen hovercraft isn't?"

"I didn't say that. This is different. It's a shakedown. It's about money. What good is a dead hostage?"

"I don't know. Ask Charles Lindbergh." She picked up a rock and hurled it at the creek, spooking his horse.

Picasso bolted sideways, yanking Daryl's arm, dragging him off balance several feet. He calmed the horse and walked back.

"Who else knows about this besides you and Roy?"

He looked at his palm and showed her the early stages of a rope burn. "Josh. He's the one who found the body."

The group of sharply dressed men, led by the woman, fanned out in the courtyard and disappeared into their rooms.

She felt his eyes on her, watching, studying her. Hiding her trembling fingers in the pocket of her jacket, she played it cool. "How's Josh involved?"

"He works for Roy, heading up the testing program."

"If Roy's involved, I have to think the place has tight security."

He nodded. "Very."

"Why are you telling me all this? I don't even think Josh's wife knows what he's been working on."

Those were a lot of data points to connect, a lot of moving parts that would have to have been tightly synced in order to kidnap the girl and steal the technology. "Why would someone do it? Why would they take the risk of getting caught? Why didn't they just steal it and take it directly to wherever they were going? Why hide it here? And ambush Jake's kid?"

Picasso nibbled the last few strands of uneaten hay.

"I wish I knew. I'm going to see an old friend tomorrow who might be able to help. You're welcome to come along."

"And why would I do that?"

"My friend is a hacker. He says he has video that shows something that might help us find the girl."

"Why can't he share it with you online? That would save you the trip."

"If he thought that was a good idea, he wouldn't have asked me to meet him in person."

"Why do I need to go? Why can't you go and tell us what he has?"

The wind kicked up out of nowhere, blowing her hair over her eyes. She brushed the strands from her face.

"You don't have to go. I just thought that since it's video footage, you might like to see it for yourself. Plus, it's a nice drive to Alpine. If you decide you want to go, meet me here in the morning. Early. Before sunrise."

Darkness had fallen and with it, the temperature. Shivering, she said goodnight, pulling her jacket tight around her torso. She stopped and turned. Daryl, now a shadow, climbed the metal stairs to the top of the trailer. She jogged to her room.

VANCE SAT in the rocking chair beneath the veranda, waiting for her. When she turned the corner, she stopped in her tracks.

"Jesus-jimminy-Christ." She placed her hand on her heart. "What are you doing here?"

"Waiting for you. I was beginning to think you were doing a dissertation of War and Peace with Cher's brother over there. You two looked pretty cozy."

"Now that you mention it, he does look a little like Cher. If she were a he." She tilted her head. "Are you jealous?"

"Should I be?"

"I hope so. That's what you get for spying on me."

"I wouldn't call it spying. I would call it politely waiting. If I were spying, I'd know what you two talked about. On that note, what were you talking about?"

She told him about their conversation.

He needed a moment to process it. "Let me get this straight: Roy is partners with the Israelis. Josh works for Roy. Mossad is funding the technology that's been stolen, and you think that's why Israeli intelligence agents are staying here? Daryl coincidentally knows an FBI agent who just happened to tell him about a murder and a stolen hovercraft?"

"I know. It sounds crazy." She dropped onto the empty rocker next to him and filled her lungs will cold night air. "What did you want to talk to me about?"

"I'm going to Miami with Jake first thing in the morning."

"I figured that was coming."

"I didn't tell you everything Sarge said."

Her eyebrows pulled to full staff.

"I think I know who GM is."

"Who?"

"Ever heard of IDR?"

She narrowed her eyes. "I don't think so."

"The Internet Date Rapist."

"Holy shit. The guy who meets women on dating sites, and drugs and rapes them? It was all over the news in Miami but I thought they had a suspect in custody."

"They did, but they let him go."

"When?"

"A week ago."

"That's crazy. Why'd they release him?"

"Good lawyers."

"That's disgusting. Good God. Do you think he could have Caitlin?"

"I don't know. His full name is Gregorio Marino."

"Should that mean something?"

"Santiago Marino."

"Oh, my God. As in Chago Marino? Tony's business partner?"

"Late business partner. Greg's his son."

She hesitated. "What if he took Caitlin? If he's been out for a week, he had time."

It was deadly quiet.

After a moment, she broke the silence. "Daryl wants me to go to Alpine with him in the morning."

"Why?"

"He says he has a friend who has some video footage that might help us. His buddy is a hacker who won't share it online."

"A hacker? With video that might show something new? You should go," he said. "That's your wheelhouse."

"That's what I was thinking, too."

The cold air sharpened his brain. He'd never mentioned Greg Marino to her. He'd left that part out, sparing her the details that Greg was the one who'd stalked Davis Frost, held a gun to skull, and busted his jaw.

Or that Marino was the one who'd tried to rip them off for the seventy-five million dollars they'd salvaged. Money they'd been trying to launder ever since. Duffle bags of dollars that felt more like a ball and chain than a path to freedom.

She stared into space, the moonlight mixing with the stars, tinting her face a bluish color. Rocking without speaking, she gave no hint as to what she was thinking, resting her forearms on the chair, both feet planted on the ground. Rocking. Forward and back.

A minute later, she stood. "I hope we're wrong." The look on her face, it was as if she were boring a hole through him. "I pray to God we're both dead wrong."

32

Gosh, her head hurt. Caitlin placed a thumb over each eyelid and pressed until she saw stars. It was dark inside the small room, but where was she? She rolled onto her side and hugged the musky pillow. Oh, God, her wrists were sore. The last thing she remembered was sitting in the cab of Mack's pickup truck.

Where was she?

She shook her head to clear it, recalling the highway sign to Pensacola. The cloverleaf. The roadside stop where he'd forced to do her *business* in the bushes. The blur of events, coming slowly into focus. He'd offered her the pain pills. The ice pack he'd made from paper towels. The pretzels. The sports drink. Then nothing.

The air inside the room was sticky and smelled of mold. The A/C unit on the wall buzzed. She stood and staggered. Something was wrong. Her head spun. Unable to keep her balance, she grabbed for the nightstand, softening her fall as she landed on her knees.

She tilted her head back toward the glow of light streaming through the sheer curtains hanging above the bed. Pulling herself to her feet, she climbed atop the mattress and reached for the windowsill.

On tiptoe, she lifted the curtain and peered into the night. Streetlamps flickered in the distance, casting misty halos on the old apartment complex overlooking a quiet street. Her heart sank. The white trailer parked curbside, she was sure it was the one that had been her metal prison.

She stepped down from the bed and walked toward a ribbon of soft light at the base of the door, emanating from the other side. Placing one hand on the knob, she twisted it slowly.

Maybe this was Mack's place. Maybe he was here. She'd find him and make him tell her why he was holding her captive. Make him take her home.

But the doorknob didn't turn. She firmed her grip on the metal ball and twisted harder. God, her wrists hurt from where the plastic ties had dug into her flesh. The handle jiggled but it didn't open. Placing one hand on top of the other, she used all her strength, fighting past the pain, squeezing and turning it first one way, then the other. It may as well have been welded shut.

She felt for the lock, running her fingers over the smooth metal ball, the kind used in bedrooms and bathrooms. Kneeling to get a closer look, she twisted the small button with the tips of her forefinger and thumb, fighting the pain, and released the lock.

Turning it slowly a half-revolution, she pressed on the door. It didn't budge. She pushed harder. This time, more forcefully. She rattled the handle. "Let me out of here!"

It was locked from the outside.

With hands clamped on the knob, she shouldered the door. Once.

Twice.

Three times.

"*Let me out.*"

The fourth time in a rage that knocked her off her feet.

She staggered to the bed and sat, rubbing her shoulder, head hanging between her knees, rocking forward and back. Her head throbbed and butterflies flitted in her stomach.

"*Somebody help me,*" she whispered. "*Please help me.*"

33

Vance tried sleeping on the second leg of the flight from Houston to Miami. They'd caught the first flight out, and after a sleepless night, he'd hoped to catnap.

Fat chance stuck on the aisle in the last row. The seat didn't recline. Two-way traffic to the lavatory treated him to a barrage of butts and zippers. The explosive sounds of toilets flushing were enough to wake his dead grandmother. Ten minutes after the jet landed, the aisle finally cleared. He passed the cleaning crew on his way off the plane.

Jake, who'd used mileage to upgrade to first class, waited at the gate. "I hate this godforsaken city."

He texted Daniel Ruiz riding the escalator to the first floor. Sarge phoned right back, telling him to meet him at Passenger Pick Up. At baggage claim, Jake railed about the prices the airline charged him to check a second bag, Caitlin's, on top of the already exorbitant last-minute fare.

At least all three bags showed up. He'd checked his gun in his suitcase, removing the magazine before loading the Glock into the TSA-approved case he'd rolled inside a pair of blue jeans.

Daniel stood next to the Jeep Renegade, and when he saw Vance and Jake exit the arrivals door, popped the hatch.

"How was your flight?"

"Uneventful," Jake said.

"I should be so lucky." Vance slung his bag into the back. "I had the aisle seat in the last row so I got to share a bulkhead with the lavatory."

Daniel grimaced, "Oh, that's rough." He looked at Jake, and twisted the diamond post in his ear. "You look like shit."

"Yeah . . . well . . . I've had a few rough days."

Jake climbed into the front passenger seat, leaving him and Sarge to load his carry-on and Caitlin's blue paisley roller bag into the back.

Daniel slid behind the wheel, his enormous belly touching the steering wheel. He powered the window down and thanked the airport cop for letting him idle in the NO WAITING zone.

It was a near-perfect March day, mid-70s with low humidity, but that didn't stop Sarge from blasting the A/C. Vance rubbed his hands together and blew on them while Daniel pointed the Jeep east into the mangle of traffic on the Dolphin Expressway.

No one despised Greg Marino more than retired Sergeant Daniel Ruiz. If that scumbag had anything to do with Jake's kid's disappearance, he'd be on it 24/7, calling in any and all favors.

Creeping along the onramp and glancing over his shoulder, Daniel played lane-change-chicken with a bright blue Porsche 911. The driver backed off and he dove in on the back bumper of the car between them. "Where's your girlfriend, the horsey chick?"

"In Texas, keeping an eye on things," he said.

"You two make it official yet?" Daniel peered at Vance through his Mr. Potato Head glasses.

"We're not engaged, if that's what you mean."

"Well, you gotta crawl before you walk. *Pequeños pasos*." Baby steps. Daniel glanced at Jake. "Did he tell you the squad used to call him One-Dance-Vance?"

Jake stared out the windshield, disinterested.

"I guess he doesn't care that you broke the record for first dates."

Ordinarily, Jake would have seized on the opportunity to torture him. But these circumstances were not ordinary. Apparently, Daniel needed a reminder. He shot a "Shut up" look at him in the rearview mirror.

Daniel tilted his head at Jake. "Where're we dropping him?"

"He's staying with me."

"You're bringing him home to meet Mama? How sentimental. With an emphasis on *mental*. Don't let the horsey chick find out. She might get jealous."

"Can you zip it, please," Jake said. "And turn off the A/C. It feels like a fucking penguin exhibit in here."

Daniel turned a button on the dash. "The best way to track a Cubano is to surveil his family. Vance knows that. Every cop south of Tallahassee knows it."

"What the hell's that got to do with anything?" Jake asked.

Daniel said, "If Greg Marino finds out Dick Courage is back in town, the first place he'll look is his mother's *casa*."

Jake contorted one side of his face. "Who's Greg Marino?"

Vance discreetly wagged his finger to catch Daniel's attention in the rearview, then ran his index finger back and forth across his throat. Damn Daniel, he had a habit of shooting his mouth off. He hadn't told Jake about Greg. Why would he without any proof?

Jake turned in his seat and faced him. "Who's Greg Marino?"

"Sarge refuses to retire. He likes to make up suspects."

Jake wasn't buying it. He asked a third time.

Sarge said, "I'm just bullshitting around."

Jake was an asshole, but he wasn't stupid. "Who is he?"

Now that Daniel leaked it, Jake wasn't going to let it go. He was trying to find his kid and gas-lighting him would require tap dancing on the head of a pin. "You remember when Davis got his face busted up?"

"Greg Marino did that?"

Daniel looked over his shoulder to change lanes. "Rumor has it he got out of jail recently."

Jesus. Daniel Ruiz was digging a deeper hole. It wouldn't take Jake long to link this news flash to the money they'd salvaged. He did some quick calculations in his head. How much did Jake know about his connection to Greg? Had he heard about the Florida license plates on the truck seen in Comstock? Did he know his daughter's fitness tracker had been found? That they'd gotten a hit on the ring?

"You think he has something to do with my daughter's disappearance?"

That didn't take long.

In a lame attempt to throw Jake off, Daniel said, "Did you tell Jake you're half-Cuban?"

Vance's blood pressure spiked. This was the price of working with Daniel. "I don't remember."

It also pissed Jake off. "What does that have to do with *anything*?"

Daniel rubbed his baldhead. "If Greg's involved, he might have eyes on Vance's mother's place."

Traffic was a parking lot.

Daniel glared in the mirror. "You really didn't tell him?"

"Didn't tell me what?" Jake growled.

He'd have liked to put Daniel in a chokehold. "It's complicated."

Jake doubled down. "Tell me what?"

"Daniel is just running all the scenarios. You know, thinking out loud."

Jake put his readers on and typed on his phone.

Guessing what Jake was doing, he did the same, pulling his mobile from his pocket and googling "Greg Marino." The top match was from the *Miami-Herald*. Headline: GREGORIO MARINO OUT ON BOND

The story identified him as the son of Santiago Marino, his uncle's partner in crime at the now-defunct Cuban drug cartel, Los Guapos.

"Shit, shit . . . SHIT," Jake yelled. He smacked the screen on his phone. He turned his head 180-degrees and glared. "I oughta smash this in your face." He slammed the phone against the dash. "Shit."

"Hey, watch out!" Vance shouted.

Daniel hit the brakes, skidding to a stop a few inches off the rear bumper of the car in front. "What'd you think? You'd rip off the most notorious drug cartel in US history, then join the Miami Yacht Club? That there wouldn't be retribution?"

Jake didn't say anything.

Vance saw the backs of his shoulders rising and falling from breathing hard.

"I never took a dime of that blood money," Daniel said.

Jake glared at him. "Shut the fuck up."

Exactly his sentiment. But Daniel was right that his mother's place was a target. The best way to trap a Cubano was to surveil his family.

It wasn't just the cops who knew it. The bad guys knew it, too.

Had he been lulled into a false sense of security? Just because the police hadn't yet come knocking with a pair of nickel-plated handcuffs didn't mean he'd gotten away scot-free. It didn't mean some agency hadn't set a trap for him. Justice. FBI. *Jesus.*

What if Greg cut a deal? What if that's the real reason his

lawyers had been able to bond him out of jail? What if Daniel didn't know? It was common practice for prosecutors to keep plea bargains under wraps.

Daniel turned and stuck his head between the seats. "Your mom lives in the Gables, right?"

"Uh-huh."

"Gimme the address."

WHILE JAKE SIMMERED in the front seat and Daniel cursed at traffic, he tried imaging how he'd feel if he had a daughter who'd been abducted by that predator. What if it happened to Lauren? Or his sister, Kathy? A rage burned in his belly. Thoughts turned to his mother. If this was Greg Marino's handiwork, she was at risk, too.

Daniel slowed the Jeep as he passed her house. A marked patrol car had parked out front. His elderly aunt stood on the stoop, front door wide open, flanked by a pair of brown uniforms. Vance's heart pounded under his jacket.

Daniel kept driving for two blocks, did a three-point turn, and drove to a side street where they could watch from a distance. The cops had gone into the house.

"There could be a lot of different reasons they're here," Daniel said.

"Yeah. None of them are good," Vance said.

The front door opened. Two cops, a male and a female, exited and headed to the walkway, and got into a brown police-issue Crown Vic. As the unit pulled from the curb, Daniel put the Jeep in drive and turned the corner, timing it so he'd pass the squad car head on, then he continued slowly toward busy Bird Road.

The female officer noticed them and stared directly at Daniel when the two vehicles passed.

Vance had the advantage from the back seat, getting a good look at her. Her partner's face was obstructed by the open laptop jutting from the dash.

"Keep driving," Vance said.

Sarge made eye contact in the rear view. "Where to?"

"They saw us. The woman cop looked right at you. Take a left at the stop sign and go around the block."

The Crown Vic had stopped on a side street and they had to pass the squad car again. This was Coral Gables. Their behavior had to look suspicious.

He saw the tall sign from the side street. "Go to the Shell Station," Vance said.

"I don't need gas," Sarge said.

"We need to buy time. We can watch and wait from there," he said.

Daniel turned onto Bird Road and drove into the Shell Station lot. When a lane opened, he backed into it.

Vance hopped out. "I'll get this." He popped the fuel cap, swiped his credit card, and followed the directions on the screen. ENTER YOUR ZIP CODE. He tapped five digits and pressed enter.

PURCHASE DECLINED.

A matching text pinged on his phone. What the hell? He recalled the fraud alerts. Had the bank canceled his card? Maybe the zip was wrong. He'd updated his information to the marina address where he'd moored his sailboat before it sank in Biscayne Bay. He pulled out his wallet, looked at the most recent address on his Florida license, and tapped a different zip code onto the keypad.

Come on. Come on. *Come on.*

Why did every upgrade make credit card machines slower? He stared at the display, tapping his thumb on the fuel handle. CHOOSE GRADE TO BEGIN FUELING lit up. The pump harrumphed. He inserted the nozzle, pressed REGULAR, and squeezed the handle.

The gushing reminded him of his sailing yacht, *The Second Wind*, destroyed during Hurricane Irma. The guy who owned the marina had been hassled by Florida Fish and Wildlife to salvage the wreck or face fines. He'd asked him to do whatever he needed to do to be compliant with the law, and promised to stop in next time he was in Miami to reimburse him for the costs. That would have to wait.

In less than a minute, the tank was full of gas.

Caitlin woke a second time, now with the feeling she was being watched. Last she remembered, it was nighttime and she was locked inside the small room. She'd tried to escape but the door was locked from the outside. She'd lain on the bed and stared at the ceiling, praying for sleep, but each time she was on the verge, a wave of anxiety stirred the butterflies in her stomach and the pounding inside her head grew into a rhythmic throb. Sleep must have come.

Eyes still shut, her lids twitched, the way they do in morning light. She opened them slowly. A man stood over the bed. Wincing, she covered her eyes with her hands, shielding them from the streaks of sunlight piercing the thin curtains high above the bed. Holding the blanket to her neck, she sprung to a sitting position and rubbed her forehead.

"I brought you some orange juice."

He had a slight accent. "Who are you?"

"Here. Drink this."

She took the plastic tumbler from him and set it on the rickety nightstand.

"The juice will help."

Swaddling her body more tightly, she swung her legs to the side and sat on the edge of the bed. "Where am I?"

"Miami."

"*Miami?*" Her voice brightened. "Are you taking me home?"

"Dream on."

She paused. "Why am I here?" She fought it but her throat constricted, her eyes welled, and streamed. "Please take me home. My parents will do whatever you want." She caught a single tear with her thumb. A resolve began to rise inside of her. "What do you want with me? Where's Mack?"

"I thought you were a smart girl." He pointed at his eyes, his fingers in a V-formation. "I'll be watching you. You can't be all that smart if you haven't figured out why you're here yet."

"I'm not stupid. What do you want?"

"Duh." He rolled his beady eyes. "Money, of course, dummy."

Dummy. How dare he. "My father will pay the money. I know he will. He'll do it as soon as you tell him where I am. You can call him. He'll give you whatever you want."

He let out a wicked laugh. "Is that what you think?"

"Have you talked to him?"

He flipped a switch on the wall; the square plastic fixture on the low ceiling oozed yellow light.

Her stomach jerked. She squeezed her arms across her chest and grit her teeth. The A/C kicked on, and with it, the hammering inside her head restarted. She dropped her chin, wincing, looking at the purple and red ligature marks on her wrists.

"I brought you a friend." He pushed the door to the hallway open.

She recoiled, clamping her knees to her chest, holding the blanket tightly to her throat.

He stepped into the hallway and herded an old woman into the small room.

"Jur awake. Don't be scared."

"Who are you?" Caitlin's eyes refilled with tears.

"Now, now," the old woman said, sitting next to her, stroking her hair. "Ju need to bathe. There's a bathroom down the hall. Come on. Let's get you on jur feet. Ju feel better with a shower."

"Who are you?" She sniffled. "I want my daddy."

"My name is Isabel. Ju need to be brave." Her tone was kindly. "Be smart, too. Now go and get cleaned up."

"Who's that man?"

"Oh, dear. Please, listen to me. Just do as I say."

The old woman squeezed her hand, coaxing her up from the bed, steering her toward the door she'd been unable to open earlier. She stepped into the hallway. The man who'd abducted her sat on a plastic crate next to the front door inside the small apartment.

Mack the pit bull glared at her. "Hey, bitch, good morning. Look who's still alive."

"I'm . . . I'm . . . I'm going . . . to . . . get cleaned up," she said, hugging the wall, sidestepping toward the bathroom.

"I got you some clothes." The other man, the reptile, snapped his head in the direction of the pit bull. "Mack, fetch the duffle bag."

He obeyed, trotting to the kitchen, returning with a black nylon tote.

Greg Marino eyed her up and down, licking his lips like a lizard, then pushed the bag at her chest. "I'm sure something will fit. I hate those ugly tights. What nice girl wears lightning bolts pointing at her pussy?" He let out a sinister laugh.

Clutching the duffel, she pulled the bathroom door shut and ran her hand along the inside of the wall, feeling for a switch. A glow of diffused sunlight coming through a single square glass block revealed a bare light bulb attached to a beaded chain. She pulled it, lighting the tiny bathroom.

Something moved behind the faucet. Two black hairs swished, the antennae of a cockroach hiding behind the pitted metal fixture. She jumped away as it leapt from the sink, ran across the tile and scaled the side of the tub.

She shook her torso like a wet dog. *Ew.*

Taking a step toward the bathtub, she peeked behind the curtain. The palmetto bug scuttled into the open drain and disappeared. She turned the hot water tap on and pulled the door snug in the doorframe, jiggling the knob to make sure it was locked, and latched the flimsy metal hook-and-eye, just in case.

Hands trembling, she put the bag of clean clothes on the floor beneath the sink. When she stood, she caught her reflection in the silver-mottled mirror: a macabre, distorted version of herself.

Pulling the tie from her ponytail, she ran her fingers through her hair and started a thin stream of water in the sink. Using her index finger, she rubbed her teeth, cupped water in her palm under the faucet, swished and rinsed.

The bathroom, not much bigger than a closet, filled with steam. She lowered the water temperature in the shower, stepped out of her track clothes, and into the tub. Curling her toes on the gritty, no-slip tape, she drew the mildewed curtain closed and added more hot water to the mix before stepping beneath the nozzle.

Tilting her head back under the showerhead, she opened her mouth, filled it with water, and rinsed it again.

Ahhh. A hot shower.

Lathering soap in her palms, she rubbed her face and chest with her hands and turned slowly beneath the spout. She wet the hardened washcloth balled in the corner. An unpleasant smell bloomed. Sitting on the edge of the tub, she crinkled her nose, then scrubbed her feet with the sour-smelling cloth.

Holding her wrists under the nozzle, the warm water massaged her bruised hands. As fresh tears flowed down her cheeks, her knees buckled and her body crumpled beneath the spray of water. Sitting on the grimy tub floor with the droplets spattering her head, she pulled her knees to her chest. The water turned pink and swirled toward the drain.

Oh, no.

How could this be happening? She'd started her cycle last year, worried about the delay, and its unpredictability. She'd not talked to her mom about it, secretly googling "Late-onset Puberty" on the 'Net.

Ninety-eight-percent of girls started their period by age fifteen. Her mother had prodded her, sharing that she'd been a late-bloomer. Most of what she'd read said it wasn't unusual for female athletes to reach puberty later than their non-athletic peers because of the effects of burning fat and the stress of competition on hormone production.

"Soon it'll be like clockwork," the school nurse had said during her routine check-up.

This was not *clockwork*.

"And don't think you can't get pregnant because your cycle is spotty and irregular," she'd warned.

Pregnant? Gosh. She was a virgin and was stunned the nurse had said that.

Had she been too frightened to notice the signs of onset? There were none. No symptoms. No cramps. No breast tenderness.

None of the things that had been warning signals the few times it had happened before.

She cupped water in her palms and rinsed the place between her legs until it ran clear. The soreness from the horseback ride had lessened, maybe eclipsed by the aches and pains from the pummeling her joints had taken inside the trailer. And the lingering pain from the cuts and ligature marks from the plastic ties. Using her thumbs, she massaged the adductor muscles on the insides of her thighs, and tilted her head back, allowing the water to drum her face.

Rolling onto her knees, she let the water splatter against her back and neck. She raised her arms overhead and stretched her shoulder muscles. Sitting upright, she lathered the last of the bar soap into her hands, working it into her scalp.

More tears mixed with the sudsy water as she rinsed her hair. Why was he holding her hostage? Her chest heaved. She cupped a handful of clear water and splashed it between her legs. It stung. She repeated it until the water ran clear.

I want my daddy.

The door thundered. "Hurry up, bitch. I need to use the facilities."

35

When they drove by the house after filling the Jeep with gas, the Crown Vic was gone. Vance asked Daniel to park at the end of the block. He got out and walked past his mom's house, scanning the perimeter, looking for busybodies. When he didn't see anyone, he motioned to Daniel and Jake to follow him and pressed the doorbell.

His aunt Sophia answered, looking up at him through cloudy eyes. "*Oh, dios mio, oh, dios mio.*"

Oh, my God, oh, my God.

She hobbled a few steps toward the door, pulling it wide enough for them to enter. "Jur mama is missing. He took her."

"What are you talking about?"

"A man. He come to the house and want to speak to jur mama." She shuffled to the entryway table and rested her gnarled hand on it, pointing her walking cane at him with the other. "The police. I ask them to find ju. I tell them ju used to be a policeman. They find ju and call ju."

Balancing on feeble legs, the cane now at her side, she

closed her eyes and held one hand in prayer, looking up, eyes closed. "*Gracias,* Jesús, *gracias.*"

"When did it happen?"

"Jesterday. Police no come until she be missing for twenty-four hours."

"How'd it happen?"

"A man come to the door. I no see him, I no see him. Jur mama. She know him."

"How do you know that?"

"She go outside and talk with him. She go. She tell me to wait inside. I wait, and wait, and wait."

"She didn't come back?"

"No. She gone." She tottered into the kitchen and pointed to the table. "Her purse. She no leave without her purse."

"Was he driving? Did you see a car?"

"No. He come to the door. I hear his voice."

"Did you see his face?"

"No. I tell you, I no see him." Sophia waggled her cane and jabbed him on the chest. "Tony bring nothing but trouble to us. And now ju."

Daniel said, "*Cualquier cosa que puedas recordar nos ayudará.*" Anything you can remember will help us.

"I tell ju everything I know." She squinted, her milky old eyes staring at the back door leading to the canal. "I tell the policemen the same thing."

Jake pulled Vance aside. "Do you think this is connected to Caitlin?"

"I don't know."

His frail aunt in her faded floral dress hobbled to the kitchen counter and leaned on the countertop. She tipped forward at the waist, balancing with one hand on her walking stick, pressing the other to her heart. "*Oh, dios mio, oh, dios mio.*"

He grabbed hold of her elbow, steadying her. "Listen to me, Sophia: I'll find her."

The look of terror on her face reminded him of the day Tony was arrested. He'd been the one who'd had to tell her and had tried to calm her down. He'd driven her to the jail in his squad car so that she could see Tony. Back then, honest Miami cops could be counted on one hand. He was one of them. He'd resisted a lot of temptation.

Drugs.

Cash.

Fast cars.

Hundred-dollar champagne.

Beautiful women.

One vice led to the other like falling dominoes. He'd seen it with his own eyes: drugs to cash, cash to fine champagne, Dom Perignon to Ferraris. Then the final sin: women as *things*. He'd seen a lot of ruined lives. Self-will run riot. He'd not succumbed to any of it.

Now, he was a money launderer. It might be his fault that his mother disappeared. Sophia's eyes bored into him, as if she knew.

36

L auren knocked on Davis' door and waited a minute, shivering in the early morning cold. She rapped gently a second time, rubbing her hands together, trotting in place, trying to get her blood flowing.

She'd stopped by his room last night and made good on her promise, delivering an envelope of cash to tide him over.

She wanted to tell him she was going on a short trip with Daryl. Maybe he was sleeping, or showering. Maybe he was out at the berm, setting up the drone to shoot another sunrise.

DARYL WINCHED and unhitched the four-horse trailer and slid behind the wheel. He backed the truck around to where she stood waiting, and powered the window down.

Passing the to-go coffee to him, she hurried to the passenger's-side and climbed in. She held her hands in front of the warm air flowing from the vents. "How'd you sleep?"

"Like a baby. A perfect thirty-eight-degree night under the stars."

"Babies don't sleep through the night."

"Well, I did." He riffled inside the center console, clearing a space for his coffee. "I got Davis' tablet back. I charged it up in my truck last night."

She fumed as he drove toward the big iron gates. "How'd you manage that?"

He fondled a feather tethered to the end of one braid. "Don't get huffy at me."

"You should've given it back to Davis."

"He'll manage. He can borrow Roy's."

Daryl turned left, heading west on the four-way. She shaded her eyes from the shards of sunlight just starting to glint from the side mirror. "Who's this friend of yours we're going to see?"

"He's hard to explain."

"What's his background?"

"It's complicated."

"Try me."

He took his eyes off the road and looked at her for a couple of seconds. "He's eccentric. If I tried to describe him, I'd never do him justice."

They rode in silence, he watching the flat road ahead, she listening to the drumming of tires. She took her mobile from her bag and typed a message to Vance. A red MESSAGE UNDELIVERABLE flashed below the green bubble. A NO SERVICE warning popped up on her screen.

"What are those?" she asked, looking ahead.

"The Davis Mountains. Part of the Trans-Pecos field, same one that created the mountain range at the ranch." He pointed at the windshield and ran his finger slowly across the peaks in the distance. "Formed by volcanic eruptions over thirty-five million years ago."

"Thirty-five million years. Wow."

"Named after the Confederate President Jefferson Davis. It's a sky island."

"What's that?"

"The way it sounds. Surrounded by flatlands instead of water. Didja know Florida's perched on a plateau that was formed by a volcano over five hundred million years ago?"

"No." She'd never heard that. "How do you know so much about geology?"

"From my father. He could track our ancestors on the North American continent back ten thousand years, which is nothing really, considering the earth is four-and-a-half billion years old. Mankind is but a blink on the geological calendar. People forget that." He glanced at her. "No one will remember you in three generations."

"Gee, what a cheery thought." She shifted in the seat and leaned against the door panel. "Do you have any kids?"

"Nope."

"Married?"

"Nope."

"Spoken for?"

"No."

He wasn't making this easy. "Have you ever been married?"

"Yes."

"Are you divorced?"

"Nope."

"Are you separated?"

"Are you writing a book?"

"No, of course not. Sorry."

He took a breath so deep his chest expanded. He exhaled and said, "It's all right. I'm a widower."

"Oh . . . uh . . . I'm sorry to hear that."

He reached for the dash and turned on the radio. The auto-dial searched for stations, stopping every few seconds to play static noise.

He turned it off, rolled the window down, and hung his elbow out, letting a blast of cold air in.

"Brrr."

"You're such a lightweight." He smiled, pulled his arm in, and powered the window up. "My wife went out to the market one night to buy coffee. She was hit by a drunk driver and killed."

Oh, God. She felt sick.

"Almost ten years ago."

Wow.

"A hit and run."

"Did they find the driver?"

"Uh-huh."

An awkward silence ensued.

"The driver was here illegally. He was released on his own recognizance."

"Did he go to jail?"

"No."

"That's terrible. Why not?"

He shook his head and shrugged. "Never showed up for the hearing. He's still out there. Somewhere."

"Is that why you freelance for Border Patrol?" The moment she said it, she wished she could take the question back.

"What? No. I freelance for them because they pay well. They trust me to track smugglers and traffickers. A little ironic, don't you think since I couldn't find my own wife's killer?"

"I don't know." She *didn't* know.

"It's why I left Arizona."

Good God. It seemed like everyone was two degrees removed from a tragedy. "I'm so sorry."

He paused for almost an entire minute before he continued: "I had to live it every day. She was six months pregnant with our first child. My mother . . . and her family . . . they didn't want to see me after that. They said every time they saw me, I reminded them of what happened."

He may as well have punched her in the gut.

"You've been married, right?"

"Yes."

"Do you have kids?"

"No."

"Why not?"

It was fair to ask. He'd just shared something very personal with her. "I guess the right situation never presented itself."

"Marriage wasn't the right situation?"

"I guess not."

"Your biological clock isn't ticking?"

"I don't know. I never heard one. I guess I always worried that some little person I was responsible for would think I was doing a bad job of parenting."

What she'd just shared with him was more than she'd ever told Vance.

"That's a weird thing to say. Children love their mothers. It's pretty hard to talk them out of it. Try taking a child away from its mother. I've seen it on the border. No matter how horrible or wonderful the mom is, the child doesn't want to be separated."

"You've seen border separations?"

"It's not exclusively a border thing. Parents are taken from their children for a lot of different reasons." He sighed. "The border's a complicated place. My people have been crossing the international boundary for thousands of years."

"Shit. Look out!" She grabbed the dash with both hands.

Daryl swerved the dually but it was too late. Her heart sank at the thumps as the tires rolled over the animal. A rank smell bloomed in the cab.

He covered his nose with the crook of his elbow. "Aw. Jeez."

Her eyes watered. She powered her window down.

He sounded like a dying man. "Roll it up."

She obeyed, folding the collar of her shirt and jacket over her nose and mouth.

As he'd tried to avoid the skunk, flats of bottled water stacked on back seat had turned over. A corner of one box pressed against the back of her seat, and the plastic-on-plastic squeaked.

She unfastened her safety belt. "I'll get it." She crawled through the center console. "Try not to hit anything while I'm back here."

Kneeling, she hoisted the flats of water upright onto the rear seat. The shrink-wrap had torn on one case and several bottles rolled onto the floor mat behind the driver's side. One bottle wedged between the mat and his crossbow stowed upright in the canvas bag.

"Shit." She climbed on hands and knees all the way onto the back seat behind him to get the loose bottle. She contorted her body, finding more stray bottles and tossed them onto the back seat.

Another had fallen into a partially unzipped duffle stuffed on top of the crossbow bag. The jacket for an airline ticket stuck out of the side pocket. She grabbed the water bottle that had fallen into the bag, opened the ticket jacket, and looked quickly. It was issued to him. He was traveling to Miami. Midday. Today.

"Is everything all right back there?"

"Yeah." She tucked the ticket back into the side pocket, crawled to the passenger seat, and buckled-up.

He laughed. "Geez, I think we stunk up the entire county."

"It's not funny. You killed an animal."

"Don't make me feel worse about it. It was an accident."

"I know."

"Sort of like you buying Mr. Pompadour's ranch."

"What?"

"How is it that you came to own it?"

She told him the story, that the purchase was unwitting. Roy was looking for temporary buyers. Vance had invested her money for her. That was as much as she was going to tell him. "In hindsight, I should have asked more questions."

"See? People make mistakes. I hit a skunk. I wasn't going to get us killed swerving to avoid it." The foul smell wafted through the vents. "I heard you got out with a nice little profit."

He knew more than he was letting on. Her phone pinged. She took it from her coat pocket. Two bars appeared. A voicemail from: MAYBE FRITZ.

She pressed the mobile against her ear. "Hey, Lauren, it's Fritz. The company doesn't want to give out any more information about the ring that came with the fitness tracker. I tried to get them to do it but their lawyer called and said you have to get a court order. If you wanna go that route, let me know and I'll give you the name of a lawyer I know who might help. Unfortunately, they'll just delay it and I know time is of the essence. Sorry. I wish I could have helped. Tell her dad I tried my best."

She slunk deeper into her seat.

"Bad news?"

Nodding, she recapped the message. She composed another message to Vance: The ring is a dead end.

Two DELIVERED messages followed, one for the one that had bounced back, and the other for the new one. She stared out the side window, hypnotized by the metal fence posts clicking past

"Roy thinks you have integrity."

"He told you that?"

"Uh-huh."

"I'm a nobody compared to him." She wasn't being modest. Roy was a decorated veteran who'd received the Medal of Honor and gone to college on a GI bill before spending thirty years on

Wall Street. "It's really something, all the service work he does for the families of police officers. Hosting retreats for disabled veterans and Gold Star families at his ranch."

"And Angel families."

She knew what Gold Star families were. They were the families of troops killed in combat. But she'd never heard of Angel families. She asked him about it.

"There're the ones who've lost loved ones to people who are here illegally."

"There's a group for that?" She'd never heard of them, but it didn't surprise her that Roy offered his ranch as a respite for them, too. "Is that how you met him?"

Daryl looked vexed. "Oh," he finally said. "You mean my wife being killed by someone here illegally? No. I already knew him before that happened."

She studied his profile, his features as sharp as the mountains ahead. The bridge of his nose jutted out, dividing his brow from his jaw, giving him an intense, warrior-like appearance.

She imagined him in spaghetti Western, riding into camera frame, bareback on a flashy paint horse while the director zoomed in tight on his sharp profile. He'd have played the strong, silent type in an old made-for-TV series.

Who was this enigmatic man and why was he going to Miami? Had he planned the trip before or after he found out Jake and Vance were going to Florida?

37

Thoughts flickered in Vance's brain like the end of an old film reel. Did Greg Marino kidnap his mother?

Jake raked his hands through his hair, "I need some air." He left the house to pace back and forth on the sidewalk, staring at his phone.

A nosy neighbor across the street watched from the window. God, he hated the way his mother's Coral Gables neighborhood had changed over the years. It had become affluent in the negative sense and new residents didn't like his Cuban family with the Anglo surname.

"Jur friend okay?" Sophia jabbed him in the shoulder. "What's wrong with him?"

He grabbed hold of the rubber tip of her cane and gently pointed it down. There was no point in trying to mislead her. "His daughter is missing. She disappeared from a ranch in Texas two days ago."

Sophia's eyes widened. "Is that where ju've been?"

"Uh-huh."

She covered her mouth with her hand and shook her head.

The roar of a V-8 engine caught his attention. A cop car sped toward the house, siren chirping, rooftop flashing red and blue lights, and skidded to a stop out front.

A woman's voice bellowed from a loudspeaker. "Stop! Do not move. I repeat. STOP!"

She was yelling at Jake, who looked like a surprised deer.

What the hell? It was the same pair they'd seen earlier. The driver, the woman, got out of the vehicle. She was big as a linebacker, maybe big enough to take him.

Jake began to wobble and took three steps like a Russian trooper, kicking his legs thigh high, holding his arms out to the side like wings, trying to keep his balance.

"Put your hands up." The cop pointed her gun at him.

Jake staggered.

"I said, *put your hands over your head*."

Jake's knees crumbled and he tried to use his hands to break the fall, but went facedown on the concrete, head bouncing on the sidewalk.

"Hey, hey," Vance shouted, walking briskly to aid Jake, hands in the air over his head.

Her partner—a wormy, short guy two-thirds her size—jumped out of the squad car. "Stop!"

He froze.

The woman cop knelt next to Jake. Daniel ran out of the house toward the sidewalk. Her partner motioned the two of them to stay back.

Jake sat up and shook his head as if parts were loose, blood welling on his brow where he'd cracked his head on the sidewalk.

Sophia waggled her cane from the doorway.

"Go inside," Vance yelled.

Jake rolled onto his knees and rubbed his head, looking at the blood glistening in his hands.

A small crowd of gawkers gathered on the sidewalk, surrounding them.

Fucking nosy neighbors.

"Is he okay?" Daniel asked.

The onlookers snapped cell pictures and recorded video. The wormy one left to disperse them. Vance read the nametag on her shirt: Officer Kagan.

Jake rolled onto his back and shaded his eyes, blood seeping from the gash on his forehead. "I'm fine."

Sophia hobbled toward them. She shook a crooked finger at Vance. "Ju bring trouble."

"You should go back inside," he said.

"Ju and Tony bring trouble."

Kagan said, "Ma'am, he's right. You should wait in the house."

Sophia glared at her, then at him, eyes narrowing to slits.

Jake struggled to his feet. "I don't know what happened."

"You passed out," Vance said.

"Does he have a health problem?" the female cop asked.

"It's not like I'm not here," Jake growled. "And no, I don't have a health problem." He wiped blood from his face using the back of his hand, and smeared it on the leg of his bright green shorts.

"What is your business here?" Kagan asked him.

"That's my question," Vance said. "What is *your* business here?"

"We got a call. A neighbor reported suspicious activity."

"A friend getting fresh air is suspicious? This is my mother's house. That's my aunt."

She tossed her head in the direction of the squad car parked curbside, then held her hand in Daniel's face, instructing him to wait with Jake. She wanted to talk to him privately.

Her mealy partner held his arms out, trying to block the

onlookers still taking pictures, some raising their hands over their heads.

"Is she *all there*?" she asked, watching Sophia hobbling up the stoop.

"What?" He grit his teeth. "Jesus. Don't tell me you're dragging your feet on this."

"Did I say that? ID, please."

She took his driver's license and dropped it in the top pocket of her uniform. "Your friend needs medical attention." She unclipped the mic from the radio attached to her utility belt and stepped way.

"Wait, don't call it in. I'll take him to the ER. It's a superficial wound."

"He hit his head pretty hard," Kagan said.

"Head wounds bleed like stuck pigs. You know that."

She paused, looked at Jake, at him, at Daniel, then turned on her heels.

He followed her. "Have you filed a missing persons report on my mother?"

"I was in the middle of it when the call came in. Suspicious activity in front of the vic's house."

"I told you, he went out to get some fresh air. Hardly nefarious activity."

Kagan glared at him. "I'm gonna give you a chance to tell me what's really going on here."

A young boy on a skateboard approached, recording video. When he saw the cop, he turned and sped away. The distraction gave him enough time to think.

"Why'd you pass the house the first time, then go to the gas station after we left the house?" she asked.

"I was surprised to see a cop car in front of my mom's place."

"Most family members rush to the scene. You didn't."

"Who called in suspicious activity?"

"I'll be right back," Kagan said.

Sophia stood on the stoop, posturing defiantly with gnarled hands on her cane, staring at them. She gave the scene one last look before harrumphing loud enough for everyone to hear. She wobbled inside and shut the door with a thud.

Kagan returned, metal clipboard in hand. She lifted the clamp and removed his ID. "What's your relation to Sophia Famosa?"

"She's my aunt."

"Are you any relation to Isabel Courage?"

"Yeah. If my last name is any clue."

"There's no need to get cocky. Any idea where she might have gone?"

"Gone?"

"That's correct."

"No."

"Is the address on your license current?"

"It's my previous address. I'll be staying here with my aunt."

"What's your current address?"

Jake huddled with Daniel. Her mealy-worm partner wandered along the walkway shooing the gawkers.

"I was moving to Texas," Vance said. "But I changed my mind."

Her eyebrows went to full staff. "Gimme a minute."

He knew why. She motioned to her partner and handed him his ID. They were calling it in.

She returned. "You're clear. Take your buddy to the ER and get him checked out."

"Will do."

"Here's my card. Call me if you hear anything new."

He walked Officer Renee Kagan to her unit. Her partner got into the passenger's side.

He wrote his number on the back of Kagan's card, tore off a

strip about as long and wide as a Chinese fortune and handed it to her. "It's my cell."

She read it. "It's not a Florida number."

"I told you, I was going to move to Texas. Long story."

"Ever miss it?"

"Florida or Texas?"

"Being a cop."

That probably came up on his background check. What didn't these days? "I don't know. It's been a long time. Sometimes, I guess."

She cracked a smile, then climbed in the cruiser. She motioned him closer. "Nosy neighbor across the street downloaded a couple of days' worth of the video from her doorbell camera. I watched it. She's the one who called in the suspicious activity. There's no sign of your mother or a possible suspect leaving the house. That's why I was asking about your aunt's mental faculties."

His heart stopped for a moment. Sophia said she heard his mother leave. "Maybe the house is too far away to activate the motion sensor."

"Nope," Kagan said from the open car window. She tilted her head at his mom's place. "My guess is they went out the back. You should talk to your aunt. You got my number," she said, pulling from the curb. "Call me if you think of anything that might help. And get your friend to the ER."

"Thanks," he said, watching until the squad car was out of sight.

The canal behind his mother's home connected to hundreds of miles of waterways. During his time on the force, he knew firsthand the canals were a favorite dumping ground for weapons, vehicles, and bodies—in that order.

He and Daniel helped Jake into the back of the Renegade. Vance followed Daniel to the driver's side for a moment of privacy. "Do you think it's weird we haven't heard his demand yet?"

Daniel ran his hand over his slick brown head. "We don't know if these two things are connected."

"Come on, Sarge. Do you really think this a coincidence? You know the stats better than I do."

Daniel twisted the cubic zirconia in his earlobe.

Of the fifty thousand people kidnapped every year, less than a hundred were taken by strangers.

"It's still kind of a long-shot," he said. "I don't know what I'd do if one of my girls or grandkids disappeared." His voice faltered. He had to stop for a moment. When he composed himself, he said, "I take that back. I know exactly what I'd do."

He'd been getting inside Greg's head. "If Marino kidnapped my mother yesterday, how'd he kidnap Caitlin in Texas?"

"That *gilipollas* can't afford to fart in public. Leaving the state would be a violation of bail."

Douche bag. "I don't think that would stop him. The problem is, that if he kidnapped Jake's daughter, he had to go to Texas to do it. If you measure the distance against the clock if doesn't work, even if he drove non-stop. He couldn't have taken my mom and Caitlin. The window of time doesn't work. He couldn't get through an airport with the girl. I doubt she'd have had ID on her. He has to have an accomplice."

Sarge leaned on the Renegade door, drumming his thumb on the window. "That's exactly what I was thinking. Let's get the show on the road."

He hurried to the passenger's-side and climbed in the front seat.

If Greg was behind it, why did he go to Texas to abduct Caitlin when he could have grabbed her here, from school, or from home? He didn't have proof that Marino did it, but every cell in his body said he did.

Was her disappearance connected to the stolen hovercraft?

His phone pinged. Two messages from Lauren appeared. They'd been sent hours apart. That was weird. The second message was important: `The ring is a dead end.`

He typed: `That's a bummer.`

She pinged right back: `Agreed. Will call when I can.`

He pecked out: `Talk soon,` pressed the send button, swiped the screen, and shoved the mobile into his pants pocket. "`Will call when I can?`" Did that mean something? He refused to let his imagination run wild.

As far as he knew, Tony was still out of the country. He didn't fit into the picture.

But he and Jake fit. So did his mother. And Caitlin. And Daniel fit, too, if only by association. Who sent him the cryptic text: `Primo - GM is out.`

"Ju and Tony, ju bring trouble." Sophia had said it twice.

38

O ther than the skunk episode, the rest of the trip to Alpine was an exercise in mindlessness.

Daryl slowed the dually to twenty-five miles per hour. Lauren rolled her window down and stuck her head out into the cool air. The truck had aired out enough that she could smell hops, and coffee, and pancakes.

Alpine was not at all what she'd expected, with indie coffee shops and craft bakeries, a small diner with gingham drapes and a red awning, an old movie theater playing *The Rocky Horror Picture Show* at midnight on weekends, and antique dealers, and art galleries.

A white silo with big red lettering jutted thirty feet into the air, advertising a microbrewery. The old four-story buildings with brick façades and vertical neon marquees anchored to wrought-iron arms cut a crisp outline against the baby-blue, cotton-balled sky.

Daryl leaned on the steering wheel and craned his neck, his chin practically on the dash. "This speed trap's a bonanza. Made a bunch of out-of-towners mad enough to start a website. The *AlpineFine* dot com. Speeders are the town's biggest revenue producers. The big counties hog all the property taxes so the small ones gotta be creative."

"I didn't even see the signs," she said.

"That's what makes it so successful. It drops from seventy to twenty-five in the blink of an eye. Set me back three hundred bucks the first time. Paid a lawyer and got a hand-written note from the local judge saying I was on probation for a year."

"Handwritten?"

"Uh-huh. Cottage industry they got going on. Having a clean driving record is important in my line of work. Plus, it's a wash. Ends up costing the same if you pay the fine or hire a lawyer. If you go the lawyer route, the attorney splits whatever the fine is with the court. Everyone's happy. Lawyer makes a few bucks, the town gets their piece of the pie, and the insurance companies can't raise your rates."

"That sounds corrupt."

He glanced at the rearview.

A sheriff's SUV rode their rear bumper

She twisted in her seat to better see.

"It would be best if you didn't do that."

"Is looking out the back window a crime?"

"Didn't say that. I don't want any trouble."

Neither did she. The crawl through town gave her the chance to look around. It was the kind of place she'd like to come back and visit sometime.

Two blocks later they were back on the main highway doing seventy on a seventy-mile-an-hour stretch of flat road. He stopped talking on the outskirts of Alpine and pushed a plastic bud connected to his phone in his ear.

A few miles later he took the white button out. "We're almost there."

"What are you listening to?"

He smiled. "Willie Nelson. Figured it wasn't your taste in music."

It wasn't the answer she expected. He should have asked. The music would have been perfect.

Uneven rows of barbed wire hung from skinny metal posts lining the highway. Daryl slowed and leaned on the steering column, craning his neck forward, looking out the passenger window.

She pressed her neck on the headrest, clearing his line of sight. He activated the right-hand turn signal and drove onto the shoulder, gravel pinging against the underbelly of the truck.

He stomped the brake pedal hard enough to put the dually into a short skid, then backed up slowly as a light-brown cloud of dirt rolled over the tailgate. A tattered strip of faded red plastic hung from the top of a metal stake. He stopped parallel to the fence and put the truck in park.

"Wait here." He covered his mouth with his sleeve and stepped out of the vehicle. He unlatched three links of barbed wire, then pulled the lines back to make a space wide enough for the truck to pass through.

He hopped in, backed the truck to the opening, then made the right-hand turn between the posts, and parked. He got out, reattached the fencing, hustled back and jumped in behind the wheel.

There was no road ahead, not even a path, just empty desert dotted with cacti and boulders. A line of mature Aleppo pines thirty feet tall looked out of place. He zigzagged slowly around the trees and low-lying vegetation, then made a lazy turn to the left, following the arc of pines planted in a semicircle.

At the end, out of view from the highway, lay a bone yard. Retired signs, railroad ties, appliances, tires, and other junk worked as a barricade around the perimeter. He parked perpendicular to a decommissioned hot tub.

If she'd been scouting for a desolate location for a video shoot, this place would have been pay dirt. An enormous gas station sign, the kind you can see from five miles away, listed against a dull green travel trailer perched on cinder blocks like an island.

She followed him on foot past a tangle of bent highway dividers, a rusty chicken coop, and mattresses stacked five-high. It was slow-motion making their way through bicycle skeletons, a pyramid of analog TVs, two toilets, and an antique wagon wheel surrounded by mountains of what she guessed to be car parts.

A newish air conditioning unit was rigged to the arched metal roof of the trailer. The only window on the backside was blocked with aluminum foil.

"Is this the time I should start getting nervous?"

"It's a little late for that, don't you think?"

"What are we doing here? This place is creepy."

"I told you, seeing a friend who might be able to help us."

He carried Davis' tablet under his arm.

"Darn it." She patted her back pocket. "I left my phone in your truck. Do you mind if I run and get it?"

"Sure. Hurry up." He held his hand high and unlocked the doors with a chirp.

She was halfway to the vehicle when she heard a shout.

"THAT YOU, DARYL?"

An old man in bib overalls emerged from around the front side of the trailer. She stopped for a second to look. His faded-blue pants legs were tucked into square-toed boots and the heavy red-white-and-black plaid shirt looked better suited for an Iowan farmer than a desert rat. The old codger took a wide stance and thumbed the straps of his overalls.

She climbed into the cab, put her messenger bag on the floor matt and peeked over the dash while Daryl talked to Farmer

John. Taking her phone from her pocket, she lay flat in the space between the seats, reached behind the driver's seat, took the airline ticket from the bag, spread it open and snapped a picture.

She jumped out of the truck, held her phone up, closed the passenger door, and yelled, "Got it."

The headlights blinked and the door locks snapped with a thump and a chirp.

The old man's blue eyes sparkled. "Hello, young lady. Ol' Daryl here, he likes to make hisself a stranger. You must be Lauren."

"Lauren, meet Kitch. Kitch, meet Lauren."

"Call me Kit." The man stuck his hand out and pumped hers. "Good to meet ya. Guessing Daryl here is looking for that video. That's the only time he comes to see me. When he wants something. That right, Daryl? Heck, it's okay. He's the only one who ever comes around. Hell, the postman ain't been here since nineteen ninety-nine. I can't blame him. Or her. Or you. I wouldn't come see me, neither. Let's go inside."

A rickety wooden ladder leaned against the backside of the trailer. They walked around a Burger King menu board and a curvaceous hood that must have come from a 1950s classic car.

He wasn't going to invite them inside, was he?

She followed them to the front side of the trailer. A shiny Suburban was parked beneath a sturdy carport. The black SUV had tinted glass an inch thick.

"You look surprised, young lady. You think I get around on a mule or what?"

"No. Of course not."

Three metal sawtooth stairs led to the front door.

Whoa.

What was this place? The interior rivaled the cockpit of a commercial airliner with floor-to-ceiling banks of electronics and flat monitors papering the walls. An efficient Ikea-like kitchen with a built-in microwave, stove, and small refrigerator occupied one corner. The big leather recliner must have doubled as the bed, a blanket and pillow neatly stacked on the footrest.

"What do you do here?"

"Kit's the original hacker. You remember the movie about the kid who accidentally hacked the military's supercomputer?"

A lump formed in her throat. "You're him?"

"I retired from that nonsense. Just do a little off-the-books work fer folks I like. And your friend Daryl just happens to be one of the folks I don't hate. Your cameraman does some good-looking work."

She narrowed her eyes and glared at him.

"Watched it in real time. Knew it wasn't Border Patrol's video 'cause it's so purdy. My stomach gets the dang whirlies watching them agents chasing *ky-oaties* and drug traffickers. What's you two doing flying that thing at Pomp's ranch?"

"Mr. Pompadour hired us to make a video."

"Fer what?"

"For the ranch."

"I know that. I mean what fer?"

"For marketing."

"That place is booked solid year 'round." Kit held his hand out. "Gimme that tablet, son."

Daryl handed him the pad and Kit connected it to a USB tethered to his computer. "I'm kinda surprised."

"About what?" she asked.

"That you forgot you was shooting Four-K. You was zoomed into a regular ol' HD frame. You been missing half the picture."

How *did* she miss this? She'd paid the big-box electronics store in New York a premium to have the new gear shipped overnight directly to the ranch. Other than juicing the batteries and downloading the apps, Davis hadn't had time to play with the new toys. The first time he'd piloted the drone was the morning Caitlin disappeared. Then the sheriff confiscated it.

She defended Davis. "It's brand new."

"Ah, don't go taking it all personally," Kit said. "It's good news."

She stared at Kit's twenty-seven-inch color monitor. He looked at a piece of paper on the console and typed in a set of numbers—time-code numbers—a shortcut to the precise frame he was looking for.

Good God.

Though small, the hovercraft looked just like the one she'd seen on the company's old website. It was in the upper right-hand corner of the shot. It wasn't visible inside the standard hi-def screen.

Daryl rubbed his jaw until red marks appeared. He stood still as a statue. "I guess this proves it was out there when she disappeared."

"Keep watching." Kit pressed the gray, reverse ARROW key and stopped on another frame. The video showed Caitlin setting her backpack down, then he reversed it so the girl would be running backward. He tapped the keyboard and zoomed out to full resolution, pointing a chubby finger on the far left side.

Daryl shifted his weight from one foot to the other; the trailer rocked slightly.

She saw it before Kit said it.

"That's the both of you." Kit was talking about her and Davis. "See? Yer about as big as ants and the four-wheelers look like Hotwheels. I'm not accusing you of nothing. I'm just a reporter helping to establish a timeline."

Kit dragged the HAND tool to the upper right quadrant of the screen on the tablet, then zoomed in. A mirror image appeared on the 27-inch monitor.

"I'm gonna slow it down. Watch the screen."

Caitlin ran into the frame, heading toward the berm.

"Watch. That damn snake moved her backpack." Kit toggled back and forth between frames, showing where she put it down when she started her run and where she picked it up when she was finished. "Like bait."

The red backpack was easy to see.

Kit hit the PLAY key. Caitlin stopped and sat on the rock where she'd stashed her backpack. The girl leaned back as if checking to see where she and Davis were.

Suddenly it looked as if the ground near the base of the berm moved. "Holy crap," she said.

"Keep on watching."

He slowed the footage to fifty-percent real time.

The ground hadn't moved, something else did.

"Now, you two pay attention."

He zoomed in tighter, blurring the video a little.

"Keep yer eyes on the far right of the screen."

Lauren stepped a foot closer and squinted at Kit's monitor. This wasn't *CSI Small Town Texas*, this was the real world and the closer Kit zoomed in, the fuzzier and less articulate the image got.

Something crawled out from under a tarp: it was clear as day. Now she understood what happened. Caitlin had been ambushed.

It was a human, a man—he grabbed Caitlin from behind and pointed something at her stomach.

Kit zoomed out enough to make the picture crisper, but smaller. "If I don't miss my guess, that's a gun. That's how he overpowered her. Pointed that gun at her belly."

Butterflies flitted inside hers.

Her captor had staged the hovercraft at the base of the berm facing south, away from the ranch, toward the mountains, west of where they'd set up the drone. None of them could have seen it happen. Not from where they'd set up. Not from the courtyard or the dining hall windows.

She didn't want to watch any more. The part when she and Davis drove away, oblivious to what was happening, was coming up next.

Kit said, "There's more. Don't go getting all mad at yourself. Y'all didn't know."

He closed the video file they'd been watching. A row of thumbnails popped up on the tablet. He moused toward the last icon, stopped on a rectangular still image of the airstrip, and clicked on it.

She'd sent Davis back out to get a shot of the private runway. He'd been pissed off and didn't want to send the drone back up because he said he couldn't get a beauty shot without the big pile of white rocks next to the airstrip ruining it. She'd pressed him to do it, saying she'd edit around it, not sure if it was even possible.

Kit opened the file and scrolled through the timeline, slowing it down, toggling forward and back with his thumb and forefinger, stopping on the frame he was looking for. He enlarged the picture.

Stunned, she looked at Daryl.

Holy mother of God.

Caitlin craned her neck as if looking for help.

"Watch carefully," Kit said. "He's gonna make her get in it."

Two seconds later, the hovercraft was airborne. Kit paused the video again.

"Jesus," she said. "Jesus. Jesus. *Jesus*."

"See that?" He put his finger on Caitlin's head and pressed the PLAY button. "It's her hat gettin' blown off in the wind."

Kit zoomed out to the widest shot. In seconds, the hovercraft was out of the frame, flying toward the Interstate, heading east.

"If I'd been paying attention, I would have seen it," she said. "I *should* have seen it happen. We could have stopped him."

She could hardly believe they'd missed it. The swirl pattern, the footprints, the lack of tire tracks, all of it fit perfectly now. But there was almost nothing to identify the man.

"Listen here," Kit said. "He had a gun. You mighta gotten her killed, or yourself shot-up. It's a good thing you went back out fer that last shot or we'd have bupkis to go on."

It was obvious this wasn't the first time Kit had seen the video. He had the time code numbers marked and flicked through them scene-by-scene like he'd watched it a dozen times before. She asked him about it.

"I told ya. I watch Border Patrol chasing ky-oaties and traffickers. When I seen this live, I called the sheriff and told him I seen a Luke Skywalker Landspeeder."

So, it was Kit who called it in.

"Why didn't he send someone out?" Daryl asked.

"I got the answering machine. Left a message. Didn't think it was smart to jammer on about a possible UFO. Didn't see the girl first time I watched. I hacked your camera guy's drone but I didn't record it. I was spying. I left my number. The sheriff called me hisself and come to visit me. He brought this here tablet and we looked at it together. I made myself a copy to study."

She should have known. That meant Manny gave the tablet to Daryl yesterday, and last night he was keeping a secret.

Kit cued the video and unmuted it.

The sound hurt her ears.

He pressed the MUTE icon. "I know, coulda, woulda, shoulda—but ya didn't. Don't beat yourself up. Them things are loud buggers. Coulda happened to any of us."

"Except it happened to me," she said.

"I heard you was trying to use that fitness gadget to help locate the girl."

Geez. Was nothing sacred or private? "You mean while spying on us, or surveilling, or whatever you call it? For all the hacking you do, what good has it done?"

Kit didn't take offense. "A Val Verde deputy found it in a trash can at a little hole-in-the-wall gas station in Comstock."

He definitely had the inside track.

"Device was smashed and outta juice by then. Just one eyewitness for what that's worth. Whole town is a time warp. No cameras. Nothing nearby, neither."

She already knew most of that and had seen the gas station on Google Earth, the corrugated metal building with two self-serve pumps.

"Saw they gotta ping from Alabama."

Was there anything he didn't know?

Daryl rubbed the back of his neck. "I'm betting dollars to donuts you know where that hovercraft came from."

Kit chuckled. "Daryl knows how much I love them donuts. Glazed, jelly-filled, chocolate frosted, sprinkles. Hell, I love 'em all. You wonder why ol' Daryl wears his hair long?"

Daryl touched a feather in his braid.

"He can hear better. And it ain't bullshit. There's a science to it. Hair hanging over your ears amplifies sound. I used to hear as good as him, 'til my hair fell out and my eardrums went to hell. Now Fabio's hair wouldn't do me a shit's worth of good."

Lauren's phone pinged. It was Vance.

How's your trip?

She turned her back to them, typed a few words, deleted them, then decided on something simpler. Good. Yours? She pushed the send button and turned back around. Her phone pinged again, this time with a question: See anything new on the video?

"Are you all right?" Kit asked her. "You look pale."

"I'm fine." She typed another message: Talk soon, and pushed the send button.

"There's a place out in the desert where they're doing the testing," the old hacker said. "And I know where it is."

Had she missed something? "Testing what?"

"The *vehicle*." He tugged on one of the denim straps holding his overalls up, looking annoyed, as if he didn't appreciate her turning her back on him to use her phone.

"Come here." He motioned her closer to his computer screen, scrolled through his browser history, and brought up a Google Earth view of something she didn't recognize.

"What is that?" she asked. "It looks like a racetrack."

Kit ran his finger over a straight line. "World's biggest skid pad. The track's nine-and-a-half miles long. It's a proving ground where a lotta the car companies test vehicles. It's hardly a secret. Even got six-degree banking fer NASCAR teams so they can test G-loads."

He typed the name of an expensive tire manufacturer into the browser, pressed the RETURN key, tapped the GALLERY tab on the website, then scrolled through a series of photos.

Daryl held a finger over his upper lip, watching.

Kit stopped on a thumbnail and tapped it, making it bigger. The photographer caught the spray from a puddle as a yellow Corvette made a tight turn around a red traffic cone.

"Is that the place?" she asked.

"Yup." He rubbed the bristles on his chin. "Place has all kinda of subterranean operations that can't be seen from satellite imagery. The secret stuff that goes on there happens underground. Offices, labs, that kind of thing."

"The hovercraft was stolen from there?"

"Well, they didn't buy it on Amazon if that's what you mean. Place is practically the Area 51 for vehicle development . . . high security, and hard as hell to hack into."

Kit waddled to the Barcalounger and sat on the armrest.

She needed a moment. "Do you have a restroom?"

"You think I use a tree?" Then he chuckled. "It's outside. Take a right. Metal shed straight ahead." He nudged Daryl and winked. "It's unisex."

THE MAKESHIFT BUILDING was constructed from scraps of freeway Armco and sheets of corrugated siding. The hinges screeched when she pulled the heavy metal door open. Inside it was sheet-rocked and wallpapered with nickel-plated fixtures and scented soaps. Almost fashionable.

She typed a text to Vance: `Got a lead.`

She splashed cool water on her face and looked into the mirror, expecting to see worse. The desert sun was doing her good. She pulled a clean towel from the rack above the sink and blotted her face.

SHE TAPPED on the front door to the trailer. Daryl answered.

"What did I miss?"

Daryl pulled the door closed behind her.

"Kit says the firewalls were breached at the site."

"What firewalls?"

"For the servers at the proving ground," the old coot said. "The place where the hovercraft was stolen. Ask me how I know."

"Okay. How do you know?"

"I had a little sneak peek myself."

He was full of surprises. "I thought you just said the place was impossible to hack?"

"Don't get fussy. 'Hard as hell,' is what I said. Not impossible. If I can do it, so can the Chinese. Or the North Koreans. Or the Russians—"

"What do you know?" she asked.

"Well, nothing really," Kit said. "'Cept I saw an email telling the recipient not to use the Internet to send anything sensitive. They planned on keeping their information the old-fashioned way, on paper in desk drawers. Smart. Only way to keep shit from walking out the door. The Israeli's have gone to a lot of trouble to keep the CAD drawings from being pirated."

"I don't care about international espionage, or drawings, or whatever you're talking about," she said. "I'm trying to help find Jake's daughter."

Kit planted both hands on his burly hips. "You might be doing both."

"That prototype is worth as much as a hundred million dollars," Daryl said.

A hundred million dollars?

"A bunch of powerful folks are very angry," Kit said.

Her head spun. "Other than the Israelis?"

"They oughta be enough to scare ya," Kit said.

Her throat tightened. She took a deep breath to fight the fear. "What does this have to do with Jake's kid?"

"Don't know," Kit said. "Not yet."

Claustrophobia set in. Kit was a big man, and so was Daryl, and three of them sandwiched inside the tight space was making it hard to breathe.

"Tell her," Daryl said. "What you used to do."

Kit frowned, as if tasting something bad.

"He's ex-CIA."

"Retired. Help a few friends out now and then."

"What did you do for the CIA?"

"Pretty boring stuff, really. Used to work overseas stopping the bad guys from sabotaging oil pipelines. You'd be surprised at how much five minutes of an oil gusher is worth on the streets of Mozambique. Daryl tell you he used to be a prison guard?"

"No. Is that true?"

"It's tit-for-tat if you're gonna be a rat fink," Kit said.

Daryl didn't answer.

"You didn't tell her you moved here from Colorado?" Kit cocked his head like Scooby Doo. "He worked at the SuperMax in Florence, Colorado. It's a special place."

Her lungs stopped. A rush of adrenaline set her face on fire. Chago Marino, co-head of the defunct Los Guapos drug cartel, was sentenced to the ADX in Florence. He'd been killed inside the prison.

"No, he didn't mention it," she said, looking at Daryl.

"The hovercraft is an Israeli Defense Department project," Kit said.

She massaged her forehead, tasting bile.

"Overseen by Mossad, the Israeli version of the deep state."

She glared at Daryl. She was mad at herself. Now she was stuck in something more complicated than a kidnapping.

Kit said, "Mossad funds dark projects the Israeli public doesn't know about. They wanted to test the thing somewhere secure. Thing's a national security risk and them Israelis live in a bad neighborhood."

"I'm confused. How could that *thing* be a national security risk?" she asked.

"It's not the hovercraft they're protecting. That old thing is just the test bed."

"I don't get it."

"It's the software. It's the next generation of, oh, heck, I don't know whatcha call it. Let's just say it's software that's gonna teach helicopters to fly themselves."

Her hands shook.

He thumbed the straps of his overalls. "There's a race to see who can do it first."

She'd have liked to head butt Daryl. "What you're saying is Roy and Josh have been working with the Israeli government developing self-flying helicopters?"

"That's the gist of it." He squeezed his fat chin. "'Cept they're testing 'em, not developin' 'em."

"Is that why a group of Unit 8200 agents is staying at the ranch?" she asked.

Kit fiddled with his phone. "Didn't know they were, but that makes sense."

Her phone pinged. A link popped up.

"Download it. Use it if you need me. Military grade encryption."

"How did you get my number?"

Daryl laughed. "How do you think he got it?"

"I'd download it if I were you, young lady."

"You're not me."

"There you go. Getting all fussy. You'll do whatever you want and I do admire you for it." The old coot shook his head. "That said, download it."

DARYL SWUNG the dually wide and roared onto the four-lane.

Her head was about to explode and when the warmth of the engine revived the faint smell of skunk spray, her stomach wretched.

She had more questions now than she had before.

She stared out the windshield of the truck.

SuperMax.

The Alcatraz of the Rockies. Where a Who's Who of the worst-of-the-worst were housed. Terrorists, domestic and foreign. Timothy McVeigh's accomplice, Terry Nichols. Ted Kaczynski, aka The Unibomber. Richard Reid, the Shoe Bomber. More recently, El Flaco, head of the Sinaloa Mexican cartel, the world's most vicious crime syndicate with tentacles around the globe.

Daryl didn't mention anything about going to Miami. She'd seen his airline ticket. Soon as they got back to the ranch she planned to corner Roy Pompadour to find out what was really going on.

39

Caitlin scrambled from the shower, wrapping the thin towel around her torso.

"I gotta take a dump." It was the reptile's voice on the other side of the door. She'd turned the water off when she heard banging.

She grabbed a handful of clothing from the duffel bag, pressed a pile of it to her chest and opened the door an inch. She was eye-to-eye with him. Reptilian slits with a bead of flesh around them, like toad-eyes.

"Give me a second." She held up the clothes he'd given her through the crack, stuffed them back in the duffle, pulled the door shut, and stepped into her dirty leggings. She pulled her dad's sweatshirt over her head and hung the towel over her shoulder. Barefoot, carrying the bag in one hand, she opened the door enough to sidestep past him. He pressed his body against hers. *Ew.* His goon followed her down the dim hallway.

Isabel stood in the doorway and ushered her inside the small bedroom, cutting Mack off with her crooked arm.

"Who died and put you in charge, you old bag," the pit bull said.

"Ju watch what ju say to that girl. *Entendido*?" She pulled the door shut. "Ju going to be fine. Never mind him. Get dressed."

Tears welled.

"Now, now." The old woman grabbed her by the shoulders and squeezed hard. "Get dressed."

Isabel stepped into the hallway to give her some privacy. She tipped her head upside down and turned the towel into a turban, sat on the edge of the small bed and sorted through the clothing the man gave her. The tags were still on them. She couldn't wear this stuff. The longest skirt would barely cover her panties and every blouse was so low cut she might as well wear a bikini top.

She stripped out of her filthy clothes, dropped the towel off her hair, wound it around her torso, and used a corner of it to check for blood. The spotting had stopped.

She bit the plastic price tag from a pair of leopard-print panties, and stepped into them. They fit. So did the bra. She tried on a skirt; it was snug. So was the sleazy top her mother would kill her for wearing.

The bedroom door flung open. She backed away, clamping her arms across her chest.

"Now, that's what I like to see," the lizard said, inspecting her. "Except for those bruises."

She cast her eyes down.

Isabel hobbled past him, eyes blazing. "Leave her alone."

"Did you call my father yet? He'll give you what you want."

"Don't be so sure," he said.

"He will. If you let me go."

He laughed. "Your dad owes me *a lot of money*."

How dare he. She lifted her head and shot him a look of pure hatred.

"Your father is a thief who stole my inheritance."

She clutched her chest. "My father never stole anything from anyone."

He guffawed and spread his arms on the outside of doorframe, leaning in and out like he was doing pushups.

Isabel stood in front of her, arms folded, glaring at him. "I know who ju are." She turned and spoke to Caitlin. "Our families knew each other. For a long time, a long time ago."

"Her father stole my money."

"You're lying. My father is a businessman!"

"No, he's not. He's a washed-up drunk who lost his fancy job. And now he's a crook. Finish getting ready. We're going for a ride." He licked his lips.

"He's lying." She looked to Isabel for assurance.

The old woman shook her head.

"My father is a successful investment banker. He worked on Wall Street."

"What's he done lately?" the reptile asked.

"I don't know jur father," Isabel said. "I'm sure he's a good man—"

"He's a con man and a thief. He stole my inheritance and I plan to get it back. Hurry up, bitch, before I ask Mack to help me."

Mack trotted behind him, chest-bumping him from behind with his squatty body. He stopped doing doorway pushups and stepped aside.

The gun hanging across Mack's chest looked ridiculous, the kind bad guys in pinstriped suits and penguin shoes carried in the old movies. Half pistol, half Tommy gun. The stock, a dull turquoise metal box with a foot-long skinny snout. A curved magazine packed tightly with pointy, copper-jacketed bullets sprouted from above the trigger.

"They stopped making these babies in nineteen-thirty." Mack slapped the metal like he was waking up a newborn.

"Don't make me use it. Especially on a gorgeous piece of work like you." He ogled her and stroked the dull wooden handle.

Isabel flung her arms from her chest, as if chasing flies. "Ju two, get out. Ju think ju scare an old woman but ju don't. Ju leave now and give us privacy."

"Fine," the lizard said. "Hurry the fuck up."

Isabel closed the door behind them. "Get ready, dear."

"Where are we going?"

"I don't know. Just hurry. Don't make him madder than he is."

Caitlin laid the loaned clothing on the bed and sorted through it, looking for a better choice. The clothes were all the same. Slutty. Her nostrils tingled as she twisted the rose-colored metal ring around her finger. She wrinkled her nose and sniffled, fighting the urge to cry.

Her mom was an assertive woman who said that her bravery came from learning to summon her big voice. The old woman was like her mother, standing up against these thugs. That's what she'd do now. She'd look for that big voice. She'd find it and start using it.

40

Vance was right about Jake's head wound: It looked a lot worse than it was. He'd taken him to one of those chain ERs where the line was short. The outpatient instructions were simple. The nurse told him to keep his blood sugar up, code for "Remember to eat."

"They're probably working on a warrant," Daniel said when they got back to the house.

The gawkers were gone. There was no sign of the Crown Vic, either.

He pulled the drapes shut. "I'm sure they're keeping an eye on us."

He wouldn't be a bit surprised if an ambitious prosecutor wasn't already out judge-shopping. His Uncle Tony had been on the FBI's Ten Most Wanted list for decades. Maybe Kagan knew. Maybe that's why Kagan acted so hinky.

What if he was the real target? What if he'd been baited into returning to Miami? What if taking Caitlin was part of a ruse to entrap him? What if Ann's accident wasn't an *accident*?

The missing hovercraft didn't square with that theory, information he hadn't shared with Daniel or Jake.

Daniel sat at the kitchen table. "I'm an active, dues-paying member of the Fraternal Order of Police. That should count for something."

"Your point being?" he asked, browsing on his cell.

"Kagan on her bullhorn out there, in front of God and everyone, yelling at Jake, making a scene."

"We're in Miami. Not Lauderdale," he said.

"Hey, now. Fort Liquourdale is northernmost Miami. She shouldn'ta let a jurisdictional detail get in the way of showing me a little respect."

Jake peeked out the curtain. "Is it a good sign or a bad sign that they're back?"

Vance looked. The Crown Vic was parked across the street.

Daniel polished his baldhead with both palms. "Great."

"What are you doing?" Jake asked Vance.

"Booking an Uber."

Daniel took umbrage. "What's wrong with my Jeep?"

"I booked a rental car. I'm gonna go get it. They'll have to make a decision."

"Between what and what?" Daniel asked.

"Between following me and staying here and keeping an eye on you."

"I need to see Ann. Either you take me with you or I'm gonna rent my own car," Jake said.

"Okay. Daniel stays here with Sophia. You come with me."

"I can't stay," Daniel said. "I got a gig tonight."

He checked the app. The rideshare was less than a minute away. He sent a message to the driver: Stop in front of the house with the for sale sign. Meet you there. "What kind of a gig?"

"Working security at a nightclub."

"Call in sick."

Sophia shook her head and poked Daniel with her cane. "I be better off by myself."

He looked out the window, and when he saw the white car slow in front of the house down the street with the For Sale sign in the grass, he and Jake hurried out the back door, jogging along the canal front bulkhead, trespassing between houses, to meet the driver.

THEY ARRIVED at the strip mall fifteen minutes before the rental car agency was scheduled to close. The front door was locked but the lights were on. Vance rang the buzzer. A full minute passed with no one answering.

"Shit. Now what?" Jake asked.

A brunette in a snug uniform trotted out from a behind a closed door. She hooked her heel on the metal kickstand and propped it open, then let them in.

He identified himself.

"Nice name," she said, smiling. "Credit card and driver's license, please." She was about to hand him the rental agreement. "How long are you going to need the vehicle?"

"Uh, I'm not sure."

"Mr. Courage, your credit card company is declining the deposit."

"Hmmm. Try it again."

"I have, sir. If I run it one more time, I'll have to confiscate it. They'll pay me fifty dollars to do it. Don't tempt me."

That was weird. He'd used it earlier at the gas station. Maybe it got skimmed.

Jake pulled his wallet from his pocket and presented his Visa and license.

Great. He'd seen all the alerts on Jake's phone. What was he thinking? Jake's credit cards were Russian roulette.

Her eyes shifted to the bloodstained gauze around Jake's forehead. She cleared her throat and looked at her computer. A moment later she handed him the paperwork with the key stuffed inside the jacket. Finally, a good surprise.

"Turn left out the door and look for a white Nissan Altima."

They switched drivers a block from the rental car agency. It was an easy half hour to Jackson Memorial. He did a three-point turn and backtracked to Northeast 1st Street, hung a left on Northwest 17th and continued beneath the I-395 spaghetti bowl. He rolled his window up and double-checked the door locks.

Cops, including retired ones, knew every back road to Jackson. He drove the shortcut through Overtown, rolling through the stop signs and red lights, past the gangbangers and crack dealers, before heading north on Northwest 12th Avenue.

He ran more scenarios in his head. Could Greg be working alone? Was he masterful enough to lure him to Miami? Did the Panamanians turn Uncle Tony over to the Feds? Would his uncle turn on him? He'd snitched on his best friend and partner, Chago Marino. Why not him?

He fixed his eyes on the windshield.

Miami was about to do its thing. A thunderhead rolled overhead and an electrical charge lit the backdrop of gray clouds hanging across the horizon. A rumble followed.

He tapped the Glock 19 holstered under his left arm. Before the trip to the ER, he'd prepped it at his mom's place, taking it out of the TSA-approved hard case he'd packed it in, loading the clip, double-checking the safety.

Raindrops smacked the windshield.

"This cloud piss is going to royally fuck-up traffic," Jake said.

Vance's phone pinged. He pulled it from his pocket. A new text from Lauren: `Coming to Miami.`

At the next red light, he typed: Why?

She didn't answer. Another minute passed. Still nothing. Something was up.

He stared at the wipers sweeping the windshield like a metronome, the red taillights ahead glowing in the mist.

The rooster tails wreaked havoc with visibility.

Conditions worsened to near tropical storm status.

Traffic lights swayed.

Did any cop in the history of policing ever quit investigating shit in their heads?

He passed Booker T. Washington High, took a left on Northeast 14th, and started to look for parking. Visibility was poor, and the signs unreadable. The buildings, a featureless collection of high-rise barracks, indistinguishable from one another, even on a sunny day.

Jake grabbed the dash. "Watch out."

Vance jabbed the brakes. A nurse in pale blue scrubs pushed a wheelchair into the crosswalk, her yellow umbrella thrashing in the wind. He turned at the sign for the self-parking garage and pressed the button for a ticket. The gate opened and he crept up the ramp leading to the concrete jungle.

Jake's phone rang. "Uh-huh, uh-huh . . . . What? . . . . Hang on." He put his thumb over the mic. "It's my ex. Stop for a second."

He put the Altima in park.

"We're in the parking garage . . . . Okay, okay." Jake ended the call. "Ann's already left the hospital."

Vance began an eight-point turn. "This isn't going to be pretty." The driver of the minivan behind them laid on the horn while he blocked both sides of the ramp turning around the tight corner.

The van driver rolled his window down, honked, and yelled.

"He just called you an asshole," Jake said.

"How do you know he wasn't talking to you?" Vance hopped out and lifted the horizontal gate by hand. Back behind the wheel, he said, "Did I tell you how much I hate this place?"

"I hate Miami, too."

"Not Miami." He raised a fist at the minivan driver who'd gotten out to scold him some more. "Hospitals. Where's Ann?"

"Home."

"Do you want to go there?"

"There's no point. She hasn't heard anything from Caitlin."

He waited for the light to turn green.

"I remember when Ann and I and used to come down with the kids every winter. Back when I worked in New York, I had a little condo in Hobe Sound. Those were good times."

All Vance could think was this was a bad time and that the same Atlantic lapped at the same shoreline as it did when his Uncle Tony co-headed the biggest drug cartel in US history. No amount of ocean water could ever clean the place up. Not then. Not now.

The Passenger Pick-Up lanes all around Jackson Memorial were clogged.

The rain let up a little. "You know what my father used to say about hospitals?"

Jake found the button and moved his seat back. "I give up."

"They're places that turn live people into dead ones."

"And I thought I was cynical."

Vance craned his head over the dash and watched for an opening. When the light turned yellow, he gunned it. The Altima fishtailed. "My father was a doctor. He would know."

Miami's days as Cocaine, Inc., brought Florida to the brink as a failed state. The name of the city could be traced to the indigenous people, the Myaamia tribe. Translated, it meant "downstream."

Apropos, he thought, since that's what people more or less said about the flow of shit.

"I really need to take a piss," Jake said. "I'm at that age where I really can't wait."

41

The blindfold was tied so tightly that Caitlin saw stars. Descending the stairs one at a time, she grasped at the pitted metal railing.

"*¿Está todo bien?*" A woman's voice came from somewhere. She repeated the question in English. "Is everything okay?"

The reptile hissed, "*Multa. Métete en tus asuntos.*" Mind your own business. "Fucking nosy neighbor," he said under his breath.

Caitlin navigated the bottom stair, stubbing the toe of her shoe on the flat walkway. "Ah."

"Keep your head down and your mouth shut." He jabbed her in the kidney with a straight finger. She arched her back, walking nervously, her fingers touching his forearm, guiding her.

They had to be near the street, close to where she'd seen the truck and trailer parked the first night when she'd stood on the bed and looked out the window. She knew from the noises, it was street traffic. A car passed nearby, and then another.

"Come on," he said, yanking her forearm, pulling her. His

pace was uneven, and with his hand now clamped to her arm, she felt his slight limp.

A truck door huffed open. "Get in."

Using her arms as feelers, she patted the air with flat palms.

He pushed down on her skull. Her head brushed the top of the frame as she leaned in, tapping her fingers, feeling for the seat. She used her left hand to balance and sit, scooting sideways onto the passenger seat.

Her stomach flinched at the smell. The truck cab reeked of Mack's sour breath. Her heart skipped as the lizard leaned across her torso, pulling the seatbelt across her chest, pinning her to the seat as he latched it. She felt the round metal of his Kimber Ultra Carry II pressing on her ear.

"Do you know what that is?"

"Uh-huh."

"Don't make me use it."

Walking her fingers over her thighs, she felt for the edge of the miniskirt and pulled it taut over her skin. "Where are we going?"

"Shut the fuck up. And get down."

She obeyed, and leaned forward, hanging her chin toward her chest.

He grabbed the back of her neck and pushed it down farther. "Keep your pie hole shut. That way I don't have to tell you to *shut the fuck up* again."

How dare he? Shut the *fuck* up? Her mother would slap her mouth for saying that.

Her door chuffed closed. He opened his, climbed behind the wheel and started the engine. The diesel coughed to life. He eased his foot on the accelerator and the F-250 rolled from the curb. If it were still connected to the trailer, she'd have felt the lurching when he pulled onto the roadway, but she did not.

The aches in her joints and muscles started all over again.

Where was he taking her? And why? The blindfold squeezed one ear. Fingers trembling, she reached to adjust it.

The punch he threw at her shoulder knocked her head against the passenger window. "Awwww!"

She raised her elbows to cover her face. He accelerated, pushing her against the seatback. He turned right so sharply she rolled toward the center console. Grabbing the underside of the dashboard, she pulled her body upright. He stopped and reached across her. The glove box popped open, slapping her kneecaps.

"Gimme your hands."

Oh, no. He spun the thin plastic around her wrists. It crackled as he pulled it tight. The zip tie cut into her skin, reigniting the burning sensation, producing a pain far sharper than the dull throb in her head.

"Do it again and I'll hit you twice as hard."

She swallowed with a gulp. This time there were no tears.

He drove without speaking for thirty, maybe forty minutes. The stop-and-go suggested he'd taken surface streets through traffic.

He slowed, then stopped and killed the engine. She felt his breath as he leaned over the center console and ripped the blindfold from her face.

Awww.

The sunlight was white and sharp. She gave her eyes time to adjust, blinking and squinting, then raised her head and looked around.

It was the truck Mack drove. Definitely the same one he'd used to pull the trailer cross-country. The empty bottle she'd drank from was on the floorboards, reminding her it was the last thing she remembered before waking up in the dark apartment.

"Hands up."

She raised them, peering out the window on her side as he snipped the tie.

Oh, my God.

She knew the place.

"Wait here." He jogged around the front bumper, his right shoulder dipping slightly from his irregular gait.

She saw the colorful sign staked in the grass in front of the horseshoe driveway: Kidz. She'd worked there over the summer. She knew the people. Teachers, families, children.

The passenger door clunked open.

"Why are we—"

"Get out."

"Why? What are we doing here?"

"Get out. Now."

She stepped onto the running board, one hand on the doorframe, the other pulling down on the back seam of the miniskirt. It was definitely the daycare center where her dad had helped her get a part-time job last summer.

"Hey." He brandished the handgun, holding it low, hiding it behind the open truck door. "Don't try anything stupid. You understand?"

"Don't point that at me."

"You need to shut the . . . up!"

Why were they here, at the place she used to work? It made no sense.

He tilted his head and flicked his eyes toward the driveway at the entrance to the one-story bungalow. "They're expecting you. You're here to pick Lizzie up."

What? "Why would I be picking Lizzie up?" She hadn't seen the little girl since the fall, when she'd quit her job to start school.

He snapped at her. "If you do one thing to make them suspicious, I'll start by killing your brother."

What?

He slammed the truck door behind her. "His name's Will, right?"

She couldn't breathe. Her knees wobbled as she steadied herself, grasping the passenger door handle. She let go and squatted, using one hand to break the fall, the other to wrestle the skirt.

His reptile eyes bored into her. "Get the fuck up. On your feet."

"Okay. Okay. All right." Her voice cracked. She swallowed hard, her windpipe constricting, face burning red hot. "Then what am I supposed to do?"

The yellow-and-brown speckles in his eyes flashed, changing shapes like a kaleidoscope. "Bring Lizzie back here, to me, at the truck. She knows you. She'll go with you. I'll be waiting."

He smacked the back of her thighs and rotated his index finger, as in "Hurry up."

She glanced at the dashboard clock. It was too early to pick up the children. His was the only vehicle on the street. He'd parked far enough away to be out of the line of sight of the daycare center's front windows.

As part of her old job, she'd escorted the children during drop-off and pick-up times. Usually, long lines of cars—fancy SUVs and luxury imports—snaked for blocks during certain hours.

Miss Jenkins was vigilant about cross-checking IDs on the preschool's app. When she worked there, she'd been taught to flag a substitute driver on the child's profile, and to use caution before letting a child to leave with anyone she didn't recognize.

Fingers quivering, she rang the buzzer.

Miss Jenkins answered. At first, she looked happy to see her, then her expression changed to one of disapproval, stepping back and eyeing the skimpy outfit.

"You girls." She shook her head and hugged her. "It's great to see you. Oh, we're so busy here. You know how it is. You're here to pick Lizzie up. She was so excited when I told her you were coming today."

A young staff member escorted the little girl to the cheerful lobby. Lizzie ran straight to her, throwing her arms around Caitlin's knees.

"That's great that you're helping her mom out," Miss Jenkins said. "I guess she had some sort of emergency. Is your mother with you?"

"Um, yeah. She's waiting outside." She flicked her head toward the door. "In the car. She's always in such a hurry, running around all the time, trying to find things for people's houses." Her mom was an interior designer who often shopped with the urgency of a heart surgeon prepping for an organ transplant.

Miss Jenkins smiled. "How's your first year in high school going?"

"Um . . . it's okay. I better not keep my mom waiting. You know how she is."

Miss Jenkins hesitated. "Is everything all right?"

Five-year-old Lizzie grabbed her hand and squeezed it. "Let's go." The little girl skipped in place.

"Everything's fine." Caitlin smiled weakly.

"Well, say hello to your mom." Miss Jenkins leaned over. "'Bye, Lizzie."

Lizzie sang, "'Bye, Miss Jenkins. See you tom-or-row."

"Good to see you, Caitlin."

The pair walked out the door, across the driveway, holding hands, then took a left toward the truck parked beyond a thick hedge.

"Who's that?" Lizzie Dinero balked when she saw the truck.

"He's my friend." She pulled Lizzie by the arm to the passenger door where he stood waiting. He'd retracted the center console to make space between the seats, gesturing to both of them to get in. As she lifted Lizzie, he stared at the little girl, his beady eyes narrowing like a snake's.

Lizzie drew closer to her. "It's okay," she whispered, helping the little girl into the space between the seats.

He started the engine.

Lizzie scooted away from him. Caitlin wrapped her arm around Lizzie's shoulders.

"Hi, honey. My name is Greg. Your daddy and my daddy used to be really good friends, a long time ago. Did you know your daddy worked for my daddy?"

Lizzie looked up with big brown eyes. "Really?" Her expression brightened. "Who's your daddy?"

"My daddy is Chago Marino. And he's dead. Someone killed him in prison."

Lizzie recoiled. Her tiny brow furrowed.

"He's playing," Caitlin said.

"It's not funny." The little girl stuck her lower lip out. Her expression changed from one of fear to one of protest. She looked at Caitlin. "Where's *your* mommy?"

"She's busy. You heard me tell Miss Jenkins she's working. Your mom will come and get you later. We're going to my friend Greg's house first."

Lizzie leaned closer to her, wrapping her arms around her waist. "I don't like your friend," she whispered.

She wanted to say "Me neither," but for now she needed to play the role of the strong person so the little girl wouldn't be frightened.

Use your big voice.

That's what her mom told her to do.

For now, she'd be quiet. She had to submit to this monster or he might kill her. Might kill them all. *Might kill her brother.*

Lizzie and Greg's fathers knew each other. But how did her dad fit into the puzzle? She'd never met Lizzie's dad and never heard of Greg's father, Chago Marino. Strange dots appeared but nothing seemed to connect them.

42

L auren pulled her hair into a ponytail and splashed cold water on her face. The idea that a hovercraft might have been used to take Caitlin wasn't crazy. She slipped out of her room, stopped at Davis' and knocked on his door, but he didn't answer. She headed to the front desk to chat with Adam.

"Have you seen Mr. Pompadour?"

"Not recently." Adam looked up from his computer, then past her with a surprised look on his face.

She turned to see what caught his attention.

Roy was huddled with the Israeli woman. When he saw her, they split.

Lauren approached him. "Can we talk? Privately?"

With an outstretched arm, he directed her to the game room off the foyer and shut the door. "I was looking for you earlier. Where'd you go?"

"To Alpine."

"With who?"

"Daryl."

"Why?"

"He told me he has a friend there who might be able to help find Caitlin." She told Roy about the full-screen footage she'd seen at Kit's, showing Caitlin and the hovercraft.

"You should have told someone where you were going."

She twisted the end of her ponytail. "I shouldn't have gone?"

"I didn't say that. But it would have been the courteous thing to do, under the circumstances."

"I figured since you asked him to help with the search, it would be okay."

"Is that what he told you? That I asked him to help?"

She paused, doubting herself, wondering if that's what he'd really said. "Maybe I assumed it."

"Have you heard from Vance or Jake?"

She told him she'd exchanged a few casual texts with Vance. "Do you know that Daryl's going to Miami today?"

The pupils of Roy's eyes dilated; his irises disappeared. "How do you know that?"

She showed him the picture she'd taken of his airline ticket. "Kit told me Daryl was a prison guard."

His pupils blew up again. "Did you ask him why he's going to Florida?"

"No. If I did, he'd know I snooped in his stuff."

"I see," Roy said.

"Have you seen Davis?"

"Josh drove him to Midland."

"What? When?"

"Last night. He asked me if he could leave. I said it was okay. There's no reason for him to hang around. We'll reschedule the shoot when things settle down."

"I understand," she said, though she didn't because Davis had promised to stick around.

"Will you text that to me? The picture of Daryl's airline ticket?"

She opened her phone, tapped the photo and sent it him. "It just seems weird."

A young woman, a guest she figured, smiled as she walked past them on her way to join friends sitting at one of the long tables in the dining hall. Roy's eyes tracked her.

"Rosa told me about your niece."

Roy didn't respond.

"I just wanted to say how sorry I am."

He stared out the window at the humpback where Caitlin disappeared. "Back when the Feds shut down the Caribbean routes, the Colombians started working with the Mexicans smuggling drugs across our border," Roy said. "They got so big they ended up putting the Colombians out of business. Drug smuggling is like water. Close off one route and it finds another. The Mexicans make the Cubans look like choirboys. They have no code of honor."

Wow. That was saying something. Miami was a scary place back when the Cuban cartels ran the city. The streets had become so dangerous it launched the original war on drugs. But it hadn't done much to stop people from buying them. All you had to do was look around. No one went to downtown Miami any more. The blatant drug dealing. The crime. The homeless. It was so sad.

"Is that what you think happened? That the cartels took her?" As soon as the words were out, she could hardly breathe.

"I didn't say that."

"Do you think it's possible?"

Roy gazed out the game room window, at the westernmost berm where Jake found Caitlin's backpack. "Of course it's possible."

There was a knock at the door. Roy answered it.

It was the Israeli woman. "Sir, may we have a moment with you?"

Roy turned to Lauren. "I hate to cut our talk short, but would you excuse us?"

"Of course."

Hand-signaling to her men to hurry, they funneled in and surrounded Roy. The woman pulled the door shut in her face. She stood on the other side, staring at it, mouth slightly agape.

If Roy hadn't set up the search ride with Daryl, she wouldn't have gone to Alpine. If she'd trusted him, it was because she trusted Roy.

"Is everything all right, Miss Gold?" Adam asked.

She forced a smile. "Uh-huh."

The landline rang. Adam ran to answer it.

She made a beeline to her room, hoping like hell Daryl wasn't spying on her. Time to talk to Vance. Alone, she tapped his number. It rang once and went to voicemail. She didn't leave a message. Next, she called Davis. His phone went straight to voicemail, too. She tossed her phone in the air. It landed on the mattress and bounced once.

DAVIS FROST LOOKED both ways before walking barefoot to the vending machine, buying a bag of potato chips and a candy bar for breakfast. Last night, he'd checked into a cheap airport motel off Interstate 20, and slept poorly.

He blotted his face with a limp towel and peeked through the drapes. The parking lot was empty. Last night it had filled with pickup trucks and oil field workers loitering outside their rooms, drinking beer.

His burner buzzed. He recognized the number. "What's your ETA?"

Karl, who'd been looking after the yacht during his trip to the ranch, had been worried when Davis first told him the shoot was delayed. He had another job lined up, moonlighting at one of the chemical plants.

"I'll be back ahead a schedule," Davis said.

"When?"

"This afternoon."

"I might have to leave a little early. I wanna spend some time with the family before I start my new gig tonight. You gonna be able to pay me or do I have to wait for Jake?"

"You'll have to wait for Jake. I hope that's not a problem."

Karl hesitated. "Do you know when he'll be back?"

"In a couple of days, I think. If I don't see you, thanks for everything."

"You got it," Karl said.

The motel shuttle ran every hour. He checked the time. Better get ready if he was going to make the flight to Houston.

43

"Oh, come here, child." Isabel did her best to comfort Lizzie but the little girl pulled away, tightening her grip around Caitlin's waist.

She wondered how this kind, old woman could protect them from Greg and his goon. The big voice she'd planned to summon, wasn't answering. Mack at the door was unfazed when Lizzie screamed after seeing his carbine and the arc of bullets sprouting from the stock. Mack told Lizzie to "Shut up," using the F-word. The little girl's eyes had widened and filled with tears.

Greg left an hour ago, but not before showing them his foot. *Ewww.*

It was so gross. He'd taken his sock and shoe off and put it on the sofa next to her, trying to stroke her thigh with it. Her entire body shuddered at the thought. She'd been taught not to stare at people with deformities but no one told her what to do if someone goaded her with a disfigurement the way he had.

Lizzie's reaction was unfiltered. "Yucky. What's wrong with your foot?"

"It's called elephantiasis. It's caused by worms."

"Ewww," the little girl screeched and recoiled. "Worms, ewww."

He was proud of it. "Wanna see me wiggle my toes?"

Lizzie leaned away and looked at it. "You don't have any toes. Even elephants have toes."

"Got two toenails. Wanna see me move them?" He moved the funky foot closer to Caitlin's thigh. Lizzie wriggled to get away from it.

His foot was a rectangular box of flesh with nails growing from a pair of two square toes. How he didn't walk like the Hunchback of Notre Dame was a mystery.

"There's no need to do that," Isabel said. "Ju put that thing on the floor. Where it belongs. And put a shoe on it."

Lizzie curled up next to Caitlin like a caterpillar and squeezed her eyes shut.

Greg stood and confronted Isabel. "Wanna touch it?"

"Stop," Isabel said. "Ju know better than to torture a child, or an old woman. I said ju put a shoe on it."

Caitlin squeezed Lizzy's hand.

"You know who I am, you old gossip. You think I don't remember you whispering behind my back? When I was a kid? Here you are now, protecting Ray's kid. I don't remember you defending me." He flicked his frogeyes at her.

That was the last thing Greg said before he left. He told them he had to run an errand and barked orders at the pit bull, leaving him and his machine gun in charge. Mack sat in the wicker chair with a cushion he'd swapped for the plastic crate, guarding the front door of the tiny apartment, the only way out.

"He knows my daddy?" Lizzie asked, whispering.

She shrugged. "I don't know."

Isabel fixed sandwiches in the dim kitchen, serving them on

plastic plates. Lizzie tore little bits of bologna and white bread, squeezing the dough between her thumb and forefinger, making dollhouse house-sized sandwiches.

Over the last couple of days, she'd eaten hardly more than a few granola bars and some pretzels. The pretzels. That reminded her of the road trip where she'd passed out in the truck and woke up in the apartment. Mack must have drugged her. There was no other explanation. Her head still ached, but not nearly as much now as it did that first morning.

Her mom and dad must be sick with worry. Lizzie's must be worried, too. If only she could find a way to communicate with someone, find a link to the outside world.

Lizzie rearranged the tiny sandwiches on her plate. "When is my mommy coming?"

"Soon, sweetie." What else could she say?

Isabel sat on the other side of the little girl. "Ju going to be fine. We're all going to be fine."

"You know him? Greg?" Caitlin asked.

"Yes, from a long time ago." Isabel sounded sad. "When he was just a small boy. I knew his daddy."

"His daddy's dead," Lizzie said, shrinking.

"I know," the old woman said.

"Does he know my dad?" Caitlin asked.

"I don't know. I don't think so," Isabel said. "He knows my son."

"Do you know my dad?" Caitlin asked.

"No. I don't know jur dad."

Lizzie looked up, puzzled, crinkling her nose like a mouse. The cast of characters was too confusing for a five-year-old. Too confusing for a fifteen-year-old, too.

She played it in her head. Greg said her dad was a thief who stole his inheritance. He knew Isabel's son. Greg said he knew

Lizzie's daddy. Then she remembered something. Her dad knew the man who helped her get the job at Kidz. He owned a yacht brokerage on the Miami River. His name was Ray Dinero.

Oh, my God. Of course. That was the connection.

It hit like a tsunami. Lizzie's dad was Ray Dinero, the man who owned the yacht place. They'd gone to his boatyard last spring when her father visited from Texas. How did Isabel fit in the picture? Who was her son? She wanted to ask, but not in front of Lizzie.

Her father wasn't a crook like Greg said. She remembered an old story. Her dad had a friend who went to prison for something called "insider trading." Lots of people hated bankers. They called them one-percenters.

Is that what Greg meant when he accused her dad of stealing his inheritance? Did he give bad investment advice that bankrupted him? Another thought crept into her head, the day she'd seen her dad in the garage with the neighbor lady. She'd have never believed it if she hadn't seen it with her own eyes. Was it possible he was a crook?

Lizzie reached for her hand and peeled Caitlin's fingers open. "It's pretty," she said, turning the rose-colored ring on her finger. "Did you see his arm?" She cowered and pointed at Mack.

Mack pulled his shirtsleeve higher. "It's a tattoo. Set me back two-grand. Betcha can't tell an Apache, from a Chinook from a Blackhawk. Probably all look the same to you."

Isabel glared at him. Caitlin shook her head.

Mack sneered. "Figures. It's an Apache. Carries a payload of Hydra-Seventy rocket pods and Hellfire missiles. The US Army's premier assault chopper. Flown 'em all. That thing I flew when I caught you?"

Her heart raced. "What about it?"

"Piece a cake. Like an IndyCar driver behind the wheel of a

golf cart. Thing practically flies itself." He licked his lips. "I'm gonna make a boatload of money. Gotta admit, the best part was ambushing you. Mighta done that just for sport."

44

The storm had intensified, turning I-95 into a carwash. Vance exited at Southwest 30th, taking the scenic route along South Miami Avenue. Traffic slowed where it turned into Bayshore Drive, and came to a standstill. Misty red halos glowed up ahead.

He checked the traffic app on his phone. A wreck blocked the southbound lanes. Alternate routes, Tigertail and Dixie Highway, were just as bad. He put his phone on his thigh and felt the vibration. Glancing down, he saw Lauren's number. He couldn't talk with Jake sitting next to him. He pressed the red button.

It buzzed again.

A blast of adrenaline mainlined his system.

Shit.

A sinking feeling set in; he debated answering it. A call from the old Dos Guapos drug pilot, Ray Dinero, wasn't random.

"Long time, no hear. How'd you get my number?"

"Sorry to call you out of the blue." Ray spoke fast, and though Cuban-born, had almost no accent. He sounded worried. "I'm glad I got you."

"How'd you know I'm in Miami?"

"Didn't. What are you doing here?"

"Visiting."

Before the Feds cracked down, the Colombians used a network of Cuban-Americans to smuggle drugs through Florida. Ray had worked for his Uncle Tony during the '80s and '90s, piloting billions of dollars of cocaine in airplanes and powerboats.

He was also the conduit to the original salvage of their chunk of the seventy-five million-dollar haul of drug cash now hidden in the hull of Jake's yacht in Texas.

"I'm looking for Jake. I need a current number."

Jesus. Jake sat next to him in the passenger seat. He hesitated.

"You there?" Ray asked.

Rain pummeled the windshield. "I'm here."

"I need to talk to him."

"Why?"

"It's personal."

It was out of character for Ray to act dodgy.

"I need a little more than that."

"I can't go into it. I need his current number. I tried the one I had and some lady in Queens answered."

"People change numbers."

"It's an emergency."

"It's an emergency." He didn't know "emergency" was in Ray's vocabulary. "What kind of emergency?"

"Damn it! My little girl is missing and there're eyewitnesses saying Jake's kid took my kid."

"What?"

"I don't have time to explain it."

"You're gonna have to try." He glanced across at Jake engrossed in the app, searching for a shortcut through traffic.

"Does this have anything to do with you being back in Miami? If it does, and you have anything to do with my missing kid, I'll kill you. I swear to God, I'll—"

"Don't threaten me."

Jake looked up from his phone.

"The daycare center my girls go to called me. They said Jake's daughter was there earlier."

"That doesn't make sense."

"I know. She used to work there. She had a summer job working at the daycare center," Ray said.

"You're sure about that?"

"Fuck, yeah. I got her the job."

Shit. "Hang on." He put his thumb over the mic. "Did Caitlin work at a daycare center?"

Jake's eyes widened. "Who wants to know?"

"Ray Dinero. His kid's missing, too."

"Gimme that." Jake snatched the phone. "Good God, Ray. Do you know where my daughter is?"

VANCE NOSED the Altima into an opening between the grassy medians dividing the north and southbound lanes along Bayshore Drive. He flashed his brights at oncoming traffic until three motorists stopped and let him across. He parked at the marina across the street from his old haunt, the Hotel Mutiny.

The wipers thrashed the windscreen and salty ocean air wafted through the vents. Biscayne Bay had turned charcoal with white-capped waves crashing against the seawall. The early afternoon sky was a lighter shade of gray.

Jake hunched over with the phone glued to his ear, scratching the back of his neck with his free hand.

Listening. Nodding. Shaking his head. Listening some more.

When he ended the call, his face was as pale as the gauze around his head.

"What was that about?"

"A couple of months ago I dropped in on Ray Dinero, to say hi to him at the boatyard. I was visiting my kids. I took my daughter with me. We were chatting and I told him she was looking for a summer job. Ray asked what she liked to do and she told him she liked working with kids." Jake paused, kneading his knuckles like dough. "He offered to talk to the owner at the daycare center where his girls go. A place called Kidz over in Pinecrest."

He'd never heard of Kidz, but he knew where Pinecrest was. An affluent, upper middle-class neighborhood east of Kendall, flattened by Hurricane Andrew in 1992, now rebuilt.

"Did she get the job?"

"Yeah. She loved working there. But it was only temporary. She quit when school started in the fall." His voice cracked, he paused, then continued. "Ray said his five-year-old went missing today. He said when his wife went to pick the girls up, the youngest was gone. The owner said she left with Caitlin. She said she saw my daughter."

The look on Jake's face was pure panic.

Vance ran scenarios in his head.

Jake shook his head. "I don't see how it's possible."

Vance did. It was the first solid clue they'd gotten. He had to play his cards very close. Greg Marino was the common denominator to all three kidnappings. The money was another link to all three victims.

"It means she's in Miami. And that she's alive."

Jake shook his head slowly, then faster and faster. "My daughter would never take a child."

He leaned on the steering column. "Did he say how it happened?"

"Ray said she was on the list to pick Lizzie up. They do it all online, on an app, for security. There must be some sort of mistake. There's got to be an explanation." He pushed his thumbs into his temples. "Ray says there's security footage showing Caitlin taking her."

Thoughts spun through his head. Ray Dinero wouldn't have this wrong. The daycare center's app must have been hacked.

"Whoever put her up to it forced her," he said.

Jake looked sucker-punched. "What? My daughter is no kidnapper. She wouldn't harm a fly. I'm positive of that. She didn't do it."

"I'm not passing judgment. But the timeline works. Think about it. We got a hit on the fitness ring she's wearing. She was in Alabama two days ago. Ray's kid knows your daughter. If she worked there, the staff knows her, too. Ray isn't attacking Caitlin. Someone's using her. Ray's trying to find his kid. Like you are."

"I feel like I'm losing my mind."

"Did he say when it happened?"

"Today. This morning. I don't know."

"Did they report it to the police?"

Jake shook his head. "Ray said the woman who runs the daycare center wanted to report it. He talked her out of calling 9-1-1. He made me promise not to call the cops, either."

That was good. "We have a solid lead now. If there's surveillance footage," he paused to word it carefully, "we might be able to prove Caitlin is in Miami. We need to go to the daycare center. I'm gonna call Ray back and ask him to tell them to wait for us. He's right. We don't want the cops involved."

Jake rolled his hands into fists. "Maybe we *should* call the police. How do we know it's not an ambush? What if someone's using the kids to get to us? Or it's a sting operation to bust us?"

"The cops would never use kids in a sting operation. No way. The courts would never allow it."

"You're right," Jake said. "We can't call the police."

"Don't forget, my mother's missing, too."

Jake's breath fogged the window on the passenger's-side. "I don't know. Maybe we should call the police."

"Listen to me." He waited until he was sure Jake was listening. "Somehow Caitlin was on the approved list to pick her up. Let's assume Ray's kid goes willingly. Let's assume there's video of it. The daycare center doesn't need the bad publicity or the legal headache. We'll convince them it's a simple mistake. It's too big a liability for them. That gives us leverage. Time to figure it out."

Jake crumpled against the passenger door. His shoulders drooped. "You think she did it."

"It looks bad. She disappears from a ranch in Texas and ends up in Miami. A little girl is kidnapped from the place she used to work. You don't know how she got here, or where she is, or where she's been for the last two days. We need to figure this out. Not the cops."

Jake chewed his lower lip.

"I know it wasn't her idea to take Ray's kid—"

"You *really* think she did it."

"I think someone is behind it and I want to know what they want and why they did this."

A car honked. He'd been blocking the covered walkway to the main entrance of the marina. There was a payphone outside, next to the building. He pulled into an open spot, parked, and called Ray.

"Wait here. I'm gonna call the daycare center." He jumped from the rental and ran in the rain, pulling the booth door closed. He googled the number on his cell, wiped the mouthpiece of the payphone with his sleeve, dropped coins into slot, and dialed.

He cleaned a circle on glass with his shirttail. This was

where his luxury sailing yacht, *The Second Wind*, went down during Hurricane Irma. There was no sign of her skeleton. He owed salvage money to the owner.

A woman answered on the third ring. "Hello?"

"My name's Vance Courage. I might have some information about the girl who went missing from your daycare center."

"Her father just called," the woman said. "He asked me to talk to you. I'll wait, but please hurry."

45

The agent leaned over the counter, funneling her hands around her mouth, baring her teeth as if embarrassed. "The ticket is twenty-six hundred dollars."

"One way or round trip?" Lauren asked.

"Round trip."

"Is it changeable?"

"Yes."

"I'll take it."

She'd already shelled out two-hundred bucks to the Uber driver to take her to the airport in Midland. She squatted and pressed her knees against the ticket counter, balancing her purse on her thighs, and pulled a wad of hundreds from a bank envelope. Counting twenty-nine bills, two-hundred extra to cover airport fees and taxes, she handed the cash to the agent. "I'd like a window seat, please."

"I'm sure that won't be a problem. Excuse me for a moment."

The rep left and returned with another person, a man with a naturally serious expression—a supervisor, she assumed. He asked to see her ID again and walked away from the counter, turning his back. He huddled with the agent for a moment. A minute later the pair returned and the man handed her license back.

"Have a nice trip, Miss Gold," the supervisor said.

The agent printed the boarding pass. "Sorry for the inconvenience." She pointed to the security lanes. "Go to the first class line."

She hurried, showing her ID and boarding pass again, and was ushered through. Walking to the gate, she stopped in the Ladies Room. She checked herself in the mirror, took a ball cap from her messenger bag and set it on the counter. Piling her ponytail atop her head, she put the hat on and straightened the brim.

Like a magician, she pulled a long scarf from her bag and draped it around her neck. She changed her mind, she stuffed it back in her bag, then riffled for a pair of reading glasses. She headed to the gate, stopping at the newsstand to buy a copy of *People* magazine.

She waited at the front of the line and was the third passenger on the plane. She stowed her bags in the overhead and slouched against the window. The flight attendant, a perky fellow with a pencil-thin mustache, offered her a beverage. She passed, asking for a blanket, instead.

When she got it, she wrapped it around her neck, took the phone from her purse and placed it beneath the magazine on her lap. Using the blanket for privacy, she tapped the photo of the ticket she'd snapped of Daryl's ticket and double-checked the picture with her boarding pass, flight numbers, and date on the ticket she'd just purchased. It all matched. She enlarged the photo to see Daryl's seat number.

A text pinged. Need to talk. It was from Josh.

It was a little late for that. She ignored the message and opened the magazine. She picked her phone back up and looked at the link from Kit. If she was going to walk a tightrope, she might as well have a safety net. She downloaded the software and sent a green checkmark to the old hacker.

Ten minutes later, Daryl Flood passed through the first class cabin heading to the back of the plane. She held the open magazine in front of her face, shoulder pressed against the window. The distance between them was good. It would give her time to exit the aircraft before he'd have the chance to see her.

The man with the thin mustache whooshed the curtain dividing first class from coach. She turned off her phone, closed her eyes and took a deep breath. The flight to Houston took an hour and a half. Hopefully, there wouldn't be any delays, giving her time to change gates without him seeing her.

46

When he ended the call with the woman at the daycare center, Vance left the phone booth open and jogged to the Nissan. Slipping behind the wheel, hair dripping, he wrestled his wet jacket off and laid it across the center console. He'd have used it as a hoodie but needed to keep the Glock holstered under his left arm, dry.

"We're good to go. They're expecting us."

"I called Ann," Jake said. "She's home. She was carjacked by some kid high on drugs."

"Carjacked? No shit. That's scary. Where'd it happen?"

"Downtown. She knows better than going there in her Jag with the windows down."

"She did that?"

"Yeah. The car's been recovered. The police have it at the impound lot. She tried to fight back but the kid pushed her down and broke her arm. She's mad as hell and worried sick about Caitlin. I didn't tell her she might be in Miami. She's looking for the box the fitness tracker came in."

"That's probably not going to help at this point."

"I know."

Traffic had thinned.

"I'm going to do a quick drive by my mom's place, see if our new friends are around." A text from Lauren pinged on his phone. `Arriving MIA on the 8 PM flight.`

Jake inflated his cheeks like a puffer fish, and exhaled slowly. "My ex got carjacked by a meth head. My daughter's missing, your mother's gone, Ray's little girl disappeared, and we're going to see if the cops are on a stakeout in front of your mom's place in the Gables? You'd think they'd have better things to do. Like go out and solve some crimes."

"You'd think."

"Shouldn't we have heard something by now? Like a ransom demand?" Jake asked.

The storm had passed and the sky had turned as blue as a robin's egg, and cooler, drier air filled the rental. No sign of the Crown Vic. He drove around the block and parked four doors down.

Sophia let them in.

Jake excused himself to go to the bathroom again. He returned and dropped the gauze headband into the kitchen trash. The gash over his left eyebrow had dried to a dark-brown streak.

"Where does Mom keep the keys to Dad's car?"

Sophia crooked a finger at the pegboard on the wall, next to the front door. He grabbed the keys to the old Volvo.

She caught up with him, tottering. "Where ju going?"

"Keep the doors locked. If I call, I'll let it ring twice, I'll hang up and call again. That way you'll know it's me. Otherwise, don't answer. Have you heard from Kathy?"

He'd texted his sister and asked her to come to the house to stay with Sophia. Now he hoped she wouldn't.

"She called. She say she very busy with the boys. I don't tell her nothing about the trouble here. I tell her everything's okay, that ju and jur friend are staying here."

"Good." He hugged her. "Don't go out and don't answer the door. I'll be back as soon as I can."

He pulled the tarp from his late dad's classic car. The engine turned over on the third try. Jake climbed into the passenger seat. Vance checked the fuel gauge. It was one of those old-fashioned red toothpicks that bounced up and down like an antique compass. Half a tank would be more than enough to get them to the daycare center.

He pressed the garage door opener on the visor and backed down the driveway.

The air conditioning blew hot. Hand-cranking the driver's-side window down, he turned the A/C to the off position, put the car in park, got out and opened the convertible top.

Thank goodness it had stopped raining, and that it was March; summertime would be unbearable, even with the top down.

It should have been an easy drive from Coral Gables to the daycare center off US-1, but Dixie Highway was mess. Vance turned on the radio. WIOD-AM was in the middle of a traffic update. A fender-bender at Dixie and 72nd Street Southwest had wreckers on the scene. A young woman with a velvety voice said the accident would slow things down through rush hour. Miami traffic could thicken quicker than cornstarch in hot water. The old Volvo was known to overheat.

He turned down the volume on the radio and asked Jake to monitor the traffic on his phone, updating him with the estimated times of arrival. He'd promised the owner they'd get to the daycare center before the place closed at five o'clock.

47

The flight attendant with the skinny mustache passed through the first class cabin, collecting trash. A minute later, football-fields of trees appeared below the wing, then the runway at Houston Intercontinental. Suddenly the plane throttled back up from five hundred feet with such thrust it pushed Lauren against the seatback with more force than during takeoff. She gripped the armrests.

"Good afternoon from the cockpit." The voice was Barry-White-silk. "Sorry for the slight inconvenience but it seems there's a plane on the runway. Air traffic control has informed us it'll be a few minutes. We're going to circle just east of the airport at about ten thousand feet and we should be arriving just a few minutes late."

Great. That would make the connection tighter, leaving less time to get to the gate before Daryl deplaned. The jet passed over a large lake and continued east. The port side wing dipped and the jetliner made a lazy turn to the west, leveled, then circled in a holding pattern. She checked the time on her phone. Ten minutes had passed.

"Where're you headed?" she asked the quiet man in the seat next to her on the aisle.

"Houston. It's my final stop. You?"

"Miami."

"I'd rather be going there. That was some move the pilot just made."

She pulled the blanket tighter around her neck. "I know. I could see the runway right under us."

"Never reassuring when something like that happens. You going home?"

She hesitated, then nodded.

Ten more minutes passed. The connection would be tighter.

The Barry White voice again: "Ladies and gentlemen, we've been cleared for landing. Sit back and relax. We'll have you the ground in just a few minutes."

The plane touched down a half an hour late, followed by more bad news from Captain Smoothie. "This is the captain from the flight deck. We're waiting for our gate to open. Weather has things backed up from here to Chicago. Thank you for your patience. Please be seated until we've turned off the fasten-seat-belt lights."

"They expect us to believe everything they say," her seatmate said. "I don't trust them. It's always about the money."

She turned her phone on. A green bubble popped up. It was from Vance. Okay. He'd acknowledged her message about her trip. She'd hoped he'd offer to pick her up, but no.

Another green bubble flashed. The sender name was UNAVAILABLE. Be careful of the thin man.

WTF? The message disappeared. She scrolled back through her old messages, then forward, looking for it, but it was gone. She closed her texting app and reopened it. The last message was from Vance.

She typed quickly: Does thin man mean anything to you? and sent it to Vance.

Folding the blanket on her lap, she stood, laid it on the seat, slung her purse and messenger bag over her shoulder, and bumped her head on the plastic overhead bin.

"Ouch."

"You okay?" the man on the aisle seat asked.

She adjusted the ball cap and tipped her neck forward, excusing herself, sliding past, between his knees and the seat-back. The flight attendant who'd helped her board the plane unloaded her carry-on. She waited like a runner in the blocks, ready to bolt as soon as the cabin door opened.

Glancing at the back of the plane, the aisle in coach had filled with passengers anxious to disembark.

Who sent the message? Did Kit send it? Or Josh? Who was "thin man"?

She felt her throat narrow.

Come on. *Come on.* Open the door already. What is the holdup?

Seven minutes later the cabin door finally opened. She pushed to the front of the line, and pulling her carry-on through the jetway, power-walked toward Gate 31-C. Daryl would be hustling, too. They had less than fifteen minutes between flights.

She arrived at the gate, glancing around, looking for Daryl. Boarding had begun and two separate lines converged down to a single one with travelers funneling into the jetway. The gate agent invited passengers from Group 5—steerage—to board, announcing the overhead bins were full, handing out claim checks. So much for first class.

She cut the line. "Excuse me."

The gate agent appeared put-out. People in line glared.

"I hate to be rude but I'm in first class and our flight was late getting in. I wanted to give you my name so you'll hold my seat." She pointed at the electronic board with the names of standby and first class passengers wait-listed. "I don't want to lose my seat."

The woman looked at her ticket, and scanned it. "Go ahead."

"I need to use the Ladies Room real quick. Sorry, but I can't wait."

"I'll need to hold your ticket. You have a couple of minutes. Hurry."

She used the line for cover and ducked into the Ladies Room, and removed the ball cap she'd been wearing, exchanging it for the scarf. Covering her head with the camel-colored fabric, she wound it around her neck, and draped the ends over the back of her shoulders. A woman washing her hands at the sink to her left, fish-eyed her. She ran her fingers around her hairline tucking in the strays.

She stood outside the restroom where she had a visual on the gate, looking for Daryl. The agent announced a final boarding call, followed by: "Passenger Gold, please check in at Gate 31-C."

Shit. She'd just broadcasted her name.

She watched from a kiosk selling cell phone chargers, and when the last few passengers straggled inside the ramp, she jogged to the gate.

"Passenger Gold, please check in at Gate 31-C."

She waved her hand in the air, trying to catch the attention of the woman she'd given her boarding pass to. A youngish man in a blue uniform waited for the okay to secure the door.

As she approached, the gate agent did a double-take eyeing the scarf on her head. Narrowing her eyes, mouthing the word damn, she picked up her two-way radio. "Wait here." She disappeared inside the jetway.

Another agent met the woman midway. She watched. The gate agent returned to the counter. "I'm sorry," she said. "Your seat is occupied."

"Then un-occupy it."

"We can't do that. We made two announcements."

"You gave my seat away? I dropped over two-and-a-half grand for this ticket."

"We have one seat left on the plane."

"I checked-in with you. You were holding my boarding pass. You can't do this."

"I can offer you a coach seat or I can call security. Your choice." The agent dangled a claim-check ticket.

She huffed. "Fine."

"I'll take care of your bag. They're holding the plane for you. Please hurry."

The fellow in the blue uniform waved them past and closed the door behind them. She followed the gate agent, running. An attractive African American woman met her at the cabin door. It clanked shut behind them and the engines started.

Head down, she pulled the scarf tighter around her neck, following closely behind the attendant. Row 38 was in the back of the aircraft. Chances were, she'd be seated somewhere behind Daryl.

The woman led the way, opening and closing bins, looking for space in the overheads. They were jam-packed. She stopped at Row 38. "There's no more room in the—"

"It's okay. My stuff will fit under the seat."

Two passengers stood and let her in.

At least it was a window seat. She shoved her purse and messenger bag under the seat in front of her. A dropdown monitor above opened and the safety video played on the screen. She watched it, thinking how much the airline must have paid for the production. Wannabe producers and directors could be found in every industry.

She looked at her phone. No new messages. She put it in AIRPLANE mode, slunk in the seat and looked out the porthole.

In less than five minutes the plane was airborne, heading east, toward Miami.

Vance drummed the wooden steering wheel on the vintage roadster. The text from Lauren gnawed at him. Thin man. It meant nothing to him.

He'd been idling in traffic with the ragtop down.

Jake wiped his brow with the cuff of his shirt. Other than taking turns bitching about gridlock, they'd ridden in silence. Jake refreshed the traffic app every thirty seconds. So far it hadn't suggested any alternate routes.

He smelled the sweet aroma of a hot radiator and checked the temperature gauge. The needle had ticked up a few notches, toward the red line.

Whoever was pulling the strings had set it up to look like Jake's daughter had abducted Ray's, a classic divide-and-conquer move.

Jake tapped the crystal on his Rolex. "I don't know if we're going to make it."

"Here, call Ray." Vance tossed his phone to Jake. "Ask him to call the daycare center and tell them to wait for us."

Jake scowled. "I'm not calling him. You do it. It's pissing me off that he's accusing my daughter of something I know she didn't do."

Vance pulled up recent calls and redialed.

Ray answered before it rang. "I'm on my way."

"Turn around. Go home. If there's surveillance, we don't need you there."

"Who's with you?"

"Jake."

"You want me to stay away but Jake's with you? He's fucking useless."

"Calm down."

The loud pop coming from Ray Dinero's phone hurt his eardrum. A thrashing that sounded like the mainsail on a sailboat flapping on a gusty day, followed.

"Shit!" Ray shouted.

"What's going on?"

"My fucking airbag—"

"Ray . . . RAY."

"What's happening?" Jake asked.

"I don't know."

"Ray?"

A grunt followed a groan, and then a series of angry snorts.

He held the phone away from his ear and yelled RAY into the speaker.

No answer. He fumbled the phone, accidentally pushing the keys, trying not to drop it. His mobile bounced off his knee and landed on the floor mat. He scooped it up and pushed it to his ear.

"Hello . . . hello . . . Vance? Are you there?"

He must have accidentally switched to a new caller. "Who's this?"

"It's Daniel."

God, Daniel's timing sucked. "I was on with Ray and lost him. I'll call you back."

"Ray's with me."

"What?"

"I can't talk right now."

"What do you mean you can't talk right now?" The asshole in front of him stopped at a green light. He tapped the horn on the Volvo. When the light turned red, the driver gunned it. "Daniel? You there?" He looked at the screen. It was Ray's phone. It pinged with a text: cops.

It switched to video chat. The angle looked up at the airbag hanging from the steering column.

"What's going on?" Jake asked.

The white blob took up half the screen. Sergeant Daniel Ruiz leaned into the shot, his face distorted from the weird angle.

Pretending to move the airbag out of the way, he looked into the camera, and whispered, "I gotta go. Keep watching." His palm covered the screen, and after he removed it, it was on a new angle facing the open driver's-side door.

He heard a voice. "You're under arrest."

He turned onto a side street and parked, watching the picture coming from Ray's phone burrowed in the deployed airbag. A tight shot of tan-colored pants filled the screen. Then an open palm pushed the airbag and phone away from the driver's-side seat.

The nose of a gun holstered to a shiny black utility belt bumped the lens. A chin came into view. He saw Kagan's face for a split second, her long auburn ponytail draped over her shoulder, then a giant thumb filled the screen, just before the screen turned black and the sound went mute.

Jake leaned over the gear knob and looked at the black screen, his face pasty, sweat beading on his brow.

Vance had to think. He typed "Kidz" into the browser. The search engine brought up the website and phone number. He pressed the CALL button.

A woman answered.

He placed his phone on SPEAKER, identified himself, and told her he was running late, stuck in traffic.

"I started worrying and called the cops," the woman said. "They said they'd send someone out."

"Are they there?"

"No. The dispatcher said she couldn't promise when they'd arrive. I'm going to call again."

"No, no, no. Sit tight. We'll be there soon. Don't do that. Listen to me, I'm a veteran of the Miami police department."

"You're a cop?"

"Detective."

"All right. But hurry. Please."

Jake pounded the dash. "Fucking-A traffic."

Didn't Ray tell her not to call the cops? His instincts kicked in. If he was going to play investigator, that meant he'd keep his thoughts to himself.

HE PULLED into Kidz's horseshoe driveway and parked the Volvo a few minutes after six o'clock.

A very worried-looking woman paced the walkway. When she saw him pull in, she hurried over and introduced herself. "I'm Cecelia Jenkins. Come inside."

She smelled like booze.

Jake pulled himself out of the sports car and lumbered up the stoop.

This time, Vance had the full bladder. "Where's your men's room?"

Jenkins pointed to a brightly lit corridor with children's drawings pinned to both sides of the walls.

"Down the hall and to the left."

Jake followed Jenkins to an office.

"Cue the video and wait for me," Vance said.

He checked for messages while walking the hallway. Nothing new. In the bathroom, he dictated a message to Lauren: text me when you land and pressed the SEND button. He washed his hands, dried them on his slacks, then met up with the other two.

The office was small and sparse, with two black metal desks on linoleum tile. Jake and Jenkins watched four flat-screen monitors mounted high on the wall. They were frozen on different angles showing Jake's daughter with a little girl.

Jake rubbed his Adam's apple, his mouth agape.

Vance dragged a metal chair closer to the monitor and stood on it. Jake's daughter was dressed like a hooker. "Can you back it up to the first scene when she entered the building?"

Jenkins recued the video and started it over. It was about two, two-and-a-half minutes total. There was no audio. Cecelia Jenkins let Caitlin in. A minute later Lizzie appeared in the camera frame, then ran to Caitlin and hugged her knees.

Jake stared at the screens.

"Was anyone with her?" Vance asked.

Jenkins shook her head. "I'm just sick about this. We take precautions to make sure nothing like this happens. But when your daughter—"

He held his hand up to stop her. "Jake's daughter disappeared three days ago."

Jenkins gasped. "Oh, my God. Why didn't someone tell me?"

"Are there any other cameras?" he asked.

"Just what I've shown you."

He heard the first few bars of an Adele song. It was Jenkins phone. She answered it and left the room.

He followed her but by the time he caught up, Jenkins had ended the call.

"Lizzie's mom keeps calling. What am I supposed to do? What am I supposed to tell her?"

"I know the family," Vance said.

Jenkins slumped into a desk chair. She opened her desk drawer and removed an airplane bottle of red wine, untwisted the cap and drank directly from it. "Oh, my God, I can't believe this is happening."

"Go home."

"I can't do that."

"Call an Uber. Go home."

"What if the cops come?"

"I'll deal with it."

"He's right," Jake said. "Go home."

"Stay with her until her ride comes," he said to Jake. "I'll be back."

He jogged to the curb, studying the line of sight, looking for houses with a direct view of the daycare center. Tips of a tall, wrought-iron fence poked from the top of a thick hedge hiding the house across the street. He approached and rang the buzzer at the gate. No answer.

The house next door, a modest bungalow with two Japanese sedans parked in the driveway, had a tricycle lying on its side partially blocking the path to the walkway. The doorbell camera was about eye level. He trotted around the trike, and as he reached for the ringer, a woman's voice came from the speaker.

"Can I help you?"

"I'm hoping you can help me with a missing child."

A fortyish brunette opened the door wide enough to see his face, then opened it wider. She wore yoga pants. A small girl looked up at him, arms wrapped around one of her mother's knees. She sucked her thumb and when he glanced down and said, "Hi, there," she hunched her back.

"You said a child is missing?"

"Yes. A girl disappeared from the daycare center across the street. I thought maybe you might have recorded something that might help us." He gestured to the doorbell camera. "Maybe a vehicle. Or people."

"I need to get my husband. Wait here." She shut the door in his face and locked it.

The husband invited him in. The man left the room, returned with his laptop and set it on the kitchen counter. His wife signed into the account and a second later a page opened.

Thumbnails populated the screen. "When it detects motion, it records."

There were dozens of them.

"Do you know what time of day it happened?" the man asked.

His wife stroked her daughter's hair. "Is it your daughter?"

Vance shook his head.

"That's awful. Do they suspect one of the parents?"

"I don't know." He looked at her husband. "Try around ten this morning."

The dad scrolled through the icons, stopping, squinting, studying. He saw it first. A pickup parked near the entrance, easily seen from the house, but hidden from the daycare center by a thick hedge. He moved closer. "Can you enlarge it?"

The husband tapped a key and the video went full screen. *Shit.* Greg Marino. He might not have recognized Caitlin, the way she was dressed. But it was definitely Marino with Caitlin in the same scanty outfit he'd just seen her wearing on the daycare monitors.

"Are you a policeman?" the little girl asked.

"I used to be."

"Then who are you?" the dad asked. "If it's not your child, what are you doing here?"

"I'm helping a friend." He pulled his cell from his pants pocket and took a photo of the screen.

"Get out of my house," the dad said.

The mom disappeared and returned with a snub-nosed revolver. "You need to get out. Now."

She advanced on him. Backing away with his hands up, he apologized for any inconvenience he may have caused.

They might call 9-1-1 and that would royally complicate shit. He fumbled for the doorknob behind his back, pushed it open, and sprinted across the street. He jammed his fingers on the buzzer at Kidz. Jake answered a few seconds later.

"We need to get out of here. Come on."

Jake handed him a USB drive. "I had her download the video."

Vance shoved it in his pocket.

Jenkins stood behind Jake, looking confused. "Did you find something?"

He talked over Jake's shoulder. "Thank you for your help. We might have a lead. I'll be in touch."

"Did someone see something?" she asked.

"Go inside and wait," Vance said. "I'll let you know."

Jenkins watched from the window as he hung a right out of the driveway, onto the main road. He told Jake what had happened, but he left seeing Greg Marino on the video, out.

At first, he looked worse. Then he brightened. "You got a picture?"

"Yeah. A shot of the screen."

The old Volvo lurched and coughed three times before taking its last gasp. "Shit." He turned the steering wheel hard right. They were only a few blocks from the daycare center.

The old car rolled to a stop, taking its last breath as it died curbside.

Jake leaned over and looked at the dash. The fuel needle rested below the red zone. "Are you kidding me?"

He pulled his mobile and sent a text to Daniel. No answer. He called. No answer. Using the search engine on his phone, he located the closest gas station, tapped the rideshare app on his phone, then copied and pasted the gas station address into the destination. A map came up on his mobile screen, showing a little icon of a car one minute away.

A Nissan Rogue approached. The driver, a woman, rolled her window down. He checked her license plate against the one on the app on his phone. He snapped the convertible top in place, rolled up the windows, and locked the doors on the old Volvo.

"Car trouble?"

"Uh-huh."

"You out of gas?"

"Yeah, gauge isn't very accurate," he said, climbing into the back seat opposite Jake. "Can you take us to Coral Gables instead of the gas station?"

She turned and faced him. "I wouldn't leave a car like that on the street."

"I'll take my chances."

"You have to change the address on your phone."

"I don't wanna do that."

"I can't change the destination. GPS tracks my trips."

"What if we go to the gas station first, I settle the tab, then you drive me to the Gables. Off the grid."

"I'm not supposed to do that."

He pulled a hundred from his wallet and handed it to her.

She turned around and studied him. "Okay. But if you're paying cash for the next trip, I can't put the address in my GPS."

"No problem. I'll talk you through it."

A squad car passed the opposite direction, heading toward Kidz, speeding but no lights or sirens.

"You gotta love it," the rideshare driver said, slowing for the cop car to pass. "Just another day in paradise."

49

"I want my mommy."

Caitlin was on the verge of tears, too, but fought them. She sat at the edge of the mattress with the little girl rolled up next to her.

After lunch, Mack had herded them into the cramped bedroom and locked it from the outside. Lizzie's sobbing had morphed into hiccups, her tiny body convulsing with each breath.

Isabel sat at the foot of the twin bed. "Now, now. It will be okay. Jur mommy will come."

Lizzie gasped between the words. "When . . . will . . . she . . . come and . . . get me?"

Caitlin moved to a sitting position and set Lizzie on her lap, tightening her arms, rocking her like a baby. "We're having a slumber party."

"No . . . we're . . . not."

She'd begged Mack not to confine them, promising not to tell Greg. He said if she kept talking, he might kill her. Might kill all three of them. Then he relented, making them promise to leave the room only to use the bathroom.

"Ju be okay." Isabel patted Lizzie's shoulder. "We take care of ju."

Lizzie calmed, turned, and looked at her, the whites of her big eyes mottled with red webs. Caitlin had a million questions she wanted to ask Isabel but how could she with Lizzie listening?

Did Isabel know her dad? Her father was an investment banker who'd lived in Miami for less than a year before moving to Texas. He wasn't a *real* banker. He'd moved to Houston because he worked in the energy business helping oil and gas companies raise money. Her imagination churned until her stomach hurt. Her father knew Lizzie's. Her dad bought his yacht from him.

Lizzie Dinero dozed and her sobs faded to the soft breathing of a small child sleeping.

The room was stifling. The window unit kicked on and the buzzing and banging started. It was no match for the humidity and the dampness of the cramped space.

50

"Stop for a second." They were half a block from Vance's mother's house and the squad car was back, parked out front.

"Do a drive-by, past the cop car," he told the Uber driver, "slow down but keep going. Don't stop."

The rideshare driver pulled slowly from the curb. "I'll drop you off around the corner. I don't know what's going on here, but I don't wanna get involved."

The patrol car was empty. She drove past the rented Altima where he'd parked it, and turned right.

His phone buzzed in his pocket. Hopefully an update from Daniel. TELEMARKETER came up on caller ID.

"We need to get out of here," Jake said.

"I'll do whatever you guys want, but you have about two seconds to decide," the driver said.

"Go around one more time," he said. "I'll tell you when to stop."

"I don't wanna do that."

Jake flashed a handful of twenties.

The driver started a lap.

"Okay, go slow," he said as they approached the house a second time.

A vehicle came up behind them. Cars parked on either side of the street made it too tight for two-way traffic. The driver behind them nosed up to their rear bumper, flashed the brights, then blared the horn.

Great. Thanks for announcing us. Just fucking great. He looked out the back window.

"Stop!" Vance shouted. Unfastening his safety belt, he opened the door and jumped out. "Come on, Jake. Let's go."

"Hey," the driver yelled.

Jake handed her the wad of cash.

Vance jogged to the driver's-side window of the car stopped behind them. Kathy looked surprised. "Stay in the car, Kat."

"Why is there a police car in front of Mom's? Have you talked to her?"

Jake got in back. He got in the front. "This is my friend, Jake. Jake, meet my little sister, Kathy."

She twisted in her seat. "What's going on? I've been calling the house and no one's answering. Is that why the cops are here? Did something happen?"

"Just drive."

She'd stopped the Subaru in front of the house. The front door opened and Kagan walked onto the stoop.

He slouched under the dash. "Go, Kat. And don't stop."

"Why are the cops here?"

"Just do it."

"All right . . . okay," she said, craning her neck, rolling slowly past the house, staring at the uniformed woman speaking to someone in the doorway. "Mom said you were coming home to visit. Who was that who just dropped you off?"

"An Uber."

"What are you doing here? Why didn't you call me if Mom's in some kind of trouble?"

"Jesus, Kat. Quit asking questions. I texted you. I asked you to come. Remember?" He had to calm down. He lowered his voice. "I'm sorry I didn't call you. Things have been a little crazy."

At the four-way stop she put the Subaru in park. "I'm not driving another inch until you tell me what's going on."

She could be a mule. "Jake's daughter was kidnapped three days ago in Texas. Mom's been missing since yesterday."

Her lip quivered. "Someone took Mom?"

Jake gripped the headrest of her seat and pulled himself forward. "That's what we're trying to figure out. Your brother's right. We need to get the hell out of here."

Kathy swallowed hard, released her safety belt and jumped out. "You drive."

Vance switched places, buckled in, looked both ways, and drove slowly through the intersection.

"Where're we going?" she asked.

That's what he was trying to figure out.

He saw the flashing lights in the rearview before he heard the whoop of the siren. They were in front of a McMansion two blocks from his mother's place.

"Step out of the car." The voice came from the cop car PA system.

"Stay here." He got out.

It was Kagan. Alone this time. She got out of the Crown Vic and walked toward him and stopped halfway between the two vehicles. "Whose car is this?"

"My sister's."

"Who else is in the car?"

"My sister and the guy who hit his head."

She walked to the Subaru and looked inside. "Where's the Volvo?"

"Out of gas."

"How'd you get here?"

"Uber."

"Why'd you take the Volvo and leave the rental?"

"I didn't want you following me."

"Where'd you go?"

"Is there a problem here?"

"Where'd you go?"

"Which time?"

"Don't jerk me around. Where were you going when you ran out of gas?"

"Technically speaking, I was on my way here."

Face-to-face she was his size, over six feet tall with broad shoulders. And she was running out of patience.

"Okay, we went to a daycare center out in Pinecrest."

"Why?"

"Jake's daughter works there."

"Why'd you take him there?"

He didn't have a good answer.

Kagan rolled a long flashlight in her palms. "Let me help you. Your mother's missing. You're an ex-detective. You went there looking for something."

"Have I done something illegal?"

"Okay. We'll play this your way." She walked to the back passenger window and tapped on it. Jake rolled his window down.

"Sir. Would you please step out of the car?"

When Jake got out, so did Kathy.

"Does your daughter work at a daycare center?"

"She used to."

"Why did you and Mr. Courage go to the daycare center?"

Vance interrupted. "Why are you harassing us?"

"I can take you downtown and we can talk there." She unclipped the mic from her radio.

"No, no, no," Jake said. "I'm looking for my daughter."

"She's missing?"

Jake glanced at Vance. He nodded.

"She disappeared three days ago. In Texas."

"And you think she's in Miami, at the daycare center where she used to work?" Kagan looked at her watch. "At this hour?"

Jake didn't answer.

"Step over to my vehicle." She walked up to Kathy who stood near the back bumper of the Subaru. "Is this your vehicle?"

Kathy nodded.

"Where're the keys?"

"In the ignition."

"Please secure your vehicle."

Kathy furrowed her brow. "What have I done?"

Vance said, "You have no beef with my sister."

Kathy powered the windows up and pressed the fob. The lights flickered and the horn beeped.

Kagan held her hand out.

"Let her go," Vance said.

Kathy held the fob in her hand, waiting to see which way it would go.

This was exactly what he'd been worried about. Either Jenkins or the neighbors across the street had called the police.

"You want me to leave my car here?" Kathy asked.

Kagan opened the passenger door of the Crown Vic. "You two, in the back."

"Don't do it," Vance said.

"What did I do?" Kathy planted her hands on her hips.

"Get in," Kagan said.

"Don't get in the car," Vance said.

"Why should I?" Kathy asked Kagan.

Kagan held the rear door of the Crown Vic open. "Get in the car."

"Not 'til you tell me why."

"Let them go and I'll go with you," Vance said.

Kagan closed the rear door on her side. She appeared to be thinking, reassessing the situation. Jake stayed silent.

"You know the drill. Either arrest them or let them go," Vance said.

"Well?" Kathy asked, "Am I under arrest?"

Kagan glared at Kathy but didn't say.

"Let them both go," Vance said.

Kagan slapped the flashlight in her palm.

"You have no issue with them," he said.

Kagan's eyes went from Kathy, to Jake, then stopped on him. "You," she tossed her chin at him, "you're riding up front with me. Let's go. And you two, you saw nothing. Understand?"

Kathy and Jake nodded.

Kagan followed him around the front bumper. He shaded his eyes from the lit headlights. The cruiser had been in a recent wreck. A triangle-shaped piece of broken plastic dangled from a hole where the headlamp on passenger's-side light cover used to be. Wires poked out. A small bulb inside the cavity looked like a cherry on a chocolate sundae.

"What happened to your car?"

"Get in," she said.

Kathy and Jake stood watching. He signaled with a flick of his neck for them to vamoose. "Check on Aunt Sophia. I'll call you later," he said, opening the passenger door and getting in.

"How's his head?" Kagan asked, settling behind the wheel of the cruiser.

"Superficial wound."

"Sorry I had to ambush you like this." She kept her voice low, watching as Kathy turned the Subaru around. "I figured you'd be back. You'll thank me later."

"I've heard that before. Never works out that way. Do you mind if I make a call?"

"Not sure I'd have grounds to stop you."

He pressed the redial button. Daniel's phone went to voicemail.

51

L auren had been the next-to-last person off the jet in Miami. Daryl waited on the jetway for his gate-checked carry-on. When she saw him, she pretended she'd left something on the plane and ran back to her seat. When she returned, hers was the only bag on the ramp. She pulled the handle and trotted past the gate where passengers waited for the plane to be cleaned and prepped for the next flight out.

She looked at the signs to the exits and spotted him on the escalator. She followed him to the train on the third level and waited on the platform before boarding the car behind him.

Minutes later, the M.I.A. Mover stopped at the rental car center. She pulled the scarf down on her forehead and slid into the crowded elevator and, facing away from him, pushed her way to the back.

The door opened to a modern steel-and-glass rotunda with brightly lit signs marking the rental car companies.

She waited for the elevator to empty and watched him from a safe distance. He joined a long line at Avis. She saw a short line to an off-brand. The service was fast and courteous.

She took the elevator, located her rental car in the dimly lit parking garage, loaded her bag, and drove to the exit where she backed the silver Malibu into an empty spot, turned her headlights off, and watched.

Fifteen minutes later, Daryl exited the garage, driving a maroon Ford Mustang.

She followed him, headlights reflecting off his back bumper, passed under the sign for I-95 south, stopped, and waited for the light to turn green. She was rummaging through her bag for eye drops when a green bubble lit up on her phone. The caller ID was UNAVAILABLE. When she read the text, a jolt of adrenaline coursed through her: `Be careful.` The bubble disappeared. She closed the text app and reopened it. It vanished the way the other warning had.

Daryl made a left at the first cross street onto Northwest 21st Street. She followed his vehicle past rows of modest single-family bungalows and duplexes with cars filling the driveways and streets. A five-story apartment complex shaped like an air conditioning unit advertised one month of free rent, the giant yellow banner—lit by a streetlamp—hung across the top floor of the concrete parking garage.

At Northwest 37th Avenue he turned right, then left onto Northwest 17th Street, passing a Honduran restaurant. At Northwest 27th he turned left again and continued over the Miami River bridge for two more miles. The right turn indicator on the Mustang blinked. Daryl slowed and pulled into a fast food restaurant and parked.

She continued to the next driveway and drove the wrong way into the exit-only, and cut the lights.

Daryl got out of the rental and went inside. She backed into a diagonal slot closest the exit facing 27th where she could wait for him and leave quickly.

She texted Vance: `In Miami. Need to talk.` She

pressed the send button. A minute later she called him. It went directly to voicemail. She ended the call without leaving a voice message.

Lauren waited in the Malibu idling at the fast food joint for over twenty minutes. That was weird. She'd seen him go inside.

Only two cars had come out of drive-thru lanes. She had a clear view to the entrance and exit. It wasn't like a tour bus stopped for food. The place was dead.

She pulled to the curb and waited for a break in traffic, drove across two lanes of traffic onto Northwest 27th and made two left turns, the second one into the fast food restaurant entrance. Daryl's rented Mustang was still there. She drove by slowly, snapped a picture of the rear license plate and continued past, looking inside the restaurant. It appeared empty.

A voice came from a metal speaker on the plastic board. "May I take your order?"

"I'll have the Southwest Chicken Salad."

"The combo or just the salad?"

"Just the salad."

"Anything to drink?"

"No. Just the salad."

She waited at the pickup window, sitting up straight, craning her neck, looking inside. It was empty.

Where was Daryl and what was he doing all this time inside the place?

"Four dollars and fifty-nine cents, please."

She handed the young man a five.

"It'll be a minute," he said.

She checked her phone. No new messages.

Reaching out the car window for the bag, she asked, "Did you by any chance see a man with long black hair inside?"

"With cool feathers?"

"That's him."

"He was here earlier. He met someone, I think." He turned his back and said it loud enough for her to hear. "Hey, does anyone remember the guy with the long hair and feathers?"

A middle-aged Latina she guessed to be the manager came to the window. "Is there a problem?"

"No. I thought I saw someone I know. The guy with long black hair."

"He didn't order anything. Used the restroom and left twenty, maybe thirty minutes ago."

"Was he with someone?"

"I don't know."

The young man returned to the window. "He was with another guy."

"Can you give me a description?"

The manager contorted her face. "No." She reached around her employee and slammed the to-go window shut.

A driver in a SUV behind her tooted the horn.

"No problem. Have a nice day," she said to the greasy to-go window and set the salad on the seat next to her.

She backed into the same spot, killed the headlights, removed the salad from the bag and called Vance. It went to voicemail. Opting not to leave a message, she typed a text: Daryl Flood is in Miami, sent it, and stabbed the lettuce with a plastic fork.

Her phone buzzed. Jesus, it was about time. She stopped chewing and swallowed a lump of lettuce. "Hey."

"How was your flight?"

"Good. How's Jake's ex?"

"Ann? She's fine. What's this about Daryl being in Miami?"

"We were on the same flight. Then we got separated."

"Why'd you fly with him?"

"That's not exactly how it happened."

"Where are you?"

"At a fast food joint. Where're you?"

He hesitated. "It's complicated."

"Are you alone?"

"No."

"Are you okay?"

"Uh-huh."

"Can you talk?"

"Not really."

"I really need to talk to you."

"It'll have to wait."

"'til when?"

"I don't know. Do you know why he's here?"

"Daryl?"

"Yeah."

"No."

"Do you know where he is now?"

"I lost him."

He paused. "Go home. I'll be in touch."

She didn't have anywhere else to go but home. "You're sure you're okay?"

"Yeah. I'll call you."

HER CONDO WAS on Shipping Avenue in Coconut Grove on a quiet residential street across from a small public park. When she arrived, a group of shady characters hung around the perimeter.

The pack of gangly young men turned away from the headlights. She'd expected to stop at the gate to manually open it with the keypad since the remote was in her car. But the metal gate was wide open and off its tracks. She drove inside and stopped.

Shit.

The passenger's-side window of her black Audi was busted out.

Parking the rental, she got out to look, and keeping one eye on the men loitering at the park, looked at the damage. The glove box was open, the interior ransacked.

A man stepped from behind the stucco façade at the condo next door, startling her. Matthew, the good neighbor who'd looked after her elderly uncle before he died, held his hands up in apology.

"I didn't mean to scare you. I'm glad you're home." He carried a roll of black garbage bags and blue painters' tape. "I was about to tape up your window. I called someone to fix the gate but they can't come 'til tomorrow. Have you been out of town?"

She nodded. "What happened?" She reached into the Malibu, popped the trunk and slung her purse and messenger bag over her shoulder.

"I don't know. There's been a bunch of smash and grabs. People are ranting about it on the neighborhood app."

He took her roller bag out of the trunk and pulled it to the stoop. She looked down next to the Audi. A thick plate of tempered glass lay next to the passenger door, twinkling like night stars.

Her fists balled. Pools of water had formed on the leather seat on the passenger's side from the rain.

"A car alarm went off. I didn't realize it was yours. I didn't see that the window was busted out until a little while ago. Did you have anything valuable in the car?"

"Just some change in the cupholder."

"That explains it."

"Explains what?"

"The tweakers."

"I don't understand."

"Meth addicts."

"How do you know that's who did it?"

"Who else would bust out a car window for spare change? The stuff is really cheap, like five bucks a hit. They're all amped up. They hallucinate and punch out car windows for dimes and quarters."

She picked up one end of the sheet of glass that used to be the passenger window on her beloved German car and dragged it onto the dirt at the base of the hedge.

The pack of thin men had vanished from the park across the street.

"Here, hold this."

Matthew handed her the roll of black plastic yard bags and tore a long strip of blue tape from the roll.

"Oh, my God," Lauren gasped.

A hooded man appeared out of nowhere and ran toward them. Matthew backed away. The stranger reached inside his jacket and pulled something out and pointed it at Matthew. He raised his hands.

Oh, my God. He had a gun and was going to kill them.

Her heart pounded. She heard a hissing sound.

"Stop!" Matthew waved his hands wildly, trying to protect himself.

He'd spray-painted Matthew's face bright red.

"Give me your wallet."

She wanted to help, but froze. Matthew grimaced, and covering his eyes with his forearm, fumbled for his wallet.

The hooded man pointed the can at her and sprayed her chest. She looked down in disbelief. "No!"

Matthew held his wallet out. The stranger pinched it open and took the cash. He sprayed a big red X on the door panel of the Audi and tossed the spray can and wallet into the hedges, then charged at her like a bull. She ran to the entryway of her condo. The hoodlum jumped into the rental, and backed out, leaving a patch of rubber five feet long.

"Oh, my God. Are you all right?" she asked Matthew.

"I'm okay." He wiped paint from his face with his sleeve, eyes closed, and spit on the ground. "Whose car was that?"

"It's a rental." The paint fumes made her gag. She looked down at her jacket, then at Matthew. Their attacker could have blinded him. "We should call 9-1-1."

"What the fuck for? The cops don't give a shit about us."

"Yes, they do. We should call them. I need to report the stolen car."

"Go ahead. Good luck with that." He looked for his wallet in the hedge. He saw the empty paint can and reached for it.

"Don't touch it. It might have fingerprints."

He laughed and kicked it, instead. "I guess you didn't hear me. Or you don't believe me. But hey, don't take my word for it. Go ahead. Call the police." He spotted his wallet and picked it up. "Maybe the rental car company will care their car was stolen."

She touched the graffiti on the Audi. The paint was still wet. She ran inside the house and returned with a damp towel, wiping most of it from the door. Jostling the driveway gate, she tried to wrestle it back on the track but it wouldn't budge. Grabbing it with both hands, she shook it like jail bars. But it was stuck.

The park across the street was vacant. A poster for a missing cat was nailed to the telephone pole. Someone drew horns where its ears were. What was going on with the neighborhood? She picked up the paint can, tossed it in the trashcan, dragged her bags inside, and double-locked the doors.

52

The call with Lauren gnawed at Vance. What was Daryl Flood doing in Miami?

Electronics flashed in Kagan's cruiser, more airplane cockpit than what he recalled from his days as an active duty detective. A laptop computer mounted to the dashboard flashed a colorful web of street maps. Her radio cackled with codes he couldn't remember.

He twisted in his seat and was reminded of the Glock holstered under his left arm. The backseat of the patrol car looked the same as it did twenty years ago. The inch-thick acrylic pane behind them was reinforced with thin metal mesh designed to shield the cops from prisoners.

"Where's your partner?"

She kept her eyes on the road. "Busy."

"Are you off duty?"

Kagan didn't answer.

"Where're you taking me?"

Still nothing.

"Do you know where my mother is?"

"The world doesn't revolve around you."

"What's that supposed to mean?"

Kagan stared at the windshield.

He slid the partition open a few inches. An odor wafted in.

"Jesus, shut that thing," Kagan took one hand off the wheel and closed it. "Smells like something died back there."

Maybe this was his day of reckoning. Collaring him for the dirty drug money he'd been laundering was the kind of thing that would turn Kagan into an overnight legend.

Except Kagan passed the exit to Miami police headquarters and asked a mundane question. "So, why'd you become a lawyer?"

"Thought I'd like it better."

"Did you?"

"Nope."

She eased left where US-1 merged with I-95, and continued north. Rows of glass towers, topped with the brightly lit names of global banks, rose like sequoias.

He gazed out the window. Motorists slowed when they saw the Crown Vic approach. Most kept their eyes glued to their windshields.

Kagan drove past colorful signs advertising luxury shopping brands, a consulate, several four-star hotels and the front office for a cruise line, closed for the night. The big white Greek Church with crosses atop its onion domes seemed out of place.

She continued to the short bridge over the Miami River. At nightfall, the water was dark matter dotted with marina lights highlighting rows of white yachts. She followed the road east where it turned into Biscayne Bay Boulevard, then hooked north past Bayfront Park.

Homeless people wandered the park at street level. A small American flag flapped in the wind, attached to the top of a blue tent staked into the grass. Next to the shopping carts—some piled four feet high with stuff—lay bodies of human beings swaddled in blankets.

"The city relocated them during the Super Bowl," Kagan said. "The organizers made a cash donation to move them during the concerts. They sent out a press release."

"The A.S.P.C.A. for people," he said.

"Something like that."

She headed east on Northeast 3rd Street where it became a one-way, and took the turn to Bayside Marketplace. He'd been there once, a touristy kaleidoscope of chain stores and restaurants. The open-air vendors were so aggressive hawking their fake watches, and cheap perfumes, and cell phone cases, he'd vowed never to go back.

Kagan stopped the Crown Vic at the end of a fire lane and backed into a spot beneath a bright light. A rent-a-cop on a golf cart sped their way and stopped adjacent Kagan's window.

"Jesus," she said under her breath, powering the window down.

"Is everything all right, Officer?"

"All good. Just taking a little break."

The security guard wasn't leaving, idling in earshot.

Kagan pulled the Crown Vic from the handicap parking spot.

The security guard drove around the back bumper. Kagan watched the rearview. He flashed the lights on his cart and turned hard to the left, trying to catch up. "HEY!" The Dixie-cup shaped light on his roof flickered blue and red.

She powered her window up. "Sherlock wants to tell me my rear bumper's banged up. I hate mall cops," she said, stomping the pedal.

Whose team was Kagan playing on?

He checked his phone. He held it up so Kagan could see the 10% battery light flashing red.

"Can I get a charge?"

"No. You need to stay off that thing."

"Where're we going?"

"The Port of Miami."

"Why?"

"Greg Marino is heading that way. I think we have a mutual interest in catching him."

Greg Marino. Wow.

———

KAGAN DROVE east onto Port Boulevard running parallel to the McArthur Causeway, and crossed the bridge linking the mainland to the PortMiami.

A message came up: `Call me. The yacht is gone.`

Fuck, fuck, *fuck*. He stared at the text from Karl Landeros, the off-duty cop they'd hired to watch Jake's yacht, the *Arm*. The screen went dark. "You gotta be kidding me."

Kagan glanced over at him. "About what?"

"Nothing," he said.

The message from Karl would have to wait. "`The yacht is gone.`" What did that mean? He wanted to call for an update. But Kagan told him to stay off the phone. Besides, he didn't have enough juice on his phone and how could he ask questions with her right next to him? The red light blinked on his phone. He needed to reserve whatever battery he had left.

53

L auren took her jacket off—ruined with red spray paint
—folded it in half and threw it on the back of her office
chair. She dialed the rental car company.

She listened to the on-hold music as she walked to the
kitchen, passing the pictures of her showhorses hanging on the
walls of the foyer. She took a mug from the kitchen cabinet,
filled it with water and set the microwave for ninety-seconds.
The auto-voice thanked her for her patience, then went back to
annoying music. She opened the cabinet, remembering she'd
run out of sugar before she'd traveled, and hadn't had time to
buy more.

She'd give them five more minutes to answer. If they didn't
care that their car was stolen, then neither did she. She'd call
her insurance company tomorrow and report both incidents.

Dropping a tea bag into the water along with a spoon, she
walked to her office, set her messenger bag on the desk and
riffled in the side pockets looking for a packet of sugar. Instead,
she found the lip balm she'd picked up near the pile of limestone at the ranch, by the runway. She set the tube upright,

searched for sugar, tore open the packet and poured it into her tea.

Stirring the tea, she fired-up her laptop and googled the off-brand lip balm that smelled like honey.

It wasn't lip balm. It was bowstring wax. For bows and arrows.

Oh, my God. Daryl Flood had a crossbow. Did he drop it there? She played it back in her head. When they'd ridden horseback, they hadn't gone to that spot.

The ranch didn't have crossbows for hunting.

What were the chances that someone else left it?

She ended the call with the rental car agency and dialed Vance. It went straight to voicemail. Again. Tilting her head against the chair back, she took deep breaths through her nose, rolling the tube between her fingers. Why was Daryl in Miami, and who did he meet at the fast food place?

What would he have been doing near the pile of limestone at the ranch?

Wait a minute. Adam told her that Daryl had delivered some sort of construction materials to the ranch.

Then she remembered when he'd unloaded his horse, the animal had kicked up a cloud of white dust from the floor-boards. Then another thought popped into her head. On the ride out to search for Caitlin, Daryl's horse pulled-up lame. A chunk of white rock had wedged into the frog in its hoof.

Damn it. Where was Vance and why couldn't he talk?

"WHAT HAPPENED TO YOUR CRUISER?" Vance asked Kagan as she continued on Port Boulevard, approaching the nerve center for Florida's cruise lines and freight operations.

"Had a little fender-bender."

"Front and back?"

"Very good, Detective. I heard you were talented. I also heard a little story about you."

His heart rate ticked up. "Oh, yeah?"

"Yeah. That your uncle is an FBI Ten Most Wanted fugitive."

Adrenaline surged. He played it cool. "You know what they say, you can't pick your relatives."

"What's that like?"

He shrugged. "I don't remember. It was a long time ago."

Traffic was light. Port operations were closed for the evening.

He powered down his window. The familiar smells of salt-water calmed him.

The world's largest passenger ship was docked for the evening, along with other floating skyscrapers lining the bulk-heads. It looked like Bloomingdales on Fifth Avenue had sailed south for the winter. He'd read about the ship with the ice rink, go-cart track, full-size basketball court, and walls for rock climbing.

"Whaddaya think Christopher Columbus would make of it?" He craned his head out the window into the cool night air, looking up, unable to see the top of the towering ship, empty now and docked for the night. Tomorrow it would fill with 6,000 passengers eager to sail to some touristy destination. Somewhere.

"I don't know what he'd think. But I think it's obscene. You couldn't pay me enough to spend a week on that monstrosity."

He had the opposite thought: that he should be standing in the all-you-can-eat buffet line with Lauren, filling his plate with Alaskan king crab.

He glanced at Kagan. Her long, auburn ponytail hung over her shoulder, softening her look under the cover of night. For a moment, she looked beautiful.

They motored past the cruise ships, toward the less glamorous tip of Dodge Island: cranes, barges, tugs.

Streetlights lit the brightly painted shipping containers neatly stacked like collectors' matchboxes, waiting to be loaded onto barges headed out to sea, or onto trucks destined for ground delivery.

Across the manmade shipping channel, neon lights glowed from the southern tip of South Beach where later, the jet set would party at the all-night clubs, dancing, drinking, drugging. And whatever that led to.

The US Coast Guard command center operated from an artificial island between South Beach and the port. To the south, Fisher's Island, a barrier reef once owned by the Vanderbilts, was now a golf course community with checkerboards of lights shining from the ten-story condos. For all the natural splendor of South Florida, residents of the richest-per-capita zip code in America had the unfortunate view of the shipping terminal.

Officer Kagan drove toward the last of the industrial lights and stopped at the water's edge. Plastic bottles glinted, bobbing at the baseline of mangroves rooted in the shallows.

Vance cracked the window, letting in the bitter aromas of hydrocarbons and saltwater and decaying sea life that perfumed the moist air.

She parked the patrol car and cut the headlights.

"Care to share what's going on?"

She turned and faced him. The fluorescent lights on tall poles mixed with the night shadows, turning her skin a bluish-gray. "Marino's heading here."

"I figured that." The shrill buzz of a mosquito broke his train of thought. He ducked, waving his hand in front of his face.

Kagan turned the ignition and powered the window up. "Had a little run-in with your friend, Ray Dinero. He rear-ended me and I hit a utility pole."

"How'd that happen?"

"I slammed on the brakes at a yellow light. You know the drill, Counselor."

"You lured him into a rear-ender. His fault."

"That's right. He went crazy. We had to arrest him for attempted assault. My partner transported him to the county jail. He had company."

"Let me guess. Daniel Ruiz."

Kagan flashed a wry smile. "Daniel wasn't leaving his man on the battlefield. Like I said. You shouldn't have quit your job."

"Why'd you ambush them?"

"Ray was going to mess things up. He's too unstable, worrying about his kid. Don't get me wrong. I'd be the same way. No, I'd be crazier. As for Daniel, he was at the wrong place at the wrong time."

So that's what happened. Ray's airbag deployed when he rear-ended the Crown Vic. Daniel had activated the video chat on Ray Dinero's phone, gambling he'd figure out what was going on. He'd seen Kagan's face but that wasn't enough of a clue. It was just as well. What would he have done if he had known she'd forced the accident?

"Here." Kagan handed him one end of a white phone charger sprouting from her dash. "Go ahead. Juice it up."

"Does this mean I can make a call?"

"Depends who you're calling."

"I'd like to talk to my friend, Lauren Gold. She flew in from Texas this evening. I was supposed to meet her." He'd also have liked to call Karl. But chatting about the missing yacht with Kagan listening wasn't an option.

He took the thunderbolt and plugged it into his phone, and when it came to life, saw more missed calls from Lauren. He twisted to the left and lifted his jacket, showing Kagan the Glock 19 holstered beneath his left arm.

"I counted on that," she said. "You might need it. But I hope not."

He showed her the missed calls with Lauren's name.

"Go ahead, but keep it short and sweet. No details."

"Excuse me," he said, leaning against the passenger door. Lauren answered on the first ring. Using his left hand to cup his face, he pressed his cheek against the passenger window to muffle his voice. "Did you get home okay?"

She was chatty, telling him about the drive to Alpine with Daryl, meeting Kit, following Daryl to Miami, to the fast foot joint. "Someone smashed my car window and sprayed me and my neighbor with red paint. Then they stole my rental car."

"Wow."

"That's all you have to say?"

"At the moment, yeah." He imagined holding that asshole in a chokehold and shoving the paint can in his mouth.

"You can't talk?"

"Correct."

She told him about the bowstring wax she'd found and the white residue in the horse trailer and the rock Daryl had removed from Picasso's hoof. And that he'd been a prison guard at the SuperMax in Florence.

"Are you there?"

He said, "Uh-huh. That's good work."

She told him she'd gone to her condo like he'd suggested. "Who are you with?"

He took his hand from his mouth and looked at Kagan. "I'm sitting in a cop car."

Kagan scowled and ran her finger back and forth in front of her neck.

"Oh, my God. Why? Is everything okay?"

"I'm not in trouble, if that's what you mean."

"Any word on Caitlin?"

"No. Stay in tonight. I'll call you when I can."

As soon as he ended the call, the airbag incident gave him an idea.

———

LAUREN SCROLLED through her contact list. She was about to call Josh back when she hesitated, swiped the screen, and called Roy Pompadour, instead. He answered on the first ring.

"Are you with Vance?"

"No."

"Thank God, you called. Josh has been trying to reach you. Have you talked to Vance?"

"Yes."

"I need you to get a message to him."

"I'll try."

"Daryl Flood is heading to a trucking company. I believe he's going to try to ship the stolen hovercraft out of the country."

She told Roy about the bowstring wax and her other suspicions.

She pulled a sheet of paper from the printer tray under her desk and wrote down the address to a place called F&F Trucking.

"Go get a burner. Your phone's been hacked."

Her heart raced. "How do you know that?"

"From Kit."

"And Vance's, too?"

"And Jake's. Call me when you get a new phone. Get that message to Vance, after you get the burner. We should stop talking now," he said, finishing with, "then go home. Be careful."

F&F was an international freight forwarding company located ten miles west of Miami International. She changed shirts, grabbed the key to her car and entered the address to the trucking company in her phone. Grabbing a blanket from the upstairs closet, she looked out the second-story window. The men who'd been hanging around the park were gone.

She swept a few chunks of glass from the leather seats of the Audi with the edge of the blanket, then laid it across the driver's-side. If Daryl Flood was on the move, she had to hurry. She pulled onto Shipping Avenue, ignoring the flapping of the black plastic bag taped over passenger's-side window.

Her phone buzzed in the center console. She looked at the screen: Vance. She let it go to voicemail. When it stopped recording, she listened to the message on Bluetooth. It wasn't a message. It was a pocket dial. There was a woman's voice in the background. Her GPS interrupted the recording. She disabled the navigation app at the red light and restarted the message.

I can't believe you told her you're sitting in a cop car.

What was I supposed to tell her?

I don't know. But that was dumb.

I was supposed to pick her up from the airport and I stood her up. She's had a rough night.

How's that?

She was attacked.

What? When?

This evening.

You mean since she landed?

Uh-huh.

Where?

In her driveway.

Jesus. Is she okay?

Yeah. She's waiting for the police to come.

The conversation was interrupted by a loud background noise.

Mwooonk ... Mwooonk.

She got home and discovered someone had busted out the window of her car. Then a thug attacked her with spray paint. That's when her rental car was stolen.

Geez. When it rains it pours. She's okay, right?

Yeah. Seeing that big cruise ship made me think that's what I'm gonna do when this thing's over with.

I'm glad she's okay. But I still hate the idea of cruise ships. You oughta fly somewhere, instead.

The message ended. Pulling over, she backed the audio up a few seconds and listened again.

Mwooonk . . . Mwooonk.

At first it sounded like a leaf blower or a wood chipper. But the way the noise trailed off in the distance didn't work. On the fourth time, it clicked. It was the blast horn of an ocean-going freighter. He'd pocket dialed her on purpose. It was a clue. He was near water. He'd mentioned cruise ships. He was at the port of Miami.

She turned into the CVS Pharmacy. The parking lot was dead. It took less than five minutes to buy the burner. She opened the box in the car, inserted the SIM card and activated the minutes. She held the burner next to her personal phone, typed Vance's number into the new one and pressed the green CALL button. Suddenly, a hand reached inside and opened the passenger door from the inside.

She dropped the phone, fingers shaking.

"Hey, calm down," Daryl said, grabbing the burner and ending the call.

"What are you doing here?"

"I've been tracking you," he said.

She took a deep breath, heart about to explode, not sure if she was more angry or scared. She saw his rented Mustang on the other side of the parking lot. It wasn't there when she'd arrived.

"I don't understand. You left your rental car at the fast food place."

"You saw me do that?"

"Well, no."

"I paid a guy ten bucks to walk out with me, then I hid, laying across on the seat until I saw you leave. Then I followed you."

"Why?"

"*Why?* Shouldn't I be the one asking you why you followed me? I saw you get on the plane in Houston. Get out of the car. I'm driving."

"Where're we going?"

"Not to the trucking company. Get out of the car."

"Why?"

"Just do it. Roy told you to go home."

"How do you know that?"

His tone sharpened. "Get out of the car."

"First, I want to know where we're going."

"Out." He reached into the center console and snatched the key fob.

"Hey, gimme that back. Drive your own car."

He got serious. "Listen to me. Vance is in danger. Get . . . out . . . of . . . the . . . car." He pressed the TRUNK icon on the fob and it popped open.

"Okay, okay," she said stepping out. As she walked past him, he grabbed her from behind, wrapping one forearm around her neck. "Get in."

"I'm not doing that." She elbowed him in the ribs.

He doubled over, angry. "Don't make me do this the hard way."

She jabbed him again, hitting him hard in the cheekbone.

"Okay, wildcat." He clamped his elbow around her neck,

bent her over, and shoved her head first into the trunk. He was about to lift her by her thighs when she bit into his forearm.

"You bitch!"

He grabbed a handful of hair, yanking her neck back to keep her from biting him again, and squeezed her windpipe until she ran out of air.

When she came to, she was in the fetal position, in absolute darkness. She lifted her head a few inches and banged it on the metal roof. Rubbing her scalp, she listened. A tear welled and rolled down her cheek. Daryl Flood had overpowered her and stuffed her in the trunk of her car.

54

G reg Marino lowered his pistol on the passenger seat, still pointing it at Tim the truck driver, who down-shifted the big rig and swung wide, angling the loaded semi toward the secured entrance.

The man at the guard shack had been waiting for them.

"You from F&F?"

"That's right," Tim said.

"ID, please."

Tim handed his worker ID card out the window.

The guard stepped onto the running board and shone his flashlight inside the cab on Tim's face, panning across his passenger's face.

Greg lowered his right hand, hiding the Kimber .45 between the seat and the passenger's-side door.

The watchman dropped onto the ground and returned with a mirror on a stick, walking around the truck and trailer, pointing his flashlight at the glass, inspecting the underbelly. He made notes on a clipboard and passed the paperwork into the cab. Tim signed the documents and the guard traded the clip-board for the ID card.

"Follow him," the watchman said, gesturing to the silhouette of another man wearing an orange fluorescent jacket.

The chain-link gate rolled open, and beyond it, an automatic gate arm lifted. Tim released the clutch slowly, steering the truck inside the compound, the engine belching and the smell of diesel mixing with the aroma of wet dog inside the cab. The old Peterbilt was sluggish, lurching in waves as Tim followed the man on the ground waving an illuminated light stick.

The guide turned and faced the front of the cab, and holding his lit baton over his head, signaled Tim to stop beneath a gantry crane hanging over the bulkhead like an enormous L-bracket.

Greg looked across the black waters of the channel at the checkered lights coming from the multimillion-dollar condos lining Fisher's Island. Soon, he'd be able to afford a place like that.

He'd departed the apartment around noon, leaving Mack in charge, and arrived at F&F Trucking around one o'clock in the afternoon.

The F&F crew was efficient, unhitching his trailer from the passenger truck and loading it into a commercial shipping container like a Russian doll. Tim had supervised the process, backing the empty flatbed up to the freight container on the ground. A series of hydraulic flat ramps unfurled accordion-style and stretched from the rear bumper of the Peterbilt to the front of the container.

Three guys operated a second truck—more a heavy-duty tow truck—with a hook on a thick pulley. They attached it to the container and lifted the edge high enough to slide the farthest ramp beneath it like a spatula. The flatbed assembly came to life, the hydraulics howling, as the chains dragged the container toward the cab. Layers of thick sheet metal rose, cables pulling the 5,000-pound container higher, ramps retracting like a dealer tapping a deck of freshly shuffled cards. When the hydraulic magic stopped, the container sat atop the flatbed. For a finishing touch, they'd secured it with cables and straps.

That took thirty minutes. He'd spent the rest of the day like a caged animal wondering what the fuck was taking so long, leafing through dated magazines, drinking stale coffee inside a grubby mobile trailer, waiting for the back office to prepare the manifest and shipping documents. The woman at reception told him that shipping to China was more complicated with the new tariffs.

He'd lied on the paperwork, listing the contents as a "recreational vehicle." FAQs on the company's website said less than four percent of all shipments were ever inspected. Even if it they did open it, the hovercraft looked like some kind of a toy.

Tim followed directions from the man on the ground, backing the tractor-trailer until it was parallel to a mountain of shipping containers stacked near the bulkhead.

Greg watched the funhouse version of the show from the wide-angle side mirror as the gantry arm dropped a giant hook. Guided by two stevedores dressed in jumpsuits, they hooked the freight container and lifted it from the flatbed behind him. The cab rose as the load lightened.

Tim jumped out to supervise on foot. "I'll be right back. Wait here."

Greg's mind wandered to the redheaded teenage girl held hostage in the dumpy month-to-month apartment he'd rented. Would he keep it another month or would he kill her when he was done with her? Would he kill the other two?

His mobile buzzed in his pants pocket, snapping him back to the present. It was about fucking time. "Are you in Miami?"

"I am," Daryl said. "Where are you?"

"At the terminal. Dropping off the goods. You got my money?"

His phone pinged. A video clip played, a shaky shot looking up at a helicopter. The camera angled down to a basket full of duffel bags on the swim platform of what looked like a fancy white yacht bobbing in the water. When the video stopped, three images followed. Still shots of stacks of hundreds stuffed into duffle bags.

"Satisfied?" Daryl asked.

He was. That crooked prison guard had almost fucked the whole plan, leaving the hovercraft out in the middle of desert. That Mack had gotten both the girl and the hovercraft was no thanks to Daryl Flood.

Greg closed the video window. "Where's my cash?"

"I'll meet you at back F&F. We'll talk then."

"You better not fuck this up. I'd hate to kill them, especially the little one."

Greg had checked with his sources inside the ADX prison to see if a guard named Daryl Flood could—in the corrupt sense of the word—be trusted.

He'd doled out millions of dollars of protection money to the Aryan Brotherhood to protect his own father up until the time his dad was killed during a routine prison movement. Dirty money was routinely funneled through the prison. That's how it worked. Flood claimed to be part of a crooked network, and when he approached him with an offer he couldn't turn down, he'd checked with his sources to confirm it.

A new intake at Florence, the imprisoned leader of the infamously savage Sinaloa cartel with access to a billion cash dollars, was running his drug empire from the inside.

International sanctions were making it next to impossible for the cartel to get the main chemical needed to produce street meth. Even the black market was tapped out. If Greg could recruit someone to steal a hovercraft in Texas and escort it to the port of Miami, Flood promised to recover the thirty-five million dollars cash he believed to be his, money that fucker Vance Courage and his friends stole from him, salvaging it from the seabed.

Flood had underestimated him, not counting on him taking hostages. Greg knew there was a risk of not getting paid; he'd been double-crossed before. This time, he took out an insurance policy on his inheritance. Having hostages would guarantee it didn't happen again.

Now, under the cover of night, Greg felt better about being gouged for twenty-six hundred bucks, the minimum cost to keep the terminal open after hours, watching the crew swing the freight container atop an awaiting barge going to Shenzhen—some Chinese port on the other side of the fucking planet. Watching the heavy equipment in action was like being a kid all over again.

Ten minutes later, Tim climbed behind the wheel. The dome light lit a thick layer of yellow dog fur covering the interior. If anything went wrong, he'd make a hairball big enough to choke him on.

55

"What's the target?" Vance asked Kagan. "At least give me that much."

"A suspected serial rapist."

"I know *who*. You already told me Greg Marino's on the way here." A pit formed in his stomach at the thought that a serial rapist had his mother and the girls. Were they still alive? If Kagan ambushed Greg here, what leverage would he have to get his mother and the other two home safely? "Why's he coming here?"

"He's dropping cargo."

"What kind of cargo?"

"Some kind of technology, shipping it to China."

It had to be the missing hovercraft. "How do you know that?"

"Officially, I don't."

"What's that supposed to mean?"

"I have a friend in the DA's office."

"And?"

"My source tells me things."

"Are you here on official police business?"

"What difference would it make?"

"A lot. I'm taking that as a no. Why are you doing it if it's unofficial?"

"I have my reasons."

"This has to be personal," he said.

"What makes you so sure?"

"Cops work off the grid if they're dirty—or if it's personal. I don't think you're a dirty cop."

"It's Jenkins," she said.

He scratched his ear. "You lost me."

"The woman, at the daycare center."

"Oh," he said, trying, but unable to add it up. "What about her?"

"She's my older brother's daughter."

"Okay. And?"

"She was on a dating site last year."

"Oh, shit." *Shit, shit, shit.*

A corner piece of the puzzle fell into place. That was Kagan's angle. Ray Dinero—Lizzie's dad—was another link. His daughters attended Jenkins' daycare place. Jake's daughter had worked there because Ray got her the job. They were all separated by just a few degrees.

"Your uncle's been on the FBI's Ten Most Wanted list for twenty years. It's not exactly classified information your uncle and Greg's father were partners in crime. When I got wind your mother may have been kidnapped, I made it my business to work the case. I knew you'd show up."

Kagan was good.

"I could lose my job for what we're doing right now," she said.

"You mean you could lose your job for what *you're* doing," he said, still processing the new information.

"Greg's license plates were picked up on a traffic camera less than a quarter mile from the daycare center, ten minutes before Lizzie was taken."

"How do you know that?"

"I already told you, I have a friend at the DA's office. My niece called the cops. I heard it come in over the radio."

"Why didn't you answer the call?"

"And do what, exactly? Write a report? Tell my brother 'I'm on it.' Get real."

"Why don't you do this the old-fashioned way and get a warrant?"

"Why? So some overpaid lawyer can get the case tossed again? Do you think it's a coincidence that a rash of sexual assaults matching Greg Marino's M.O. magically stopped when that piece of crap was being held in the county jail? How many more do you think went unreported?"

"Probably a lot."

"He's very careful. He doesn't leave forensic evidence. The women, he drugs them, they can't remember what happened."

He already knew these details.

Kagan drummed her fingers on the steering wheel. "I have a special dislike for rapists. There's first class seating for them in hell."

A second message from Karl Landeros pinged on his phone: u get my msg.

He typed yes and pressed the send button.

His brain was stuck in gear trying to think of what to do about the message from Karl when his phone buzzed again. The number was unfamiliar. A local Miami prefix. He pressed the red button and dismissed it.

"That piece of crap spent half the day at a trucking company out west of the airport today," Kagan said. "He dropped off a trailer and arranged to have it loaded into a freight container."

"How do you know that?"

"The good folks at the trucking outfit are working with law enforcement."

"What law enforcement?"

"The D.E.A." She paused. "Greg's consigned a freight-forwarder to swap cargo containers. It's going down here. Tonight."

How did Drug Enforcement fit into the picture? "What's the swap?" he asked.

"Something coming from China. Supposedly a cargo container filled with fifty-five-gallon drums."

"Filled with what?"

"Chemicals."

"For what?"

"Some kind of banned additive to manufacture street meth. It's hard to get, even on the black market."

"Who's the buyer?"

"The Sinaloa cartel."

"I don't understand."

"Which part?"

"Why didn't they ship it directly to Mexico? Why take the chance going through a US port of entry?"

"China agreed to stop the illegal export and Mexico agreed to stop importing the stuff as part of US trade negotiations. But the Chinese always cheat and the shit's been slipping through the Mexican ports. D.E.A's been looking for a way to catch 'em red-handed. The art of deception is revered in Chinese culture."

"Stick to the point," he said.

"Whatever Greg's got, the Chinese wanted it bad enough they used the Aryan Brotherhood to broker the deal."

"It's a hovercraft."

Kagan's eyes widened. "What?"

"I'm pretty sure Greg jacked a developmental hovercraft from an R and D facility in Fort Stockton, Texas."

"You shouldn't have quit your job."

He shook his head. "I don't need to be paid to go after pieces of shit like him."

Kagan raised her eyebrows. "Good for you. The rest of us have bills to pay."

Headlights turned onto Port Boulevard. Kagan squinted through a set of field glasses. "It's showtime."

She started the engine and crept along the shoulder, hugging the concrete barriers, lights out. She parked five hundred feet from the entrance to a freight terminal with a lighted guard shack, shaded her cell with her jacket and checked for messages. She typed quickly with her thumbs and sent a text.

"Turn yours off," she said, following suit. "No lights."

The trucker slowed, then turned wide and stopped in front of the guardhouse.

She peered through her binoculars. "He's checking ID and inspecting the rig."

A moment later the gates opened and the steel pipes sprouting from the roof of the cab puffed black smoke that slowly dissipated beneath the white cone of light coming from the streetlight marking the entrance.

"Greg Marino?" he asked.

"Yes. He's the passenger."

"If you've been tracking him, that means you know where the hostages are."

"It's not that simple."

"Simple?"

"He's got muscle on the place. A crazy Army chopper pilot. Convicted felon."

Shit. A chopper pilot could easily have flown the hovercraft. "How do you know that?"

"What does it matter? What's important is that we can get him."

All he could think is that this cop might get them all killed.

56

Davis Frost dropped anchor on the *Arm & A Leg* in about fifty feet of water near a decommissioned oil platform off the Gulf of Mexico. While captaining the yacht for Jake, he'd seen the supply helicopters making routine flights to the offshore oilrigs, delivering provisions and transporting people.

He'd agreed to pay a premium price for one-way service to the Lake Jackson Airport where he'd chartered a six-passenger prop plane run by a freight dog who took cash and didn't ask questions.

He'd been transferring the cash hidden in the hull of the yacht into big waterproof dive bags for weeks leading up to the trip to West Texas. He'd ordered the bags online months ago, complete with the logo he'd designed himself for his imaginary company, Fisheye Dive Adventures.

He'd raised the dive flag on the bow, a signal to the helicopter pilot he was ready to go. The chopper hovered fifteen feet above the yacht, blades huffing, churning the water to white caps, and dropped an empty basket. He held on as the wind rocked the boat, loading the empty basket with the bags of money he'd stacked on the teakwood swim platform. The crew winched and transferred the bags in through the open door of the chopper.

He took his cell from his pocket and recorded fifteen seconds of video. Starting on an angle looking up at the helicopter hovering overhead, he tilted down inside the basket filled with bags, pressed the red button and stuffed it back in his shorts' pocket. He'd taken a series of still shots earlier, documenting the unzipped duffle bags filled with banded stacks of hundreds.

On the final batch, he'd loaded the last two dive bags and climbed inside, exhausted, the basket twirling, the scene below him a pinwheel of blue and white. A pair of athletic men hauled the last two duffle bags on board, then pulled him to safety.

The Sikorsky gained altitude, and turned northwest, toward the shoreline. He looked back once at Jake's million-dollar Maritimo yacht, now just a dot of white. The youngest man, the muscle, handed him a headset. He listened to air traffic control clear them to land at the regional airport.

Scrolling through his phone, he selected the video he'd just shot and three good still shots of the dive bags filled with cash and texted them to Daryl Flood.

This was retribution. He'd taken the lion's share of risk and done the heavy lifting on the salvage job. Camping on Boca Chita Island, feeding the mosquitoes, locating the wreck, hauling a boatload of heavy transport cases from the seabed into his old twenty-three-foot Dusky fishing boat.

He'd trusted Lauren and she'd sold him a bill of goods, telling him they were working on a corporate video for a business that made watertight transport cases.

The company, she'd said, had sunk a powerboat off the coast of Miami twenty years ago as a time capsule to prove the integrity of their products. They wanted to open the cases during a live webcast, hoping to attract a big audience.

If ever a load of shit had been dumped on his head, it came from that story.

He'd spent a week in the hospital with a broken jaw, and six more weeks on a liquid diet with his mouth wired shut. When he looked in the mirror, he saw that his mouth had healed on an angle. Lauren said it was his imagination: another load of crap. Worse, his jaw ached 24/7 from an untreatable form of temporomandibular joint pain.

Meanwhile, Lauren, Jake, and Vance bought a luxury guest ranch. Jake drove a Porsche 911 GTR and lived on a sixty-foot yacht. Lauren bought a condo in Coconut Grove. And when Vance's million-dollar sailboat sank during Hurricane Irma, he shrugged it off.

What did he get beyond his life flashing before his eyes and a broken jaw? Ten thousand bucks. Big whoop.

It didn't take long to discover the cash hidden in the belly of the *Arm & A Leg*. The trio knew he was working for peanuts, captaining a floating vault filled with enough cash to get him killed.

When Lauren dangled the West Texas video shoot in front of him, an opportunity opened up. Once she proposed the dates, he manipulated the schedule, tweaking things here and there.

Lauren had the same blind spot she'd always had. Vance had stayed at the Texas ranch after they sold it back to the previous owner and Davis knew she wanted to see him. He used it to his advantage.

Jake had promised Caitlin a father-daughter bonding trip to the ranch. As soon as Jake firmed the date, he reminded Lauren she'd promised to hire him to shoot the marketing video. The owner, Roy Pompadour, wanted them to come later in the springtime when the desert was in bloom. But Davis knew Lauren would jump at the chance to go sooner. To visit her blind spot.

When Greg Marino had come within a hair of putting a slug in his skull when the bullet jammed in the chamber, Davis had pissed himself. Marino went crazy, pistol-whipping him, busting his jaw.

When the chance to get even with that monster arose, he'd vowed to seize it.

Jake's kid disappearing? That was never part of the plan.

57

I t was pitch black inside the trunk. Lauren tightened her abs and pulled her knees to her chest. Panting, and gasping for air, she slowed her breathing by counting, staving off an oncoming panic attack.

I have to get out.

I have to get out.

I HAVE TO GET OUT.

Rolling onto her knees in a cat stretch, she swept her hands around inside, feeling for objects, trying to recall what she'd left there. Riding boots. A crop. Spurs.

A Christmas gift bag from her trainer filled with horse brushes.

The Audi bounced, hitting a speed hump, or a pothole, throwing her airborne, thumping the back of her skull on the metal lid. Rubbing her head, she scooted toward the passenger seat bulkhead. The rear seats opened to carry skis. Fumbling her fingers along the felt-covered divider, she pinched the metal latch and released it.

The opening was much too small to escape but it gave her a line of sight to Daryl behind the wheel.

The tire iron.

Where was it?

She'd called roadside assistance last year to fix a flat and hung around while the tow truck driver changed it. Scooting 180-degrees on her side, she felt inside the molded compartment next to the passenger's-side rear tire. A roll of toilet paper. A gallon plastic bag with a combination lock. Stretching her right arm, she felt the opposite side of the trunk. No tools.

Then she remembered. The spare was stored in a recessed space beneath her. That had to be where the jack and tire iron were. She scooted on her hip, contorting her body, making room to feel for it. Her left hamstring cramped. She grit her teeth, keeping quiet, waiting for the pain to pass. Folding her body more and more tightly into a cannonball, there still wasn't enough room to open the tire well.

She reached for the plastic bag and removed the padlock. It was one of those heavy round ones shaped like an old pocket watch. She put the bag in her jacket pocket and palmed the heavy lock in her hand like brass knuckles.

The car stopped. She peered through the gap. It was big enough to put her forearm through. Daryl got out. She held her breath, and craning her neck, pushed her ear nearer to the opening.

It smelled like salt air. She heard water lapping against a bulkhead. A tear welled and rolled down her cheek. Was he going to kill her, dump her body in the water?

Why didn't she do what Roy Pompadour told her to and get the information to Vance? Why didn't she do what Vance told her to do? Go home and stay inside. Instead, she drove west to the outskirts of town, to a part of the city she didn't know, with a broken window. She hadn't been following Daryl Flood. He'd been tracking her. How could she have been so stupid?

GREG WATCHED Tim shooting the shit with the skeleton crew, taking their sweet-ass time—on his dime. How the fuck long did it take to pick up the container he was trading for the one they'd unloaded, and drop it on the flatbed behind him?

His stomach heaved at the aroma of wet dog. He opened his window. A swarm of mosquitoes filled the cab. He cranked it up and reached into the side pocket on the driver's side for the can of bug repellent. He pressed the nozzle, filling the air with a bitter smell. Gagging at the blend of wretched odors, he opened the cab door, stepped onto the running board and sprayed himself from head to toe.

Reaching inside the top of his boot, he removed his Kimber .45 and stuffed it down the front of his pants. Time to get this show on the road.

VANCE SAW a second set of headlights coming from the mainland, LEDs, the blinding white lights of a passenger car.

"Shit," Kagan said, throwing the cruiser into reverse, backing into a driveway.

The car passed slowly. A black Audi.

Kagan's mobile buzzed. She looked at it under her jacket. The driver in the Audi continued slowly toward the end of the peninsula.

He felt for the Glock under his jacket.

Kagan saw him. "Don't be stupid."

"What's that Audi doing here?"

"It's backup."

"Who's in it?"

Kagan didn't answer. The driver U-turned at the end of

Dodge Island and crept toward them, lights dimmed.

"I'm getting out," he said.

"I wouldn't do that if I were you."

"I'm not you."

He hopped over the concrete barrier and crouched near a thicket of mangroves growing at the shoreline. A cloud of mosquitoes took flight, swarming his face, the shrill buzz piecing his ears. He waved his hands, slapping his face, scratching his arms.

Beneath the industrial lights on the other side of the road, the crane lifted a container onto a barge like a Tonka Toy.

The Audi stopped parallel to the concrete barricade, a few hundred feet away from where Kagan had tucked the car in backward. He drew his weapon, and pointing it at the ground, peered over the barrier. A man got out of the Audi and jogged to the squad car, his long black hair blowing in the breeze. Daryl Flood climbed into the passenger seat of the Crown Vic.

He stayed low, using the barricade for cover, watching, then made his way toward the Audi. The front passenger window was busted out. Using the shadows for cover, he climbed over the low wall, and crept around the back bumper to the driver's-side and peered into the cockpit. Lauren's purse was turned over on the passenger seat.

Staying low, he used the car for cover and moved back to the rear bumper. Taking one long step across, and a second one up and over the barrier, he landed heels-first on the other side. Squatting, he placed his hand atop the barricade, using it as a guide as he moved closer to the Crown Vic to spy on Kagan and Flood.

Something landed on the road and clattered a few feet from him. He jumped at the noise, heart racing. He backtracked to see what it was. A silver padlock glinted on the asphalt. He heard a muffled voice coming from the direction of the Audi. He squatted, and crouching, made his way back to the driver's-side, out of Kagan and Flood's view, and listened. He crept to the rear bumper and tapped the trunk lid. A pounding sound answered. He placed his ear next to the license plate.

"Help," a woman's voice said. "Help me. Get me out of here."

Good God. Lauren was locked in the trunk. He couldn't help her. Not now. He shaded his phone with his jacket and typed a quick text, `Hold on`, and pushed the send button. He heard the ping coming from near the busted-out window. Then he remembered he'd seen her purse dumped on the front seat.

Shit. He waited a minute. The Audi was parked down from the terminal, closer to the dead-end tip of the island. If Marino tried to get away, she'd be far enough away from the action. She'd be safe, but she'd have to tough it out in the trunk.

Slinking, he peeked around the rear bumper of the Audi. The interior of the Crown Vic was dark. Moving slowly, he took a position on the other side of the barrier and hunkered down to watch.

The tractor-trailer lights lit the compound as it turned around inside and approached the exit facing the guard shack. The driver waited at the gate. It lifted and he motored toward the chain-link fence waiting for it to slide open.

Kagan started the engine and accelerated, tires spinning, drag-racing across the road, jamming the brakes, sliding parallel to the fence, and blocking the exit.

The truck driver sounded the air horn.

Vance covered his ears.

The automatic chain-link fence began to roll open.

The passenger in the truck popped up like a gopher and fired a round, hitting the windshield on Kagan's cruiser. The doors on the patrol unit flung open and Kagan and Flood rolled out, then scrambled for cover on the passenger's-side of the Crown Vic.

BOOM.

A flash of light from inside the Peterbilt. The door opened and the driver fell out from behind the wheel.

Kneeling, Vance deactivated the instant-on red laser on his Glock. Using the barricade to steady his hands, he lined his right eye with the metal sight, ignoring the mosquitoes buzzing his face and stinging his arms. He didn't have a shot.

Kagan and Flood hunkered down, and split ways. She moved to the front wheel well, he to the rear bumper. On cue, they took potshots at the semi's cab. One bullet struck the windshield. The shooter disappeared under the dash and pointed his weapon out the window, unloading six blind rounds.

One slug smashed into the barrier less than a foot from Vance. He hit the dirt. If his calculations were right, the shooter had no more than three rounds left without reloading.

He squatted in the moist grass, scanning the perimeter.

The Peterbilt roared, building torque, the silver roof pipes belching black smoke, the cab bouncing like a lion on a leash. His guess, the driver was going to drop the clutch and ram Kagan's cruiser.

Crouching in the shadows, he climbed over the barricade and zigzagged, creeping up on Kagan, holding the Glock steady at eye level.

Greg was behind the wheel, holding the brake like a top fuel dragster, heating the tires, the fronts smoking, the engine building RPMs, the cab seesawing slightly, the heavy load working as a counterweight.

He dropped the clutch. The semi lurched forward, T-boning the cruiser, pushing it thirty-three degrees as if opening an enormous door. Kagan and Flood leapt backward, staying low.

The truck stalled.

Ruh, ruh, ruh.

The crankshaft wouldn't turn over.

Ruh, ruh, ruh.

On the third try it roared to life, exhaust pipe covers flapping, hacking gray smoke, ramming the Crown Vic a second time, pushing it sideways, opening the gap another foot. The driver backed the load up a few feet and doubled down, jamming his foot on the gas, pushing the squad car harder, rotating it an inch at a time like a stubborn turnstile.

Daryl crouched behind the Crown Vic, staying low, moving as it moved, keeping cover.

Vance looked for Kagan. She was gone. He advanced in the darkness, unseen, across the road, past the police cruiser, to the passenger's-side of the Peterbilt, getting one foot on the running board. The fenders quaked and the engine screamed as it struggled to push the crumpling Crown Vic out of the way.

He gripped the window frame and peered into the cab.

This time he wasn't going to play nice. Not like the last time when he'd left Greg Marino cuffed in a storage unit, betting wrongly he'd planted enough evidence to put him away.

The patrol unit swung farther sideways, smashing into the utility pole, stopping the semi like a giant shim. Greg wrestled the gear knob with two hands, looking for the reverse gear, whites of his eyes flashing, teeth bared like a rabid animal, jugular pulsating.

Now or never.

He took his time, rested the nose of the Glock on the window frame, and took a shot.

Greg screamed and rolled backward, grabbing his kneecap, groaning, kicking up a plume of animal fur.

Vance dropped from the running board and squatted, swatting bugs, looking for Kagan, waiting for her to make a move.

The truck idled, then stalled.

What the hell? What was taking so long, what were Kagan and Flood doing? He sat on his heels, shoulder against the searing heat of the wheel well, breathing tire smoke, heart pumping.

This sucker wasn't getting away.

Staying low, using the front corner of the grill for cover, he popped up for an instant, assessing the situation. No sign of Kagan or Flood.

Crouching, he reversed direction to the three-foot gap between the cab and the cargo where two axles and eight wide tires supported the weight of the freight container. He squared his shoulders and leaned back, twisted quickly and glanced through the opening, then dropped back.

No signs of life.

Suddenly his feet went out from under him. He hit the ground facedown, used his hands to break the fall, but dropped the Glock. Digging his fingers into the pavement, he searched for anything to hold onto as something reeled him under.

Two powerful hands gripped his ankles, dragging him under, the broiling underbelly of the truck heating his back.

Kicking blindly, he broke one foot free and stretched his torso, wriggling his legs, fumbling with his hands, stretching his arms, and reaching for the gun too far way.

Uh-oh.

The engine re-fired. A glob of oil dripped onto his pants, burning the skin on the back of his thigh as 1200 pounds of torque began to twist above him. He scooted on his stomach. Tire smoke bloomed and wafted, a dense black fog blinding him. Coughing, he crawled facedown toward the center of the underbelly, diesel engine gasping and howling, tires turning faster.

A pair of hands clamped his windpipe. He rolled onto his back. He couldn't breathe. Clawing at the hands, he peeled two fingers back and bent them until they snapped. Jamming his elbow into the chest of his attacker, he glanced up at the drivetrain and rolled to the left, rotating his body, staying between the axles as the front tires climbed on the hood of the Crown Vic.

The smoke dissipated. He measured the space above him, a foot, maybe. He pressed his cheek to the ground and twisted his neck, studying the angle like a pool hustler. Rolling onto his belly, he rotated his torso as the truck crept forward, changing its trajectory, six pairs of massive tires turning in unison above him, spewing dirt and gravel.

He inhaled through his sleeve, held his breath and closed his eyes. When he opened them, a silhouette crawled at him like a croc. He rolled onto his left hip and heeled it in the skull.

His assailant levitated, as if being pulled up by an invisible force, hoisted by the neck, screaming. He scooted out of the way, letting the body drag by, one eye watching the wheels. The driver made a hard turn to the left, the body swung right, into the oncoming path of four giant wheels on two axles.

Clunk-clunk. Clunk-clunk.

His stomach roiled. The body broke away, and the human hair attached to the drivetrain, brushed his face.

He lay still as the semi tractor-trailer passed over him, and completed its turn onto Port Boulevard.

He scrambled to his feet. Spotting the Glock lying in the gravel he scooped it up and activated the laser. The truck gained speed, groaning, topping out first gear, about to drop into second when he jumped the board on the passenger's-side. Staying low, he peered into the cab. Testing the laser on the ground, he raised his sidearm, nosed it through the passenger window, took general aim, activated the laser more precisely, and shot Marino in the right hand.

His ears rang from the blast of the 9-millimeter.

Marino dropped both hands from the wheel and rolled sideways, howling.

A burly man in an orange vest, the truck driver who'd been

shot inside the cab, ran to the driver's side and opened the door.

Twenty, maybe thirty men outfitted in black D.E.A. gear emerged from the shadows. Two armored vehicles rolled toward them and stopped in front of the semi tractor-trailer, in a V-formation, blocking it. A Coast Guard helicopter hovered above.

"You okay?" the truck driver asked him, peeling off his orange vest, revealing another beneath it, D.E.A.-issue.

"Uh-huh. You're D.E.A?"

"Yeah. Who are you?"

"My name's Vance Courage."

"Good work." He patted his flak jacket. "Hurts like hell and gonna have a bruise big as a cannonball. Close range knocked the shit out of me. I'll take care of this. Go help the others."

Daryl Flood stood over the body on the ground. He lifted the head.

Oh, God. Half of Officer Kagan's scalp was missing, her police uniform looked like a gunnysack filled with human parts.

"She was working with Marino?" he asked over the helicopter chuffing above, confused.

"Nope. Revenge job," Daryl said. "Marino raped her brother's daughter. But don't quote me." He shook his head and looked away.

"Then why'd she go after me?" Vance asked.

"I tried to stop her."

"From going after *me*?"

"Yeah. She knew you could have put him down, that you had the shot and you didn't take it. What a pity. She should've let justice take it from here. We got him."

Justice. Man-oh-man. She'd almost gotten both of them killed. "Is the hovercraft here? Is that what he dropped off?"

"Yep."

"Why'd he steal it?"

"Shipping it to the ChiComms."

"I didn't think he was smart enough to put something like that together."

"He didn't. It fell in his lap. Tel Aviv doesn't mess around when it comes to intellectual property theft."

So that's what Unit 8200 was doing at the ranch. "Tel Aviv? What's their connection to the D.E.A.?"

"It's part of a sting operation that started inside the SuperMax at Florence."

Lauren told him Daryl had worked there. "You're undercover? With the D.E.A.?"

"That's right." Daryl slapped him on the back. "Needless to say, we had a few screw-ups." He looked at the shipping container on the flatbed blocking the road. "We got the goods and can prove the Chinese were bypassing sanctions. That was the mission. Didn't figure he'd start taking hostages. Or that anyone would get killed."

"Wait. I still don't understand. What was Greg going to do with that?" He gestured to the freight container filled with the substance needed to make street meth.

"Marino thought F&F would handle it from here."

"F&F?"

"The trucking company. F&F's a front."

"For who?"

"The D.E.A. Everyone thinks opioids are the crisis. Don't get me wrong. It's still a problem. But street meth coming up from Mexico is the biggest scourge. Ever heard of El Flaco?"

"Sure." Everyone had. The head of the Sinaloa cartel, extradited from Mexico to the US and sentenced to life at the SuperMax in Colorado.

"He's running his organization from prison. The Justice Department thinks he has access to a billion dollars and he's been shopping the black market for chemicals. The Chinese have been sneaking it directly into Mexico but now that the

Mexican government has to answer to D.C. or face economic sanctions, they tightened down their ports. We wanted to find a way to stop them from exporting the shit illegally. So we dangled technology in front of them."

"How does Marino fit the picture?"

Daryl shook his head. "There was some crazy rumor going around Florence that Marino thought his dead drug lord father left sunken treasure for him."

"Seriously?" He felt the adrenaline.

"Yeah. The Aryans told us some retired cop, Fort Lauderdale, I think, was helping float the rumor. We used it and told Marino we could recover his imaginary money for him. He wanted El Flaco to guarantee him thirty-five million dollars. Can you believe that? We sent a message back that for thirty-five million the Sinaloans could hire an army of thugs, and they might just kill Marino for having the balls to suggest it. Marino saw the logic."

Vance felt a lump in his throat.

Daryl wasn't finished. "I went around you guys and asked Lauren's buddy, Davis Frost, if he could fake a video for us. Davis did a damn good job. Had this yacht he wrangled somehow. Hired an oilrig supply chopper. Did a hell of a job staging it. Everything, including the money, looked real. He charged us a pretty penny, but it worked. Boy, coulda fooled me."

"Huh." He stuffed his shaky hands in his jacket pockets. "Why'd you plant the hovercraft at Pomp's?"

"I couldn't exactly meet him at the Dunkin' Donuts parking lot and do a transfer. There's a lot of surveillance out there with all the R&D and testing going on and not a lot of places to hide. Pomp's place was the best option. Plus, we had a tracking device on it."

"A guard was killed."

"Not part of the plan."

"You knew where Jake's kid was the whole time?"

"That was *never* part of the plan."

"Jesus." He raked his hands through his hair. "Since when did Beijing start doing business with the prison gangs?"

Daryl laughed. "Stanford economists, biochemists from Kansas, the Aryan Brotherhood. Any sell-out will do."

"Why'd the Chinese want the prototype that badly? That they'd take the chance of pissing off the US government?"

"That's not what they're after. It's the software for a self-flying helicopter they want. The Chinese promised to manufacture them and sell them to El Flaco's cartel as a bonus if they'd help transfer the technology to them. Can you imagine?"

There was still a missing piece. "The technology belongs to the Israelis, not us."

"Roy Pompadour's niece died of a meth overdose. He tried everything to help her. Beautiful young girl, in and out of rehab, life ruined. Such a tragedy." He shook his head. "Ninety-percent of it crosses the southern border. Production and distribution are run by the Sinaloans. Mr. Pompadour is a personal friend of the Israeli Prime Minister.

"His express intent was to severely impact the cartel's supply chain. Mr. Pompadour is just sick about the collateral damage. But it's taken a lot of meth off the street. Hopefully, it'll spare a lot of other families."

That was a lot of intel to ingest. "I hope he's right. He has enough money and influence to bend the rules. At least you got that piece of garbage off the street."

Daryl looked at the last text on his phone. "Can you believe it? Kagan's final words were to me. I need to go figure out who's going to notify her next of kin. Oh. One more thing. Tell Lauren I'm sorry. I couldn't take the chance she'd blow my cover." He rolled his sleeve up.

Vance raised his eyebrows. "She bit you?"

Daryl handed him a phone. "It's Greg's. The address for the safe house's in it."

"You don't need it?"

"Been downloading data for days. Gotta a guy who's good at it. Tell Lauren he's the one who sent her the cryptic texts. Tell her we were looking out for her, all of us, especially Mr. Pompadour."

"Is your guy the guy in Alpine?"

"I guess she told you about him."

"Yeah. Who is he?"

"Ol' Kit. Ever see that old movie about the kid who almost started a war hacking into the DOD computers?"

"Seriously?"

"Seriously. Retired CIA. Plus, he's an FOP."

"Hmm." Friend of Pomp's.

"I'll text you the passcode for Marino's phone. You better get her out of the trunk. I'd like to have a head start before you let that wildcat out."

Vance turned to leave.

Daryl stopped him. "Be careful. The guy at the house—he's armed and dangerous. Chopper pilot, ex-military. He's got a bad case of PTSD. But he's no killer. At least, not so far."

The puzzle was complete—but for one thing. Was Jake's boat really missing or did Davis borrow it for the fake video? The dinner he didn't eat almost came up.

He jogged past the mangled wreckage that was the Crown Vic, toward Lauren's Audi parked in a safe spot down the road, away from the wreckage.

El Flaco. Thin man. Of course.

He inhaled deeply and opened the trunk. She looked terrified. A wave of emotion washed over him. Fuck the money. It wasn't worth it. He looked away and dabbed a tear from his eye. Then she bitched him out and it sounded beautiful.

58

Vance approached a strobe of red lights. A uniformed cop stopped him. Daryl said something and the officer waved him by the semi tractor-trailer full of a chemical he couldn't pronounce. He tapped the brakes on the Audi as an ambulance pulled out in front of him, siren wailing.

He gave Lauren the password to Marino's phone. She keyed it in and held it so he could see the screen. `You are 23 minutes from home.`

He scrolled through his mobile and dialed Daniel.

"Where are you?"

"En route to the port. Been listening to my scanner. Something big's going down."

"I guess you made bail."

"Ray Dinero made bail. I was just along for the ride."

"You're a little late to the party." He handed the phone to Lauren and asked her to give Daniel the address to the safe house.

In the win category, he'd helped stop the hovercraft from going to China. A federal investigation would reveal the source and identity behind the shipment from China. As for the rest of it, God only knew.

HE ROLLED to a stop across from an old, two-story apartment building. The dumpster behind it overflowed with trash. An abandoned shopping cart lay in the footpath leading to a stairwell.

Lauren got ready while he waited for Daniel.

"Are you sure you want to do this?"

"Not unless you have a better idea." She flipped the visor down and the mirror lit up.

She applied lipstick and used her finger to smear it, then drew wide black lines around her eyes and rubbed them until she looked like a raccoon. Opening two more buttons on her shirt, she reached into her bra and rearranged her breasts, making them look larger. She finished by rolling her jeans to her calves, tying her shirttails above her naval, and kicking off her shoes.

He felt a pit in his stomach. "Do you think this is a good idea?"

"You mean me going barefoot or the whole look?"

Headlights appeared in his rearview. Daniel turned his lights out and parked behind the Audi.

The trio climbed the stairs to apartment 13B; a little boy stopped to stare. His mother urged him to keep moving.

Older kids on bikes circled the parking lot. Telemundo blared from an open window, and the aroma of roasting meat wafted from an open apartment door, the occupants pulling it shut as they passed.

Everyday sounds stopped, a sign that the dwellers knew something was going down.

The walkway on the second floor ended at a corner unit overlooking the street where they'd parked. The white metal door had dimples, old marks he recognized as coming from a police baton. He held his hand up. Lauren and Daniel stopped and waited as he crouched, passing beneath the window and the peephole. The blinds were drawn and the lights were out.

Squatting, he looked over the rusted railing to the walkway below, checking for witnesses. He backtracked, ducking below the window, signaling Daniel and Lauren to follow him to the narrow walkway between buildings where he could scout the backside of apartment 13B. He spotted a small window near the roofline.

Two men speaking Spanish exited apartment 12B and walked around the corner. He smelled marijuana before he saw them. The younger of the two, surprised to see them, flicked the joint over the railing, into the hedges. He held his finger to his lips and waved them off.

He leaned back, shading his eyes from the streetlamp in his periphery. The narrow window near the roofline was eight feet up, about two-feet wide and a foot-and-a-half tall.

He gestured toward it and whispered to Daniel, "I need to look inside."

It was eerie quiet.

He placed his heel in Daniel's cupped palms, bounced twice, then jumped, grabbing the lentil at the base of the window. He peered inside, balancing on his fingertips.

Squinting, he waited for his eyes to adjust. Two people sat at the edge of a twin bed. He saw the outline of a child's head resting on the pillow. He tapped on the window and ducked.

Daniel grunted, forearms wobbling.

He raised his head. Caitlin stared up at him. He held his finger to his lips. Her eyes got big and she cupped her hands into a big heart shape, smiling.

Vance kept his voice low. "They're inside. Caitlin saw me. They're okay."

An attractive woman in a pair of short-shorts crossed the street and walked toward the U-shaped courtyard.

"Wait here," Vance said to Lauren and Sarge, trotting down the back staircase, slowing his pace on a path intended to intercept the woman. He needed her to think their meeting was an accident.

She spotted him first. He strolled past, then stopped for a moment and glanced around. She took the bait.

"You looking for someone?"

"Sort of. Do you live here?"

She cracked her chewing gum and raised one hip. "Uh-huh."

"It's my cousin's birthday. I was hoping to surprise him."

She backed away a step.

"He doesn't know I'm in town. Come here." He motioned her closer, beneath the upper deck walkway. "So, he won't see me."

She kept her distance.

"I need a favor."

"What kinda favor?"

"Knock on his door for me."

"Why would I do that?" she asked, eyes darting.

"I'll give you a hundred dollars."

She turned her head sideways. "That's too easy."

He took a crisp hundred from his wallet.

She narrowed her eyes.

"Look, I don't have all day. My cousin's gonna go to work any minute."

"That's all I have to do?"

"Yeah. Just knock on the door."

"Pay me first."

He handed her the hundred. "What's your name?"

"Gloria."

"Okay, Gloria, after you."

At the top of the stairs, he held his hand up and motioned her to the doorway of 13B. Gloria stood in front of the peephole, swiped red lipstick, patted her hair, held her knuckles up—poised to knock—then looked to him for the okay. Her eyes widened when she saw him un-holster the Glock.

"Shhh," he whispered, then mimed a knocking gesture.

Gloria rapped on the door, waited a second, kissed her open palm, and blew it at the peephole.

The door opened.

"Hey, there. I heard it's your birthday."

Mack stepped out onto the walkway, his weird gun slung over his shoulder.

Vance pounced, catching him off guard, and rammed Mack's squatty body into the metal railing. Gloria dashed down the stairs. Mack leapt to his feet, spun, and dove toward him. He ducked to the left as Mack belly-flopped on the walkway, the Mauser breaking free and skidding on the cement.

"Fuck," Mack said, rubbing his chin.

Daniel grabbed the carbine and knelt, holding his pistol on the ex-Army helicopter pilot.

The blinds on the window next to the front door twitched. He saw two hands spread the slats, and an eyeball peering at him. "Oh my God," his mother said opening the door, "jur here. Oh, my God . . . oh, my God."

59

J ake's ex stared into space, resting her broken arm on her knee. He'd braced himself for the riot act. But it didn't come.

A nurse in the ER called their names. Ann adjusted the blue denim sling over her shoulder. He reached for her good hand, helping her to her feet.

"The doctor would like to see you."

She led them through a corridor where a second nurse in scrubs directed them to an office at the end of the hall.

"I wonder what's going on," Ann said.

He shook his head and pulled the brim of a ball cap lower to hide the gash on his forehead.

They stood in front of a mahogany desk, red buttons flashing on a desktop phone. Medical school diplomas hung on the walls.

A man in a tailored suit entered and held the door for a younger woman dressed business casual.

"I'm Dr. Hamilton," he said. "This is Detective Valdez. Please have a seat."

"Is our daughter okay?" Jake asked.

"Your daughter will be fine," he said. "Please, sit."

"Of course," he said, helping Ann.

"She's been examined but I think she should undergo further evaluation."

"Why?" Ann asked, "Why can't we just take her home?"

The doctor looked at Valdez and nodded, giving her the go-ahead.

"I'm with SVB, the Special Victims Bureau."

"Special Victims Bureau?" Jake asked.

"We investigate sex crimes. Your daughter should be seen. We have a special unit at Jackson Memorial."

"For what?" Jake gripped the chair arms. "Was she . . . assaulted?"

"We don't know," Valdez said. "One of the men who was holding her hostage is a suspected serial rapist. He's in custody. We'd like to do a rape kit. To get DNA."

"Did she say she was assaulted?" Ann asked.

"No."

The doctor scrambled to his feet. "I understand how you must be feeling."

A vein pulsated in Jake's head. "No, you don't. You have no idea how I'm feeling." He was in a fog, his head throbbed and his stomach roiled. "No tests."

"She has superficial lacerations on her wrists and some bruises," Valdez said.

His heart pounded under his shirt.

"She reported some spotting during—"

"I said, *no.*" He mopped his brow with his sleeve.

Ann's lip quivered.

"She may have been drugged and won't remember what happened," Detective Valdez said. "She's underage. We need your permission."

The doctor leaned forward, one hand on the desktop. "We could examine her here, if that would make it easier."

"Did you hear him?" Ann asked. "He said, no. You will not use our daughter to solve your case."

"Then a least give her Plan B," Dr. Hamilton said.

Jake raised his brows. "Plan B?"

"It's the morning-after pill," Ann said.

"For what?" he asked.

"To prevent pregnancy," the doctor said.

He stood, nostrils flaring. "My daughter will never know we had this discussion. Do you understand?"

Valdez nodded.

Dr. Hamilton said, "I'm sorry for your situation."

"Come on, Ann. Let's get out of here."

60

D avis Frost had watched from the porthole as the Cessna descended over turquoise water, touching down at Owen Roberts International Airport in Grand Cayman. The man behind the wheel of an awaiting black Tahoe asked to see his US passport. The pilot loaded the Fisheye Dive Adventure bags into the SUV.

Five minutes later, he arrived at a four-story, white Art Deco building where he was led into a private room with a large vault. His phone buzzed in his pocket.

"How'd the pilot I referred work out?" Daniel asked.

"Good. I'm there now. They're gonna be mad the money's missing."

"They'll get over it."

"Did they catch him?"

"Yep. Charges are gonna stick this time."

A man in a suit walked in. "Oh, pardon me," he said. "I'll give you a minute."

Davis held his hand up. "Hang on." He turned his head for privacy. "I'll text you the details when I'm finished up here." He ended the call.

The man in the tailored suit handed Davis an envelope. "Insert the drives into a secure computer and follow the prompts."

The banker held his hand out and Davis shook it. "Here's my card. Thank you for trusting us to manage your assets."

MID-FLIGHT TO MIAMI, Davis inserted the thumb drive into his laptop. A few minutes later he looked at the balance in his Cayman account. The rush of dopamine was better than any drug he'd ever done.

At baggage claim at Miami International Airport, Davis recognized him. Sarge had been there that day in the storage facility in Plantation Key when Greg Marino had almost killed him. He'd sat in a puddle of his own urine, tasting blood in his mouth, wholly prepared to meet his maker.

He handed the envelope to Sarge and headed to the gate to catch the next flight back to Grand Cayman.

61

Vance followed Lauren to the body shop to drop the Audi for repairs. While he waited, he opened the convertible top of the old Volvo. Then he activated Greg's phone and watched the video that Davis faked for the D.E.A., the one Daryl had forwarded to Greg's phone.

The reason it looked so real was because it *was real*. When it ended, he played it again, and again, and again, watching the duffel bags of money winching skyward toward the chopper overhead. He'd spoken with Karl, the cop who'd been watching Jake's yacht, and learned the *Arm & A Leg* had been located by the Coast Guard, unmanned and anchored near a decommissioned oil platform south of Freeport, Texas. He'd underestimated Davis. In a big way. Talk about the last laugh.

Driving the Dolphin Expressway east to the MacArthur Causeway linking Biscayne Bay to the mainland, he glanced at Lauren looking skyward, eyes closed. It was the sort of day where the sky met the sea as a single blue backdrop. He felt for her hand and held it for a moment.

From the mainland, a series of bridges linked the chain of

artificial islands dotted with signs for tourist traps. He passed the exit to the underwater tunnel built at the southeastern end of Watson Island, meant for passengers heading to the cruise lines.

He slowed the vintage Volvo. Across the channel, the port of Miami bustled with semi tractor-trailers loaded with freight, rental cars, tourists, tankers, and cruise ships with their baritone horns wailing across the bay. Hordes marched up the gangways, stopping on the upper decks to admire the view.

Beyond the cruise ships, a steady stream of semis rolled toward the working end of Dodge Island where stevedores loaded and off-loaded cargo. He followed the bridge a dogleg north across the last two manmade islands, one operating the ferry service to Fisher Island; the other, the Coast Guard base station.

Yesterday, it could have ended differently.

He downshifted the Volvo as he approached Alton Road, turned north, and stopped at the valet sign. The yellow stucco building with arched green awnings and a clay-tiled roof had a line outside the door waiting for lunch.

"Joe's Stone Crab? Can we afford it?" Lauren asked.

It was a legit question now that she knew Davis Frost had made off with their money. "That's what credit cards are for," he said, shrugging.

He got out and hurried to the passenger door, opening it, taking her wrist. With his hand on the small of her back, he led the way, holding the door for her, and stopped at the maître d' stand.

"Table for three," he said. "It's under Courage."

"Nice name."

"Thanks. I hear that a lot."

The man at the stand checked his name off the list. Even at

lunch the place was packed. "Have a seat at the bar. It'll be a minute."

She sat on a stool next to him. "Three?"

"Daniel invited himself."

She furrowed her brow. "And you didn't say no?"

"Like he would have taken no for an answer."

"I suppose." She scanned the restaurant. "I thought it would be fancier."

Joe's was laid out, and lit, like a cafeteria.

The maître d' seated them at a table for four covered with a black-and-white plastic tablecloth, and bibs with blue bow ties at each setting.

Vance's phone pinged. You buying?

Daniel stood over him with his mobile in his hand. *"Como estas, primo,"* he said, pulling up a chair and sitting next to him.

Primo. "You sent those texts to me? I should've known."

"When I found out Greg Marino was out on bail I started snooping around, asking questions." Daniel twisted the post in his ear. "Did you think I'd keep my nose out of it?"

Daniel keep his nose out of other people's business? "Not a chance," Vance said, reminded that Flood said a retired cop had been pushing the rumor at Florence.

The waiter stood over them, pen in hand.

"May we have a moment?" Vance asked.

When the waiter was gone, Daniel said, "I have a friend at the SVB. She went to the hospital last night to talk to Jake."

"Jeez. I can't imagine," Vance said.

When the waiter returned, he and Lauren ordered. Daniel opted out.

"You're not going to dine with us?" she asked.

"No." He reached into his pants pocket and set three thumb drives on the plastic tablecloth.

Lauren picked one up. "What are these?"

"Your money. Deposited into a Cayman bank."

"I don't understand," she said.

"The gold drive is for you. Davis thought it would be a nice touch, you know, gold for Gold."

"Davis did this?" he asked.

"He took a cut. Ran it by me first. I thought it was fair."

"Ran it by you first? What about running it by us?"

Daniel shrugged. "He took ten percent. You should thank him. As far as I'm concerned, he performed a *muy* valuable service."

"My God. He could have kept all of it," Lauren said. "What would we have done then?"

She was right. Vance picked up the two silver drives and dropped them into the inner pocket of his jacket, still numbed out from the events over the last few days.

Daniel stood. "Enjoy your stone crab."

"Wait," she said. "Where's Davis?"

"Grand Cayman."

"He's staying there?"

"Far as I know." He ran his head over the top of his smooth, brown head. "See you around."

When Daniel was gone, she asked, "Are we in the clear?"

"You mean if the money's in an offshore account?"

"Yeah."

"If it's true, there'll be a money trail. Clear will never be an option."

The waiter interrupted, carrying food. "Stone crab with melted butter for the lady." He set a plate of shiny orange and black claws in front of her. "And cold, with lemon, for the gentleman," he said.

A sweet aroma wafted from hers.

She picked up the crab cracker and put a claw between the metal teeth.

"Allow me," he said, taking it from her, snapping the hard shell and setting the cracked crab on her plate.

Using a skinny fork, she scooped a hunk of tender meat, dipped it in the liquid butter and put it in her mouth. Head tilted back, she closed her eyes and chewed slowly.

He gave her a minute, running his hand inside his jacket, feeling the pistol holstered under his left arm and the pair of thumb drives inside his pocket. His and Jake's.

Yesterday, he could defend their fortune with a rent-a-cop and a 9-millimeter. He'd have to reevaluate. Their new nemesis would be The System: different, more complex, and faceless, with long tentacles and unlimited resources. Run by governments and corporations, nearly impossible to tell where one began and the other ended.

Some *muy* valuable service Davis had done.

"What are you thinking?" She'd drifted back.

"Nothing." He smiled, filling the crab cracker with the biggest claw, clamping it until his hand throbbed and the shell snapped. "That's not true." He squeezed fresh lemon over the cold, white meat. "How would you like to go on a trip?"

"Where to?"

"Anywhere you want."

"I've always wanted to go to Belize, to see the Great Blue Hole." She held up her gold thumb drive. "We could go anywhere."

It wouldn't be as easy as she seemed to think. Not with these tracking devices tethered to the global banking system. Why say it aloud and spoil the moment? "Pick a place," he said, "any place, and we'll go."

"What about Area 51?"

Something funny was a welcome respite. "Cute."

"What about Grand Cayman? I think I know someone who might be a good tour guide. We could dive, maybe swim with the stingrays."

He smiled. "Like I said, we'll go anywhere you like. Belize, Grand Cayman, it all sounds good to me."

ABOUT THE AUTHOR

Karen S. Gordon is an emerging author of action/adventure series, Gold and Courage. If you enjoyed *Express Intent,* or have comments you'd like to share, she would appreciate you leaving a review at the portal of your choice. *Express Intent* is the third installment of the Gold & Courage Series.

The adventures of Vance Courage and Lauren Gold will continue . . .

Please sign up for Karen's newsletter at karensgordon.com.

Thank you. Without you, the reader, none of this would be possible.

ALSO BY KAREN S. GORDON

The Mutiny Girl

"An outstanding debut thriller that has it all: misdirection, intrigue, murder, and family. Captivating and engrossing." — *The BookLife Prize*

"A taut, thrilling drama told exceptionally well." — *Steve Berry, NYT Bestselling Author*

"An engagingly written series starter with a bounty of plot twists and Miami vices." — *Kirkus Reviews*

Killer Deal

"A ripped-from-the-headlines legal thriller that John Grisham fans will love. Highly recommended." — *BestThrillers*

" . . . a fast-paced thriller . . . an intriguing look at the hunger for power, the ego of control, the persistence of greed, and two unlikely heroes whom we can cheer for . . ." — *BookTrib*

Express Intent

"Fast-paced, evocative and urgent from the get-go, Express Intent is the best Gold and Courage series book yet." — *Bestthrillers*

www.ingramcontent.com/pod-product-compliance
Lightning Source LLC
Chambersburg PA
CBHW030545260626
47157CB00006B/2203